NEVER
an
AMISH
BRIDE

NEVER
an
AMISH
BRIDE

*A Honey
Brook Novel*

USA TODAY BESTSELLING AUTHOR

OPHELIA
LONDON

Entangled Publishing, LLC
10940 S Parker Road
Suite 327
Parker, CO 80134
Visit our website at www.entangledpublishing.com.

Amara is an imprint of Entangled Publishing, LLC.

Edited by Stacy Abrams
Cover design by Elizabeth Turner Stokes
Cover art by Tom Hallman
Interior design by Toni Kerr

Print ISBN 978-1-64063-906-5
ebook ISBN 978-1-64063-907-2

Manufactured in the United States of America

First Edition July 2020

AMARA

GLOSSARY OF PENNSYLVANIA DUTCH WORDS AND PHRASES

ach: oh, or oh no

aye: yes

bobbeil: baby

bruder: brother

daed: father

danke: thank you

Englisher: non-Amish

fraa: wife

Gott: God

grossmami: grandmother

gut: good

gute mariye: good morning

guten tag: good day

jah: yes

kapp: bonnet

kinnah: children

liebchen: sweetheart

maam: mother

mein freund: my friend

mutza suit: a formal, collarless black suit worn by Amish men

nay: no

Ordnung: a set of rules for the Amish, varies by congregation

Rumspringa: "Running around." A period in an Amish teenager's life before baptism when they are allowed greater freedom.

wunderbar: wonderful

ye: you

NOTE FROM THE AUTHOR

Ten years ago, my sister moved to Hershey, Pennsylvania, a thirty-minute drive to Lancaster County. Ever since my first visit to Amish Country, I've lived in awe and admiration of the "plain" culture and its unique lifestyle. In researching for this novel, I spoke with a woman named Mary Garver, who grew up near an Amish village and still has many close friends who are Amish. Along with some hilarious stories—one about her being one of four people named Mary sitting at a dinner table of five people—she gave me wonderful insights about that particular community's *Ordnung*, along with other rules and traditions specific to them. For example: individuals reading from the Bible aloud, "hands off" courtships, and the use of electricity for business purposes. From that, I learned that Amish congregations/communities can vary greatly in their unique customs and practices—which are often unwritten and not taught in church. This fascinated me further, yet what I did see in all the different groups was a love and devotion to God, family, and hard work. I've grown to love the Amish people and their desires to live good lives full of service and fortitude. This book is dedicated to them.

CHAPTER ONE

Esther Miller stood at the screened back door, shading her eyes from the sun. The comical scene playing out before her had become almost common: Louisa shooing away Levi from the house. Only this time, her best friend was chasing him off with a pitchfork.

"Lou!" Esther called through a laugh. "You nearly caught him that time!"

"Ach jah," Louisa muttered. "Crazy boy thinks he can sneak in here and steal my hot cross buns whenever he wants." With herculean strength, she jammed the pitchfork into the ground. "If I actually catch him, I might—"

"Kiss him?" Esther said.

Louisa whipped around, her black prayer *kapp* nearly sliding off her bun. "Kiss him? Well, I never."

"But you might." Esther patted Lou on the shoulder as she walked by and back into the sunny kitchen. "I'm kidding you," she added a moment later. Louisa had become so testy lately when it came to jokes about Levi, making Esther wonder if there might actually be something between them. As far as she knew, her best friend hadn't been interested in being courted by anyone since last summer.

Despite that near-engagement, Lou had hardly seemed to mourn the loss at all.

Esther envied that.

Her Jacob had been gone for nearly two years, and Esther still didn't know how to move on. "Closure," as the *Englishers* called it. The English bookstore in town had a section of hardbacks all about it. Not that she'd dare read one.

"It was *Gott*'s plan" had become the standard answer whenever she'd talk about it with Bishop Abram—the leader of their congregation—or with *Maam* or her sisters.

In her heart, Esther knew this was true, but still, she hadn't been able to allow his memory to leave her heart.

Why was it *Gott*'s plan that her betrothed be taken from earth so early? He hadn't seemed very sick, but then suddenly, it was over. All their plans, her entire future, had washed away like bubbles rinsed off a dinner plate, down the drain...

And mere weeks before their wedding day.

In fact, the lovely light-purple wedding dress and apron Esther had hand made for the occasion still hung on the inside door of her closet, waiting to be worn.

By now, it had gathered a thick layer of dust.

Here she was: the tragic twenty-three-year-old non-bride with a wedding dress she would never wear, dried flowers that would've been used as simple decorations for the ceremony, and a cellar full of canned goods that were meant to be the newlyweds' winter storage.

Two years later, she still sensed pity in the eyes and voices of her married friends and neighbors. Where did she fit in now? For the past few months, Esther had begun to feel completely out of place, even within her own family.

"Let me help you with that," she said, needing to get her mind off Jacob, for she'd been dwelling on the disappointment much more often these days. She playfully wrenched the apple peeler from Louisa's hand after watching her nick her finger for a third time. "You've never been able to peel properly."

Lou rolled her eyes with a smile. "And yet, I make the best-selling jam in all of Lancaster County." She paused, the proud smile disappearing off her face. "Well, some say that. I didn't mean to brag."

Humility was a high priority in their Amish order. Next to *Gott*, family, and hard work, there was no higher attribute than a modest heart.

At the moment, this was something else Esther wasn't perfect at. Though she'd rather die strung up like a scarecrow in the middle of a cornfield than admit it, she, too, was a bestseller. *Maam* had taught her to make soap when she was just a girl. She smiled to herself—with maybe the tiniest touch of pleasure—whenever she thought about that blue ribbon and that nice big check she'd received on her nineteenth birthday. In fact, she was making nearly enough money now to start her own business, instead of just renting a stand at her cousin's home-goods store.

There she went again, boasting to herself.

"So?" Louisa cut into her thoughts. "You haven't said a word about the wedding."

Esther stared at her for a blank yet foggy moment. Was her best friend actually asking about her nonwedding two years ago?

"Is Sarah letting you help at all?"

"Oh." Those clouds of confusion parted, though a different kind of storm settled in. "Not really."

Louisa turned to her. "Goodness. When's the wedding?"

"Third of November, a Tuesday."

"First of the wedding season." She bit her lip. "Two months away."

Esther picked up a towel and began wiping off the counter, really hoping for a subject change.

She'd already happily married off an older sister and brother, but the thought of Sarah's upcoming wedding felt different—made her a little sad, maybe—mostly because Sarah was a year and a half younger than Esther.

Despite our closeness in age, Esther thought as she continued peeling, *my sister and I could not be more different. While I've tried—okay, sometimes unsuccessfully—to follow the example of* Maam *by being devout, soft-spoken, and kind, Sarah's always been a bit more...how to put it? Difficult. Maybe even brash.*

Another small wave of sadness washed over her, not wanting to think ill of anyone, least of all her own sister. Still, their dissimilarities were sometimes glaring.

They also greatly differed when it came to planning their weddings. For Esther, she'd wanted to involve the whole community. Jacob's proposal had come so suddenly—almost too late to fulfill all the classes and lessons required before a couple could wed. Both families had been excitedly planning for the whirlwind of preparations ahead.

Then suddenly, there would be no wedding.

"Sarah likes things done her way," Esther said to Lou. "Exactly the way she wants. I love my sister with all my heart," she added, "but she's left so much till the last minute because she doesn't like to delegate."

"Well, it is her wedding," Lou said. "Can't blame her for wanting it to be perfect."

Esther would never admit this to anyone, but secretly she was relieved that Sarah hadn't asked for her help. Anna, their elder sister, had been married for a while, and Esther had enthusiastically helped her with her wedding preparations. This time— marrying off a younger sister before she herself was married—was almost painful; even harder with Jacob's death and her disappointment fresh in her mind. She knew it was unkind, but Esther truly believed the less she had to do with the wedding, the better.

"What color is her dress?" Lou asked.

Esther immediately pictured her own purple dress hanging in the closet. "I don't know."

Lou frowned. "You haven't seen it?"

"She hasn't made it yet. I don't think she's even picked out a color."

For a moment, the two friends stared at each other before both cracked up laughing.

"Good gracious!" Lou said, wiping away a tear. "The poor girl's going to be in a terrible rush. She's never been a keen seamstress."

"Nor have I," Esther admitted. "It took a good three weeks for me to get my dress ready, and that was with *Maam*'s and Anna's constant help. Jacob's mother's, too."

"Maybe it's meant to be a surprise," Lou said. "Like how *Englisher* women won't let their grooms see their wedding dress before the ceremony."

"Seems a strange tradition," Esther said. "And their gowns are so lavish. All that white lace, and they wear it only once."

"Jah."

For a moment, both women stood in silence. Esther didn't know what Lou was thinking, but for just a second, she imagined herself in one of those white gowns. Would Jacob have thought she was beautiful?

Surely not. When he'd returned from *Rumspringa*, he was as pious as the bishop.

"I suppose it's a good thing we make our own plain wedding day dresses," Lou said, breaking into her thoughts. "And then we get to wear them to every church service for as long as we want."

Again, Esther pictured that purple dress—the one she would never get to wear. "Or for as long as they fit," she joked, not wanting Louisa to notice her mood change. "How's the music coming along?"

Esther knew this would be a good subject, as Lou was in charge of the youth choir, and they'd been working on their songs for the upcoming weddings for weeks. Louisa's enthusiasm was the perfect distraction for Esther's wandering mind.

"I wish you would sing with us," Lou whined while mixing a bowl of blackberry compote with a wooden spoon, sending a burst of both tartness and sweetness into the air. The scrumptious-looking dark-purple concoction would be canned and used at Sarah's wedding supper, as well as the other weddings that season.

"No, thanks." Esther chuckled under her breath. "I'm too old for that group now. I'd feel like their grandmother." She dropped another peeled apple into the bowl of water. "Besides, I haven't sung in years. Jacob didn't like it."

Louisa stopped stirring. "You sing like an angel."

"I think that's why." Esther smoothed down the front of her blue apron until her hands slid into its pockets. "You remember how spiritual he became at the end. He thought my singing was wicked." She shrugged. "Feared I'd show off too much. I suppose I understand what he meant. That was at the beginning of our courtship. I doubt I've sung a note since."

"Well, that's silly—you should." Louisa grinned. "And in *my* choir."

"Maybe next wedding season," Esther said for the third year in a row. "Speaking of Jacob…" Knowing the subject had gotten stale with her friends and family, she kept her eyes fixed on the floor. "I've been having a hard time lately. I…I understand that everyone has a mission in life—I do, I know that. But, well, Jacob was so young…"

"I know," Louisa replied, picking up her spoon and beginning to stir again.

"I don't understand—"

"Esther," Lou said without looking at her. "It was *Gott*'s will. *That* was His plan for poor Jacob."

Esther bit the inside of her cheeks, wanting so much to rebuff this—this unsatisfactory answer—

but knew she mustn't. Even though they were best friends, she didn't want Lou or anyone to know what was truly bothering her.

Suddenly, the pressure of a heavy rain began building behind her eyelids. It wasn't the death of her fiancé that made her want to sob. It was the thought of her struggles *because* of his death. Doubting her faith was something she'd never expected to feel. Ever. She loved her church. She loved her community, family, the connections she'd had her whole life.

But after everything that had happened, did she still truly believe?

And if she did, *what* did she believe?

There were still so many unanswered questions that it had become a topic no one would talk about, leaving a depressing confusion to sit heavily on her chest like a bale of hay.

"Okay, I really do have to go," Esther said. "I need to take my new batch of soap into town."

"Oooh, what kind did you make?"

"Clove."

Louisa's eyebrows shot up. "Is that allowed? Your wildflower soap smells light and fresh; isn't clove too strong a scent?"

Secretly, Esther had wondered the same thing, but the oils she added to scent her soaps were so deliciously beautiful, how could they be improper, even to plain folk?

"I add only the tiniest of pinches," she said, then quickly backed up, holding the screen door open. "See you tomorrow?"

"Jah," Lou said, still wearing the troubled expres-

sion Esther was trying to ignore. "See you later."

So far, it had been a mild Pennsylvania autumn, but today the sun was full out, warming all of creation. For a moment, Esther imagined what it would feel like if she peeled back her *kapp*, allowing the breeze to blow through her hair. Instead, she made sure the pins holding it were securely in place over her tight bun.

Maam was in the kitchen homeschooling Esther's three youngest siblings at the long wooden table. They were studying a poem by William Wordsworth. Esther grinned, grateful for the progressive education she'd received at home. *Maam* loved poetry and never shied away from teaching the English classics. Quotes from the Bible, along with Shakespeare and Keats, were needled into throw pillows on their sofa. Though *Maam* did tend to flip those to their blank sides whenever Bishop Abram would visit.

After Esther had finished her formal education at eighth grade, her father had built her a little nook off the end of the kitchen—her own soapmaking lab. Even when not filling orders, she considered it her hideaway whenever she was feeling down.

Over the last year, she'd easily tripled her inventory. Her cousin couldn't be happier, because those heavier-scented soaps had become very popular, bringing more and more customers and tourists into Yoder's Home Goods.

Esther blindly grabbed a box of two dozen from her stash, waved goodbye to *Maam*, and left out the back. There was no sign of *Daed*, which meant he was deep in his garden, harvesting the autumn melons for the weekend's farmer's market.

The walk from her house behind Honey Brook Creek to town wasn't far. She wouldn't ask *Daed* to stop working to give her a ride in the buggy, and she'd always been miserable at riding a scooter bike, especially one-handed. There were a few times, however, that she'd hitched a ride in a car with Lou's cousin, who'd left their order to marry a Mennonite from Icedale. Though Esther was well over twenty, she'd never asked her parents if those joyrides were appropriate. It was one of those things she'd rather ask forgiveness for than permission.

It wasn't long before the first small storefront came into view. Catching sight of the bright redbrick building on the south side, like always, Esther automatically steered herself to the north side of the road.

She hadn't stepped foot in that building—not in the six months since that *person* had begun working there. First of all, she hadn't been sick, so why would she need a medical clinic run by *Englishers*? Secondly, not only had that *person* been away from Honey Brook, Pennsylvania, for ten years, but the mystery that surrounded the mere name of Lucas Brenneman still haunted the community.

He was Jacob's older brother. She wasn't sure why, but if ever his name was mentioned in a whisper at a quilting bee or canning frolic, she felt a knot in her stomach. After all, Jacob lived with Lucas for more than a year before he'd asked to court her. Then he'd proposed. A few months later, her poor sweet Jacob went up to heaven.

Her community wasn't much on gossip, making

Esther wonder how many folks actually knew he was back in town. For, as far as she knew, no one had spoken to him since his sudden return to the area, not even his family. It wasn't a proper shun— because Lucas hadn't been baptized before he'd left on *Rumspringa* all those years ago. And because he'd never returned, folks assumed what wickedness he'd been up to, as well as the wickedness he'd exposed his younger brother to.

At the age of sixteen, Lucas had flown on an airplane to stay with his cousins in New York. In their church, *Rumspringa* wasn't frowned upon, but when word came that Lucas wasn't coming home, the common "running around" tradition made everyone wary. No one knew where he'd gone, since he'd never bothered writing to his poor parents.

Which made it an even bigger shock when Jacob had announced he was taking *Rumspringa* at eighteen with the intent to visit Lucas. The elders of the church were opposed, and though Jacob had had hours of council, there was nothing against it in the community's rules, the *Ordnung*.

When Jacob had returned a year later, he hadn't talked much about his time away from home or about Lucas. He'd heard some music, watched some TV, and even gone to Disney World, but that was all he'd been willing to share.

Almost subconsciously, Esther's gaze slid across the street to that redbrick building. Another gust of wind blew against her body, almost as if it were warning her away from what she suddenly wanted to do—needed to do.

What had really happened to Jacob? What had

Lucas done to his younger brother, and why—after only a year away from home—had he come back so different? Esther knew she couldn't go on wondering. It was making her miserable.

Perhaps, if she was brave enough right this second, she could finally get some answers.

Before she lost her nerve, and while grasping the boxes of soap under one arm, Esther clenched together the top of her wool cape and marched due north.

MEDICAL CLINIC, the sign read over the double doors of the redbrick building. A gold plaque was glued to the window. After the names of three doctors, the list ended with: Lucas Brenneman, physician assistant.

Esther sucked in a deep breath and pushed through the doors.

A receptionist desk sat in front, behind a sliding glass window. There was no one at reception, nor were there any patients in the lobby. Esther was ready to ring the little bell on the counter when the door leading to the back began to open.

"Sorry," someone spoke, "we're closed for lunch." A tall man with dark hair, wearing a white lab coat, came into view. *Less than thirty years old*, she considered, *and friendly looking, maybe even handsome—for an* Englisher. He was holding a spoon in one hand and a carton of cottage cheese in the other. "I forgot to put up the sign— Oh." He lowered the spoon, leaving a dollop of cottage cheese clinging to one side of his mouth.

Memories suddenly flooded Esther's mind. The lanky, lean boy spiking a volleyball right at her face.

Her grinning partner at the cornhole tournament giving her a high five after they'd won. Sharing a book at Bible study. Trying unsuccessfully to catch his eye during youth singing time.

Esther's throat went dry, while her heart beat like a drum the second she locked eyes with Lucas Brenneman.

CHAPTER TWO

It gave Lucas pause whenever plain folk came into the clinic—rarer than a five-star restaurant in these parts. But this blond Amish woman with the large blue eyes and fresh-looking complexion stopped Lucas dead in his tracks. She reminded him of someone he knew very well—or maybe used to know. Before it drove him crazy, he was forced to drag out the mental file of when he'd been a kid living in this very community, the mental file he did not like opening.

But her eyes...

For a moment, he let his mind go slack, allowing locked-up memories to freely flow. A girl chasing a bunny. A young teen bringing him a pie after he'd broken his leg. A face watching him from behind her Bible.

His brother's one true love...

Moses Miller's Esther, he thought, somehow remembering the nickname, for there had been four Esthers in their community, one being his own grandmother.

"Sweet Esther," he said quietly under his breath, remembering how he himself had shortened her nickname from Moses Miller's Esther, to M&M's Esther, to simply Sweet Esther.

Though three years apart, they'd grown up together. He hadn't been blind back then; he'd noticed how she'd look his way, paid extra attention, and tried to sit directly across from him in youth group. But, since about the age of five, his brother Jacob had been rehearsing how he'd ask out Esther on their first date.

There was never a thought of muscling in on his brother's girl, no matter how pretty her eyes had been.

As she stared at him from across the lobby, donning the traditional black heart-shaped prayer *kapp* common for single Amishwomen in Lancaster County, Esther was not wearing the smile he remembered. In fact, her mouth was hanging open, not moving since she'd gasped at the sight of him.

How could he blame her? Though he'd moved back six months ago, Lucas had been careful not to infringe on Honey Brook, his community for the first sixteen years of his life. Whenever he could, he did all his grocery shopping and car repairs in the neighboring town of Intercourse, or even Hershey, hoping to avoid any awkward moments.

Like this one.

"Morning," he said, then gave her time to un-thaw before speaking again. "Esther Miller?" When she didn't reply, it was Lucas's turn to feel awkward.

"Hallo," she finally said, shifting her body weight.

After another moment, Lucas snapped fully awake. "Do you need a doctor?" he asked, the obvious reason for her visit finally dawning on him.

Ever since he could remember, it was uncommon for the Amish community to seek out English doctors. Therefore, if Esther Miller had done so, something must be very wrong.

Stepping up, he ignored any embarrassment.

"Are you ill or hurt? How can I help?"

Esther blinked hard, as if waking up. "Oh, no—no! It's not that."

"You're okay?" He gave her a visual assessment, though it was difficult to see if anything looked out of place by how thoroughly her traditional Amish clothing covered her. Plain gray dress down to her lower calf, blue apron, black cloak, black prayer *kapp*—the color signifying that she was single. Under the *kapp*, her hair was the fairest blond, growing lighter since he'd been away. Her cheeks showed the rosiness of a sunny summer.

"Yes," she said, straightening her posture. "Perfectly okay. Hale, even. Not a single cavity or freckle."

Lucas almost smiled at the detailed reply, even though he hadn't been big on smiles lately—being so near his father again.

"You're Lucas Brenneman," she said.

"I am." He even flashed the name badge on his lab coat.

"You look different." She tilted her head to one side, while her shoulders visually dropped in relaxation. "The same but different."

"I could say that about you, too."

Finally, her lips curved into a smile that reminded him of simpler times. "Please, no. I was just a girl when you—"

She cut herself off, maybe fearing the mere mention of the subject was taboo.

"When I left," he finished for her. He didn't know how to continue, and she still hadn't said why she was there, standing in the middle of the lobby clutching two boxes in one arm, eyes staring at him as if he had something strange hanging out of his mouth.

After a moment of silence, she lifted a hand, gesturing toward his face. "You have something right there."

Her gesture caused him to touch his tongue to the side of his mouth. Quickly, he dipped his chin, wiping the entire area with the back of his hand. "Cottage cheese," he mumbled, feeling a little dopey and quite like that sixteen-year-old he'd been the last time he'd seen her.

"Almost like the strawberry ice cream."

"Pardon?" he said.

"After the Chupps' barn raising, you got into the homemade ice cream and smeared it all over your face like a mud pie."

Lucas stared at her.

"We were just kids," she added.

"I remember," he said, crossing his arms. "It was strawberry."

"Like I said." She exhaled a light, feminine giggle.

He couldn't help smiling now, picturing the scene nearly perfectly. "We got in so much trouble—Noah Otto and me. I had to do all the early-morning milking for two weeks." He felt his smile grow, which seemed a little strange, since he'd worked so hard at not allowing himself to dwell on his childhood.

"I interrupted your lunch," Esther said. "Sorry about that."

"It's no problem. Are you delivering something?" He gestured at the boxes she held.

"Soap."

"To me?"

"Why would you ask that?"

This was getting weird. If the woman simply wanted to gawk at him—at the man who'd left family and home ten years ago, only to return without warning and without seeking reconciliation from family or church—hadn't she seen enough?

"Mr. Lucas," she finally said, using a formal, very non-Amish title. "I wonder if you have some time. I need to talk to you." She bit her lip, appearing suddenly unsure. "I think."

He felt his eyebrows lift. "Talk?" he repeated. *To me?* "The clinic doesn't open again for almost an hour. Would you like to come on back?" He nodded toward the door behind him that led into his office.

She clutched the boxes in her arms like they were protecting her. "Can't we talk right here?"

He tried hard not to smile again. According to their *Ordnung*, it was okay for two single adults to be alone. Yet perhaps Esther Miller found it unnecessary to be secluded.

"Would you like to sit?"

She glanced at the chair he offered but shook her head. "Have you ever heard of closure?"

"Of course," he said, not knowing where in the world she was going with that.

"Good, because…well…I need it. And I'm sure this all seems utterly out of the blue, my showing up here like this, *jah*? I haven't seen you since…that last day. But I have questions, so many that my mind is full of them."

Questions about him? About where he'd been since he'd left on *Rumspringa*? Hadn't his mother shared with the community all his letters? For years, he'd written home at least once a month. Though he never received a letter in return, he kept writing, knowing his mother would feel more at ease if he kept her updated. When he'd written that he'd come back to Honey Brook, however, with no response, he finally stopped.

"Well," he began, unsure of where to begin. "My cousins in New York invited me to stay with them. I'd always planned on going there for *Rumspringa*, so—"

"My questions," she cut in, "are about Jacob." She paused to take in a deep breath. "I want to talk about Jacob."

Lucas felt a cold hand reach into his chest and squeeze.

During his time away, he'd gotten word that Jacob and Esther were engaged. He'd been pleased for his brother—securing his childhood crush for the rest of his life. Even though he knew that life would be short.

The hand around Lucas's heart clenched tighter.

Their future was never to be. Lucas had known that all those plans his little brother had shared when they'd been together would be nothing more than daydreams.

Because of our father.

The thought still turned his stomach.

Especially since he knew Jacob wouldn't have told anybody about what had happened when he'd come to him, and he'd begged Lucas to never share it, either. As far as Lucas knew, that dark secret had died with his brother.

"I can't help you," he said, snuffing out that tiny glimmer of light from his past.

Her lips dropped into a frown. "But I need to know. I need to know so much about so many things. Other things!"

"What *other* things?"

"Well, for starters, there's the youth choir and all that wasted food we'd been gathering!" she exclaimed. "And what about my dress? It's still my favorite. What do I do now?"

Frankly, the woman wasn't making sense.

"He was so young. And it was over like that." She snapped her fingers. "All of it. Why? When you love someone, are you supposed to just stop? Bishop Abram and Mother say the same thing every time."

Lucas opened his mouth, ready to give the righteous, pat, Amish knee-jerk answer he remembered from years ago: "It's all God's—"

"Stop!" Her shout made him flinch. "If you say it's *Gott*'s will, I'll throw something at you."

Completely taken aback, Lucas couldn't help smiling, finding her burst of anger not only amusing but completely out of character for a traditionally submissive Amish woman.

Still, he couldn't help teasing her. "Miss Esther, our lives are in God's—"

He had to swerve out of the way when she threw a brick of soap at him. Then another. He caught the next with one hand.

This pint-sized plain woman had a flaming hot temper.

"I'm sorry," he said, knowing he'd taken it too far

when two blazing red patches bloomed across her cheeks. "I couldn't help it. Forgive me."

"Fine," Esther said. "Please just give those back," she added, referring to the three bars of soap she'd hurled at him. He quickly picked them up and handed them over. While doing so, Lucas noticed each had a very pleasing smell. Something earthy but not quite like the lightly scented soap his mother used to use at home.

Curious, he was about to inquire, but then hints of a warning in her eyes returned.

Better ask about it later.

Later? What later? It's probably bad enough she's here right now. She's got to be worried about being seen.

Still unsure of the point, he knew that whatever it was that had caused her to step through those glass doors must've been very important.

"Go on," he said after an inward shrug. "I'm listening."

Esther was still breathing hard, her temper not quite under control. But she began speaking... something about flowers again and *that dress*. And then all the whys, just as before.

Honestly, Lucas was having a difficult time following her train of thought. She was speaking so quickly, gesturing with her free hand. "I'm good at making these," she continued, holding up one of the bars of soap. "But the Bible, and Bishop Abram—"

"Abram King?" he couldn't help interrupting. "He's your current bishop?"

Esther's eyebrows bent in confusion at being cut off. *"Jah."*

"Huh." Lucas rubbed his chin. "Once, he thought I'd vandalized the side of his barn when I hadn't. In fact, I'd been away from home that entire day. He still blamed me and told my folks." He shook his head. "Sure hope he's more forgiving now."

"Anyway," Esther said after a long pause, probably ignoring his words completely, "the bishop and the *Ordnung* and the Bible say it's wrong, but I don't understand why I should feel guilty."

Despite her rambling, Moses Miller's Esther had grown up to be mighty cute. Cuter even than the Englishwoman he'd taken on two dates back in New York. But he quickly thwacked that out of his brain. It was a waste of thought—she'd been engaged to his brother. Girls like that were hands off *forever*.

Plus, she was Amish. Absolutely no point in giving her any kind of second thought.

Fortunately for him, Esther continued to weave an un-follow-able story, pausing only to ask another *why?* Most of the time, it didn't seem Lucas needed to contribute more than a nod here or there. Even though he'd told her he would not talk about Jacob, she apparently needed to vent about a bunch of other random things.

Maybe it was as simple as his had been the first door she'd come to.

He swallowed a bit of laughter when he thought how she'd chosen his door.

Because…he had questions of his own. He'd been away from home for ten years. How was his family? His mother? Did his brother Jeremiah grow up to be the carpenter he'd always dreamed of being? Lucas became lost in his own thoughts until

Esther suddenly took a large step toward him.

"Please," she said, her voice sounding choked. "Please tell me."

Their sudden closeness caused his chest to feel tight. "I'm sorry," he began, "I wasn't paying—"

Before he could finish, the front door flew open. Stephanie, the clinic's receptionist, entered.

Esther jumped a full foot back from him, as if Lucas was deathly contagious. "Never mind," she whispered under her breath, cheeks turning pink. "This was a mistake." A split second later, she spun around and practically raced out the door, her cape flapping behind her like a superhero's.

Lucas stared, wondering if she would trail glitter like a comet.

"Hey, boss," Stephanie said, dropping her keys on the counter.

"I'm not your boss," he said for the hundredth time.

"Did I interrupt something important?"

He shook his head, keeping his eyes fixed on Esther as she crossed the street.

Stephanie followed his gaze. "Is she from…?"

"Yes."

"So pretty. Like one of those painted dolls. The porcelain ones, ya know?"

"No," Lucas said, watching as she walked toward Yoder's. "I mean, yes—yes, she's pretty. I can see what my br—" He forced himself to blink out of his ridiculous haze. "We've got patients," he said to Stephanie.

"Not until one o'clock."

Lucas ran a hand through his hair, scratching at

the back, a bit disturbed about where his mind had wandered. "Get the files for me, please."

Stephanie shrugged, chewing on a wad of gum. "Anything you say, boss."

While thumbing through the blood work of his next patient, his thoughts easily slid to Esther Miller, wondering if he'd ever see her again.

CHAPTER THREE

"Mortified." That was the word Esther kept whispering under her breath. Absolutely, completely mortified.

Why had she just barged in there? With barely a thought!

She paused in the middle of the street to shudder. What in heaven's name had she been thinking? She turned her face away when a buggy pulled up alongside her. She didn't bother looking at the passengers, knowing how red her face was.

Mortified.

Remembering why she'd come to town in the first place, Esther quickly ducked inside her cousin's store. There was a bit of a crowd at Yoder's, and Esther was more than happy to get lost in it, her mind still spinning fast over what had just happened with Lucas.

Lucas Brenneman…

She had thrown soaps at Lucas Brenneman!

"Esther. Esther!"

But lying low, even temporarily, was not in her future. A short, squat woman bounded up from behind the bakery counter.

Leah had been running Yoder's Home Goods for nearly ten years. Her family converted to the Beachy affiliation when Esther was a child. This highly progressive group of Amish were allowed certain secular luxuries, like owning businesses in town, women working outside the home, and electricity.

Leah was beaming like always, smiling ear to ear. "Is that a new batch for me?" she asked, glancing excitedly at the boxes.

"'Tis!"

"Did I tell you, the box you brought in last week sold out in two days? That's got to be a record. Not even Louisa's jam sells so fast."

Esther tried not to feel prideful, and she would never tell Lou that Leah was keeping track of their sales like a competition.

"Really?" she said, picturing all those happy people peeling open the handmade wrappers of her soap. Inhaling the lovely fragrances. Rose, lavender, and geranium were her most popular scents. Wildflowers. Very safe and obedient. Well within the rules about such things in the *Ordnung*.

Another twinge of curiosity at the thought of more exotic scents made Esther's heart speed up. Stifling that desire was getting harder and harder.

Temptation is everywhere, Bishop Abram was fond of preaching.

"They fly off the shelves," Leah added. "It's made such a huge difference for business. I can't thank you enough."

"That so?" Esther smiled, stepping back so a group of tourists could pass by. "I'm so happy they're helping your store."

"I have a check for you in the office." Leah grinned. "It's nice that you're allowed to have a bank account. I told you carrying cash, even around here, ain't safe."

Esther nodded, remembering the time she'd been followed by some English teenagers almost all the way home right after she'd been paid quite a lot of money. After that, it hadn't been difficult to convince *Daed* to add her to his bank.

"What did you bring me this time?"

Esther set the boxes on a stack of Lancaster County T-shirts with a picture of a horse and buggy on the front. "I was experimenting," she said, opening the flaps.

"Heavens!" Leah exclaimed. "I can already smell it. It's positively delicious!"

"Clove," Esther said. "I was thinking for Christmastime. I don't know. Too strong?"

Leah picked up one of the prettily wrapped bars and waved it under her nose. "Don't change a thing."

Esther looked at the floor, feeling a huge smile stretch across her face.

"Excuse me." They both turned to see a woman in a flannel shirt, gold sunglasses holding back her short hair. "What is that?"

"Soap," Leah said before Esther could speak. "Handmade only two miles away. One hundred percent organic."

"May I?" the woman asked, displaying an open palm. Just as Leah had, the woman held the bar up to her nose and took a deep breath, sighing in bliss afterward. "This," she whispered, "is the best thing I've ever smelled—including Chanel. Did you make it?"

Esther nodded. *"Jah."*

"Are they for sale? Now?"

"Of course!" Leah burst.

"How much?"

"Two—" Esther began, but Leah cut her off.

"Three, um, *four* dollars a bar."

Esther froze. There was no way anyone—even a rich English tourist—would spend four dollars on a simple bar of soap. Esther felt guilty charging two.

"Four?" The woman nodded, a smile appearing on her face. "Hillary, Gretchen, check these out. Authentic Amish soaps—handmade. And only four bucks each."

"Seriously?" Two more women approached. Leah quickly handed each a bar. "Ooh, nice," one of them said. "It smells like Christmas."

"Right? Think of how they'd make your bathroom smell."

"Spa city, baby!"

"How many do you have?" the flannel shirt woman asked.

"There're two dozen in each box," Leah said. "Two boxes."

The woman's grin stretched wider. "I want both."

"Hey!" her friend said, elbowing in. "You can't have them all." She glanced at Esther. "Unless you have more?"

"Sorry," Esther replied, flabbergasted. "This is all I brought."

"We have to at least split the boxes," the friend suggested. "We're not coming back this way."

The flannel shirt woman sighed and rolled her eyes. "Fine. We'll split."

"OMG," the third woman said. "I'm a blogger, and I'll definitely feature these soaps on my next post. They're totally amazing! Do you have a mailing list? I'd love more."

Esther opened her mouth to answer.

"Yes," Leah said. "Of course!" She momentarily slipped to the back and returned with a clipboard, paper, and pen. "Jot down your name and email address. We'll let you know when we have more in stock."

"Amazing." The woman beamed. "They smell so delicious, I almost want to take a bite!"

"Don't do that," Esther said, grinning. "They're made for washing, not eating."

"She's adorable!" the flannel shirt woman said. "This whole shop is fantastic."

"Thank you." Leah's huge smile made her eyes go squinty. "I can ring you up at the counter if you're ready to check out."

While she escorted the three women—their carts full of jams, shoofly pies, and multiple jars of pretzel dough—to the cash register, Esther covered her mouth with a hand, her body swaying slightly.

What had just happened? Never in her life would she think her soaps could be so popular. After all, she made them in a tiny cubby in her mother's kitchen. Even when she'd allowed herself to imagine success, her dreams had never gotten this far. What would *Daed* say? Should she even tell him?

Of course, Esther. Why would you think of hiding this from him?

She knew the reason why. *Daed* was afraid success would go to her head, fill her thoughts with ideas that led to pride, and thence temptation.

"So much for your record, cousin," Leah said when she returned.

"Huh?"

"It took two days for a box to sell out last time." She put an arm around Esther's waist. "Today, we didn't even get to put them on the shelf!"

"But, Leah, I can't believe you doubled the price. I reckon that's a sin of selfishness."

Leah patted the side of her hair. "That's good salesmanship. I have to keep on top of trends in commerce. Like it or not, your soaps are the current hot commodity." She paused to massage the back of her neck. "Mercy me… Who on earth am I going to find to make you a catalog?"

Esther laughed, feeling ever so proud—in a humble way, of course.

"Back to this," Leah said. "What brilliant, addictive fragrance will you come up with next? Better be a good one, and the stronger the better—you know those are the real money-makers. Business is all about making money, cousin."

"That's true," Esther said in agreement, though feeling the slightest bit conflicted between wanting to please Leah and perfectly follow the *Ordnung*. Despite what she knew was obedient, she grinned as she left the store—cooking up new combinations in her head. The smile wobbled some as she eyed that redbrick building. The trip to town might've started out as an embarrassing mess, but it had ended on a high note.

Praise to Gott *for bestowing upon me such a gift. May I try to stay humble and use my talents to serve Him.*

The inner prayer felt false, causing sudden fatigue in her limbs. Why couldn't she be content with a peaceful, simple, unselfish life like everyone else she knew? Was there something wrong with her?

The thought made the constant heaviness in her soul feel even heavier. Once clouds appeared over her spirits, they just kept rolling in. Why hadn't she been more adamant about answers from Lucas Brenneman when she'd had the chance?

Only he knew what happened when Jacob had been away from Honey Brook, before he'd gone to live with the Lord. Only Lucas Brenneman knew why poor Jacob had returned home like that.

She slowed her walk as she glanced back at the clinic. Surely now he was busy with patients and had written her off as a plain old Amish girl—indistinguishable in a crowd of Anabaptist folk. He'd been wearing jeans and a blue-striped collared shirt under his lab coat. Not in the least bit Amish anymore—not that she needed proof.

Though she would've had to have been blind to not notice how striking he looked—handsomer even than when they were teenagers. Nice, broad shoulders, darker, wavier hair, taller and sturdy like the Douglas firs behind her house. An appealing man like that could really take up space in a room... and space in her mind.

As she passed by a grove of trees, she stopped walking and pushed out a long, heavy breath, knowing she had absolutely no business thinking about Lucas Brenneman in that way.

To temporarily shoo away those dark clouds, once home, Esther helped her mother with the schooling of her younger siblings. Abraham was stumped by an arithmetic problem that Esther was more than happy to help work out. Math was never her interest, yet when it came to making soap, the arithmetic and miniscule amount of chemistry she'd learned in school were surprisingly helpful, especially when doubling a batch—like she planned on doing the next day.

"You're in a good mood," *Maam* remarked after the children had gone outside to play. "Anything special happen?"

Deciding to keep all of today's events to herself for now, Esther only shrugged. "A trip into town."

Her mother smiled and tucked a loose piece of Esther's hair into her *kapp*. "Well then, seems you should find reasons to be in town more often."

CHAPTER FOUR

Early dusk fell as Lucas turned the keys in the ignition. Headlights weren't needed yet as he drove toward home, but out of precaution, he turned them on anyway. He didn't live so far from town that his truck was really necessary. While he'd been away, however, he'd gotten used to the convenience.

And, since everyone around here thinks I'm going to hell in a handbasket, why does it matter?

He shifted into third gear. *They have no idea what's truly in my heart. The choice I made all those years ago was the right one. I feel that in my soul.*

Even if no one else understands.

Passing the road that led to the Millers' farm, Lucas's thoughts drifted to that conversation with M&M's Esther. He still didn't know what that had been about. The one topic she had spoken clearly of was what had happened to Jacob.

For Lucas, that was an impossible subject to divulge.

Still, it was probably highly beneficial for his psyche to connect with anyone from his childhood, for old wounds still cut deep. The choices his father had made back then. Jacob, too. And the one choice Lucas had known he'd had to make.

Good for the psyche, he repeated in his head.

Just that morning, he'd lain in bed, thinking about the day before, the good he'd done, the mistakes he'd try not to make again, and the goals he had for that day—the closest thing to saying a prayer like he used to. He'd thought about his family and home, all he'd left behind when he'd made that choice at sixteen.

Why had he really returned to Honey Brook? He could've taken a job anywhere. Why this place? Why…if he still had bitterness in his heart toward his father? It had been six months, and he still hadn't reached out to anyone.

As he idled at the one stoplight in town, Lucas recalled a woman he'd treated earlier that day. She'd come in with a sprained wrist, bruised rib, and fat lip and told him a fable about falling down the stairs. Lucas was too familiar with the ways of the world to be fooled by a story like that. If she'd been treated by anyone else at the clinic, they would've called the sheriff. But Lucas's inner Amish heart couldn't do that. He'd grown up believing that all problems— even the serious ones—were to be solved within the community, and no one ever intruded on another's private issues.

Then he remembered a patient from a few months earlier. Same types of bruises and scarring, only this woman had been plain. X-rays showed she'd had two arm breaks before, and neither had healed properly. As he'd been writing her a prescription that he knew she'd never fill, a burning wave of resentment pushed through his bloodstream.

He still could not understand why, when modern healthcare was so close to their village, they chose not to take full advantage.

As today's patient was about to leave, Lucas had taken a moment to block her way out of the exam room. "I promise you, I will call the authorities if this happens again," he'd said firmly, making sure she'd met his gaze. "Such an action goes against everything I believe in. That's how serious I am."

A tiny tear had trickled down the woman's cheek. "I know."

"Is there somewhere you can stay?"

The woman dipped her head, then nodded. "I think so."

Lucas finally stepped out of her way. "Go there now, not home."

"Okay," she said, her voice thick. "Thanks."

While hanging a right hand turn, Lucas released the kind of exhale that came only after a very long day. As he pulled his truck around the back of his house, it was dark inside. He still hadn't installed the security system that turned lights on and off to make people think someone was home. Not that he expected much crime in this neck of the woods, but it was best to be prepared. He'd had one of those security systems at his apartment in Queens, though it still hadn't kept him from getting robbed twice.

He didn't like dwelling on those days. Although he'd felt back then that he'd been on the path God had intended for him, he struggled daily, worrying that he'd disappointed the most important people in his life.

As he shrugged out of his coat and switched on the light, he thought about Esther again, oddly wishing her visit had lasted longer. He hadn't realized until now how much he'd been aching to talk about Honey Brook. Did his family miss him? Did they have anything in their hearts for him besides betrayal?

The thought made his head throb, so he grabbed the remote. The flat-screen on the wall came to life, set on the Food Network—but was there any other channel? For Lucas, it was the sole reason he had cable.

It was a baking competition, a rerun Lucas had seen twice, so he found a show he'd recorded and pressed play. As usual, he chuckled along, especially at the part when the judge of the show got in the contestant's face and swore up a storm, throwing the poor wannabe chef out of the competition.

Only once in a blue moon did Lucas feel guilty for using modern technology and advances. There was still a huge part of him that believed in the simplicity of plain living and the spiritual reasons behind it. Sometimes when he laughed at profanity or a crude joke, he caught himself, inwardly reprimanding that his mother would not approve, that he'd fallen far away from the clean-minded spiritual life he used to live. The lifestyle he thought he'd live forever.

The show ended, but Lucas hadn't been into it. Perhaps the crassness had bothered him more than usual. Probably because of that visit from Esther. Yes, he hadn't stopped thinking about it since he'd gotten home, whipped up his favorite Bobby Flay seared steak, and finished the evening with one of those shows that features family-run restaurants.

Maybe he'd see her again. If he did, what would he say? From what he'd gathered, she came into town to sell soap at Yoder's. Now that he recognized her, he made a vow that next time he saw her, *he* would ask *her* to talk.

He felt a strange flutter of anticipation in his chest as he got ready to turn in, still keeping with the Amish custom of asleep at dark, up at dawn. The plan was curiously comforting. Perhaps it would give him what he'd been craving all these years.

CHAPTER FIVE

Traces of the sunrise were barely visible on the horizon when Esther popped out of bed. The September weather warming the air as she hummed to herself, she flew through her morning chores.

Having something wonderful to look forward to always put Esther in the best mood. Combing through young Eve's thick hair was usually a chore no one enjoyed. But this morning, Esther cooed and cajoled her little sister while gently working out the tangles.

"Something's up with you, *jah*?" Anna, Esther's married sister, asked as they stood side by side at the sink, washing the breakfast dishes.

Esther bumped her sister's hip. "*Nay*, there's not."

"Then why have you been grinning all morning like Auntie Rosie's horse?"

Esther tried to hide her smile by keeping her chin dipped, staring into the bubbles.

Anna had married John three years ago. Their courtship hadn't lasted long, and even though Esther had known her older sister was ready to be a *fraa*, she'd had a hard time letting her go. For years, the two sisters had shared the room at the top of the stairs, talking long after even the crickets had gone to sleep. Wednesdays had become precious to Esther, as that was when Anna came to visit.

"Can't a body be in a good mood without causing the Spanish Inquisition?"

Anna glanced at her. "The what?"

"Nothing." Esther blinked, forgetting that her sister hadn't received the same kind of education as Esther. Early on, *Maam* must have sensed something in Esther, for her last years of schooling were steered toward literature and even world history. Esther had found it fascinating—mesmerized by stories of the American pilgrims risking their lives for freedom, the courage and miracles of Anne Frank, and even the centuries of war between England and France told by Shakespeare.

What Esther had loved most, however, was the poetry. Her mother would give Esther a poem to read and study, to pick apart for hidden meaning about *Gott* and nature. At bedtime, *Maam* knelt by her bedside and recited that poem word for word, images dancing through Esther's young mind.

"A thing of beauty is a joy forever…"

"To see the world in a grain of sand, and to see heaven in a wild flower, hold infinity in the palm of your hands, and eternity in an hour…"

"Motherhood: All love begins and ends there…"

"Trailing clouds of glory do we come from God, who is our home…"

Even today, the beautiful words lived deep in Esther's soul. Sometimes when she felt down, she'd force herself to recite one.

"How are you feeling?" she asked Anna, taking control of the conversation. "You're getting as big as wee Abraham's pig." She gently rubbed a hand over Anna's growing belly.

"Not funny," Anna said. "Last week, John had to

help me off the sofa. I couldn't get up on my own."

"You're loving it." She handed Anna the final dish to dry. "Every time I see John, he's walking on air."

Anna giggled. "He's more excited than I am."

Her sister went on to tell about the crib her husband had finished sanding and the rocking chair that Simon, their older brother, was working on.

"Sounds like the nursery is all but ready. Just needs a baby."

"I'm working on it." Anna sighed as she stepped away from the sink to take off her damp apron. "The other day, we were talking about maybe moving to the other side of the Baker's mill. It's real close to Simon."

"Jah?" Esther asked, helping her sister untie the wet knot. "But you love your farm. You finally got a good corn harvest last fall."

"Aye," Anna said, her voice light and wistful. "But right now, we're pretty far away from family. Simon's got the three boys and little Rebecca. This wee bundle will be close to their same ages." She removed a clean, white apron from a drawer. "We want to be around the younger cousins." She frowned while trying to maneuver the apron ties around her belly. "If you'd had *kinnah* with Jacob, we'd stay right here—" Anna cut herself off, her face ashen white. "Oh, Es."

Esther put both hands over her cheeks and turned away, feeling heat pulsating beneath the skin.

Anna moved toward her sister. "I'm sorry. I didn't mean to say…"

Esther dropped her gaze to the floor, ashamed

and guilty over something that was no fault of her own.

"Esther, please." She felt Anna's hand on her shoulder. "I can't believe I... My mouth just goes sometimes. I wasn't thinking."

Esther took a moment, breathed out a long exhale, then lifted her chin stoically. "It's okay."

"No, it's not." Anna stomped her foot, tears filling her eyes.

Esther didn't wish for her sister to feel shame at what she'd said. After all, it was the truth. She and Jacob should've had two *bobbeils* by now, and one on the way. The perfect ages to complement Anna's future family.

Dear Gott, *please forgive my doubts and take away my fear. Help me have faith in your plan for me.*

She paused her inner prayer, hoping to feel something. Anything. When nothing came, she pinched her eyelids together and sucked in a slow breath. "You better rest now," she said to Anna. "Just over two months before you're due. Why don't you take some knitting out to the porch? It's mighty sunny."

"Nay," Anna said stubbornly, still blinking back tears.

But Esther was already leading her toward the back door. "I'll bring you some hot tea."

Anna's eyes brightened. "Juniper?"

"Of course."

After she'd dragged the knitting basket to the chair where she'd placed Anna, Esther filled the kettle with water and settled it over the woodstove.

Then, once Anna had her tea, she went straight to her soapmaking nook at the back of the kitchen.

Today began so brightly, she thought, blinking furiously at the tiny tears invading her eyes. She knew of one sure way to knock away those tears like spiking a volleyball.

First the lye, then the coconut oil—the fancy brand she'd had Leah order online. After carefully stacking each item on the counter, she pulled down a small box. Measuring, stirring, boiling, whisking… As the recipe progressed, the time came to add that final ingredient. Instead of the usual amount, Esther doubled it, filling the kitchen with the fragrance of spicy, warm clove.

After she'd poured the mixture into its molds, she set out to make a second batch. Triple the size this time. After all, even with all the battery-operated fans going, each batch took nearly a week to set up properly.

And if Leah wanted more, she'd give it to her.

Hours later, while pouring the final mold, Esther's mind began to slow from its frantic speed. *Why am I so determined to want what is not righteous?* she thought, staring down at the rows of the overly fragrant molds. *Why can't I use my talent to enjoy what I'm allowed to do?*

Her soul felt a familiar heaviness. If she couldn't control her will enough to obey the simple rule of limiting the scents in her soap, how else might she sin in the future?

For the first time, Esther allowed her thoughts to wonder if being baptized into the church, and thus keeping those very important covenants for the rest of her life, was what she really wanted.

Not allowing such a horrible thought to plant seed, she quickly cleaned up her nook, changed into a clean apron, grabbed a box of lavender soap from the top shelf, and headed to put on her cloak.

The second she opened the front door, she jumped and screamed. "Amos!"

Her soon-to-be brother-in-law stood shaking on the steps, face as white as the underclothes hanging on the lines. "Sarah," he muttered.

"What about her? *Maam!*" Esther called over her shoulder. "Amos, what happened to my sister?"

"What is it?" *Maam* said, gently pulling Amos inside. "Has something happened to Sarah? Where is she?"

"In the carriage," Amos said. "She's been to see old Eliza Fisher."

Esther stood on her toes to see a buggy parked by the fence. Eliza Fisher was the community's healer. The eccentric old woman wasn't someone most folks just dropped in on. If Sarah had seen her, something was wrong. She pushed past Amos and ran toward the buggy. "Sarah," she called out. "Are you okay? Can you hear me?"

Sarah suddenly appeared, slowly sitting up as if she'd been reclined back in leisure. A white ice pack sat on her lap.

"What…? Is anything wrong?"

"I'd say so," Sarah said, displaying the ice.

Maam came up, followed by Amos and pregnant Anna. "What happened, dearest?"

Sarah moaned. "We were at his mother's." She tipped her head toward Amos. "Showing Sister

Mary that I can too put up peaches—despite what everyone says." She turned her gaze to Esther, but Esther didn't dare reply. "I was *trying* to move the canning pot off the stove—"

"She wouldn't let me help," Amos cut in.

Sarah glared at him. "Because you're helpless in the kitchen."

"Gracie was standing right next to you."

Sarah sighed again. "You sister is too obsessed with that horse of hers to know anything about canning."

"You were moving the pot, and..." Esther prompted, needing to hear the end of the story to make sure her sister was really okay, and also, admittedly, so she could take her soap into town as planned...

"She picked it up." Amos actually chuckled.

"With your bare hands?" *Maam* said.

Sarah pressed her lips together and stared up at the sky. "I was *distracted*. And do not laugh at your fiancée." She turned to Amos, who immediately dipped his chin and removed his straw hat. "*Maam*, Eliza Fisher says...she said I mustn't use my hands." Sarah displayed the pads of her fingers. All eight of them were marked a mean red and looked as painful as a barbwire cut.

"*Aye*," *Maam* said, examining them. "This does look like a pretty good burn. Deep second degree, I'd say."

"What does that mean?" Sarah asked, looking panicked.

"Well, from what I understand, it affects the second layer of your skin, not just the top layer. And see, you're getting blisters already."

Sarah snatched back her hands. "It feels like they're on fire."

"You need to keep applying ice. In a few days, they'll feel better, but the blisters will be there for a week or two, I fear."

"That's what Eliza Fisher said. She said I can't do anything that engages my fingers. She said they need to rest till at least mid-October."

"That seems mighty extreme," *Maam* said. "But I'm not the expert. You don't want the blisters to pop—that'll take twice as long to heal and may scar."

"Scar?" Sarah said, quickly returning her hands to the icepack. "I can't be scarred on my wedding day."

"Which is why you need to rest," *Maam* said, coaxing Sarah down from the buggy. "Take my arm."

"I want Esther's," Sarah said with a pout in her voice. "Help me, will you, Es, darling?"

"Sure," Esther said, allowing Sarah to loop an arm through hers, then lay her head on her shoulder. It felt good to be of service, but knowing Sarah's personality, Esther couldn't help sensing something else was coming. The other shoe was about to drop, as the English saying goes.

"Es," Sarah began, her voice almost too sweet. "I've been thinking. Since old Eliza said I can't use my hands, and now *Maam* is saying I must take it easy…"

"Jah?" Esther said, a warning tingle at the back of her neck.

"Well, since you have only that old soap of yours to keep you busy, I wonder—well, I mean, I'm sure you'd be ever so happy to plan my wedding."

Esther stopped walking. "Your what?"

Sarah turned in to Esther's body and gave her an overly tight hug. "Oh! I knew you'd come to my rescue." She gave another lung-collapsing squeeze. "I've already mentally planned everything, so now it's just a matter of execution. Anna, you can help some, of course. And even Gracie if she ever comes out of that horrible horse stable."

"Sarah, why me? Why not *Maam*?"

"*Maam*'s starting to take in some of the village's *kinnahs* to homeschool."

Esther turned to her mother. "What?"

Maam smiled with a twinkle in her eyes. "We talked about it as a family last week. Have you forgotten already?"

"Uh, *nay*, I do remember something about that." Esther held her fingers up to her temples, massaging the oncoming headache. She did recall that her mother was going to be much busier going forward, especially in the evenings, when she'd be preparing her school lessons for the next day.

"Sarah," Esther continued, still trying to think straight, "I'm really not—"

"Oh! And we must go shopping tomorrow. You know, if I'm up to it."

"Shopping for what?" Esther said, her mind swimming, trying to get a hold of the conversation while also straining to ignore the tears just behind her eyelids and the pressure in her chest, the constant reminders that her younger sister was getting married before her.

Sarah pulled back and looked at her as if she was missing an obvious answer. "Material for my dress, of course," she said. "You get to make it for me."

And there went the other shoe…

• • •

After an hour of trying ever so subtly to get out of it, Esther finally agreed to plan Sarah's wedding. Sewing the dress from scratch would be the biggest challenge, since traditional Amish weddings were not like the *Englishers'* ceremonies.

Leading up to the day of the wedding, there would be several ceremonial announcements and meetings and meals—nothing Esther couldn't handle with a bit of help. The wedding itself would take place at their home. Some might mistake an Amish wedding as a traditional church service, for there were sermons, prayers, lessons, scriptures, singing, and a final blessing. After that, the women prepared the big meal while the men set up the tables. Weddings were indeed a community affair.

Their sect was slightly different—adding a youth choir during the ceremony. The church leaders hoped that getting teenagers involved would help them become interested in joining the church earlier.

Isn't it bad enough having to see my own wedding dress on a daily basis? Esther thought as she walked toward town—slightly slower than she'd planned, feet heavy as lead. *But now I have to make my sister's?* And it wasn't as though Sarah was the easiest person to work with, let alone the most gracious.

The afternoon wind picked up, and without her cloak, Esther walked at a brisker pace, pumping her arms, the invigorating exercise making her heart beat fast and sweat pool at the base of her neck. To take her mind off the wedding, maybe she'd talk to Leah about adding another shelf to her soap display at the store. After all, she'd said it herself: they were the hot commodity. Whatever that meant.

She'd talk about anything to distract herself from thinking about making the wedding dress— *Ack, Esther!* Before she'd had the chance to correct the prideful thought, two hands grabbed her elbows. The next moment, she was spun around.

"Will you come with me?"

Even while startled and gasping, Esther easily identified her accoster.

Lucas Brenneman.

He appeared as out of breath as she, like he'd dashed at a sprint into the middle of the street just to grab her. When his hands gripped her tighter, she glanced down at them, causing Lucas to immediately let go. For a moment, they simply stared into each other's eyes, neither of them blinking.

Esther couldn't think of the last time she'd been touched like that by a man. She could still sense his strong grip on her skin like a phantom, causing her to feel warm all over, maybe even a little eager for him to touch her again.

"Come where?" she asked, breathless from the fluttering of her heart.

But he was already walking.

Too stunned to think on her own yet, she followed, curious but also…it was the mysterious Lucas Brenneman. Talk about distractions.

When she'd been a silly girl, she used to think he might resemble Gilbert Blythe from the *Anne of Green Gables* books: a very handsome young man with dark curly hair, a kind yet mischievous glint to his hazel eyes.

The twenty-six-year-old Lucas might've still been a fair comparison, if Gilbert Blythe had the broad shoulders of an iron worker and two days' worth of scruff on his chin, his eyes brown like a bar of Hershey's chocolate.

She was still a silly girl now, allowing herself to think of him in that way, feeling the rapid beats of her heart as he glanced back to make sure she was following.

He led her to his clinic, holding the glass door open. Just like the other day, no one was inside. He didn't speak at first but was pacing back and forth across the lobby floor, hands on hips, examining his shoes. Out of politeness, Esther didn't speak but waited for enlightenment as to why he'd practically snatched her off the street.

"I'm sorry if I frightened you," he said, still pacing. "I saw you out the window and…" Finally, he stood in place and looked at her, hands still on hips. Esther was surprised to notice how nervous he looked. Nervous to talk to her?

"Please," he said, rubbing a fist over his chin scruff. "Would you tell me about my family?"

CHAPTER SIX

If Esther Miller was appalled by his actions, she didn't show it. Though she did seem pale from the shock he gave her, and her cheeks had dots of a rosy color, she stood firmly in place, not making a run for the door. It had been a complete impulse when he'd seen her from the window.

Okay, that wasn't true for, not too long ago, he'd promised himself if he saw her again, he would ask to talk.

"Your family," she repeated.

"Yes. My brothers and sisters." His palms felt a little clammy as he rubbed them together. "My mother."

"Well, your *maam* is wonderful, always kind to me when we see each other. She and my *maam* are bosom friends, you know. Or…" She hesitated. "They mightn't have been so close before you…"

"Left," he finished.

"*Aye.*"

"Why are they close now?"

His heart grew unexpectedly light the moment Esther smiled. "Well, three weasel brothers were causing real havoc in your momma's henhouse. One day, *Maam* was calling at your place when all three weasels showed up. Quick as lightning, your momma grabs the rifle and starts shooting. Of course the pesky creatures scatter to all corners. But the story goes that for the next hour, my and your mother took turns flushing out those weasels like you'd flush a quail from a bramble bush."

Lucas couldn't help covering his smiling mouth. "No way."

"*Aye!*" Esther laughed. "Can't you picture the scene? Those two women—mothers of thirteen *kinnahs* between them—bellies down in the dirt, waiting for one of *Gott*'s creatures to appear in their crosshairs."

Lucas rocked back on his heels and heartily laughed. "That must've been a sight."

"Oh, *jah*. It was all the jolly talk for months on Sunday evenings. Your brother Caleb says he tracked a wounded one ten yards before it died. He returned home with only the skin."

"Caleb did that?" He felt a belly laugh coming. "But he's just a tyke. How did he keep up?"

"Caleb's nearly fourteen. Almost as tall as you."

This comment hit Lucas like a blow to the head, his laugh cut short.

Of course he knew time passed in slow-paced Honey Brook just like everywhere else in the world. So why was it shocking that his youngest of siblings was nearly grown up?

After years of confidence in his decisions, inklings of regret poked Lucas in the stomach. His family would be completely different now. If he passed them on the street, would he even know them?

He paused that train of thought to look at Esther. He'd recognized *her*. Easily. And they weren't even family. Another ache churned inside him—because they'd almost been family. If she and

Jacob had married, they would've been in-laws.

But he'd died. Even after all they'd done during those months of *Rumspringa*. He'd failed his little brother.

"B-Bridget has twins!"

At the exclamation, Lucas snapped back to the present. Marbling red on her throat, Esther might've looked as anxious as he felt.

"Twins?"

She nodded, slapping a big smile on her face. "Born on Christmas Eve, if you can believe such a blessing. And they're gorgeous."

Bridget had barely begun to court boys when he'd left home. And now she was a mother.

"Your sister has them raised so well. There aren't two more polite and pious girls in all of Honey Brook, though neither can seem to keep their shoes on. Martha, the quiet one, is learning to sew and stitch, while Lydia, oh heavens, can that girl sing! It's the highlight of every Bible study."

Lucas allowed wonderful images to bob inside his mind. Two little girls—who looked exactly like his sister—running barefoot through the dewy grass, picking wildflowers, giggling, learning to pray and study, and be the apples of their parents' eyes.

"Thank you," he said without thinking. When he looked at Esther, she was smiling warmly, no longer pale or embarrassed. "You have no idea how badly I needed to hear that."

"I think I might," she said, her voice quiet.

Maybe she did. After all, while brooding over the time that had passed, he'd felt dark and gloomy and full of wasteful regret. Perhaps she'd seen that on his face and jumped in with the story about Bridget's twins.

Surprisingly insightful for someone who was… well, he'd been about to say just a teenager. But M&M's Esther was no longer a child, a not-so-small fact that he realized every time he looked at her pretty face.

"Lucas," she said. "Do you ever think about just going home? I'm sure your mother would love it."

"I think about that all the time," he admitted. "But they don't want to see me."

"How do you know?"

"I wrote my mother dozens of letters, but she never wrote back. Not once. I think that's a pretty solid indication they're done with me." It was strange saying the words out loud, like it was no longer a secret.

"You *didn't* write to her."

"Yes, I did."

"But, well, no one ever mentioned that—I mean, not that it was any of my business, but the talk has always been that she didn't get one single letter from you."

"What?" Lucas gazed at her confused expression, feeling rather baffled himself. Why did his mother not admit he'd written?

"Do they know you're here?" Esther asked.

"I have no idea, though it was in my last letter, but if she never…"

"Don't you think you should let them know? Maybe write another one."

Lucas sighed in perplexity, pushing his fingers through his hair, knowing he needed a cut and a shave. "I don't think so."

"If you decide to reach out, I can help—I mean, I'll go with you, if you'd like."

"You're very thoughtful." Her kind words caused a lump in his throat. "Sorry, again, about kidnapping you."

She exhaled a feminine laugh. "It's okay. We're not allowed to learn self-defense like the English girls, but I did see part of a karate movie at Leah's once." She made a karate chop in the air. "Next time, you might not be so lucky."

"I'll remember that, Kung Fu Panda."

"Panda?"

"Never mind." He chuckled and dipped his chin. "Don't ask me why I'm suddenly thinking this, but do you remember the time you ran over to our house because you heard something in your barn?"

Esther blinked twice, as if jogging her memory. "Yes," she said, sitting down in a chair. "My folks were over at the Lambrights', looking in on their new *bobbeil*. Simon and Anna were on their own dates that night. I was alone with the *kinnahs*."

"And you heard something banging in the hayloft."

"Yes, I…" Those blue eyes suddenly flashed toward Lucas, and he couldn't help grinning. "What…?" She pointed at him. "What did you do?"

"Nothing," Lucas said, letting his eyes drift off to the side. "Nothing *much*."

"Lucas Brenneman. Tell me what you did!"

He stared down at his palms and laughed. "It started off as a contest to see who could hit the hacksaw hanging on the wall with the most rocks. A kind of misplaced target practice. When we saw the flashlight coming, we hid."

"You hid?" She stood up and walked toward him, probably attempting to look menacing, but she was too darned cute to pull that off. "What were you doing in our barn in the first place when your father had that huge cow barn? And who was *we*?"

Lucas had to think for a moment, the memory still not all the way clear. "It was Noah Otto."

Esther sighed. "Oh. Him again."

Lucas laughed hard. "He and I got into a lot of trouble when we were kids. I'm sure he was the bad influence on me."

"Noah Otto moved to Ohio a few years ago," Esther said. "He's deacon out there and runs a foster home for orphans."

"Okay then. I suppose *I* was the bad influence."

"Finish the story," Esther said, taking her seat again. "You said you hid when you saw me come into the barn with a flashlight."

"We didn't know it was you yet," he said, his heart lifting as the memory returned. "We thought it might be your pa, so we didn't make a sound."

"And then?"

"Once we saw it was you, I guess we tried to…"

"Frighten me."

"More like scare the dickens out of you." Lucas couldn't help laughing, not only at the memory, as clear now as if he was watching his favorite episode of *Iron Chef*, but also at the slight tick to Esther's mouth. Was she angry with him? Or was she trying not to laugh?

Just in case it was the former, he raised his hands

in surrender. "In my defense, we were only kids."

"And whose idea was it to make the howling noises?"

Lucas had to think for a moment; then he jabbed a thumb at his chest.

"I see." She crossed her arms. "Exactly what kind of animal were you trying to be?"

"Hmm…" He tapped his chin with one finger. "I believe it was an aardvark."

"Aardvarks don't growl."

Lucas shrugged. "We didn't know that. I think we'd read about them in a library book and thought they looked ferocious."

"Boys," Esther said, shaking her head. Then she looked at him, her lips pressed together as if trying not to smile. A moment later, they burst out laughing in unison. Lucas's soul hadn't felt light like this in years.

"An aardvark," she said, holding her hands out to her sides. "It's too much."

"Up until then, I'd had a very limited education."

"And now you're an expert on African nocturnal mammals?"

Lucas chuckled again. "Well, I don't like to brag, but I now know that aardvarks are not related to anteaters. Another fact: though they don't actually growl, they do make a noise."

"Fascinating," Esther said. "And what might that sound like?"

"I suppose it's a sort of grunting when they're looking for food."

"Like a pig?"

Lucas pointed at her. "Exactly like a pig."

"Though a bit more guttural, I'd think," she suggested, a new smile twitching at the corner of her mouth.

"Yes. Very guttural."

Esther puckered her lips then pushed them to one side. "Hmm, I'm not sure what you mean. Would you mind demonstrating?"

"Well, you know, kind of a soft…" Lucas Brenneman, professional physician assistant, actually snorted. Just to make a girl laugh.

And what a payoff.

Esther Miller tipped her chin and did a loud, though strangely dainty, snort-laugh of her own, her cheeks flushed the color of a rosy sunset. Lucas hadn't seen or heard anything so free and happy since…well, maybe since he'd left home.

"Sorry, again, if I scared you," he said.

"That was a long time ago." Esther pressed a fingertip to her eyelashes.

"I meant earlier on the street."

"Oh." She rubbed her arms, probably along the areas where he'd grabbed her.

Her eyes were bright, and Lucas was grateful for the jokes. But also for the joyful memory they'd shared. The way his attitude had been lately, he didn't expect that a conversation about home could be positive.

A few moments of silence passed between them.

An old college friend of his once said that the earth is populated thanks to awkward pauses between two people. He might've been naive at the time, but Lucas knew what that meant now, which made him feel even more awkward—and a little hot beneath his lab coat. Because Esther Miller was not only a grown woman, but quite attractive.

And Jacob's fiancée!

"Is there anything else you want from me?" Esther said.

The question caused Lucas's awkwardness to warp into panic. He didn't want her to go yet. Glancing at the clock on the wall, he knew his colleagues would be returning from their morning conference any minute.

"You were off somewhere before," he said, noticing the box she'd set on the chair next to her. "I hope I didn't make you late."

"Nay."

"Is that more soap?"

She picked up the box, gripping it tight. "How'd you know it's soap?"

"Because you threw three bars at my head."

"Oh." Another rosy blush began creeping up her throat, but her eyes were merry. "I won't apologize for that, you know."

"I'd never expect you to." He waited a moment, then asked, "May I?"

Perhaps a bit begrudgingly, she opened one flap of the box and handed him a bar wrapped in silver paper with a purple bow. He held it under his nose and inhaled.

"Odd," he said.

Her eyes widened. "Odd?"

"It smells like a meadow. With flowers."

Esther released a loud exhale with a definite touch of sarcasm. "That's the point. If you read the wrapper, it's labeled lavender."

"You don't say. What will they think of next?"

She huffed again. "Give it back."

Lucas held it out to her but, at the last second, lifted it above her head, just out of reach.

She stopped her forward motion and tilted her chin to meet his eyes, narrowing her eyelids. For a moment, Lucas feared he'd placed himself in the middle of a Bruce Lee movie.

Having the wisdom to not poke Kung Fu Panda, he gave it back.

"Thank you," she said hotly. "Still the big bully, I see."

"When was I a bully to you?"

"You mean besides the volleyball game when you picked me last? And the time you and Jacob kept hiding my prayer *kapp*—Jacob told me later you talked him into it. Oh, and let's not forget about the wild aardvarks in the barn."

It was like watching a movie of his own life. For the past few years, Lucas had worked so adamantly to block out thoughts of home that he'd actually forgotten the happy memories. He realized now just how many there were.

"I know you have to go," he said when she'd straightened the boxes in her arms. "But I wonder if…" He scratched an eyebrow before going on, unsure how to phrase the question. "Well, if you wouldn't mind talking another time."

Esther's eyes narrowed skeptically, and she opened her mouth to speak.

"I mean, only if we happen to run into each other on the street again," he said, hopefully cutting off her oncoming refusal.

Unless something in their *Ordnung* had changed, they were allowed to be alone together. Lucas would respect the community's rules out of respect for Esther. When she didn't answer right away, he worried she might not deem it safe to meet again with an outsider. The thought disappointed him more than he'd expected.

"You mean if I happened to be delivering more soap to Yoder's on Thursday?"

"Why not Wednesday?" he asked, the words out before he thought them through.

"Because…" Esther took in a deep breath, held it in her cheeks, then blew it out, as if preparing for a measles shot. "Because I have to make my sister's wedding dress because she burned her fingers and can't use her hands—"

"Is she okay?" Lucas couldn't help interrupting, his medical training kicking in.

"Oh, she's fine."

"But you said she can't use her hands."

"She's not *supposed* to—not for almost a month."

"Have you seen her fingers? Were there blisters?"

Esther shrugged. "Some, but they're mostly just red now. And she uses her hands all the time, by the way, when she thinks no one's looking."

The annoyed tone in her voice made Lucas want to laugh.

"Who told her she can't use her hands?" he couldn't help asking.

"Old Eliza Fisher."

Lucas ran the name through his memory. "Holy cow, she's still alive? She seemed a hundred years old when I was a kid." He almost added that there was no way their community should rely on someone like Eliza Fisher if they had serious health issues. Even plain folk deserved the best medical care possible.

Why don't they just come to the clinic to see me? How can I get them to trust me?

"So anyway," Esther went on. "I have to make my sister's wedding dress."

"Ah, you mentioned that." Lucas nodded, not comprehending why that would be such an awful thing for her. Then again, there was probably subtext he was missing. "Okay."

"It's a long story."

"A frustrating one, I take it."

In reply, she groaned and rolled her eyes up to the ceiling, making Lucas want to laugh.

"Maybe you can tell me about it on Thursday."

"Yeah." Esther swayed her body. "Maybe."

As he watched her cross the street, he considered what a surprise the visit had turned out to be. Yes, he'd been after answers, but the stories and pictures she'd planted in his mind were even more than he'd hoped for.

Then their short conversation the other day popped back into his mind. As he recalled, he'd been plenty sharp when she'd asked about Jacob, even though she'd probably had to gather major courage just to pull open those glass doors in the first place.

Knowing his old community and how private his family could be, she was probably truly clueless about what had happened to Jacob. After how kind she'd just been to him, Lucas couldn't help feeling he owed her something.

Not everything. But something. Even though he knew if he shared his secret, it would surely bring her pain, not closure.

CHAPTER SEVEN

"You promised your sister."

Esther sighed. "I know, but—"

"A promise is a promise," *Maam* said in a sing-song voice while laying writing notebooks on the table.

Esther straightened one. "Don't you think I'd be more of a help here with you? With all your new students? And what does that phrase even mean? *A promise is a promise…*"

"It means you gave your word, and that means a lot in this family." *Maam* began putting out yellow pencils. "And lower your voice, sweetie," she said while glancing toward the stairs. "You don't want to hurt your sister's feelings."

For a split second, Esther felt a tiny pinch of guilt for trying to get out of the task. *"Jah,"* she said a moment later, dropping her voice. "But it irks me to no end that she thinks I have so much spare time to just plan someone's wedding. *I* have commitments, too. My days are very busy."

"And yet you just offered to help me with the schooling."

Esther bit her lip. She knew it was a lost cause to fight. In fact, her whole conversation with *Maam* had been while she'd been tying her cloak and fastening her outside black *kapp*, readying herself to call Sarah downstairs so they could go material shopping.

"Did you know Leah sold two boxes of my soap before I'd even set them on display?"

Maam put on her little round glasses and began thumbing through a book. "I believe I heard something about that."

"She wants me to make more. It's ever so good for their business. I'm helping their whole family—the community!"

"That's very charitable of you, sweetie. But is it bringing you closer to the Lord?"

Esther stopped tying and looked at her mother. "What?"

"All things are to be done for the praise of *Gott*. Everything in life is to worship Him."

Esther felt a knot in her stomach. Not once had she thought of her soap that way. It was an escape for her, something to do and have that was all her own. Must she really turn even that over to the Lord?

Though the question pressed against her heart, she wasn't ready to speak her doubts aloud to *Maam*. Or to anyone. She just wanted to live her life, hoping maybe all her questions would somehow disappear.

"I...I want to do better," she said, humbling herself. It was as much as she could say without stretching the truth. "Do I have to stop making my soap?"

"I didn't say that," *Maam* replied, organizing the pens in her apron pockets—the children would be showing up for school any minute. "I simply want you to remember the commandments. Put no other gods before me, and love the Lord thy God with all thine heart."

"I do," Esther said, a lump of shame forming in her throat. She didn't like feeling this way. She didn't ask to have doubts about the church, or lingering heartache over Jacob, or pride about her soap.

But her struggles were growing more intense every day.

And now she had to plan Sarah's wedding?

"Would you pick up some small bandages while you're in town?" *Maam* asked, shaking Esther out of her daze.

At the mention of medical supplies, her thoughts shot to Lucas. Should she confess that she'd seen him? Spoken to him, twice? And that she had every intention of meeting with him again?

"Okay," Esther said, then shut her mouth. Today wasn't the day for surprises or confessions. *Maam* was preparing for new students, *Daed* was working hard on the harvest, and from the sound of it, Sarah was finally making her way downstairs.

Esther felt her shoulders relax. For only a moment.

"I can't find my gloves," Sarah said, stomping into the kitchen.

"I thought you weren't supposed to cover your fingers yet."

Sarah looked at Esther. "What if I'm cold?"

"Are you?"

"Esther, if I'm outside, I might be. I need to be prepared. Who knows what could happen with you driving the buggy."

Esther inwardly sighed and tried to remember what her mother said about keeping her word, and what the preacher said last Sunday about showing unbridled charity toward others, and what the Bible said about not killing.

"Where going?" little Benjamin said, tugging at Esther's cloak along with her heartstrings. "I come, too? I help."

Esther bent down and picked up her little brother, traces of oatmeal at the corner of his mouth. Which, of course, made Lucas pop into her mind again. That tiny dollop of cottage cheese.

"I come, too?" Benjamin repeated.

"Aww." Esther gave him a squeeze, then spun in a circle. "Not this time, buddy." She ruffled the top of his head, noting that he needed a haircut. Perhaps she'd do that later today.

"No tagalongs," Sarah said. "It's going to be stressful enough."

"We're shopping for material," Esther said, hoping to defuse her already stressed-out sister. "It's a happy occasion."

"We see things so differently," Sarah said, literally peeling Benjamin from her arms and putting him on the floor. "I've never found much happiness in sewing."

Remembering back to when she'd made her own wedding dress, by then Esther had sewn five dresses on her own, and maybe a dozen blankets, and over twenty burping clothes for all the new *bobbeils* at church. By no means did she have the skills of a professional seamstress, but she could surely make a simple dress fit for a wedding.

Plus, she'd loved Jacob and had been excited to marry him—excited to start a new life. Making her dress had been a way to show that. When she thought about it now, she couldn't remember what that felt like. Was she still in love with him? Or had the two years since he'd gone weakened those feelings?

And was that a sin? Was she meant to move on, or was she supposed to be devoted to him forever?

Too many of the same questions made her temples throb.

"You can take my gloves," Esther said, pulling them from a drawer and passing them to Sarah.

"Thank you," Sarah said as she began putting them on. "Well, they're not quite as soft as mine, but they'll do. Can we go?"

"Peanut's hooked up and ready."

"Esther! Can we please not take that mule of yours?"

"What's wrong with her? She's stronger than any of Pa's horses and so much sweeter."

Sarah rolled her eyes but headed for the door. "She needs a good wash with some of that soap you're always working on."

"Oh, *jah*? Which scent do you think she'd like?"

Sarah breathed out a snort-laugh. "Heavens, whichever's the strongest. Some of that perfume the English woman at the bank wears. You can smell her a mile away."

"Two miles," Esther tweaked.

The sisters glanced at each other, then dissolved into laughter.

As they climbed into the buggy, Esther happily considered that maybe today wouldn't be as bad as she'd been dreading. Maybe Sarah would have a good attitude and they'd have a wonderful time building memories.

• • •

Two hours later, Esther was ready to climb aboard Peanut and ride away, leaving Sarah behind to drown beneath a pile of fabric samples. All these years, Esther had thought her sister was a perfectionist, when it turned out she was plain old indecisive.

"I still don't know," Sarah said, holding some heavy blue cotton up to the light. "Does the color suit me?"

"It does," Esther said, leaning back against a table of flannel, her feet sore from standing. "It's only slightly different from those other three blues over there."

"I like blue, but I don't want to look pale."

Never one to preach at her younger sister, Esther did not explain that Sarah shouldn't be fretting over what she looked like. She was beautiful before *Gott*, and Amos loved her, and the covenants she'd be making to the church were the most important thing about her wedding day.

All the youth had been taught this lesson since their first prayer meeting. And *Maam* had always been a flawless example of modesty and humility and obedience. Why, in Esther's estimation, their mother practically walked on water. Except for the tiny incident of making Esther follow through with her promise to Sarah, *Maam* was pretty near perfect.

"The deep blue matches the hue of your eyes," Esther said, recalling the headline of an article in an English women's magazine with a glossy cover. "And makes your skin look creamy and your cheeks lily—I mean, *rosy*."

Sarah turned to her. "Is that *gut*?"

"Oh, *jah*," Esther replied with a sage nod. "You'll look right smart in your black apron, matching Amos's suit to a tee."

"Black apron," Sarah repeated, staring off into space. "I do like the idea of matching."

Esther didn't have the heart to remind her sister that all brides in their order wore black aprons over their wedding dresses and all grooms wore black suits, bow ties, and tall hats. If the notion of matching helped Sarah make a decision, Esther was all for it.

"Your stockings will be black, too," Esther added.

"Who cares about my socks?" Sarah replied.

Okay...

"I like this one the best," Esther tried again, picking up a random piece of blue fabric. It was thinner than the rest and looked the easiest to cut and sew. "Should we get it?"

Sarah tapped a finger to her lips. "I think not." She pushed past Esther and to a table of thicker fabrics, practically denim. Definitely *not* easy to cut and sew. "I wish they carried the same purple of your wedding dress."

Esther froze in place, her hand still outstretched. "What?"

"You know it's the prettiest color and nicest material they've ever carried here." She exhaled a moan. "I don't see why I can't just wear *that* dress."

Esther felt her mouth fall open. "Be…because it wouldn't fit you. And because…it's my dress."

"But you're not using it, not even on preaching Sundays. It's just hanging in your closet doing nothing. Don't you think it would look nice on me?"

"Sarah." Esther closed her eyes, needing to concentrate on breathing. "You cannot wear the dress I made for my wedding day on your wedding day. You just can't."

"Fine," Sarah said. "Oh, look! This is it. This is the one." She was holding up a bolt of heavy blue cotton.

Esther wouldn't care if the material was coarse winter fleece with satin trim, she was just happy her sister had picked one. "I love it," she said, forcing a great big smile.

"Do you really, sister?" Sarah looked almost vulnerable, which seemed out of character. It wasn't usual for her to care what Esther thought about anything.

"I love it," Esther repeated, wearing a genuine smile this time. "You'll be the most beautiful bride in Lancaster County." She put an arm around her sister's shoulder and drew her in to her side. "More beautiful than any *Englisher* in a silly white gown and veil."

Sarah pressed her lips together. "*Danke*, Es," she whispered, causing a lump to form in Esther's throat. She did want Sarah's wedding to be a wonderful, memorable day. And if it took a little coaxing and tender self-confidence prodding to make her sister happy, where was the sin in that?

Esther was about to add that she'd promise to brush Sarah's long hair with one hundred silky strokes on the morning of her wedding, when Sarah said, "We better buy a lot of extra material in case you mess up."

CHAPTER EIGHT

The guy in the yellow shirt raised his hand. It was his third question in a row. "Aren't your marriages arranged?"

This time, Lucas didn't bother reminding the classroom that he no longer considered himself officially Amish, that the "your" pronoun in Yellow Shirt's question was misplaced. "No," he simply said. "Teens can begin dating, or *courting*, as they call it, when they're sixteen. They can court as many partners as they'd like and decide who they want to marry."

"You get married that young?" Yellow Shirt didn't raise his hand.

"It's extremely rare for anyone to marry under eighteen. Depending on the state, I believe that's against the law. They usually wait until early to mid-twenties."

"What's up with those beards?" This question came from the back of the room.

"It's nothing more than a tradition started during the Civil War," Lucas replied. "In most Amish sects, it's customary for a man to begin growing a beard once he's married."

"But no mustache?"

"Never."

"Why not?"

It wasn't a difficult question, but when Lucas had agreed to give a short Q&A, he thought the topics might be less superficial. Then again, the basic questions were probably the precise reason why his friend and colleague, Dr. Gregory Browning, had asked Lucas to give the lecture.

Hershey Medical Center was less than an hour drive from Honey Brook, Intercourse, and other Amish villages. Lucas had to admit it was an inspired idea to educate the doctors, nurses, and interns at the teaching hospital about the growing population of Amish and Mennonites. Apparently, over the decade since he'd been away, the local clinics were treating more and more plain folk. Gaining even a basic background of these patients was highly beneficial to all involved.

And how often did a teaching hospital have their very own Amish medical expert?

At least it will look good on my résumé, Lucas had thought after he'd agreed to the one-time Q&A.

"The Anabaptists of the late eighteen hundreds didn't want to look like soldiers. Also, the tradition goes that the original German and Swiss Amish wanted to distinguish themselves from other religious groups—which explains the absence of mustaches and also the bowl haircuts."

"Yeah, what's up with that hair?" Yellow Shirt again.

"It's obviously *tradition*," a young medical intern in the front row answered. "Haven't you been listening?" She turned around to face Yellow Shirt. "And stop being so ignorant and insensitive. This is *his* heritage; these are *his* people." She pointed at Lucas.

Again, Lucas's knee-jerk reaction was to explain

that he no longer practiced the Amish religion or lifestyle. "Any other questions?"

The classroom fell silent, and people were definitely squirming in their seats.

"Come on," he coaxed, attempting to lighten the mood. They'd already covered the use of buggies, one-room schoolhouses, the plain clothing, no zippers, and very few buttons. He'd even mentioned that the women make their own wedding dresses. Obviously, the only reason that had come to mind was because of Esther. Even while standing in front of the class, he couldn't help smiling when he thought of the aardvark story and her shocked expression when he'd told her he'd been in the barn that night.

"Anyone? Come on," he continued, holding his arms out to the sides. "I'm here all day."

Spatters of nervous chuckles.

A man wearing a denim jacket slowly raised his hand. "Do you believe in God?"

Once more, Lucas ignored the incorrect pronoun. "Yes, they do," he said. "All their religious beliefs are based on the Bible—Old and New Testaments. Their faith in *Gott* is highly important."

Even though he hadn't been to a proper church meeting in years, did that mean his religious beliefs had changed so much that he had to make it a point to distance himself by changing that pronoun? By the way he was talking, it sure seemed like it. Did he still believe in God, the Ten Commandments, and the Sermon on the Mount?

"How did you say that word?" the intern at the front asked, dragging him back to the present.

"What word?"

"God? It sounded different."

Lucas replayed his earlier sentence. "Oh." He rubbed his chin. "Um, yes, it's pronounced slightly different. *Gott*—a hard *T* instead of a *D*."

"Is that Pennsylvania Dutch?"

"More like it's derived from the accent," Lucas explained, all the time wondering why his tongue had slipped to the old pronunciation. He hardly even thought in reformed German anymore. "If you've driven around the countryside," he continued, not wanting to dwell on why he might've made that mistake, "you've probably noticed the bedsheets and clothes hanging on the lines. This is because they don't use electricity. Though some homes may have a propane tank—"

"The Amish bakery I go to has electricity," someone said.

"Well, in situations like that, it's common for an Amish family to team up with a less conservative sect, like a Mennonite family. Most Mennonites in this area are allowed to use electricity."

"My cousin's Amish neighbor has a computer in his barn," said someone from the back corner. "And a phone."

"That's… That seems odd," Lucas said.

"Actually," an older man with a trimmed gray beard standing by the wall began, "it's not at all unusual for Amish families to have a phone outside their home—in a barn or even built onto the side of their house."

Lucas had no idea what the man was talking about. Back when he'd been a teenager, there'd been a handful of new order Beachy Amish families who used some electricity or built phone booth shacks near their property lines, but he'd never heard of any family in his community using modern technology.

"You said you've been gone for ten years," Yellow Shirt said. "A lot's changed, right?"

"Apparently," Lucas said in a low voice, trying to wrap his brain around the concept.

"The dairy farm by my house is all electric. I asked the owner about it once, and he said the FDA won't let him sell milk unless the whole plant is refrigerated."

"That seems…logical," Lucas said with a nod. Maybe he wasn't such an expert after all.

For another thirty minutes, he answered questions as best he could, though now he wasn't at all sure he was giving current information.

For a religion that has been based on the same strict traditions for a few hundred years, how has so much changed in a single decade?

While the room emptied, Lucas packed up his notes and laptop. A few people gave him a quick thank-you, and the female intern who'd sat in the front stopped to give him a big smile, which Lucas barely returned. His thoughts were still lost in all the info *he'd* gleaned from the class.

"Rough day?"

It was the older man with the short gray beard.

"I've had better." Lucas pinched the bridge of his nose. "Thank you for attending, by the way."

The man slid his hands into his white lab coat. "I wouldn't have missed it. High time we heard a lecture from…well, from someone like you."

Lucas lifted a polite smile, feeling about as Amish as Gordon Ramsey. "I reckon I'm not as much of an expert as I used to be."

"You did fine. It was interesting. Fascinating, actually."

Even with the compliment, Lucas's mood refused to lighten. "That's very kind of you."

The man took a step toward him. "I'm sincere. We see more and more of you plain folk these days. In order to treat a specific type of person, it's vital to know as much about them as possible—medical history. I'm sure you agree."

"I do." Lucas set down his computer bag. "That's the whole reason I'm here. A friend of mine who works at the med center asked me to do this seminar. You might know him—Greg Browning."

The old man smiled. "Doctor Browning has worked with me on several projects. I asked him to set this up."

"You did?"

When the man smiled again, lines crinkled the sides of his twinkling eyes. "I'm Griffin Ballard. I head the lecture committee. Please, call me Griff." He extended his hand.

"Nice to meet you, Griff," Lucas said, shaking his hand.

"I suppose you have some questions for me now."

Only about a million, Lucas was about to utter. But he didn't, knowing exactly why he'd been asked to do the Q&A. And despite some rocky moments, he was glad he'd done it.

"Are the plain folk who seek professional medical help coming in for basic needs or only bigger issues?" he asked.

"It varies." Griff sat on a chair, turning it to face Lucas. "Fortunately, we see far less childhood disease than we used to. Vaccines aren't as frowned upon now."

That's wonderful news to hear, Lucas thought as he remembered vividly one of his baby sister's playmates getting tetanus from a construction site and quickly passing away. It shocked the community, yet he couldn't recall if any action was taken at the time. Did that incident cause the brethren to rethink their strict policy?

"Expectant mothers are relying more and more on certified midwives," Griff added, "instead of untrained women in their neighborhoods."

Lucas sat down across from Griff. "A few days ago, I treated a woman with injuries that looked like they came from abuse. Is that becoming common?"

"About as common as the rest of the world," Griff replied. "Maybe a bit less, though. I do envy their strong devotion to family and faith—*your* devotion. I'm sorry, I had a hard time determining if you're still a follower of the religion."

The question made Lucas shift in his seat. "Not, um, no…"

"Forgive me." Griff put a hand on his shoulder. "That was a very personal question. I shouldn't have asked."

Lucas exhaled, grateful for not having to answer any further. Because…he wasn't sure. He hadn't gone to church in years, he seldom read from the

Bible, and he couldn't think of the last time he'd actually knelt down to say a proper prayer.

But did that mean he didn't believe in the celestial Creation of the world? Or heaven and hell? Or that God could answer prayers? Even if he felt like he had no business praying because of the bitterness in his heart almost too heavy to carry?

Lucas felt a tightness in his chest.

"We had a case just a few months ago," Griff said, interrupting his gloomy thoughts. "A young Amish girl was brought in with swollen glands, high fever, and blood in her urine."

Lucas's spine stiffened as he leaned forward to listen.

"Turns out it was only a nasty case of mono, but when other diseases were brought up, her parents had no problem discussing potential treatments."

That old resentment flared up, making his head hurt and his stomach churn. Resentment aimed directly at his father. Was he still so close-minded today?

"What a relief," Lucas offered so he wouldn't speak what was truly on his mind. "Sounds like good progress has been made. I hope it continues."

"I honestly believe that with you working at the Honey Creek clinic, this area will gain even more trust in the professionals." He began stroking his beard. "Especially if you come back to do another lecture."

"Me?" Lucas said.

Griff nodded. "After hearing you today, I'm actually thinking of adding a lecture series to the curriculum. Continuing education for the local docs, as well. Anyone who wants to learn."

"Oh," Lucas replied, a little dumbfounded. "You want me to teach a class?"

"Well, there won't be books or homework," Griff said, his eyes twinkling again. "But the information you presented today is imperative to this area, while your background and personal knowledge is unprecedented." He leaned forward. "Like it or not, you're *the* subject expert."

Though the idea had been sprung on him, Lucas couldn't find a reason to disagree. "How often? I already volunteer here twice a month."

"Let's double that," Griff suggested. "Two days to volunteer, two days to lecture. Wait." He scratched his beard. "I think I'd like to make the lecture series once a week. The money will be good and you'll truly be making a difference."

Lucas didn't care about the money. In fact, he might've offered to do it for free. "Sounds good." He pulled out his cell phone and opened the calendar app. "What days?"

As the two men worked out the new schedule, Lucas got even more excited. If the head of the lecture committee thought he had important knowledge to share, he wouldn't shirk his duty.

"So, would you like it to be a Q&A like today?" Lucas asked.

"Maybe some basic questions at first," Griff said, "but I'd like you to delve deeper. Tell us more about the current health habits, traditions, and overall way of life of today's local Amish."

Lucas got that sinking feeling again. Was he really the right person for this?

"I know there were some bumps in the road today," Griff said with a wink. "I suppose that means you'll have to do your research. Reach out to your people." He stood to leave. "From what you were saying earlier, it sounds like they're wonderful folk, caring and generous. You shouldn't have any trouble reconnecting with them."

• • •

As he drove home, Lucas kept the radio off. The raunchy lyrics of even the mildest pop songs were getting on his nerves. Besides, he needed to think. How was he supposed to reconnect with "his people"? Only Esther Miller acknowledged that he was back in town. Even after all those letters to his mother, had his own family written him off?

He ran a hand through his hair, remembering what it had been like to have that infamous bowl cut. Sure, it looked strange to the *Englishers*, but when he'd been a kid, it was how all his buddies looked. It hadn't been strange at all.

As he neared town, Amish farms began popping into view. As he passed one—set way back on its lot—he noticed a power line reaching from the main road of restaurants and stores straight to its barn. He knew who lived there, or who used to live there. The Mast family made the best cheese in twenty miles. He'd grown up snacking on the leftover curds and dry ends. No cars in the gravel driveway, but two buggies and a tractor. Plus, a big handwritten wooded sign. Yep, white cheddar and cottage cheese were on sale today.

Huh. Had Yellow Shirt been right? Was it not rare now for Amish farms to have some source of power? As he was about to turn off the main road and head for home, something made Lucas keep driving straight instead.

Slowing down, he slid on a baseball cap and sunglasses. Not much of a disguise, but he knew it'd be best if he wasn't recognized. Just around the next corner, up a rolling hill, a red barn with a green roof appeared in the valley, then the white house with the summer pond. The same straight rows and rows of beet plants.

Lucas shifted his truck into park. Far enough away that he wouldn't be seen, he stared down at the barn, the pond, the crops, the house that might still have the drawing of a sheep named Dan on the back of the closet door.

He felt a strange sense of relief when he noted the absence of any power lines. Hearing a bark, he glanced toward the barn, seeing two dogs run out the double doors. A tall man in a blue shirt, black pants, suspenders, and straw hat followed them out.

Lucas stopped breathing.

The man filled a bucket at the water pump, then walked to the side of the barn, pouring it into the horses' trough. Next, he stood on the base of the wooden fence, reached out, and stroked the nose of a brown pony. It didn't look too big. Maybe a late summer foal, ready to be trained to pull a pony cart.

That used to be Jeremiah's job. And he'd been teaching Lucas. Jacob would've been next in line...

Lucas swallowed hard, leaning forward to watch the tall man throw a rubber ball for the dogs to chase. The cows must've all been milked and the other animals fed. The clusters of zucchini plants and pumpkins were larger than he'd ever seen. It must've been a leisurely moment for the farmer, one of the few before the October harvest.

Suddenly, the man aimed his gaze toward Lucas, shading his eyes with both hands. Even though they were a good sixty yards away from each other, Lucas couldn't help sinking down in his seat. Even if he'd been seen, there was no way the farmer would've recognized him.

Not after ten years.

Yet, the farmer didn't look away. In fact, he began pacing forward, past the pig sty and chicken coop, even past the old outhouse, as if he was going to march up that hill and straight to Lucas's truck.

But that was crazy. When the man stopped to shoo a few loose hens, Lucas started the engine and drove away, watching in his rearview mirror how the man, too, had stopped but was still looking out toward the road. Lucas pressed on the gas, kicking up gravel.

It was only a coincidence and was not about to be some cinematic reunion between father and son. Lucas felt like an idiot to think for even a split second that could happen. The bitterness and blame he felt toward his father was stronger than ever.

Jacob used to climb that tree. And splash in that pond. And chase the new spring piglets around the yard. In some way, his father had taken that away from him.

Lucas gritted his teeth until his jaw ached, wanting to push the bad memories away. Otherwise, he might not survive in Honey Creek. Could he ever figure out how to forgive him? Lucas bet a day's pay that he was considered dead to his father—or at least gone forever.

What was it that Griff Ballard has said? That "his" people were wonderful and generous? And they'd be ever so easy to reach out to.

As simple as that.

Because of his upbringing, full of love and all the comfort he needed, and by truly generous people, a part of Lucas believed in the theory of reaching out.

But in the flesh, it was not at all simple.

Not for him. Was it shame that kept him from moving forward? Would the old bitterness stay stamped on his heart forever?

Almost like a lightning strike in the middle of the road, Lucas thought of Esther Miller, pictured her smiling face—the same one he remembered from years ago when he'd thought of her as nothing more than the girl his brother had a crush on. Was she an enigma, or might others from the village be as open?

He bit down harder on his back teeth, knowing the pride in his heart would never allow him to be vulnerable. He was content to reconnect with Esther, reminisce over some of the good times and share funny stories. She was easy to talk to and didn't make him feel uncomfortable about being home. She'd even seemed happy to see him.

His cell rang. He pulled it out and read the face. "Hey, Greg."

"How'd it go today?"

"I'm not sure whether to thank you or punch

you in the mouth."

Greg laughed. "I heard great things. You're a celebrity around here."

Lucas pulled the truck over to the side of the road and parked. "It was an experience, I'll give you that." He rolled down the window, letting the light September breeze blow through the cab.

The two men talked, Lucas filling Greg in about Yellow Shirt, the smiling intern, and then about the job offer from Dr. Ballard. "He wants you bad, man," Greg said. "He's been looking for an Amish expert for years."

I'm not an expert anymore, Lucas wanted to say. But his self-inflicted pity party had gone on long enough. "I'm glad I can help," he said instead. "It's a good cause. The Amish are pretty secluded folks, and if something about them seems secretive, it's usually because they want it to be."

"I hear that."

"But there should never be a question about offering help with health and taking care of any population's general well-being," Lucas continued. "We mustn't allow traditions to keep professional medical care off-limits. That's devastating to families and communities."

He was beginning to get frustrated again, hot under the collar, so he leaned his head out the window and took a few slow, deep breaths.

"Sounds like they've got the right man for the job," Greg said.

Lucas laughed, mostly at himself. "Maybe."

"Buddy, I've known you for years. You've got the best bedside manner of anyone I know, and your dedication to research is unsurpassed. I never understood why you didn't go on to finish med school and become a doctor."

At the time, research was all Lucas had been interested in. And when Jacob had gone home after staying with him for *Rumspringa*, Lucas saw no reason to continue down the path of advanced education.

"Who needs the headaches of those MD initials? I'm satisfied with PA."

Greg laughed. "That's no lie, man."

The friends wrapped up the call, and Lucas resumed his drive home, grateful for his buddy's confidence in him.

As he pulled into the driveway, he thought again about Esther. Just the day before, he'd boldly asked if they could meet again. And she'd said yes. At the time, he'd simply wanted the pleasant feeling of connection to continue. She'd brought a calmness to his soul he hadn't felt in years. Was it selfish to want that again?

When he sat down on his couch, out of habit, he reached for the TV remote, ready to catch up on *Cake Boss* or *Master Chef* or any of the other food shows that addictively lulled him into a zoned-out state every night.

Instead, he noticed his Bible on the bookshelf on the other side of the room.

Without wondering why, Lucas walked over and picked it up, running a hand down the smooth, worn leather cover. Over the past ten years, it had been moved from box to apartment and box to apartment four times. Never once had he not unpacked it and given it a place on the bookshelf. Yet, it had been far too long since he'd opened it.

The clock over the fireplace ticked loudly as he continued to run his hand over the leather, one finger tracing the gold lettering. Inside the front cover, he'd see his mother's handwriting, as well as his *grossmami*'s—*Maam*'s mother. Notes and messages from them would fill the margins and headers.

He'd received that Bible on his tenth birthday, and he'd carried it to every church service and scripture study for the next six years. As a youth, he'd underlined his own favorite verses in St. Matthew, Romans, practically all of Psalms. There was one particular passage from James that he used to recite to himself before his nightly prayers.

Lucas closed his eyes and bowed his head, straining to remember the words. Though seemingly just out of reach, he simply could not remember them. Instead of letting another rush of frustration take over the moment, Lucas sat down in his favorite chair, his heart beating faster as he flipped open to nearly the end of the book, scanning for those verses in James that had so inspired him once upon a time.

CHAPTER NINE

The hours couldn't fly by quickly enough for Esther. Knowing it was the day she planned to meet Lucas made the humdrum activities seem almost exciting. Even consulting with Sarah for the fourth time about the style of the wedding dress was bearable. She'd already laid out the pattern and blue material, ready to be pinned, then cut out in the morning when the light in the sewing room was best.

The rest of *Maam*'s students had already gone home to help with chores. Only sweet little Abraham was left. The more time it took for her brother to finish his long division, the more impatient Esther became. It wasn't his fault she'd made secret plans.

No, not secret. That would be sinful. She had plans that she just hadn't told anyone about yet. A woman was allowed time to herself, after all, *jah*? She glanced down at Abraham's work.

"Carry the two," she said, then ruffled the top of her brother's hair.

"Stop it," Abraham said in a mopey voice.

"Stop what?" She mussed his hair again.

"Stop your teasin'!" He knocked her hand away.

"Temper…temper…"

"Ma!" Abraham whined. "Make her stop."

Their mother glanced up from the letter she was writing at the far end of the table. "Behave, you two."

"I *am*!"

Esther lifted her eyebrows innocently. "So am I. But your freshly cut hair is too irresistible." She bent down to kiss his cheeks and pinch the back of his neck.

"If he stabs you with his pencil, don't you dare get blood on my wedding dress," Sarah said, blowing on her fingertips.

"Ack, Sarah," *Maam* said. "Such violent talk."

Abraham wiggled away from Esther, pushed back from his chair, and stood.

She laughed. "You don't relish your big sister kissing you?"

Abraham stuck out his tongue. "I don't like no one—"

"*Any*one."

Her brother's face turned red. "*Any*one—ugh!"

Esther was laughing now. So were Sarah, Benjamin, and even *Maam*. "I'm gonna get you," she said, chasing her brother around the table, Abraham only inches away from her grasp. His wails and pleas made Esther tease him more. Just as she was about to catch him and cover him with kisses, *Daed* appeared at the back door.

"What," he said, removing his straw hat while wiping his boots on the mat, "is going on here? Who's making a racket when it's schooling time?"

For a moment, nobody moved. Then, betraying them all, Sarah said, "Esther started it."

Still out of breath, Esther glared down at her sister. "You do want armholes in your wedding dress, right?" she whispered. The sinister part of her heart thought that might make a great joke, repaying

Sarah for being such a pain in the backside all week.

"Esther." *Daed* pointed at her. "Come here. You, too, son."

For a moment, Esther feared her father might actually be upset. True, it was school time, but it was so warm today, and the battery-operated fans in the room weren't helping in the slightest.

"Outside with me," he said. "Now." Then he glanced over his shoulder. "All of you. Sarah, Benjamin. Evie!" *Daed* called out until their curly-haired little sister came down the stairs. "Mamma," he added, "you too."

Maam pressed her lips together in a smile and followed them out the back door. Sitting on the patio was a large ice chest filled to the brim with brightly colored Popsicles.

Abraham gasped. "For us?"

Papa laughed. "Of course! Can't expect you to get much done on a beautiful day like today. If it's okay with Momma, I say we play the rest of the afternoon."

All eyes shot to *Maam*. "Well," she said, running her hands down her apron, "I suppose we shouldn't waste such a perfect autumn day."

Whoops and shouts erupted as hugs and kisses were shared, then on to the tasty cool treats.

Even Esther took the time to sit on the edge of a bench after choosing a strawberry-flavored Popsicle, her chin tilted toward the sun. She loved hearing the *kinnahs*' laughter, Sarah's advice to Evie, as well as her parents chatting behind her. After a few minutes, however, and maybe after too much sugar, her younger siblings' laughter grew boisterous. Playful shrieks floated from around the corner by the barn where the youngsters and *Daed* had disappeared.

"What's that ruckus?" asked *Maam*.

"I'll check," Esther said. Before she could take two steps toward the barn, out jumped the *kinnahs*, Abraham holding the garden hose. They were soaking wet. After not too many seconds, so was Esther.

"That's for teasin'!" Her brother laughed, spraying Esther in the face. The cool water felt so marvelous that the sneak attack barely bothered her. Not until all—including Papa—were covered head to toe in mud did the water fight conclude.

"Out to the barn," *Maam* ordered. "Let me hose you off before you dirty up my clean floors."

"Mother!" Esther suddenly remembered. "May I take my bath now? I've got, well, I'm going into town this afternoon, if it's okay."

"What time?" she asked, tugging off Benjamin's muddy shirt.

"Three," Esther said, silently praying that there would be no further questions. She'd been taking soap into town so often lately that she hoped that would be the assumption.

"Better hurry," *Maam* said.

"Do you want a buggy?" asked her father, working to get the mud out of his beard.

"Are you sure?" Esther asked, rather surprised.

"Plowing's done. The mule's been resting all day."

"*Danke, Daed,*" Esther said. "I really appreciate it."

Practically tearing off her muddy dress and apron, Esther ran bathwater—warmed by the solar panels that lined the roof—and grabbed a bar of her clove soap. In no time at all, she was clean and dry, dressing carefully in a plain pink dress and blue apron. Though she didn't try to stand out, she thought the light color looked good on her.

Having done it dozens of times, she had no trouble getting Peanut the mule into her harness and the buggy ready to go. She thought about that crack Sarah had made about her mule needing a bath. Esther thought she smelled like fresh soil, hard work, and love.

As a precaution in case her parents were watching, she took a box of soap with her, as if hand delivering it to a customer was her purpose for needing the buggy.

But, since no one was around to even wave her away, she set off down the road. Esther assumed she should feel guilty for not telling her mother the exact truth. Was there an implacable hardness in her heart now that kept her from feeling even the slightest bit of remorse for her actions?

Maybe this was what the deacons warned about during the preachings. Would the little white lies add up until she didn't know what was true anymore? She wondered what Sarah or Louisa would say if they knew what she was up to. Actually, she knew exactly what they would say, which made her gently pull back on the reins for just a moment—reconsidering the adventure.

Would she someday look back and wonder if this was her first real step off *Gott*'s path? At the terrifying thought, she pulled hard on the reins, causing Peanut to whinny.

"It's okay, girl," she said, talking sweetly to the mule while her heart beat hard. She didn't want to be disobedient. She wanted to be at peace, to have perfect faith, to not keep thinking about how much fragrance she might get away with adding to her next batch of soap, and also to not feel like she wanted to cry every time she thought about Sarah's wedding dress. "Everything's okay," she cooed to Peanut. "We're just going to turn around ever so slowly."

At first she thought her eyes were playing tricks on her. An Englishman in a black sweatshirt with the hood up was standing along the shoulder of the road, an arm held out to his side, his thumb extended like a hitchhiker.

"Going my way, pretty lady?" he said. Esther held tight to the reins as he approached the buggy.

"Oh, for heaven's sake." An indulgent relief flooded her body at the realization it was Lucas. "What on earth are you doing out here like this?" she said, trying not to giggle at his appearance.

He looked up and peeled back his hood. "Figured you'd be coming down this road. It's a shortcut to town." He peered into the buggy. "Got more soap, I see."

"Special delivery to Yoder's."

"Uh-huh." Lucas held a hand up to Peanut, letting her smell him; then he stroked her nose. "You're going there now?"

"Well…" Esther bit a thumbnail out of nervous habit. "I must admit, I was actually about to turn around for home."

His eyebrows mushed together, displaying an

expression of confusion, then unmistakable disappointment. Esther wasn't sure how either made her
feel.

"I see," he said. "I thought we—"

"I know," she cut in, not forgetting her reason for
wanting to retreat. "I know we said we'd talk some
more—and I really want to."

"You've still got questions," he said.

She nodded, biting her nail again.

"So do I." Lucas stood in silence, then turned his
attention to Peanut. He scratched behind her ears,
then patted the side of her head. When Jacob had
been alive, he'd held strong to the old Amish belief
that the measure of an animal's creation was to toil
and till the earth, to work *for* man.

Lucas pulled a sugar cube from his pocket and
fed it to Peanut. The mule swallowed it whole then
began nudging Lucas, wanting more. It was terribly
sweet watching him treat her favorite pet so kindly,
differently than how others in the community had.

He looked up at her. His eyes were a soft brown,
lighter than his younger brother's. It made Esther
blink hard when she realized she was comparing the
two Brenneman brothers. She actually flinched
when she realized she preferred Lucas's looks.

Did that make her unfaithful?

"You're leaving, then?" Lucas asked.

Esther kept her gaze away as she nodded.
"Where will you go?" she asked.

"Same place I was headed. A friend of mine in
Nickel Mines had a litter of kids. Triplets," he added.
"I thought you might want to see them, but since—"

"Three baby goats?" Esther's own shriek of glee

almost startled her, and she nearly gave herself whiplash. "I'd love that! Can we go?"

Lucas laughed and ran a hand through his hair. It, too, was lighter than Jacob's, thicker, even, and had curls on the ends. But Esther must stop all these comparisons. Admiring her dead fiancé's older brother couldn't possibly be the Christian way to gain the closure she desperately wanted.

"Do you mind driving?" Lucas said, glancing up at the empty space next to her.

"Not at all." Her smile grew as Lucas nimbly climbed onto her small buggy and took his seat. He smelled of pine and clean shampoo.

"Is this okay?" He gestured at how close they were forced to sit.

Keeping her grin in place, she aimed her gaze forward. "I'm a big girl, Mr. Lucas." She clicked her tongue, causing Peanut to trot.

"I see that," he replied. "Decent driver, too. Very safe and slow for such a wide, empty road." When she glanced at him, he was grinning.

Esther was never one to back away from a challenge. She'd been riding on and driving with Peanut for nearly seven years. She knew exactly what the animal was capable of. Clicking her tongue again, she gently whipped the reins. "Let's go, girl," she said. "Show him what you've got!"

As Peanut picked up the pace, iron and springs clinked, and wind whipped into the coach of the buggy, ruffling Esther's cloak. When they hit a small bump, Lucas laughed and actually gripped the railing on the side of his seat as if worried he'd fall off.

"Woo-hoo!" he cheered as the road flew by, making Esther giggle, prompting Peanut to go faster.

The wind on her face was exhilarating, and her heart sailed like it always did when she rode with abandon—another thing of which Jacob hadn't approved. At the thought of his name, Esther lost her nerve and pulled back on the reins, slowing Peanut to a trot.

"Had enough?" she said to Lucas.

"I take it back—you're a fantastic driver," he said. "That was a blast!"

"Danke." She laughed, catching her breath. Esther hadn't felt this comfortable with a man since…well, since Jacob. "How much farther?" she asked, not wanting awkwardness to set in.

"We're almost there. I think you broke a speed record." He gave directions, and after no time, they were pulling up to a small farm.

At first glance, it looked plain, but then Esther noticed the big white truck behind the barn, as well as the satellite dish for watching TV. She'd been in plenty of English homes, though it was always an adjustment at first. She didn't want anyone to feel uncomfortable, and never really relished explaining her lifestyle to curious outsiders.

"There's Eric," Lucas said as he hopped off the carriage and took the reins to hold Peanut steady. "Hello, to the house!" he called.

A middle-aged man with light hair wearing overalls came around from the side of the house. "Lucas! Glad you could make it!"

Still keeping hold of the reins, Lucas reached a hand up to Esther. For a stupid long moment, she stared at it, thinking this would be the first time she would purposefully touch the grown-up Lucas.

"Plan on staying up there forever?" he said in a quiet voice. "Or do you prefer to climb off yourself?"

"No. Um, thank you," she said, sliding her hand into his. She couldn't help but notice the hard roughness, silently wondering why a medical person's hands would be so worn. "Much obliged," she added after landing firmly on the ground.

"May I take care of the mule?" he asked, already leading Peanut toward the fenced-in field where two horses and a cow were grazing. Esther followed behind Lucas, watching him first shake hands with his friend, then lead Peanut inside the fence.

"This little jenny's tuckered out," he said to Eric. "Mind if she gets some water?"

"Help yourself." Eric patted the mule on the rump.

"Oh, *I'll* do that," Esther said, not used to anyone else taking care of Peanut.

"I got it," Lucas said with a crooked grin. "I do remember how to handle animals."

She unleashed a jolly laugh. "Okay, but keep an eye on her. She'll drink for an hour straight if you let her; then she won't want to move for two days."

Lucas nodded, squinting from the sun. "Esther, this is Eric Leigh. We met at the clinic when I first moved here." The man smiled and nodded, extending his hand for her to shake, no awkwardness at all. "Eric, meet Esther Miller. We grew up together."

Eric stopped shaking and gripped her hand. "Not Moses Miller's Esther?"

"Why, yes," Esther said, surprised at hearing the nickname.

Lucas stepped closer. "You know each other?"

"No," Esther began slowly.

"Yes," Eric cut in. "Or I've heard of you. You make the soap at Yoder's."

Esther felt herself standing a little taller. "I do."

"Boy, oh, boy. My wife can't get enough of it. She'd buy out your entire inventory if given the chance."

"Honest?" Esther couldn't stop the smile from spreading across her face. "I'm so pleased to hear that."

"Smells pretty good, huh?" Lucas added in.

"I'll say. There's one that reminds me of my granddaddy's rose garden. Takes me back some years, I tell ya. Shoo, y'all," Eric added when a half dozen chickens began pecking around their feet.

"Do you know if your wife has tried the clove?" Esther asked, wondering if that was something Leah would say to a customer. Commerce, and all that.

"Can't say I remember that scent."

Esther grinned. "Well, I just so happen to have a fresh box in the buggy that you can give to her."

"That's real nice." Eric bowed. "But I'm sure she'd appreciate it better coming from you. Vivian! Vivy, babe, come on out here."

"You're famous," Lucas whispered, giving her a nudge.

"I am not." She laughed softly. "But folks sure love the soap these days. My cousin who sells them, she keeps asking me to make them smell stronger, but you know how the church is about that."

Lucas cocked his head to the side. "No, I don't.

Or I don't remember."

"Well, I suppose it's difficult to be submissive if you smell like perfume." She ran a finger under her chin thoughtfully. "I'm trying to be obedient. I mean, I *want* to be—"

Just then, the back door flew open, and a tall woman with a blond ponytail appeared. She wore a pink sweater and white jeans. Esther couldn't imagine wearing something so immodest, but she tried very hard not to judge outsiders, for they lived a completely different lifestyle. Perhaps not better or worse, just different.

"Hi there," she said, walking over. She looked much younger than her husband. But again, Esther was not to judge.

"Viv, you know Lucas, of course."

"Sure." Her smile was big and bright. "Nice seeing you."

"And this…" He took a pause and actually gestured at Esther with both hands. "This is Esther—"

"Hey there. Good to meet ya. I'm Vivian Leigh—like the movie star, but I'm just a housewife." Vivian's high laugh sounded like sparkling diamonds.

"You didn't let me finish," Eric said. "Her name is Esther Miller."

Vivian's expression was blank for a moment; then her eyes lit up. "*The* Esther Miller?"

"Yup." Eric grinned and hooked his thumbs around the straps of his overalls.

Vivian's gaze shot to Esther. "You mean my future best friend in all the world, Esther Miller?"

"The very same."

"Ohhhh...my goodness," she said, jumping up and down while clapping. "I love your soaps. They're my very favorite thing ever. I swear, I can't get along without them."

Trying to push past the sudden shyness brought on by being the center of attention, Esther lifted a smile. "Thank *ye*," she said. "Um, I brought you a box—two dozen hand cut. I hope that's not too many. It's a new fragrance, clove—"

"Are you serious?" Vivian eyed the box Lucas had just appeared with. "You brought it for...me?"

"Jah." Esther motioned for Lucas to hand it to Vivian before the woman burst.

"Omigosh, this smells amazing," Vivian said, sniffing the air above the box. Esther could smell it, as well. And she had to admit, it was pretty amazing. "Thank you. Oh, my stars, thank you, Miss Esther Miller!"

The next moment, Esther was yanked into a hug. Vivian was laughing, or maybe it was that laugh-cry folks sometimes did when they couldn't make up their minds. Her skin smelled like honeysuckle soap, which made Esther want to laugh-cry, too.

She heard Lucas's quiet laugh, and Eric cleared his throat. "Sorry," Vivian said, finally letting her go. "I didn't mean to...wrinkle you. I'm just so, well, I'm overwhelmed, that's the only way to put it."

Feeling a bit overwhelmed herself from all the attention, "You're welcome" was all Esther could utter.

"What can I do for you?" Vivian asked. "Would you like a drink—some tea? Won't you please come inside?"

"Actually," Lucas said, "I brought her to see the goats."

Just as before, Vivian's eyes went wide as sunflowers. "You like kids?" she asked Esther.

"Yes." Esther smiled, trying not to look too excited. "I adore them."

Vivian jetted toward Esther, this time to grab her hand. "Come with me. They're the cutest we've ever had."

"She treats them like pets," Eric said to Lucas as the men followed behind.

"They *are* pets," Vivian said, walking so fast toward the house now that she was practically dragging Esther. "You think I'd let them sleep out in that dreary old barn of yours?"

"She dresses them up," Eric continued. "All three were in pink tutus yesterday. I hope none of the neighbors saw."

Brand-new baby goats in pink ballerina outfits? Esther almost couldn't catch her breath, she was so thrilled. Before they'd even reached the house, she heard faint bleating, making her heart skip a beat. The scampering of tiny hooves on hardwood floor made her want to run the final steps.

Vivian opened the door, allowing Esther to enter first.

Better than an avalanche of golden retriever pups, she was greeted by three of the softest, furriest, tiniest, most adorable kids she'd ever seen. Without even thinking, she dropped down to the floor.

If this is my "punishment" for telling a tiny white lie, she thought while allowing herself to be smothered, *it just might be worth it!*

CHAPTER TEN

Lucas wished he had a camera. Remembering his phone, he whipped it out, ready to capture the moment. But he stopped just short of snapping the first picture, recalling the strict policy plain folk had about not wanting to be photographed.

Even if that policy had softened, he should at least wait and ask Esther's permission first. So he slid the cell into his pocket and simply enjoyed the scene playing out before him in real time.

Esther's happy squeals were so high-pitched, they might've registered on the Richter scale. If he didn't know better, he'd think she was suffocating under the three baby goats.

"I want to take you home with me," she cooed in baby talk, snuggling the kid with white and brown markings. The little guy stuck out his tiny tongue and bleated. Esther giggled and hugged him harder. "No, I want *you*," she said, moving to the kid whose coat was black as coal. She kissed his face and fell backward when the kid started nuzzling under her neck, following his natural instinct to butt heads. "Glory be!" As Esther rolled over to stand, she squealed anew as the smallest of the kids actually jumped onto the flat of Esther's back, as if climbing onto a stump.

By now, her heavy outer prayer *kapp* had come untied and the pins holding her hair were loosening. Still giggling in bliss, and while somehow holding all three goats on her lap, she looked up at Lucas, strands of blond hair falling over her eyes. "This one needs your attention."

"Okay," he said, walking over, then squatting down beside her. Esther giggled as the black goat stood on his hind legs, balancing his front hoofs on the front of Lucas's shoulders. When he began licking Lucas's face, his first instinct was to turn away and stand up. But because of the gleeful hysterics coming from Esther, he didn't have the heart.

"Whoa," she said as another kid jumped up to lick her face.

"You okay?" he asked, automatically reaching out to take her arm, making sure she was steady. The touch was brief, and because of the goat trying to lick up his nose, she probably didn't notice his face flush hot as his hand clutching hers lingered longer than necessary, an additional squeeze on purpose this time.

"I don't think I'll be the same after this," she said. "My life is complete!"

Same here.

Lucas couldn't help chuckling. While gazing at Esther's smiling face, sitting so near to each other that he could've reached out and stroked her smooth, pink cheek, he couldn't imagine seeing anyone as happy as her ever again. Strange how glee could make someone look more attractive. Or maybe he was simply more attracted to Esther in that moment *because* of her happiness.

Either way, though, it was futile to feel any sort of attraction. After giving the kid a semi-awkward hug, Lucas stood up and took a few steps back.

"Esther, sweetie," Vivian said as she slid onto the floor, belly down. "You can come over any time. Ya hear me—whenever you want."

"Really?" Esther said, a bit of hair caught in the corner of her mouth.

"I'm knitting them Christmas sweaters—don't you say a word," she snapped when Eric groaned. "I can give you the pattern if you want, and you can make some of your own."

"I'd love that! Tiny goat-size Christmas sweaters. Have you ever heard of anything so adorable?" Once again, she looked up at Lucas, grinning ear to ear like a carefree child.

For a moment, he thought back to that first time they'd seen each other at the clinic. There'd been flashes of the girl he used to know, but until now, he hadn't seen her in full bloom.

That day, she asked me about Jacob, he thought while watching Esther hold up the front legs of the black goat, making him walk on two hooves like a toddler. *And I promised myself I would talk to her about it. That's what we're supposed to be doing right now.*

Instead, he'd thrown the ultimate distraction at her—three of them.

He genuinely did love watching her play with the kids, but all he was really doing was putting off a promise he'd made to himself, because when he finally got around to telling her the truth, he knew how badly it would hurt her.

He did not want to betray his brother's memory, but how much longer could he keep the secret?

The other night, he'd found the passage in the

book of James that he used to love as a kid. He'd read it over and over until it was nearly memorized again. After that, he'd stayed up late, thumbing through the thin onion-paper pages, pausing to read the verses marked in yellow—those had been the ones from his mother.

Ever since then, he hadn't stopped thinking about that old Bible; how it had felt so good in his hands, like a lost friend he'd found. Even the smell brought back fond memories of being on a road to a completely different life.

What would his life have been like if he'd stayed on the first path? Would he be married and raising Amish babies? Back then, he'd courted a few girls from church, given them rides home in his buggy after the singings on Sunday nights, but he'd never met anyone special.

His gaze drifted to Esther. For the past hour, she and Vivian had been chasing the goats around the large living room and open kitchen. Up and down the carpeted stairs. Her eyes were glowing bright and her cheeks were a fresh pink. She looked...

As quickly as it had come, again, Lucas wiped the ridiculous thought from his brain, refocusing on his conversation with Eric. The two men had retreated to the sofas in the corner when the goat races began.

"Have you been keeping up with your physical therapy?" he asked his buddy.

Eric rolled his left shoulder up and back a few times. "Whenever I remember."

"Still stiff?"

"Only when it rains." Eric smiled.

Leaning forward, Lucas clasped his hands together and rested his elbows on his knees. "How have you been treating the pain?"

Eric dropped his gaze to the floor for a moment, then glanced up. "Ibuprofen and Tylenol, that's it."

As subtly as he could, Lucas visually examined his friend, looking for any of the telltale signs from when he'd first treated Eric six months ago. No shakes, excellent color, seemed calm and in control. Focused.

Lucas exhaled in relief and sat back. "That's great, man. Glad to hear it."

"Thanks to you," Eric replied. "I don't know how I would've gotten out from under—*Ouch!*" A blue rubber ball hit him squarely between the eyes. "Viv!"

"Sorry, hon," Vivian said, crawling over to retrieve the ball. "That was meant for Teresa."

After rubbing his eyes, he moaned in mock exasperation. "She named the goat after a nun."

"The most *famous* nun," Vivian cut in, tossing the ball to Esther, who quickly lobbed it up to the first landing, causing a minor stampede of goats climbing over one another up the stairs.

"Are they pygmies?" Lucas asked Eric.

"You have to ask?"

Lucas chuckled. "They're smaller than a cat."

"Surprisingly cleaner, though. Actually, they're not that bad. Makes my Vivy happy, and there's nothing more important than that."

Lucas couldn't help noticing the intensely loving look on his buddy's face as he glanced across the room at his wife. For the first time in his life, Lucas regretted being single.

"Well, I hate to say it," he added a few minutes later, "but we should probably get going."

Esther froze like a statue, then pushed out her bottom lip. "Oh, no."

"So soon?" Vivian echoed, sounding just as disappointed.

"It's starting to get dark." He gestured at the window. Esther rose onto her knees to look outside, then sank back to the floor just as the black goat leaped into her lap. She wrapped her arms about him, burrowing her face into the side of his neck.

Lucas really wished he could take a photo. But instead, he'd work hard at keeping this picture solid in his brain for as long as possible.

Which should not be difficult.

"They love you so much," Vivian said. "I wish you could take them home with you, but, since that would literally kill me dead, I guess you'll just have to come back."

Esther laughed, then rose to her feet. "I guess I will, then," she said, smoothing down her dress. Vivian looped her arm through Esther's as they walked to the door, talking in low whispers with the occasional laugh.

"Can I get that sweater pattern?" Esther asked. "I already know what color scheme I'll use for little Milo here." She scratched the brown and white kid behind his pointy ears.

"Of course," Vivian said. "Gimme your email address. Oh, wait." She bit her lip and glanced away, blinking. "Um…"

"Email it to me," Lucas jumped in, then turned

to Esther. "I'll print it out for you."

"Danke," she said, a slight wobble to her smile.

He didn't want to put an uncomfortable damper on the afternoon, so he quickly added, "Maybe you can make one for me, too." He grinned. "It's been a long time since anyone's knit me a sweater."

"Har-har," Esther said. "A sweater for you would take too much yarn and way too much time. I still have to make my sister's darn—" Suddenly, the bright smile on her face froze, and she sealed her lips together. "Well, anyway, it was lovely to meet you—all of you." She gave Vivian a hug, waved goodbye to the goats, then walked out the door.

Following suit, Lucas shook hands with Eric and gave Vivian's shoulders a squeeze. "Thanks for everything," he said, trailing behind Esther, who was already leading the white mule toward the gate. "I'm sure we'll be back soon."

"I hope so," Vivian said, standing on the porch watching Esther, eyebrows pulled together. "Everything okay?"

"Yeah." Lucas nodded. "She's fine, thanks again. We had a great time!" He quickly jogged to the fence where Esther had the mule by the reins, heading toward the buggy. "Let me help."

"I've got it," she said, sounding a bit frustrated, and then he heard her sigh. "Thank you," she added, handing him the reins. Together, they bridled the leather ropes around the mule and attached the yokes. The animal gave no fuss, as if she'd done this a million times.

"Bye!" Lucas called once they were both in the buggy. He waved over his head to his friends just when Esther clicked her tongue, prompting the mule to move forward.

"What's the hurry?" he asked when they were a few yards down the road.

"It's getting dark. Like you said."

"You're telling me you've never taken a buggy ride at night?" It was meant to be a joke, but Esther only stared at him, then glanced away.

Way to go, man. Lucas gave himself a mental thwack to the skull. *Of course she's been out at night. With my own brother.*

A few moments of silence passed between them, but Lucas was determined to not end the evening on a down.

"I think we should sneak back in the middle of the night and steal Bubba." He gave her a nudge. "Maybe they won't notice, eh?"

She didn't make a sound at first; then Esther laughed inside her throat. "It's *Bubbles*," she said, "not Bubba. Of all names…"

"She calls the goat Bubbles?" He scratched his chin. "And I thought Bubba was strange."

Esther switched on the buggy's headlights, illuminating the gravel road before them. "Bubbles is a perfect name for him."

"It's a *boy*?"

She narrowed her eyes. "It just so happened that when he bleats, little bubbles float off his tongue and he tries to catch them, and then… What are you laughing at?"

"You." Lucas sat back. "I've honestly never seen anyone so excited about goats."

Finally, that smile was back. Just seeing it made

calmness settle his body.

"*That* was a blessed day," she said, lowering the reins to rest on her lap, causing the mule to slow its trot.

"I had fun watching you."

She pulled at the ties of her bonnet, maybe out of habit, then exhaled. "I feel so blissed out right now." Her voice was light and dreamy.

"Where did you hear that term?"

"Read it in a book."

"You read books about being blissed out?"

"I read about a lot of things," she said. The moonlight was bright, so Lucas clearly caught the twinkle in her eyes. "Thank you for bringing me."

"Anytime," he said, meaning it.

For a few miles, they talked nothing but baby goats. Well, she did most of the talking, and Lucas wouldn't have it any other way.

"Eric's a nice man," she said, just as they neared the outskirts of Honey Brook. "You two met at your clinic?"

"He came in with shoulder pain but..." He paused, considering the ethics of sharing the case. Since Eric practically preached it from the mountain tops, Lucas was pretty sure his buddy wouldn't mind Esther's knowing.

"Actually, he'd hurt his shoulder the year before. He was after a fix."

"You mean drugs?" Lines ran across her forehead.

"Besides the hospital in Hershey, we're the only place in fifty miles that has oxycodone."

"I've heard of that." The creases on her forehead

deepened. "It's addictive. People can die from it."

He nodded. "Yes, it's very dangerous. And it's never meant to be prescribed for more than a few months at the very most. Unfortunately, though, some doctors misuse their credentials, which is bad for everyone."

"Eric was addicted?"

He nodded again, recalling that day with perfect clarity. "Once he knew he was not going to get one single pill out of me, he was willing to talk about rehab and physical therapy. It was pretty bad at first, but he had Vivian and his extended family to help."

"And now he's clear?"

Lucas couldn't help chuckling. "I think you mean clean."

"Oh." She smiled, the moonlight reflecting in her eyes. "Yes, clean."

"Sober as a judge," he replied, then noticed her frown. "Sorry, that's a saying. Yeah, Eric's totally clean, getting healthier and stronger by the day. Modern medicine isn't something to be afraid of," he couldn't help adding, making sure she knew she shouldn't rely solely on people like Eliza Fisher, or whoever the community's "healer" was now.

"Perhaps not," Esther said. "Moderation in all things."

"Very true."

It was quiet for a moment, then Esther began chewing on a thumbnail. "Aren't you so grateful we don't have that problem? You and I."

"Problem?"

"*Jah.*" She pressed her lips together. "We're plain, clean-living folk. We live off the land and work hard, take care of our own. Folks are more likely to crave fresh, homemade chicken stock soup than drugs. Our people have lived like this for a hundred years. Aren't you truly grateful?"

For once, Lucas did not feel the desire to correct the collective pronoun. It touched something deep in his heart that Esther claimed him as one of "our people." He wanted to thank her for that but couldn't muster the words. A moment later, however, he did feel the urge to amend her comment.

Despite what I've been feeling lately, I'm not Amish anymore. I'm still so different from her and from her family—from my family.

"You, um, might need to get out now."

Lucas blinked and focused his eyes. The buggy was stopped a few buildings down from the clinic. Without his noticing, they'd passed the gas station, firehouse, and probably his parents' property line. He felt a slight tightening in his chest when he remembered watching his father from his truck the other day. What would have happened if he'd opened the car door and walked down that hill?

It probably would've made things worse than they already were. Or maybe, he'd be able to see his mother...

Before he got too carried away, he focused on the street. The shops were dark and empty except for the ice cream parlor that stayed open late for the teenagers to gather.

"Sorry," he said. "I guess the end of the drive sort of snuck up on me."

"Me, too," Esther said, fiddling with the reins. "This wasn't how I thought it would go...meeting with you today."

He nodded in agreement. "Can I ask you something now?"

"Okay."

"Right before we left the goats, something seemed to bother you. You mentioned your sister, then, I don't know, your mood changed. Was I reading you wrong?"

"Nay." She sighed. "But it's nothing—no, it's not nothing. It's definitely a very important something." She sat up straight and looked right at him, voice firm. "And I don't see why I shouldn't talk about it."

"Okay," he said, not knowing how else to answer.

"She's getting married soon and she asked me to sew her wedding dress—which might not seem like a big deal to you, but she's younger than me, and with Jacob gone I just wish—" She stopped talking and they both turned at a sound coming from behind them. An open buggy was heading their way. It looked like some teens out for a joyride, but Lucas knew they should not be caught together.

"Go on," he said, wanting so badly to take her hand. Offer some kind of comfort, even at the mention of his brother. He knew it was only a matter of time before he'd confess to her what had happened before he'd died. From the very beginning, Lucas knew that what Jacob had done in secret would hurt her badly.

His worry now was, would she hate him, too?

"Better not right now," she said.

"Is this Sunday a preaching Sunday?"

"Yes. Do you want to come?"

He smiled but bowed his head. "No." Reading a

few scripture passages and feeling reminiscent about home was not enticement enough to endure all the scrutinizing eyes showing up at a preaching would bring.

"I ask because I wanted to know if you're free. What is your schedule on Monday?" Lucas had his regular shift at the clinic and was volunteering at the Hershey Med Center in the afternoon.

"I'm… Well, I'm doing some things in the morning, wedding things, but I'm free after supper."

Lucas thought fast, knowing he needed to steal away before the approaching buggy got any closer. "How about getting together at my house?" He paused, gauging her reaction. "It's not far."

"Oh." She was back to chewing on her thumbnail again, while her other hand was pushing into her collarbone. "I think that will be okay."

Lucas was almost shocked. He didn't think she'd go for it.

"There're some things I still want to ask you," she added. "And things I need to tell you."

"Same here."

He was aching to know how his family were all getting on. Was Jeremiah married with children now, like Bridget? What about his younger siblings? Were they courting or already engaged? He suddenly remembered the letter he'd received from Jacob, saying that he'd proposed to Esther Miller and she'd accepted. His brother had been so overjoyed, and so in love with her.

"It'll be totally platonic—on Monday," Lucas felt the need to add, ready to spring off the buggy.

"What does that word mean?" she asked, blinking up at him with round, curious eyes.

He ran a knuckle under his chin. "Long story short, Plato was an ancient Roman philosopher. He had a theory that—"

Esther burst out laughing, then elbowed his ribs. "I know what it means. You just seemed far off for a second, so I made a joke."

"Nice one," he said, feeling his chest rumble with a chuckle.

"And Plato was Greek." She elbowed him again, so near him now that he caught a whiff of her scented soap. *She smells like vanilla—like a sugar cookie.* His mouth began to water, and when she smiled at him, the sensation in his chest felt anything but platonic.

CHAPTER ELEVEN

"Home already?"

Esther froze in place when she heard *Maam*'s voice. She reckoned everyone was upstairs preparing for bed.

"Already?" she said. "It's nearly eight o'clock." Heavens! Why did she bring up the time? What if her mother wanted to know where she'd been the last four hours?

"Yes," *Maam* said, coming out of the kitchen to meet Esther by the wood-burning stove. Looked like a fire had just been lit, and the room smelled of fresh cinnamon rolls. "I thought you might be on a date."

"What?" Esther felt blood rush to her cheeks. "Wh-why would you think that?"

Maam smiled and adjusted the white lace kerchief covering her hair bun. "That wouldn't be so strange."

Esther sank onto the sofa, already feeling the weight of the conversation. "But...Jacob," she couldn't help saying.

"It's been two years." *Maam* sat beside her. "Maybe you've mourned your poor Jacob the proper amount of time."

Esther didn't know what to say. She'd been working so hard to get over the disappointment, to forgive Jacob for leaving her, to understand his death and why *Gott* allowed it. Not yet had she felt that "closure" everyone talked about.

And she'd surely not reached the point where she considered courting.

Too easily, she pictured a particular tall, vigorous, light-brown-eyed man who she'd spent time alone with three days already this week. But those hadn't been dates. She and Lucas were only…helping each other. They both needed a friendly ear, someone to talk to about their problems.

Totally *platonic*…

She pictured him again, smiling when they'd joked about the goats' names. Was that a tiny flutter in her stomach? If so, why did the next feeling fill her with guilt?

He'd talked to her about treating his friend through addiction, like a professional doctor would have—someone with a formal, modern education. Someone who lived in the modern world, drove the cars, knew the slang, and would never think of returning to the plain life. Like hers.

"I'm not ready yet," she said to *Maam*, not sure if that was the complete truth.

Maam squeezed her hand. "When it's time, the Good Lord will whisper it to your soul and fill you with His spirit."

Even though she nodded, Esther wasn't sure of the truthfulness of that, either. She hadn't felt *Gott*'s presence in months. Did He no longer care about her questions and struggles? Had she gotten used to filling that void with making soap?

"I better go to bed," she said, needing to be alone with her thoughts, for she had many of them tonight.

"Yes, you've got an early morning."

"Do I?" she asked, tossing the strings of her prayer *kapp* behind her shoulders. Then she remembered. "Oh, the wedding dress."

"She may not speak it aloud," *Maam* said, "but your sister is very grateful for your help."

A small part of Esther wanted to laugh, but sarcasm always left a bitter taste in her mouth. So instead, she lifted a small smile and tried to feel gracious. "Did you know she asked if she could wear *my* wedding dress?"

"Well, that's not our tradition, but it would be a sweet gesture of you. I know she's always loved the color of your dress."

"Mother," Esther said. "I made that with my own two hands. It's important to me."

"I know, dearest. I didn't say you had to let her wear it, I only said it's a sweet gesture."

"Okay," Esther said, guilt from the childish outburst heating her body. "I'm sorry, *Maam*. I'm still having a hard time with…things."

"She loves you," her mother added. "She really does."

Esther blew out a long breath. "I love her, too." Without another word, Esther climbed the stairs, pausing for a moment to peer into Sarah's room. Her sister lay on her back, one leg hanging over the side of the bed while the other was tangled in the sheets. Her light brown hair surrounded her head like a halo.

Tomorrow will be a good day, she thought as she quietly undressed in the bedroom next door. *I'll pray hard for a positive attitude and for patience and love. Surely* Gott *will bless me with that.*

• • •

Maybe she should've added fasting along with that prayer. Then again, fasting for forty days and forty nights like the Lord had done would still probably not have changed the outcome.

It had been difficult enough to cut the blue fabric perfectly along the pattern lines, but nearly impossible with four sets of eyes watching every move she made, let alone Sarah's anxious breathing and gasps the few times Esther had cut a bit outside the lines.

"Are you stopping already?" Sarah asked as Esther began carefully folding the material still pinned to the pattern.

"Jah," she said, holding a safety pin between her teeth. "I promised *Maam* I'd help with the vocabulary lesson; then I need to fill a new soap order— Leah's been waiting. After that, I have some errands to run."

She wanted to stop by Rebecca's Yarn Barn to pick out the softest lamb's wool for the kid goats' Christmas sweaters. When she'd see Lucas next, he'd give her the pattern so she could start knitting right away.

A tiny flutter tickled her tummy again when she thought about him but, since she couldn't determine what that flutter meant, she ignored it. After the *kinnahs* left at the end of their schooling and she'd washed up the lunch dishes, the flutter was still there. And, since she knew the recipe by heart, her body practically went into autopilot when she escaped into her nook to make a double batch of soap.

The flutter carried on even through her walk to visit Anna with canned sugar peaches and a loaf of warm cinnamon bread. But thanks to the lively conversation during supper, when Benjamin practiced counting to one hundred by fives and Eve sang it to the tune of "Amazing Grace," Esther was finally able to forget about any flutters.

• • •

By Monday, the dress and all its layers were cut out, and Esther had sewn up two sides, working hard at the tricky inner seams so no stitches showed, as was the Amish custom. Sarah had also chosen her four wedding attendants. Anna—bless her pregnant heart—had volunteered to make those dresses, as it was the true Amish custom for the bride to make all of them.

Even though Esther was to be one of those attendants, there was no way she could have made two dresses in such a short amount of time. It would be a miracle if the wedding dress was finished.

"You taking the buggy out later?" *Daed* asked, startling Esther while she'd been slicing brownies in the kitchen after a supper of roast beef, creamed potatoes, and roasted beets. His question made her nearly nick her thumb.

"If it's okay," she said, barely glancing at her father.

"Where are you going?" Sarah asked, taking one of the brownies.

"Yeah," Benjamin inserted when Esther didn't answer quickly enough. "Can I come, too? I'll learn to drive my own pony cart soon."

"Not tonight, Benji," *Maam* said, setting a glass of milk in front of him. "Big sister's got her own plans."

"Like what?" Sarah pressed, licking the fudge frosting off the top of her brownie.

Esther knew she couldn't get out of answering this time. Would she tell another white lie or confess everything right there on the spot?

"Don't ask so many questions," Eve said. "She might be meeting a handsome stranger for a secret date."

Esther couldn't swallow and stared helplessly at her sister while a million words ran through her head like an explosion of alphabet soup.

"She very well could be." *Maam* winked at Esther. "And that's none of your business, Little Miss Nosey." She pointed her reading glasses at Sarah. "I need you to measure these for my lesson tomorrow." She laid out some strips of cardboard cut into different sizes.

"*Maam*, you know I mustn't do anything that might damage my…" She held up one hand and wiggled her fingers, fudge on the tip of a pinkie.

"You don't need to use the pads of your fingers for this. Run along and find the box of rulers."

The second Sarah disappeared into the crafts room, *Maam* shot Esther a glance and cocked her head toward the door. Esther took the hint and reached for her cloak and black bonnet. "Be careful," she said in a low voice, giving her another wink.

Esther had no idea where her *maam* thought she

was going tonight; she was just grateful for the distraction. "I will," she said, quietly slipping out the back door.

Peanut seemed to sense another early evening adventure, for she was nodding and whinnying, just busting to get out, as Esther entered the stable. In a flash, she was hooked up to the buggy and Esther was riding away from home, the map to Lucas's house that he'd drawn for her the other night tucked into the folds of her dress. She'd taken this very buggy to see Jacob many times after they'd become engaged, but something about *this* buggy ride felt different.

The man was mysterious, though Esther felt no danger. Thanks to Peanut's quick clip, it didn't take long until she came to the final point on the map.

Out of nowhere, she had a flash of the first time they'd seen each other, when Lucas had that spot of cottage cheese at the corner of his mouth.

Mercy me, that was adorable.

But a thing like that would've been adorable on *any* man, she added forcefully. Lucas was just so… okay…*attractive*. And he was such a good sport to take her to see the kids, and he even had a jolly sense of humor. What was it he'd called her the other day? Kung Fu Grizzly? Or was it Koala? Teddy Bear?

Streaks of a yellow and orange sunset striped the sky, causing Esther to feel a bit of that heavenly spirit that used to fill her not too long ago. She missed it.

As she drew nearer to the house, she spotted his truck. Instantly, that silly girlish flutter in her stomach increased, which made her bite her lip to regain her sensible wits.

Not at all Amish anymore, she repeated to herself. Before she could stop her brain, she was imagining what life would be like if she left the church like Lucas had, left her family and all her friends. Left the traditions she held so dear.

A hot pressure pressed in her head, yet she couldn't determine if it was out of fear of leaving her life or from sadness for a future she was so worried was coming that it was unstoppable. The weight of a boulder in her stomach made her swallow hard; then she nearly jumped out of her skin when Lucas began reining in the mule.

"I said hi," he called, shading his eyes from the bright sunset. "Twice, but you didn't hear me."

"Aye," she said, hoping he wouldn't be able to read whatever her expression showed.

"Deep in thought?" he asked, holding the reins with one hand while opening the door to the buggy with the other.

"Thoughts? Oh, no! None!"

He chuckled. "No thoughts at all, huh. That doesn't sound like the Esther I know."

She couldn't help smiling. "You're teasing me again."

"Only because I know you like it." Yes, she did. And the comment made her press her smiling lips together and turn into the wind. It was then that she noted he was wearing black wool pants, a blue long-sleeved shirt, and black shoes.

"Why are you dressed like that?" she asked.

"Like what?"

She waved at him. "All you need are suspenders and a straw hat and you'd look nearly like my pa."

He glanced down at himself as if he hadn't looked in a mirror all day. "I see what you mean. Maybe I've been living plain all these years but kept it a secret."

"Pretty well-kept secret," she said, gesturing at the satellite dish on his roof. It was a joke, but Esther couldn't help smiling to herself, wondering if he knew he was the most Amish non-Amishman she knew.

His house was painted a light gray and had a green shingled roof. It wasn't large, but the land was lush. A sturdy bench swing sat on the spacious wraparound porch. A small herb garden and a big potted tomato plant sat in a shady corner.

Lucas opened the front door. After stepping in, the first thing she noticed was that the house smelled like him. Like pine and leather and...something almost earthy, yet clean. Most of all, though, it smelled like hard work and sunshine. For a moment, she wondered how she might capture such heavenly scents in a soap.

"Would you like a tour?" he asked.

Her curiosity piqued. "Sure."

Heavy blinds—common in plain homes—were pulled back, showing large windows.

"Well, this is the living room." He paused to rub his smooth chin. "Or the family room—sitting room. I guess I don't know what it's called."

A deep-cushioned blue sofa sat on the far side of the room. Across from it was a comfy-looking armchair and a rocker. Under one of the big windows sat a short armoire, dinged up as if it had traveled thousands of miles. Beside another window was a bookshelf, lined with volumes that appeared both recent and ancient. The obvious centerpiece of the room was the black wood-burning stove built into the large stone hearth. Above it, an enormous TV screen.

"Living room," Esther said, trying not to fixate on the TV and other obviously modern electric-powered devices in the room.

"Thank you for the clarification." Lucas bowed his head.

Just like the other homes in the area, the kitchen was part of the living space. One big room. A small table with two wooden chairs sat in the middle, separating the cooking area from another bookshelf—this one with hooks and pegs for coats and hats. The countertops were granite, which surprised Esther. She couldn't help running a hand over the cool gray surface.

"That's one of my upgrades," Lucas explained. "Along with this." He walked to the sink and turned on the faucet. "This place was piped with only a water pump when I bought it."

"Wow," she said, unable to stop herself from joining him at the sink to run a finger under the water. "This must've belonged to a Swartzentruber family," she said. "They live much plainer than we do."

"I remember," he said. "Luckily, the man I bought it from had already added indoor plumbing." He pointed his chin toward a closed door off the kitchen that Esther surmised was the bathroom.

"Luxurious," she said with a smile. "Do you watch many TV shows?"

"Not really. Especially not now that my schedule's gotten busier. In fact, hmm, it's probably been over a week since I've turned it on." What he'd just said seemed to give him the need for a second of inner thought. So Esther didn't interrupt. A moment later, he reached for the TV's remote control and pointed it at the screen. It flickered with a bright white light but then went black again.

"Sorry, I wasn't thinking," he said, dropping the remote onto a chair. "You don't watch TV."

"No," Esther said. "But I'm interested in what you enjoy. Do you have a favorite?"

She noticed a little smile brighten his face, which made her curious. This must've been an important subject to him.

"I do—or I did," he said. "It's a cooking competition. Contestants come on the show and learn how to make a specialty dish from scratch in front of a room full of people and judges and TV cameras, then—"

"Why didn't their mothers teach them how to cook?"

Lucas's mouth hung open, no words coming out, until he tipped his head back and laughed. "That…is a very good question," he said, pointing at her. "Clever girl."

Esther didn't think what she'd asked was necessarily clever, but she felt cozy inside knowing she could make him laugh.

"Would you like some water? Or tea, maybe?"

"Tea would be nice."

He practically flew to the other end of the room, filled a kettle, and adjusted the switch on a shiny silver gas stove. "I wish I could surprise you again, with a closet full of baby ducklings this time, but you said you had some things to ask me." He looked at her, then away. "Would you like to start?"

Instantly, all those questions and concerns she'd been repressing the last few days bubbled to the surface. She felt her palms go clammy and her throat dry up—not quite ready to begin. But if she didn't dive in to what she'd been dying to talk about, she might chicken out forever.

"Lucas," Esther said, nerves making her hesitant. "When I first brought up Jacob, I sensed you didn't want to talk about it, and I respect that. But you must know how I…" She exhaled. "I need to know what happened when he left to stay with you."

"You'd like those answers now," he said.

She nodded.

After a sigh, he switched off the stove and walked to the living room. "We should sit for this."

CHAPTER TWELVE

As instructed, Esther sat on the blue sofa, while Lucas sank onto the rocker across from her.

"To start with, he was never really a healthy little boy," Lucas began, as if he'd planned out exactly what to say. "I first thought something might be wrong when he was about thirteen. He couldn't run as fast as me or the kids his age. He seemed weak."

"Jacob, you mean?"

"Yes. Some even teased him about it."

Esther sat very still, not remembering anyone being unkind to him. Then again, she wasn't with him every hour of every day. An older brother would've been the true expert. She leaned forward, listening more carefully.

"I was past the eighth grade, so already done with school, and was working at the mill full time," he continued. "But I asked my mother if I could go to the library for some books. My last year of school, I'd become obsessed with science and biology—growing up on a farm, it's inevitable. But it wasn't a sick cow that made me want to study; it was my brother."

"You thought Jacob was sick all the way back then?"

Lucas nodded. "I suspected. I was only fifteen and had extremely limited knowledge and experience—basically only farm know-how. There were a few times when Jacob was so weak, he couldn't get out of bed."

"Honest?" She sat back, ashamed of herself that she'd never noticed anything like that when they'd been younger.

"I'm not surprised you didn't know. My parents were good at hiding it. The church says pride is a sin, but even I knew my folks didn't want anyone to know something was wrong. When I turned sixteen, I could actually do something about it."

"Is that when…" Esther began but couldn't finish.

"When what?"

"Is that why you left home? Because of Jacob?"

"Yes."

She wrapped her arms around her body and leaned farther back, away from him. "You couldn't bear having a brother who wasn't perfect?"

When he stared at her, a little notch cut into the skin between his eyes. "I left at sixteen because of Jacob, but not because I was ashamed of him. Of *course* not. Esther, I left to help him."

"How? You went to New York for *Rumspringa* and never came back."

He dropped his chin, both hands raking through his hair. "I knew you didn't know," he muttered under his breath. "No one knew."

If he'd planned out what he was going to say to her, he'd clearly already gone in a different direction.

"Esther," he said slowly, "I didn't come home after *Rumspringa* because I went back to school. I got my GRE in six months, then applied for college. Somehow my test scores were high enough to get me into NYU at seventeen. I lived with my cousins while taking classes, studying health and biology… human anatomy. My last year of undergrad, I worked with some very understanding professors at the medical school. Because of my…" He paused. "My unique upbringing, many doors were opened, and I was able to study medicine with the best in the country. That's why I asked Jacob to come to me for his *Rumspringa*."

"Wait a second." She pressed a hand to her forehead. "You're telling me that you ran away from home to become a doctor?"

"I'm a PA, not a doctor," he said, holding out both hands. "I couldn't sit idly by and watch my brother get sicker and sicker. My parents are very traditional; I knew they'd never take him to a certified medical professional, so I had to become one. It was the only way I could help."

Esther shut her eyes, trying not to sway, trying to take it all in.

"Back then," Lucas continued, "folks in Honey Brook didn't have phones in their barns or even business cell phones like they do now, so it took some creativity to reach Jacob. When I did, it was easy to convince him to come to me for his *Rumspringa*, even though he was already eighteen. He wanted to get better, because he wanted to propose to a girl."

Esther felt blood rush to her face. "Me?"

"He talked about you nonstop."

Esther couldn't dwell on that now; the pain might cause her to burst into tears. "Go on, please."

"The first two weeks we literally lived at the hospital running tests." He paused to take in a deep breath. "It wasn't long before the bone marrow biopsy came back with very clear results. To put it simply, Jacob had cancer."

Esther easily noticed that his voice shook at the word. She, too, felt a jolt, but of fear and a whole lot of confusion. "Cancer," she said, the word tasting foul on her tongue. "I…had no idea he was *that* kind of sick. Did he know?"

There was a pause first; then Lucas nodded. "I told him right then."

Wait. Wait. He knew he had cancer and didn't say one word about it? Never mentioned it in a single letter. It felt as if she were being poked with a hot branding iron. *We began courting when he got home. We were close—told each other everything.*

Obviously not everything, she added, now feeling icy cold all over, the betrayal very real.

"He didn't tell me back then. No one did. Why?" After a split second of thought, she couldn't help turning to Lucas, looking him dead in the eye. "You could've told me."

"No." He ran a knuckle over the bridge of his nose. "Jacob made me promise I would never breathe a word about it to anyone. Ever. I couldn't break that vow. He begged me."

Esther took time to consider this, breathing through her nose, trying to both process and calm down. "People can get better, *jah*? Cured. I heard if it's caught early, it will go away."

"Not in every case," Lucas said, sounding regretful. "And we didn't catch it early."

"Right," Esther said with a sigh. "What kind of cancer?"

"Leukemia. It's in the blood."

"I know." She bit her bottom lip. "Go on."

"Because of Jacob's background, NYU was very interested in his case. It's not every day an Amish kid walks in for treatment. In order to treat his kind of leukemia, he basically needed brand-new blood."

"How…?" Trying to imagine what that meant, Esther felt her gaze drift to the side.

"Let me explain. In order to get new, clean, cancer-free blood, he needed someone else's clean, cancer-free blood."

She sat up straight. "Like from a blood bank? That's simple, right?"

Lucas shook his head. "Unfortunately, this kind of blood donation is more complicated. Instead of whole blood from a bank, it needed to be a bone marrow blood donation—and those are rare. Patients with leukemia put their names on a list and wait for someone to offer to donate their bone marrow. That list is very long. Some people have been on it for years."

"Did you put Jacob on the list?"

Lucas nodded. "The very first day."

"So…" She blinked about a dozen times, trying to make sense of it. "No one helped him, and that's why he died?"

"Like I said, it's complicated. Bone marrow has to be a perfect match. Going on the national list is one thing, but it's a long shot. The best matches come from a family member."

"Oh." She blinked again. "His family was here."

"Not everyone."

Slowly, the dark confusion in her mind brightened to understanding. "You. You matched."

"We were the perfect match."

Without thinking, she reached out and took his hand with both of hers. "Lucas, you did that? You donated your own bone marrow?"

He looked up at her, their gazes locking just before his brows pulled together, his lips pressing into a hard line. "He was my brother."

Esther squeezed his hand, feeling tears in her throat, gratitude in her heart for the selfless action, for this utterly selfless man. She knew it was painful for Lucas to tell her these things—to break a promise to Jacob—while also realizing she would need to know the truth. As she felt his skin against hers, giving his hand another tender squeeze, she realized she'd never felt so understood by another person in all her life.

"What happened next?" she asked.

Lucas swallowed before continuing. "The blood transfer was a success, but he needed further treatment to make sure the cancer was gone. Have you heard of chemotherapy?"

"Yes." Her voice felt weak. "That's when the doctor feeds you poison to kill everything in your body."

"That's one way of looking at it. But the medicine is very specific—it's not meant to kill everything, just any traces of the cancer."

She nodded. "Okay."

"Jacob's body responded well to the weeks of chemo, and he seemed to be getting stronger. We all kept track of him, hoping the cancer would be gone forever. The thing is…" He stopped when his voice began to shake again.

"Lucas, you don't have to tell me." Esther squeezed his hand tighter, reading the pain on his face, not wanting to add to it.

A moment later, he squeezed her hand back. "I want to. I want you to know everything—someone should. *You* should." He bowed his head and took in another deep breath. "Jacob's leukemia had a mutation. That means we couldn't be sure it was all gone because the treatment wasn't as specific as he needed. All we could do was wait and hope."

"When he came back home," Esther said, recalling a specific memory, "he told us you'd gone to the beach."

"We went to Florida for a few weeks. He needed sun and relaxation and to get as strong as possible. I fed him as much as he could stand." He paused to chuckle quietly, perhaps reliving a private memory. "I made sure he ate the healthiest foods on the planet. But we also had a lot of fun. We went to Disney World and down to the Keys. He swam in the ocean and started building real muscles. Then one morning, after almost a year, he began vomiting and couldn't stop. I rushed him to the hospital, but…"

Esther let go of his hand. "The cancer was back."

"Yes," he whispered.

"Because of the mutation."

He nodded. "I begged him to do another round of chemo and some radiation this time, but…"

"He refused." Just thinking the words made hot tears fill her eyes, helplessly flowing down her cheeks. "He wanted to go home."

She tried to blink away the tears, tears for sweet Jacob, but also for the man sitting across from her. The man who'd done all he could—even given of his own body—to save his brother's life.

CHAPTER THIRTEEN

"Yes, he wanted to go home," Lucas said. "How did you know?" While waiting for her answer, he laced his fingers together and squeezed, feeling raw and exhausted from sharing the painful story. Even with Esther. Because he knew she deserved to know, even though by telling her, he'd broken the only promise Jacob had ever asked of him.

His soul felt black with guilt for so many things. Didn't matter that he knew he'd done the right thing.

"He seemed different when he came back," Esther replied. "I don't know, more open and yet private, like he wanted to be alone more often. He seemed stronger—but maybe just spiritually. He was more devoted to *Gott* than ever. Honestly, that was what made me fall for him most when he returned."

Lucas couldn't help flinching. Of course she'd been in love with his brother. "How else was he different?" he asked, needing to speak.

"He was pious, more reflective. Everyone assumed he would work with your pa at the farm, but he took a position as a bookkeeper at the Roths' egg farm. Most days, he sat in an office instead of working outside. He was quieter and simpler, maybe even overly reverent."

Lucas recrossed his legs. "You liked that about him."

"I wanted stability. Someone strong in the church. Maybe I wanted someone who would never be in danger of getting injured in a tractor accident. So when he proposed, I agreed. I loved him, too, of course, but now I'm so…"

He waited, not wanting to interrupt if her emotions were making it difficult to speak.

"I'm just so…*furious*!"

The word made him balk. "Furious?" *At Jacob?*

"Yes!" She rose to her feet, fists clenched, her face flushing red. "He knew he was sick, and he still proposed—without telling me." She looked him right in the eyes, hands on hips. "He asked me to marry him knowing he was going to die."

Lucas slammed his eyes shut. Everything she was saying was true, but the way she'd put it made his brother's intentions seem so diabolical.

"It's understandable that you're upset," he began, wanting to defuse her anger if he could.

Esther actually blew out a sarcastic huff. "Upset?"

"Just…slow down and think for a second, okay?" he asked, holding up his hands in surrender.

She huffed again but then crossed her arms and shrugged.

"My brother was a good guy—he was private; we know that. Maybe he wanted to keep you from worrying over him, if he could help it."

"Okay, but—"

"Esther," he said, feeling tightness in his own chest. "You knew his heart. Do you honestly think he set out to hurt you?"

"Does it matter?"

"I think so. He loved you, you can't doubt that.

He must've had his reasons for not wanting you to know."

Esther was chewing on a thumbnail, swaying back and forth as if mulling over the idea. She didn't speak for a while but walked to the window, gazing outside. Her back was to him, but Lucas noticed when she swiped at her cheeks.

He didn't know how to help her any further. He'd known the truth would change her life forever, which was one of the reasons he'd been putting it off since the day she'd first asked.

And now, just as he'd feared, she probably blamed him for not telling her, for not saving Jacob. For failing everyone.

Suddenly, Esther turned around to him, her face no longer red.

"I might not have known all his secrets, but I did know his heart, and he was pure. Thank you for reminding me of that." She blew out a breath, looking heavenward. "Whatever his reasons were, they weren't malicious." She dipped her head and pressed a hand over her chest. "I forgive him."

Though he'd hoped her angry attitude toward his brother would soften, Lucas was surprised by how quickly her forgiveness came. Would she forgive *him* for his part in the secret, too?

Would his own heart be as forgiving toward someone he felt had done him wrong?

He pictured his father. Would he have stopped him at sixteen if he knew Lucas was not coming back? Did he care back then? Did he care now?

For the moment, however, Lucas had to put aside his emotions. He couldn't worry about the burden he still carried for not being truthful from the beginning or wondering how much she held him responsible for the secret.

"I know you're still upset," he said, "and this is very difficult, but I have some questions for you now."

"Yes?" she said, looking calmer, breathing steadily. Forgiveness must really be a balm for the soul.

"If it's okay, would you tell me when he got sick again?"

"Like I said, I thought he seemed healthier when he got home, though he did little physical work. We courted for nearly a year; then just a few days before the official presenting at church, he proposed. Honestly, I was ready to get married, ready to start a new phase of my life. I wanted a home and children." She turned her eyes away, perhaps not wanting him to see her expression. "The change came so quickly that it shocked everyone."

"Change?"

Esther nodded. "The wedding was coming up, but Jacob wouldn't leave the house, not even to see me. Your mother said he needed rest, but then your father took him away to a farmer's market for a few days. I didn't understand why, if Jacob was too sick to leave his bed. It was confusing."

"Go on," Lucas said, knowing there was more to the story.

"When they came back, Jacob was pale, so pale and weak. When I was finally allowed in the house, he couldn't even sit up on the couch. Bishop was there. Everyone was praying, and your mother—"

Suddenly, she cut off. Lucas was relieved. He also

needed a moment to catch his breath.

"He went to heaven that night," she continued. "It happened very fast—or seemed to at the time. We had the funeral and it was over. No one talked about it with me, like it never happened."

"I'm sorry," he said. Although the sentiment sounded feeble, he felt the need to apologize for so much more. "I'm so very sorry, Esther."

"I'm sorry, too," she replied. "Lucas, I think I understand."

Somehow, in that moment, her words made it possible for him to turn off at least a small part of the energy that had been hiding secrets in his heart. "Thank you for telling me," he said. "I know it was difficult."

"You told me some tough things, too."

He dropped his chin to stare down at his wooden floor, needing to unburden even more. "I can see why you were troubled that first day. I'm ashamed for the part I played in it taking so long for you to get answers. You didn't deserve that."

"I'm sure your folks would like to know the whole story, too."

"Tell them." Did keeping his promise to Jacob about not telling his parents about his diagnosis and treatment matter anymore?

"I think *you* should."

"I can't…" He shook his head, feeling thorns in his throat. "I can't…face him."

"Your father?"

Lucas rose to his feet and began to pace. "He should've done something back then. He should've taken Jacob to a hospital when he first started showing symptoms. That was his duty, not mine—I was a kid. Ever since I've been back, I've been trying to understand why he didn't reach out for help. Was he worried about his reputation or that he'd get in trouble with the church? Was that worth the life of his son?"

Though the words made him want to put his fist through a wall, something about saying them aloud lessened their strength. Now that he'd shared his frustrations, the secret no longer had power over him.

He looked at Esther, who was pressing her palms together as if in prayer while observing him. Why had he chosen to share with her? And not sought out one of his brothers or even his mother? Or just kept it to himself for another decade.

"Give it time," she said, walking over so she was standing before him.

"I've been here six months," he said, attempting to lighten the mood.

"More time," she added, her lips curving into a smile. He was breathing even easier now, more weight off his shoulders.

"How about that tea?" he said.

Esther smiled bigger and rolled her eyes. "I could really use some right about now." She displayed her hands—they were shaking.

"Are you okay?"

"I think so." She balled her hands into two tight fists. "Leftover adrenal."

"Adrenaline," he said, then felt stupid for correcting her. "Me too. Feel this." Without thinking, he took one of her hands and pressed it over his heart.

"See how fast it's beating?"

Esther stood frozen, her shoulders unmoving from holding her breath, blue eyes focused right on his. He felt almost dizzy, too drained of energy to stop the impulse. Feeling really stupid now, he dropped her hand and took a step back. "Sorry."

"It's okay," she said, though her voice sounded a bit strangled. "Um, *jah*, your heart's beating very fast. Do you need to rest? I can make the tea."

"I'm absolutely fine," he said, touching a fist to his chest. "I do know how to boil water." For a moment, he thought about offering to whip up one of his favorite peach cobbler recipes for her, straight from Emeril Lagasse's website. But then he reconsidered. Tea was polite and proper, but he shouldn't push his limits any more than he already had.

Despite how they'd talked about Jacob and cleared the air about Lucas's role in his *Rumspringa*, Esther had still been his brother's girl. Making her completely off-limits.

"Ya know what?" he suddenly said, pushing the tea box back into the cupboard. "I'm feeling a little tired."

"Oh?"

"Do you mind if we call it a night? I've got a busy schedule tomorrow and—"

"I understand," Esther said, walking over to get her cloak she'd hung on a peg by the door. It was a nice reminder of another reason she was off-limits.

Amish and non-Amish didn't mix. Sure, they could be friendly neighbors and help each other out when needed, but anything more shouldn't even cross his mind.

If he rejoined the church someday, under differ-ent circumstances, that would be another story. In order to do that, Lucas would have to give up the comfortable and convenient modern luxuries he'd grown accustomed to. Something about being with Esther that evening, however, made the thought of living a plain life not daunting in the least, though giving up a career in medicine would feel like cut-ting off one of his arms.

The biggest obstacle when it came to returning to the church was that Lucas would also have to confess and forsake his sins (or what the church considered sins) to the leaders of the church. And, since there wasn't a bone in his body that thought what he'd done was wrong, a true reconciliation would never happen. Especially since he still couldn't forgive his father.

"Want me to drive you home?" he said, suddenly noting how quickly darkness was coming on.

"No, thanks," Esther said while tying a knot at her throat. "But I appreciate the offer."

Less than a minute passed and she was out the door. Another minute later and sounds of the buggy driving away faded into the distance.

He hadn't offered to help hook up the mule. He'd just stood there and let her do it all herself. "That's not the gentleman my mother raised me to be," he said aloud, opening the door. But she was long gone.

They say confession is good for the soul, Lucas thought as he stared out into the night. While he did feel some relief at finally divulging Jacob's secret to one of the few people who truly deserved to know, his heart felt heavy, like he was missing something obvious.

For a moment, he thought about jumping in his truck and chasing down the buggy, needing more time with Esther, needing her to understand his feelings. How the last thing he'd wanted was to make her sad.

Before she'd left, they'd made no plans to meet the next day...or ever. Now that she'd gotten her answers about Jacob, had they fulfilled their need for a relationship?

CHAPTER FOURTEEN

The sun was up, and pleasant smells of turned earth and mowed grass greeted Lucas as he closed his front door. His coworker, Steve, would be by any minute.

This was the first time he and Steve would be at the Hershey Medical Center at the same time. Usually, one was there in the morning and the other in the afternoon. It was convenient to carpool today, and Lucas looked forward to getting to know his work colleague a little better on the hour-long drive.

It was also the first time that Steve would see where Lucas lived. It wasn't exactly in an Amish neighborhood, but close enough. Steve seemed like a nice guy; maybe he wouldn't say anything.

Lucas shaded his eyes as he saw the red sedan turn onto the road, dust flying up from the tires. He raised a hand to wave, but the red car drove right past him. Lucas whistled loudly between his fingers, causing the car to stop, then reverse. Looking directly into the driver's side, he made sure Steve saw him.

"Hey," Lucas said, climbing into the car, watching out for the fancy leather upholstery.

"Hey, dude," Steve said, glancing past Lucas and at his front yard. "You live here?"

Lucas tried not to roll his eyes. "Yep."

"Always?"

"Bought the house, barn, and property when I

came to work at the clinic six months ago."

"Seriously. Huh." Steve put the car in gear, did a tight turn, and pressed hard on the gas. Lucas didn't say anything but wondered if any of his plants were damaged from flying gravel.

"Nice car," he said, mostly out of politeness.

"Isn't she something?" Steve said, stroking the wood-paneled dashboard. "Brand-new. Drove her right off the lot."

Lucas frowned. "Sorry, I was talking about your car."

"Yeah."

"You called it she…her."

Steve stared at him. "Yeah, man. That's how you refer to cars. By the feminine pronoun."

"Huh." Lucas scratched his chin. "I've never heard of that."

There was a brief pause; then Steve burst out laughing. "I didn't know you were a jokester."

Lucas figured Steve was about thirty-five. Maybe younger. He'd been an MD for four years and ended up at the clinic when one of his colleagues at the hospital where he'd been working nights told him about the job opening. From what Lucas gathered, Steve didn't have the disposition or drive to work trauma or ER. Though his flashy red sports car certainly stood out, maybe this slower life was a good fit for him.

"This place is driving me crazy," Steve blurted. "Know what I mean?"

"Hmm?"

Steve sighed. "There's nothing to do here. If I wasn't a workaholic, I'd be heading back to civilization as fast as I could."

Nothing to do? Lucas thought. Why, in this part of the country, there was always something to do. Chores were never-ending—though not in a bad way. He could spend hours fixing up his place: planting, mowing, patching holes, fixing chicken wire… He stopped himself before his dream to-do list got out of hand.

"What do you do on your days off?" Steve asked.

"Work," Lucas said. *And sometimes cook*, but he didn't feel like oversharing.

"Yeah? More time at the Med Center?"

"Sometimes," Lucas replied. "But I meant at home. I'm repairing some fence right now; then I'll finish the wraparound porch."

Steve gawked. "You're doing that yourself?"

"Who else?"

Steve laughed. "Dude, hire somebody. Just look around; plenty of those kinds of people dying for work."

Lucas's chest felt tight, and he knew he needed to keep his temper in check. "What people?"

"You know…" Steve lowered his voice. "The cloak-wearers."

Maybe Steve wasn't such a nice guy after all.

"You've seen them. They don't come into the clinic much, but they're all over. The laundry lines, the buggies, those weird bicycles with no pedals—"

"Scooter bikes," Lucas corrected. "Most plain homes don't have electricity, so that's how the laundry dries. Cheaper electric bill, even if they do."

"But what a pain, right?"

"I guess," he said noncommittally.

Steve shifted his car into a faster gear. Luckily, buggies and scooter bikes didn't use that stretch of road this time of day, otherwise, Lucas would've worried someone would get run down.

Steve put on his sunglasses. "I don't know, man. Maybe I made a mistake moving here. I thought it would be an adventure, but nothing ever happens in this place. Like literally nothing. Snoozeville."

Lucas mentally counted off all the challenging and interesting things that were probably happening in his former neighborhood just today. Yes, he had an important job now, but was it any more important than the families who owned the dairy farms? Or built handcrafted tables or grew rows and rows of beets?

Or soap that smelled like Christmas?

Before he let his mind wander—because Esther was a subject he shouldn't allow himself to dwell on—he pointed out the window. "See that bakery? For more than twenty years, people have traveled from all over the country for their pies and specialty desserts."

A bemused expression sat on Steve's face. "I didn't think Amish people could sell things for money."

Lucas felt his eyebrows pull together. "Where did you hear that?"

"I don't know. I've been here only a couple of months." Before Lucas could launch into all the successful Amish industries found within fifty miles of Honey Brook, Steve added, "And what about the women? It's like we have to cruise all the way to Philly to hook up with anyone decent."

Lucas got what Steve was talking about but didn't know how to reply. "There are women everywhere," he finally said, logically.

"Yeah, but I've yet to see a legit gorgeous woman around here." He grinned. "It's probably sick to even admit this, but I do check out the local talent from time to time." He paused to laugh. "I'm a man, right? And they can't hide everything under those potato sack dresses and hats—"

"*Kapps*," Lucas corrected unapologetically. "The women make all the clothes themselves. Did you know that?"

"Had no idea. Guess that gives them something to do besides watching the grass grow."

Lucas feared if he opened his mouth, he'd say something his mother would not be proud of. Instead, he waited for a few miles to pass, then smoothly changed the subject to why they were trapped together in that stupid car in the first place.

"How long have you been lecturing at the Med Center?"

"This is my third class," Steve said. "It's a pretty cool gig. What about you?"

"Fourth time for me."

He looked at Lucas. "I heard you're, like, a subject expert."

Lucas shrugged, nonplussed.

"I know it's important to give back—since it's a teaching hospital connected to the medical school—but there are so many other things I'd rather be doing." Steve turned toward Lucas, lifted his glasses to display an arched eyebrow. "Like maybe checking out some of those *pies* in the store back there. I like a girl who's good with her hands. Know what I mean?"

That was it. Lucas *could* stomach Steve talking about how he didn't find the area entertaining, but he would not permit him to talk about Amish women that way. Fighting of any kind was still against his nature, but he was this close to knocking the guy's teeth out.

"You're being incredibly rude and crass about folks you don't even know," he said, keeping his voice steady. "What you're saying is disrespectful."

"What's with you?" Steve gawked at him. "Are these people your pets or something?"

Lucas felt the muscles in his arms, fists, and throat tighten. "Pets?"

"Yeah. Are you their protector or…" His voice trailed off. "Wait a second. You grew up around here."

"Not around." He held heavy eye contact. "Here."

"In Hershey, you mean?" Steve asked as they finally pulled into the parking lot.

Lucas slowly shook his head—hoping the gesture appeared just a little bit threatening to the guy. "Honey Brook, Pennsylvania. Born and raised."

"Oh…I had no idea."

"Obviously."

"Look man, I'm…well, I didn't…"

"Save it." He had three inches on the guy and probably fifty pounds of muscle due to the last six months of his pounding in fence posts and sanding slats to repair his front porch. But he was not going to punch him, no matter how hot his blood was boiling. "Drop me off here," he said, gesturing toward the curb by the ER entrance.

"Sure, sure." Steve finally did seem nervous, obeying Lucas's command in a flash.

After climbing out of that deathtrap, Lucas turned back to Steve. "Look, I know you didn't fully understand what you were saying. You're uneducated about the subject—that's no crime. Maybe if you spend more time in the community, you'll learn how hardworking and industrious the folks are around here. You'll never meet a group of people who care more about their neighbors, their families, and their beliefs. Nowhere else in the world."

"Sure, Lucas. Sorry."

"I forgive you," Lucas said, noticing instantly how the heavy blackness in his soul lifted. Remembering, too, how quickly Esther had forgiven Jacob.

Before leaving Steve, he added, "Maybe you wouldn't be so uneducated if you sat in on my lectures."

"What do you teach?"

"Sensitivity Training: Insight into the Amish Population. For some people, it should be required." He shut the door, turned on his heel, and left.

He tried very hard not to smirk as he walked away. Then again, it wasn't every day he got to tell off a jerk right to his face. He did wonder why he'd been so protective, almost to the point of physicality. Then he remembered how Esther had spoken to him as if he was still Amish, still living and believing all the teachings and traditions of the church.

As if nothing had changed.

Well, he was reading his scriptures again. And just that morning, he'd knelt by his bed and tried to talk to God. It had been awkward at first, and Lucas felt like his words weren't even reaching the ceiling, let alone heaven.

But he'd kept trying, and after a while, he'd sensed a stirring in his chest he'd assumed was gone forever.

And it had felt good.

CHAPTER FIFTEEN

After knocking several times with no answer, Esther slowly pushed open the door. "Lou? Anyone home?" It was after lunchtime, so her best friend should've been washing up after feeding her four perpetually hungry brothers.

After working most of yesterday helping Sarah plan the wedding day lunch and dinner menus, Esther had actually gathered the nerve to tell Louisa what she'd been up to the last two weeks. Never great at keeping secrets, she shook out her hands in preparation, getting rid of any final jitters.

The living room was empty, but muffled sounds of a conversation floated in from the kitchen.

"Lou, are you—? Oh! Sorry!"

Louisa and Levi jumped apart from each other. There hadn't been time for Esther to see clearly what she'd interrupted, but she could've sworn Levi was holding her hand.

"Esther!" Lou's face was bright red as she stared straight ahead. "He wasn't... I mean, nothing's going on." She shot a glare at Levi. "I told you never to come here again. Go now, before I call my father to throw you off the property!"

Levi, looking amused and oddly confident, tipped his hat to both of them, then left out the back door, whistling the whole way.

"And don't come back!" Lou called after him, wiping her hands on her apron. "I mean it, you hear?" She sighed in what was obviously forced frustration. "Oh, that man. I really should tell *Daed* how he's been coming here uninvited—"

"Uninvited?" Esther said with a sly smile. "Confess it, Lou; you're sweet on him."

Louisa whipped around. "*Sweet? On him?* That's insane. Why, that's..." She began wiping down the already clean kitchen counter. "That's just the wildest talk I've ever heard!"

"Uh-huh," Esther said. When it was evident her friend wanted nothing more than to suddenly rearrange the living room furniture, Esther wordlessly helped her move a heavy armchair. After a few silent moments, she said, "You could do worse, you know."

Lou didn't look up. "Don't know what you're talking about."

"He's tall and handsome."

"Who?"

Esther rolled her eyes. "You know exactly who. And he's the best around at metalworking. My *daed* bought his last two buggies from Levi. They never break down, and *Daed* says they're the sleekest in three counties. That's a noble skill."

"I suppose," Lou said, dragging the armchair back to its original spot.

"Talk is, he'll inherit his uncle's business when they retire to Ohio next year. With his good reputation and all the plain folk around here, he'll make a fine living for himself...and for anyone else who might live with him."

Louisa looked at Esther and planted her hands on her hips. "Esther Miller, what on earth are you going on about?"

"I saw you two—right here. I wasn't spying, but you certainly weren't trying to hide it. Any of the *kinnahs* could've walked in. Or your *maam*."

"They all went to a neighbor's after lunch." Lou spoke softly as she looked down at the wooden floor. "Won't be back till nearly suppertime."

"So you planned for him to—"

"We didn't *plan* anything."

"We?"

"Stop it, Es." Lou groaned. "It's nothing."

Finally, Esther walked over to her friend and touched her elbow. "It's obviously not nothing. He's been coming around your place for years. We all thought he'd ask to court you two seasons ago."

"Ya mean there's been talk?"

"Nothing bad." Esther gave her friend's elbow a gentle squeeze. "And mostly from Eve and her friends."

"Your little sister loves to gossip."

"Courtships are interesting to folks."

Lou groaned again. "How will I face everyone? This is so mortifying."

"There's nothing to be embarrassed about. And if you want to talk about mortifying, listen to how I—"

Like pulling a boiling pot off a hot burner, Esther completely lost her nerve. No way was she ready to breathe a word about being with Lucas. She loved her best friend to bits, but Eve wasn't the only one around who loved gossip. If Louisa caught the slightest whiff of this, it would be spread all over the village like a wildfire.

In that moment, she felt much more protective of Lucas than herself. He'd been in Honey Brook for six months. If he'd wanted his family to know, he would've told them himself, especially after all he'd shared with her the other night about his father.

"Finish," Lou said, looking up at her. "What about being mortified?"

"Nothing," Esther said, becoming fascinated by a blue-glazed pottery bowl on the table. "This is so pretty. Didn't you want to move this chair?"

"Es?" Her friend stared at her as Esther felt blood rush to her cheeks. "You're blushing."

She cleared her throat. "I most certainly am not."

"Ohhh. You've got a secret. You better tell me. I'm your best friend."

"I'm *your* best friend. Explain to me what I walked in on?"

Lou immediately sealed her lips together and let out a low hum. "Maybe we should change the subject."

Esther exhaled. "Good idea."

"So!" Lou exclaimed with an animated grin. "Tell me about the wedding. Is your sister over the moon excited?" She sat down at the long wooden table and patted the chair beside her.

"It's tough to tell with Sarah," Esther said, taking a seat. "She gets real excited when she's bossing me around. *Nay*, I take that back—yes, she's very happy. Amos was over this morning. They sat on the porch swing for hours, just laughing and whispering." She leaned closer to Lou. "I saw him kiss her twice."

Lou lifted her eyebrows. "Scandalous."

"It's was cute, actually. Romantic."

"Es, I haven't heard you talk like that in a long time. Anyone special in your life?"

Lucas had definitely become special to her, but not in a romantic way.

He wasn't a practicing Amishman anymore, he still hadn't reconnected with his family, and most importantly, he was Jacob's older brother. If she felt romantic about him, wouldn't that be terribly improper? Not to mention a waste of time…

"No," she said. "Not really."

"But there is somebody?"

Esther didn't know how to answer honestly, but she definitely didn't want to lie. "Maybe," she slowly offered.

"But you don't want to talk about it yet."

"Not yet."

Lou smiled. "I understand perfectly."

Esther's heart slowed from its nervous pace, and she slumped her shoulders in relief. "So how's choir rehearsal going?"

"Fine," Lou replied, filling a teakettle. "To be perfectly honest, there isn't much talent this year. All the best voices have married off, and for some reason, married women—even the youngest ones—don't think it's their place to sing with the youth." Lou scooped heaping spoonfuls of tea, adding them to a pair of porcelain mugs.

"Maybe they feel too grown up." Esther sighed. "After all, folks around here think I'm an old maid."

"That's nonsense," Lou said, handing her a stirring spoon. "I'm two months older than you. What does that make me?"

Esther laughed at first, but too soon, her thoughts turned sober. "Even before Sarah officially announced her engagement at the publishing, I'd been feeling left behind."

Lou adjusted the flame over the propane burner. "I have just as much to do around here as I ever have. More jam orders, and I make visits to the neighbors almost daily now since my mother's foot treatment. What in the world would I do with a husband?"

They cracked up laughing. "Shhhh," Esther said. "Don't let Bishop hear that kind of talk. He might take it upon himself to marry you off to a nice young man in another district."

"I think he's satisfied that I'm staying busy and not making trouble for the community."

"You truly never feel like you don't fit in?"

Lou squinted while concentrating on retying her apron. "Why should I?"

That's a very good question, Esther thought. *Why do I, then? Why does it sometimes feel as though I'm looking for a way out?*

The thought caused a familiar and very heavy weight to sit upon her heart. Besides making Leah ecstatic every time she dropped off a new batch of soap, the only bright spots in her life lately were when she'd been with Lucas. And it was useless to feel romantic about him.

Still, she couldn't help remembering how he'd looked at her the other night at his house, and how she'd felt…understood in a way no one else had made her feel.

"Es, I know I've asked this a dozen times, but

would you reconsider singing at the weddings? For me!"

Esther shook her head as another feeling washed over her. Even though he'd been gone two years, Jacob had drummed into her head that her voice was too beautiful to share. It would make her proud and stand out.

"*Nay,*" she said. "It brings me no joy anymore."

Lou nodded. "If you change your mind, it's never too late."

"*Danke, mein freund,*" Esther whispered, throat tight. Before her mood sank another notch, she added, "I better go. *Maam* will need help with supper." She didn't add that, since she had plans that evening, she herself would be missing from the dinner table tonight.

Before departing, the women shared a tight hug—the kind only two best friends could share. Both with secrets the other may never learn.

CHAPTER SIXTEEN

After closing the clinic at noon, Lucas remembered Eric had asked him to drop off an audiobook about overcoming addiction. His buddy had requested one with a Christian angle. Lucas had no trouble choosing which book.

He slid on his sunglasses and turned on the radio as he drove toward the small village of Nickel Mines. When the lyrics of the song made him feel uncomfortable, he switched to a classical station, then turned off the radio altogether, preferring to meditate on his day.

Eric was out mowing the front yard when Lucas arrived. "Hey-o!" he called out, pointing to a spot on the gravel for Lucas to park his truck. After "hiding" the keys above the visor, Lucas walked toward Eric.

"Brought you that book," he said. "Audio, just like you wanted, ya lazy bum."

"Excellent," Eric said, pulling out one earbud. "Thanks, man."

"You're welcome. How's it going?"

Eric shrugged and turned the loud motor to idle. "Some days are better than others. It's probably a blessing that I have three acres and only a pushing mower."

"Probably a huge blessing." Lucas laughed. "Anything I can help with?"

"Just pray for me, dude," he said, staring toward

the sun. "I try my best, then leave the rest to the man upstairs."

"I didn't realize you're religious," Lucas couldn't help saying. "You never mentioned it when I visited you in rehab."

Eric shaded his eyes. "I suppose it's not something I talk about very often, but lately... Well, we've lived in Amish country for years. Not like anyone around here would do a double take because we're Christians."

"Yeah," Lucas said, agreeing wholeheartedly.

Besides a few select people, no one knew how deep Lucas's religious roots ran. Well, his coworkers knew, plus anyone who'd ever sat in on one of his lectures at the Hershey Med Center.

Even though he wasn't practicing any particular religion, why didn't Lucas talk about what he used to believe? What he still believed even after being away from the church of his youth. Had his core beliefs changed?

He had a feeling he'd be mulling over that question for a while. "I will pray for you," he said, clasping a hand on Eric's shoulder.

The two friends talked about Eric's mower for a minute, then about the changing fall weather. "The girls are all inside," Eric added.

"Girls?" Lucas looked toward where Eric was pointing.

Eric rolled his eyes, then laughed. "It's worse than before. They're playing dress-up."

"Who?" Lucas asked, feeling like he was missing a joke. "What girls?"

"Miss Esther," Eric said. "And she brought her

sister. Viv's out of her mind excited for the company. Last I checked, they had those poor kid goats dressed like bunnies. Fluffy tails and all."

Lucas whipped off his sunglasses. "Esther's here?"

"Thought that's why *you're* here."

"No, I…" He trailed off, glancing down at the audiobook in his hand.

"Viv'll love that you dropped by." He pointed his chin toward the house. "Go on inside. Maybe you can talk some sense into those crazy females."

The news was dumbfounding, though Lucas shouldn't have been surprised. When he'd brought her there before, Esther had gone bonkers over those tiny goats, and Vivian had made her practically swear in blood that she'd come back.

Giving Eric a final wave, he jogged toward the house.

Before he'd even reached the door, he heard the giggling.

"This way, Milo. Come here, boy. Come to Auntie Esther."

Lucas was already laughing as he opened the door. "Is it safe to come in?" he asked, poking his head around the corner.

"Lucas, sweetheart!" Vivian called out. "Just look at all this cuteness!" She was holding up one of the goats. Instead of a bunny costume, the helpless thing was dressed as a fat pumpkin.

"I heard about what you've been doing," he said, giving Vivian a half hug after she'd slid over to him across the hardwood floor in her stockinged feet. "Eric's ready to call a psychiatrist."

"Oh, whatever." Vivian shoved the goat into his arms. "She's been thinking about you all day," she said in a low voice.

Lucas lifted his eyebrows. "This thing?"

"No, you silly boy." Probably trying to be sly, she slid her gaze over to Esther, who was sitting on the stairs, pulling a black cat costume off a goat.

He chuckled through an exhale. "How do you know what she's been thinking?"

Vivian shrugged and gave him a nudge. Lucas didn't need the hint. "I better grab that," she added when the phone rang.

"Hi," he said to Esther, carrying the goat toward the staircase. She was surprisingly soft and yeah, okay, cuddly. "Why am I not surprised to see you here?"

Esther smiled up at him. She was wearing a long black skirt with a brown sweater on top. The sweater looked like it belonged to a much larger person, maybe her father. It was covered in goat hair.

"Hey," she said. "What are you doing here?"

"What do you think?" He held the tiny animal away from his body, so the goat was facing him. He immediately began licking Lucas's nose. His tongue felt warm and rough. Despite being raised around all kinds of animals, it was starting to gross him out. The way it was making Esther laugh, however, he was not about to stop.

"Milo," Esther said. "You must allow him to breathe." She was by his side, taking the goat into her arms. "We talked about this, remember?" The goat gave a little bleat, then stuck out his tongue.

"Children," Lucas said, shaking his head in playful frustration. "Sometimes they just won't listen."

"It's this modern generation. I blame all those cooking shows on television." She smiled, gave him a wink, then walked away.

He knew his smile was huge and didn't bother trying to hide it. He was really starting to love hanging out with Esther. She was fun, made him laugh, and didn't treat him like…well, like he assumed the Amish folk would treat him.

Only a few days had passed since he'd seen her, but he couldn't deny how being around her made him feel good, especially after talking about Jacob. They'd both been carrying that burden too long. He wished they were alone so he could tell her, well… he didn't know exactly what he wanted to say.

When he heard her giggle—being smothered by all three goats—another soothing wave swept up his body, followed this time, however, by a slow-burning type of warmth spreading through his chest, just from being near her.

"I'm actually glad we ran into each other," he said, following behind as she walked toward the couches.

"We seem to do that a lot," she said.

"Yes." He sat on the other side of the couch so she wouldn't feel crowded, even though he knew how good it would feel to sit right next to her. "This time, we couldn't have planned it better." He allowed the smallest, brown-and-white kid to climb onto his lap like a kitten. "They are pretty cute," he admitted, scratching her behind the ears.

"They're adorable," she said, cuddling one to her

chest. "The very best remedy for a bad day."

Catching the tone in her voice, he held the goat back from licking his forehead so he could face Esther properly. "You're having a bad day?"

She was looking down, her lips pushed to one side. "Kind of, yeah." She took in a deep breath, then let it out. "I almost stopped by your—"

"Who are you?"

They both turned to see a girl, maybe thirteen, standing halfway down the stairs.

"Eve," Esther said, gently pushing all the goats off her lap so she could stand. "How did you like Vivian's powder room? Isn't it pretty with all the lilac wallpaper? It's your turn to pick the next costume for this little guy." She pointed at the tan baby goat as he rambled away.

"I need my inhaler," the girl said.

Lucas sat up straight at attention while Esther rushed to her. "Having a hard time breathing?"

She nodded.

"Is it allergies or asthma?" Lucas asked, unable to not get involved at any mention of a medical issue, knowing he could treat either ailment at the clinic, and even more grateful they had such a valuable resource close by.

"Allergies," Esther said, wrapping an arm around the girl. "I'm sure it's the goat hair. You'll feel better when we're outside. Lucas, this is my sister Eve; she's been a big help with Sarah's wedding. She makes it so much fun."

"Very nice to meet you," Lucas said, smiling at the description. From what she'd mentioned to him earlier, he knew full well that Esther was not having *so much fun* planning her sister's wedding.

"Evie, this is Lucas. He's a friend...of Eric, Vivian's husband."

"Hi," the girl said, leaning into Esther's side.

It was fine that she'd introduced him as Eric's friend, and not *her* friend, and definitely not a run-away Amish.

"Do you love these baby goats as much as your sister?" Lucas asked, kneeling down to pet one that had wandered over, while keeping an eye on Eve's wheezing inhales. They didn't sound deep enough to be asthma. She probably really did simply need to be outside and breathe some clean air.

"They're called kids," Eve corrected, which made Lucas smile.

"You're right. My mistake."

"So many *Englishers* today," Eve said quietly, but not too hushed that Lucas didn't hear.

Though she was mostly correct, something roiled in Lucas's gut, knowing he wasn't grouped at all with the Amish people. Not that he should be.

"I think we'd better go," Esther said. "Do you have a spare inhaler in the buggy? Why don't you go get it?"

Her sister nodded, then went out the back door.

"Y'all leaving?" Vivian was standing under the high arch leading to the kitchen, a phone pressed to her ear.

"Eve's not feeling well," Esther said. "But we had a marvelous time."

"Promise you'll come back soon," Vivian said, giving Esther a one-armed hug, still holding the phone. "And you—" She stabbed Lucas in the chest with one finger. "Bring dessert next time. You know I love your chocolate ooey-gooey butter cookies."

"Yes, ma'am," he said, wondering which of his recorded Food Network shows had that recipe. His thoughts wandered further as he wondered if he'd turn on a TV ever again. "I promise."

Together, they walked toward the barn. Lucas must've been preoccupied to have not noticed Esther's white mule by the gate, as well as her buggy. Eve was sitting on the top seat, using her inhaler. He watched for a moment, noticing how her breathing became slower and more even. After a few breaths, she jumped down off the buggy.

He couldn't help wondering the circumstances that got her that prescription. Had she been to his clinic or another medical professional?

"Hey, I forgot to say goodbye to the kids!" Eve exclaimed. "Can I go back inside for just a minute?"

"Sure," Esther said, holding her sister's chin in her hand for a few seconds. "If you're feeling better."

"I am! My lungs are wide open now." With that, she took off running toward the house.

"Make sure you knock first!" Esther called.

Since Eve was gone, Lucas moved his examining attention back to Esther. Her skin was clear but her blue eyes looked a little tired.

"Can I ask you something?" he said, scratching the mule behind her ears. "You implied you're in a bad mood. Or you were until you got here." He nodded toward the house. "Is there anything I can do?"

"No," she said, the shadow under her eyes growing darker as she lowered her gaze.

He patted the mule again. "Want to talk about it?"

Esther breathed out, then began massaging her temples with both hands. "You know how Sarah got hurt and now I'm in charge of her wedding."

Lucas nodded. He'd heard a whole lot about that lately.

"It's been...a challenge."

"Why?"

She sighed again, and Lucas wished he could go back in time and not bring up the subject if even talking about it made her frustrated.

"I've married off one sister, and now Sarah's engaged. I've stood as attendant to three of my girlfriends' weddings, and I can't even count how many cousins. It's hard."

"Always a bridesmaid..." Lucas said, allowing his voice to trail off, knowing Esther wouldn't need to hear the rest of the common saying. Then he felt sick—what a tactless thing to say. "I'm sorry," he said, bowing his head. "Please go on."

"Not too long ago," she said, "I planned my own wedding, which never happened. I know it sounds selfish, but is it fair that now I have to plan my younger sister's?" She started picking at a spot of chipped paint on the buggy. "I'm sewing her wedding dress, and every stitch reminds me of *my* dress. I'm trying not to resent the whole thing, but I'm only human."

"You've mentioned your dress more than a few times. I don't understand."

"Jah," she said, blinking up at him. "It's just hanging in my closet like a dead...purple...hay sack.

What am I supposed to do with it?"

"Wear it?"

Her mouth fell open. "My wedding dress?"

"Oh. Sorry." *Wrong answer.*

Hmm. Okay, she was upset about her wedding dress, and it was hanging in her closet like a dead purple hay sack. Got it.

"It's a reminder," she finally said, sounding calmer after the burst of emotion. "I'm about to marry off a younger sister. And Anna is having a baby." She sniffed. "Lou's got a secret beau, and all I have is a dress I can't wear."

"Maybe you could give it to someone," he suggested.

"My wedding dress?"

Okay, okay, very *wrong answer.*

"It's a symbol," she said.

"Thought it was a reminder." He couldn't help grinning, hoping to lift the mood.

"It's a *symbol*," she repeated, "that my life isn't going the way it's supposed to."

He slid his hands into his pockets. "Whose is?"

For a long moment, they looked at each other; the longer the silence lasted, the more Lucas got that feeling again, the one he knew was a foolish waste of time.

"I haven't admitted that to anyone. Not *Maam* or Anna or my best friend." Finally, Esther looked up. "I can't believe I told you."

"If you want, I can tell you something I haven't told anyone."

"Okay," she said, seeming a bit more upbeat.

Before continuing, he thought the words out in

his head. "I don't believe in fate, but do you think there's a reason we keep running into each other? We're both going through difficult things." *Understatement*, he wanted to add. "But talking to you helps me. Helping you through your problems helps me, too. Though I don't know why."

"Seems too simple." She tilted her head to look at him. "You're very easy to talk to and, I don't know…it's like I know you'll keep everything confidential. I can tell you anything."

"I hope you mean that."

Puffy white clouds and a blue sky were Esther's background, making her look like a painting or fancy book cover. There was something more he longed to say, but those words were not coming.

"Okay, I'm ready now," Eve said, climbing onto the buggy. "Can I hold the reins this time?"

"Sure, Evie," Esther said, but her big blue eyes were still fixed on Lucas.

No, he did not believe in fate, nor in the ability to read minds. At that moment, he was very relieved for that second part.

"*Danke*. I guess I'll see you later," she said as Lucas held open her door and kept the buggy steady, dying to reach out and help her take a seat.

"When?"

"When what?"

He couldn't help smiling. "When will you see me later?"

She smiled in return, then shot a quick glance at Eve. But she was occupied with a gray barn cat who'd jumped onto her lap.

"Tomorrow's pretty busy—wedding stuff." She

lifted a toothy grin that made him chuckle. The quick look they shared and held made his heart beat in his chest, and it was becoming difficult to even swallow.

"I've got a full schedule, too," he said, needing to break the silence. "What about the next day?"

"Leah's been waiting for my new batch of soap. Vanilla clove—extra heavy on the clove."

Lucas noticed the excitement that flashed in her blue eyes, but a moment later, she was chewing on her bottom lip. He wasn't sure what to make of that. "Will you be delivering it to her?" he asked instead.

She nodded. "Right after lunch."

"Maybe I'll see you then."

"I'm driving," Eve said as the mule began to pace forward.

"Goodbye, young lady," Lucas said, moving to stand in Eve's eyeshot.

"Bye," she replied, way too focused on making the mule do a tight turn than speaking to an English stranger.

"Bye-bye," Esther said with a giggle.

Lucas slid his hands in his back pockets and watched until they disappeared, well aware of the warmth of longing flooding his body. After they'd gone, he glanced up the hill behind him to see Eric tackling the back lot with his push mower. He was about to head up there to offer some help, or at least bring him a bottle of water, when he glanced at his watch.

Shoot, I gotta get going.

After bending the speed limit just a hair, Lucas

reached home right as a big red van pulled up to the curb.

"Brenneman?" the driver asked, meeting him in the driveway. He was consulting the iPad in his hands.

"Yes. Lucas Brenneman."

After studying the electronic screen for another minute, the driver glanced up at him. "You're canceling service?"

"Yep." Lucas nodded, feeling only the tiniest twinge of regret for the decision.

"We're removing the satellite dish?"

"Please."

"Oh. Well, all right, I can make that happen." The driver chewed on the gum in his mouth. "Mind if I ask what you're getting instead of Dish?"

"Nothing," Lucas said.

"Not even local cable? I can give you an antenna for that. Got some in my van."

"No, thank you," Lucas said, leading the man toward the house. "In fact, do you happen to know anyone who might want a sixty-inch LED smart TV?"

CHAPTER SEVENTEEN

"It smells like a spice factory in here," Sarah complained, fanning her face. "How much of that stuff are you using?"

"I think it's pleasantly subtle," Esther said, trying not to make eye contact with her mother.

She knew it was *probably* too potent, and that she could very well get into hot water over it if the bishop happened to show up. But she didn't care. When Leah had stopped by to drop off Esther's latest check, she said how well the stronger-scented soaps were selling.

"I honestly can't keep them on the shelf," she'd said. "And the catalog will be online in a few days. Get ready for the spotlight, cousin!"

"I'll open a window," Esther said to Sarah, instead of simply telling her to go outside if the smell was so distasteful.

That morning, she'd been working on the wedding dress. Half the inside panels were done. If she wanted to keep her sanity, Esther needed to figure out how to find some kind of pleasure in the task. Yes, she was helping her sister, and the good book said Charity Never Faileth. But Esther did not feel pure charity in her heart.

At least not yet.

Then she'd remembered what Lucas had said before about her own wedding dress. How she should just wear it herself or give it away.

Men, she'd thought while loading the new bobbin with heavier blue thread. *They don't understand traditions. Especially not Englishmen.*

Was Lucas really still an outsider, though? He'd mentioned to her on more than one occasion something he'd read in the Bible recently. Hadn't he also mentioned he was praying again? He was working on his spirituality—she could feel that just as strongly now as when they'd been together at Vivian's, when they'd been so easy and comfortable with each other, almost like they were best friends.

Best friends, but more... Esther couldn't help thinking, knowing she was kidding herself every time she denied that being around Lucas made her feel soft, and pretty, and warm all the way down to her toes.

Lucas had also spoken so tenderly about Jacob and how strong his faith had been.

During those conversations, Lucas certainly hadn't sounded non-Amish.

Esther knew in her heart that if he'd just reach out to someone in his family—okay, maybe not his father, at least not at first—but if he would make a tiny effort, she knew it would pay off, for she knew how much joy being with family could bring.

Well, most of the time...

"I'm going out later, if it's okay," Esther said while tying the last purple ribbon on a soap wrapper. "I don't need the buggy."

"Are you meeting *him*?" Eve asked.

Esther whipped around to her little sister, finding Evie grinning like the cat that swallowed the canary.

"Him who?" Sarah asked, helping *Maam* fold

clothes she'd just pulled off the line.

"The *Englisher* from the goat farm. They were talking."

"It's no one," Esther said, waving a hand dismissively. "Don't know what she's talking about."

"Him, who?" Sarah repeated, this time directed at Eve.

"Um...his name was...it started with an L... Luh-luh...Levi!"

"Levi." Sarah frowned. "You don't mean Levi Sutter?" She pointed at Esther. "Levi Sutter is Lou's beau, or he practically is. She's your best friend! And he's not an *Englisher*."

"He's not her *official* beau," Esther replied, realizing too late that was the dumbest thing to say. Then again, it was better than telling them the correct name.

So I ran into Lucas Brenneman, she imagined herself saying nonchalantly. *I've actually met with him four times, once at his house. Alone. I'm sure everyone's okay with that...*

"Esther, I can't believe you're stealing another girl's boyfriend," Sarah said. "What if Lou thinks he's going to propose?"

"I don't"—she was at a complete loss for words—"know what to say."

"Well, it's shameful, Esther." Sarah snapped a towel in the air. "And just a few weeks before wedding season begins. What sort of example are you setting?"

"Maybe it was Leo?" Eve said. "I'm not good with names."

"Hmm." Sarah planted her hands on her hips.

"Wonder which innocent woman Esther stole *that* boy from."

"I'm taking these boxes to Leah," Esther said to her mother while her two younger sisters continued their squabble over *L* names.

"Don't be home too late," her *maam* said. "Your heavy cloak is by the door."

"Thank you."

Just as before, her mother was letting her leave—assuming she would be home after dark—without knowing where she was going. Wouldn't *Maam* try to stop her if she really thought she was off to meet a mystery man? Or did she think Esther was part of some secret book club or sewing bee? Or maybe a budding author like in *Little Women*?

As she walked down the lane, she wondered what Lucas had planned for them today. She got excited thinking they might go back to Vivian's to play with the goats…but they'd been there two days ago. Surely he had a different plan for them.

They'd been at his house once, so maybe it was her turn to come up with something to do. As she stopped to watch a flock of blackbirds pick at something across the road, her gaze couldn't help drifting farther up the path, then picturing what was around the corner.

Suddenly, she knew exactly what she was going to do. And stubborn old Lucas would play along whether he liked it or not. It would take one little pit stop along her way into town. Just a few short minutes would set her plan in motion.

As she turned to cut through a field, Esther couldn't help grinning to herself. After all, wasn't there a quote about how serving others in need makes your own worries and troubles go away?

She could definitely use some of that today.

After another lecture from Leah about how Esther should be making soap full-time now—which she did not need to hear—Esther sat at a little table just inside Yoder's Home Goods so she could watch for Lucas out the window.

It didn't take long before she saw him step out of the clinic and lean against the door. No white lab coat, just black pants again and a dark gray sweater. If he let his hair grow out, then cut it in the bowl style, he'd almost look—

She jumped when Lucas tapped on the glass right in front of her face. He waved and laughed, mimicking how she'd jumped. Esther couldn't help giggling, then glanced behind her to see if Leah, or any of the Amish customers, had noticed.

"Hi," he said, entering the store. "Is this all right?" He must've seen the worry on her face after he'd come in. "Do you not want to…"

"*Nay*, it's fine." She bit her bottom lip. "Um, Lucas, I wonder if you'd run an errand with me."

He lifted his eyebrows. "Sure. Where to?"

"I borrowed a book from a friend and, wouldn't you know it, I've already read the silly thing. I'd like to return it."

"Sounds good. Do we need my truck?"

"It's not far." She stopped to grin. "Besides, I have these." She bent down to grab something under the table, then came back up holding two pairs of Rollerblades.

Lucas frowned in confusion. "Are you serious?"

She nodded, ready to turn blue in the face explaining why she wanted him to skate with her. But Lucas did not need any convincing.

He picked up the larger pair—obviously meant for him. "I haven't bladed in more than ten years. You?"

"To be honest, I haven't since Jacob asked to court me." She didn't bother explaining that he hadn't approved of the spirited mode of transport or entertainment. "So it's been a long time for me, as well. But I'm sure I remember how."

"Me too. Ready?"

After returning his grin, she rubbed her hands together. Lucas sat in one of the chairs at the little table, and they began lacing their skates. She'd borrowed them from Leah, who had several pairs in various sizes for her delivery boys, who preferred blading during the summer months. Esther had guessed at Lucas's size. From the way he stood up, testing them out, she'd guessed right.

Hooking her knapsack over her shoulder, then gripping the back of the chair, she stood slowly, trying to stabilize her footing. When she'd been young, she'd loved using skates, and had gotten pretty good at it, faster than Lou and Anna, even Noah Otto. One night after the youth singings, when Esther had been no more than twelve, she'd challenged Jacob to a race. She'd beat him by a mile—which now made her feel horrible, knowing the physical advantage she'd had over him.

"Hey, you're a natural," Lucas said, gliding beside her, body bent at the waist, hands clasped behind his back.

"I'm just trying not to fall on my face in front of you," Esther called out, the chilly air blowing against her cheeks. This probably would've been a better idea a few months back, but she made sure her cloak was fastened tight as she raced to catch up to Lucas.

"You're fast," she said, trying not to sound out of breath. "This isn't a race."

"Sorry," Lucas said. Then suddenly, he slowed way down, slow enough that she passed him easily. A moment later, she felt him behind her. The second he placed his hands on her hips, a shock wave zipped up her spine, making the back of her neck tingle.

She blinked hard, hoping she wasn't about to faint and then roll down the hill.

"How's this for a better pace?" he asked, moving his hands up to her shoulders, then gently sliding them down to her elbows, holding her so they skated together.

Esther couldn't breathe, yet her heart was beating a million miles a minute. "It's…nice," she managed to get out. "F-fun."

What a ridiculous understatement, she thought, purposefully slowing her pace so his body touched hers, just a little. *Does Lou think it's "nice" when Levi touches her?*

"Which way next?" he asked, letting her go, then coming up to her side.

When her eyes cleared, she noticed they were at a three-way stop.

"Left," she said after coughing slightly, missing how his closeness had brought such warmth.

He gave her a thumbs-up, then took off at a faster pace than before, perhaps regretting their closeness. They passed two buggies and a group of *kinnah* who'd just been let out of school.

"Relax your hands," Lucas said, falling beside her again. "Like this." He flared out his fingers, moving his arms gently back and forth. "Like you're swimming."

She longed for him to simply take her hand and show her what he meant. Anything to cause him to touch her again.

"I've been swimming only once," she said, needing to remember that platonic promise she'd made to herself. "And all we did was float in inner tubes. We didn't use our hands."

Lucas laughed. "Well, now you'll be prepared for it." He skated forward quickly, then slowed. "Up this hill or around the bend?"

"Up," Esther said, then pumped her arms to skate past him. Maybe it would be better if he wasn't paying too close attention to where they were going.

It was tiring, going uphill, but having a goal made it feel easier for Esther. When she reached the top, she slowed to a stop, not so gracefully skating off the road onto a patch of grass. Lucas followed, his hair mussed from the wind. He looked five years younger and about a thousand worries lighter.

"Now where?" he asked, rubbing his palms over his knees.

Esther took a beat, then wordlessly gazed to the farm way down the dell.

Lucas's face went white. "This is where you

brought me?"

"I need to return the—"

"Esther." He moved farther back from the road, farther away from that farm. "That's my parents' house."

"I…borrowed the book from your mother."

He tilted his head. "You saw my mother?"

"I see her quite often, Lucas. All of them. Even your eldest brother. Peter moved up to Swartsville for a job last year, but he still comes home to visit every preaching Sunday."

Lucas wasn't moving, and Esther wasn't sure if that was good—that he was taking everything in— or if he was about to blow up.

"Your sister actually lent me the book."

"Sister." Lucas kept staring toward the house. "Which…?"

"Hannah." She smiled. "Hannah Anna Banana."

"Banana?"

"There were three other Hannahs in her grade. Jacob came up with the nickname."

Lucas took one step toward the house, still only a blank expression on his face. "Must've been after I'd gone."

"She's twelve now, almost as tall as my little Evie."

A second later, she heard him take in a sharp breath; then he lifted a hand to pinch the bridge of his nose. "I understand what you're trying to do," he said, eyes closed. "I appreciate it, but I can't go down there."

"Why?"

He lowered his hand and looked at her. "Should

I explain it again?"

His tone made her flinch. "No, but—"

"Did you tell them I'm here?"

"No," she said firmly. "I promised you I wouldn't do that."

He nodded and let out another deep exhale. "Let's go."

"Lucas, please." She was not about to budge. "We're here now. I'll go inside with you. It'll be easier if—"

"How long have you been planning this?" he asked. "Tell the truth."

"I didn't plan anything. It came to mind as I was on the way into town. I was thinking how you took me to see the goats; then later we went to your house… You've planned things, and I thought it was my turn. That's what friends do."

"Don't you have friends of your own?" he said, his voice sounding strained.

"*Jah…*"

"They're probably all Amish, too, right? Why don't you hang out with them?"

Esther allowed the words—the subtle insult—to run circles through her mind. Was he accusing her of something? Or was he simply pouring salt on her already open wound?

CHAPTER EIGHTEEN

Lucas felt so angry, so betrayed that he couldn't think straight. If he'd wanted to reach out to his family, didn't Esther know he would do it himself, on his own timetable? He didn't need her to hold his hand.

Just as regret at his misplaced rage began mentally punching him in the head, Esther burst into tears. *Oh no*, he thought, trying to replay his words to her, but all he could remember was the hot flash of anger.

"I don't fit in," Esther blurted, turning away.

"What are you talking about?"

"What you just said about my friends." She glared at him, wind blowing back her cloak. "I thought you of all people would understand."

Him of all people? *Does she think I feel like I don't fit in, either?*

Well, did he?

When he took a split second away from his own anger, he actually thought about what she'd said. Sure, he was almost literally a fish out of water, but what confused him was why *she* would feel out of place.

As a teenager, he remembered her as being pleasant, fun-loving, and kind to everyone. Nothing glaringly out of the ordinary now, either. In fact, she was rather...well, he quite enjoyed being with her. A woman like Esther should feel welcomed anywhere.

Before he forgot his manners altogether, he realized he owed her a pretty hefty apology. Her plan had been misguided, but she'd been trying to help.

"What do you mean you don't fit in?" he asked. "Do you want to talk about it?"

"No," she snapped. He knew he deserved it. He'd snapped at her to mask his own insecurity.

"Come here," he said when her crying increased. "Behind those trees, there's a place we can sit." Without thinking, he took her gloved hand and looped it through his arm. They'd been coordinated in their Rollerblades, but neither of them was great at walking on grass still wearing them. She plopped down on the wooden bench Minister Bender had made when he'd been a kid. One night, he and his four brothers had snuck out here to carve their names on the legs. Without needed to check, he knew Jacob's was on the leg closest to Esther.

"I don't know what I'm doing," she said.

"I can untie these for you, then," Lucas said, attempting a very lame joke. Esther didn't even react.

"I'm so mixed up, and I hate feeling this way."

It was like the first day at the clinic. Words rushed from her mouth, but nothing made sense. Okay, she felt lost. What about the dress? How dare Sarah. And what did she really believe? Why had *Gott* taken him?

Jacob, he thought. *She's talking about Jacob, and she's…crying.*

The thought of Esther still missing his younger brother to the point of tears—even after all she knew—made his stomach clench. She'd been engaged to him. They'd been in love. Had his thoughts gotten so carried away since he'd seen her through the window at Yoder's? Or as she'd been skating alongside him? Or practically any other time they'd been together?

She'd belonged to his younger brother. The brother he'd have done anything for—even leave the most important people in the world to him.

"I feel myself getting restless," she said, interrupting his thoughts, "questioning the simplest things, and I sometimes wonder if our way of life is *Gott*'s plan for me."

Lucas sat up straight. He surmised she was going through something confusing, but it must've been serious if she was even considering leaving the church.

"Talk to me," he said.

After wiping away a few more tears, and after a few more deep breaths, Esther said, "I'm not sixteen anymore. I had my courtship and my engagement—that part of my life is over, it seems. I'm obedient and charitable and I love *Gott* so much, but I don't know where or how I fit in."

She was talking so fast, unloading so much information that Lucas wondered how long these worries had been building up.

"I'm floating," she went on, "drifting in the gray, and I have no idea anymore if *Gott* has a plan for me. Then I think, maybe that means I'm to carve my own path, but what if it leads away from home? I pray and I pray, but I have no peace. I don't know what to do." She looked at him, fingers clasped. "I'm scared, Lucas."

Finally, those muddled words made sense. It wasn't about a dress, or about where he'd been the last ten years, or even about Jacob.

Esther was doubting her faith. The idea shocked him.

From that simple discernment, the weight of her heavy heart caused his own heart to feel heavy.

"It's ironic," he couldn't help saying as he continued to untie her skates.

"What is?"

"You're asking *me* for advice about this. I *did* leave home, and then…things changed and I left the church, too. I've lived as an *Englisher* for years."

"But you came back."

Her words gave him pause. "Not to repent of my sins to the brethren and ask for forgiveness—you know that's the only way I'd be fully accepted again. And not to return to the plain community."

"But your family…" She glanced through the trees toward the home where he'd grown up.

"They don't want to see me," he said, feeling like the words were on repeat. "I'm a disappointment."

"How do you know what they're thinking?" She clasped her hands over her knees and leaned forward, red circles rimming her blue eyes. "There must be plenty of places for you to work. Why did you choose Honey Brook?"

Her question shouldn't have been difficult, but it was. Maybe he'd even mentally been avoiding the implications of coming home when he'd taken this job.

Was his subconscious protecting him from something? Or preparing him?

Esther was gazing down at him, so open and eager.

Back then, he'd prayed a lot, too, about what God's plan was for him. When he'd made that choice at sixteen, he remembered how unsure he'd felt at the time, yet very sure. And scared. So, so scared.

Suddenly, the words from James and Exodus and the teaching of Paul swam around in his head so much that he almost couldn't see.

Then his thoughts became clearer than polished glass. "Esther," he said, "this is a very important subject—for both of us. I don't have answers for you right now, but in a few days, I know I will."

• • •

Hours later, Esther had left for home before him, probably hoping he might walk down to his parents' house on his own. But Lucas had no intention. His steps were steady, however, as he walked through the trees, passed dried rows of corn ready to be cut for the grain.

Besides the glow of gaslights coming from the front windows, the whitewashed house was dark. He'd sheared his first sheep here, and when he'd first started attending youth singings on Sunday nights, practically every volleyball game was in this pasture behind the barn.

A light flickered and he saw movement inside.

As he walked down the gravel path, Lucas felt nervous, but now, as he stood on the doorstep, then knocked three times, all nervousness vanished.

This'll probably end in nothing anyway, he thought as the door began to open. *He was in his sixties when I left home. There's no way he'll recognize me now…*

"Lucas Brenneman."

"Minister Bender," Lucas said, not bothering to feel shocked. "It's good to see you."

The old man's beard was longer, and white as snow, while the hair on his head was nearly gone. He wore a blue shirt, black vest and pants, and black slippers. It was nearly eight o'clock at night, after all.

"Oh, my." He chuckled, stroking his beard. "I haven't been minister nigh on these ten years. Come in, please. I heard something a few months back 'bout you being in Honey Brook, but, since your folks never mentioned it, I thought it was a rumor."

Lucas stepped into the cozy parlor. "I've been here since April."

"Been by to visit your mamma?"

He dipped his head. "No, sir."

"Brother," he corrected, sitting on a rocking chair. "Call me Brother Sol."

Lucas's heart stung at the request. "Thank you."

"Have a seat," Sol said, gesturing to a tan couch covered in yarn-tied quilts. "Push all that to the side. My granddaughter's been learning to crochet. Apparently, I'm the sole benefactor."

If he'd been more polite, Lucas would've inquired as to which granddaughter, but there'd been so many — one of them named Hannah like his own sister.

"Since my Gracie Mae passed on three winters ago, I seem to be the sole benefactor of everything in my family."

"I'm sorry," Lucas said, lacing and unlacing his

fingers. "I didn't know about your wife."

Sol bobbed his head up and down. "Well, she'd been ill for a while, weak as a kitten at the end but still sharp as a tack, mind you. I would've kept her with me forever, but the good Lord's will had a mere fifty years in mind. I didn't doubt His will then, and I don't now." He smiled and gave Lucas a wink. "Trust in the Lord with all thine heart, and lean not unto your own understanding."

"I never understood that scripture," Lucas confessed.

Sol began rocking in his chair. "Ya ever have a real difficult decision to make?"

Lucas actually laughed. "Once or twice."

The old man puckered his lips and nodded. "Did you ponder over it for hours and hours? Maybe even days and weeks?"

"Yes."

"Did you make the decision and then take it to the Lord?"

"Um, no," Lucas admitted. "I kind of did it the other way around."

"Did you feel peace with your decision?"

Lucas thought back. "Not peace, but at the time, I definitely felt that God—*Gott*," he corrected himself, choosing the more familiar, spiritual Amish pronunciation. "I definitely felt that *Gott* understood. He didn't send down an angel to stop me or…cure what ailed my soul."

"Because you were raised well, by righteous, goodly parents. *Gott* trusted you to live your life, to give unselfishly, to treat others kindly, and to always show your love to Him through your actions." He tapped his own chest. "With all thine heart."

Taking a long moment to drink in the powerful words, Lucas smiled. "You've always had a way of explaining the Bible. Especially to the youth. You were my favorite minister."

"Well now." Sol began rocking faster. "We're all given different gifts of the Spirit. What do you think yours is?"

"I don't know. Healing, maybe? The gift of teaching."

Sol smiled. "Both very precious. And powerful." He leaned forward. "But I don't think that's why you sought me out tonight, when you could be eating your ma's pot roast and stewed tomatoes."

"I did want to ask you about a story in the Bible." He waited a beat before beginning. "It's in Luke chapter fifteen."

"Ah." Brother Sol nodded and laced his fingers. "The return of the Prodigal Son."

CHAPTER NINETEEN

Esther checked her wristwatch for the third time. Silly mule was taking her sweet time. If they kept this pace, she'd be late to Lucas's.

Stop it, silly heart. Don't go beating a mile a minute just because I thought his name. Lucas was a friend—that was all he could be. They were helping each other, a mutually beneficial arrangement.

But he had looked adorable when they'd been Rollerblading a few days ago. And then when he'd gotten serious about finding answers for the both of them, her heart felt pretty close to melting.

To free herself of those kinds of thoughts, it helped when Esther recalled a happy memory with Jacob. Once, he'd arranged a sleigh ride for just the two of them. He'd seemed so strong and capable, and because of the cold, his eyelashes had frozen. They'd sledded all the way to the diner in Bird-in-Hand, where they'd ordered potato soup and hot cocoa.

Dwelling on that memory, however, didn't seem to help this time. And after clicking her tongue to get Peanut to a faster clip, her heart did another set of quick trots when she remembered to where she was racing.

Back to that gray house with the comfortable couch and warm wood-burning stove.

The overcast October afternoon brought with it a chilly breeze—hints of the cold weather to come.

Daed had talked at lunch about a storm passing this way, but it must not be much, since he didn't fuss when she'd spoken of harnessing the mule. She was glad she'd worn her heaviest cloak, thick black outer bonnet, and warm gloves, as she grasped the material at her throat when another gust of wind shook the small buggy.

"Whoa," she said, steadying sweet Peanut. The mule shook her head but corrected her footing. Wanting to get out of the wind, Esther gently wiggled the reins, coaxing Peanut to pick up the pace. Another gorgeous golden twilight sky led her east toward their destination.

Maybe hearing the buggy and Peanut's clomps, Lucas came into view in his front yard. It was certainly the pounding of the hoofs and not her heart that made Esther gulp for air.

He waved, but with the quick pace she was traveling, she was nervous to let go of the reins. Instead of waving back, she gave him the biggest grin she could.

"Hi!" she called.

"Hello! Want a hand?"

"Please!"

He opened the door of the buggy and she happily leaped out, taking a quick moment to inhale as she passed him... Clean and crisp, yet woodsy with a touch of sweet. She filed it away inside her mind, convincing herself that the lingering was nothing more than research for a new soap fragrance. Maybe a whole line for men.

"Don't you own any bright red sweatshirts?" she asked, noticing his black pants and dark blue pull-over. "How about a nice neon yellow snow jacket?"

"What's wrong with this?" He pulled at the neck of his sweater.

"If you're not careful around here, you might be mistaken for any number of Anabaptist sects. Someone might hitch you up to a plow."

She was rewarded for her silly joke by one of Lucas's belly laughs.

"Would it bother you if I dressed more plain?" he asked. "I'm not in the church anymore."

"Not at all." She observed him, unabashed now. "You'd look…" *Handsome,* she wanted to say, picturing him wearing a traditional wide-brimmed hat. "Comfortable. Which you should be when you're at home, *jah*?"

The smile he shot her made a light bulb turn on in her chest.

And then there was that time Jacob gave me a bouquet of daisies, my favorite flower…

"What about you," Lucas said, rubbing his thumb and index finger over his chin. "You look… um…happy."

A grin tickled the corners of her lips. "I am! My ride over was chilly but exhilarating. We got going pretty fast, faster than the other day with you."

"I believe it." He patted Peanut. "Your cheeks are glowing and your eyes are like…"

"Like what?" she asked when he didn't finish.

"Sapphires." He dipped his head and kicked a rock. "Sparkling blue."

She felt her smile stretch wider at the compliment. And for some reason, she could not recall one Jacob memory.

Lucas twisted the reins in one hand, displaying long muscles along his forearm, which Esther would've had to have been blind not to notice. "Remember that oversized art book your brother checked out of the library?"

Esther thought for a moment. "The one about Greek mythology?"

"Exactly. There's a photo of an exotically beautiful woman riding bareback on a horse. It's stuck with me all these years."

"What did she look like?"

Lucas sent her a playful look that made her skin tingle, then gazed off to the side. "Big eyes, dark eyelashes, long legs. Her ears were tall and pointy and her nostrils flared too much—"

"Lucas!" Esther covered her giggling mouth. "You're describing the horse."

"Oops." He grinned. "Well, the woman in the painting was fair-skinned with blushing pink cheeks. The brightest blue eyes. Her hair was waist-long and tangled, blowing away from her face and flowing down her back." His gaze turned to her. "Her hair was red, I believe, but still, you make a pretty good resemblance."

It took a moment for his words to register. Lucas Brenneman thought she was exotically beautiful?

"*Danke,*" she said, suddenly feeling shy. Vanity was one of the seven deadly sins. Still, she couldn't help but bathe in his words for a nice long moment, her heart nearly beating out of her chest.

He's too much of an outsider, she told herself when the silence between them felt alive. *Has living in the modern world for so long turned him into a great big flirt?*

Out of nervous habit, she reached for the ties of her head covering, but they weren't there. Not until then did she realize—due to her high-speed chase against the wind—her prayer *kapp* had blown off and was probably crushed on the side of the road. Leaving her head and hair completely exposed.

Realizing the impropriety way too late, Esther froze in place, while basking in the heart-fluttery feeling of Lucas's gaze glued to her at her most vulnerable.

CHAPTER TWENTY

Lucas knew it wasn't gentlemanly behavior, but he couldn't keep his eyes off Esther. "I haven't seen your hair down since we were children," he observed, allowing his gaze to linger on those wild tresses—just like in that painting. "It's lighter now. Like wheat in the—"

Before he could finish, Esther spun around so her back was to him, sweeping up her hair. In a flash, it was tied into a bun.

"Lucas Brenneman, you shouldn't say things like that—it's not proper."

Of course not. But how could he ignore her hair? Even the most pious man in the Old Order would at least notice.

Out his kitchen window, then from his front porch, he'd watched as she'd galloped toward him like an angel sent to rescue him. It was going to take a lot of complicated recipes to get that image out of his head. More realistically, though, some mighty fervent prayer.

"It won't happen again," he said, then quickly added, "but I won't take it back."

What's the matter with you? This is Moses Miller's Esther. The love of Jacob's life. Not a little girl but a woman trying to find her way. She's confused but wants to please Gott. *Unlike many plain folk, she has interests outside their basic traditional way of life. She makes soap and appears to be quite successful at it.*

For a moment, he wondered if Jacob had known all of this about her and appreciated her talents. He couldn't help mentally giving his shoulder a friendly punch, feeling good that *he* appreciated them.

Still, it was dead wrong on every level to flirt with her, or to have these ridiculous thoughts, as fleeting as they were. He made a vow then and there to never forget who she really was: an Amish woman who'd been engaged to his brother.

When the mule kicked the side of the gate, Lucas snapped himself back to reality. After securing the gate and giving the animal some water, he walked toward the house.

From the way she jumped when she saw him, Esther appeared as if she'd been caught in deep thought as well. Though surely not in the same direction his had been.

"Coming in?" he said, holding open the front door.

"Yes!" she said with a breathy gasp.

"Make yourself at home, please."

After taking a few steps in, Esther stopped in place, her eyes moving over the room. He'd tidied up since she'd been there a few days ago. He'd even brought in daisies from the backyard and put them in a vase—the only thing in the room that didn't scream "bachelor pad." He'd also built a fire, which he assumed she approved of, since she wandered straight there and sighed contentedly.

Even this deep into the fall months, Lucas hadn't once turned on his electric heater. He preferred the fireplace, its crackles and sparks bringing back childhood memories.

"Temperature's dropping tonight," he said by way of explanation.

She exhaled what he hoped was a hum of approval. "Lucas?" She wrinkled her nose. "Is something burning?"

Quick as lightning, Lucas raced across the room and slid a pot off a hot burner, trying to keep his mutters under his breath.

"Conducting experiments?" Esther giggled, coming to his side.

"Heating applesauce," he explained, staring in defeat into the pot. *If* Top Chef *could see me now…* he thought, then caught himself wondering what rerun of that show would be on tonight. Didn't matter. His dish was long gone. No regrets.

Esther took the pan from him and gazed in at the black crispy substance. "Maybe less fire next time."

"I think I ruined the pan."

"It's salvageable." She walked the pan to the sink and filled it with water. "Let me teach you a trick." She placed it back onto the hot burner.

"It's already fried to a crisp."

"When this water comes to a boil, it'll be a cinch to scrub clean." As it began to bubble, she took a small scrub brush and easily scoured away the stuck-on remnants. "See?" She held it up. "Good as new."

"It's a miracle."

"Simple chemistry." She grinned, picking up a hand towel.

"Let me do that."

She rolled her eyes. "Please, I know how much

men loathe washing dishes."

"I have to because I live alone."

"True." She shot him a smile that went straight to his heart.

"Sorry again," he said, "about the other day when we were skating. I know you were only trying to help."

"I'm sorry, too. I didn't mean to interfere—I mean, I obviously *was* trying to interfere; I just shouldn't have been."

Lucas couldn't help chuckling. A big smile stretched across Esther's face, then she glanced at the kitchen table, her brow furrowing in confusion.

She'd noticed the two place settings he'd laid out and could probably smell meat roasting in the oven.

"Are you expecting someone?"

"You," he said. "I thought we'd enjoy a meal together this time."

"Oh." More confusion clouded her expression, and he was still a bit baffled by the decision himself.

It had been an impulse to cook for her. Though too early for suppertime, he hoped it would make her feel more comfortable than last time, especially after he'd nearly snapped her head off the other day.

Besides, he hadn't hosted anyone to a meal at his house yet. It was time he tried harder—one step at a time—to see how it would feel to be home to stay.

"Is that okay?" he asked, wondering if he'd overstepped his boundaries by about a hundred miles.

"It's okay." A timid smile brightened her face. "It smells delicious. May I?" She touched the handle to the oven.

"You might want to put on your anti-fire gear first."

"I think it's safe." She removed the lid of the ceramic Dutch oven. After the steam cleared, two thick-cut pork chops appeared, perfectly browned on both sides—his own spin on Paula Dean's pork chops with garlic and honey-glazed pears.

"These look wonderful!" she exclaimed.

Lucas felt his shoulders relax. "They should be done now, if you'd like to pull them out." He backed up so she'd have room on the counter.

"Do you have a platter?"

He quickly handed her his best one.

She helped herself to a knife on the counter and carved through one of the chops. As steam escaped, she bent her face down and took in a long inhale. "Perfect," she whispered. "Where did you get such fresh meat? I didn't notice any pigs out back."

"Duerksen's farm."

"The Mennonites in Blue Ball?"

He nodded, then waited, knowing she'd figure out his motive without him saying another word.

"Because you're worried about being seen in Honey Brook."

He nodded again. "Even though we've got the best farms in all of Pennsylvania—*they*," he corrected. "*They* have the best farms."

"Why did you do that?" She leaned a hip against the counter. "Why did you change 'we' to 'they'? You live here. This community is just as much yours as, well, your family's."

Lucas didn't want to get into that subject with Esther again. He was having a hard enough time processing what he and Sol had discussed the other night.

"Habit, I suppose," he finally said. "But I'm working on it. Why? Trying to get me to run myself out of town?"

"Not at all." Esther smiled. "I want to keep you around so I can taste more of your yummy cooking. Now, bring me a plate before everything gets cold."

"Yes, ma'am."

Esther piled on thick slices of the pork, added a pinch of salt, then reached for the skin-on mashed red potatoes keeping warm on the stove. "Did these come from Duerksen's, too?"

"How did you know?"

She poked a finger in for a sample taste. "Mmm. They must have something in the soil over there. All their potatoes, sweet potatoes, squash, and carrots come out so nice." She shot him a look. "Never tell Papa that."

Lucas laughed. "You have my word."

"What about these?" she asked, holding up a jar of canned pickles.

"Those are from a shop in town. The display is right across the aisle from a stand of soaps that smell like heaven."

Esther's cheeks flushed pink as she tossed her head back and laughed, exposing her long bare neck. Lucas swallowed hard, trying not to stare.

"And the bread?"

Taking a moment to clear his throat, he said, "I made it."

She lowered the knife. "You did not."

"I promise. And I'm dismayed at your doubt."

He took the knife from her and cut a thick slice from the loaf that still hadn't cooled all the way, then slathered on a generous layer of homemade honey butter. "Tell me what you think."

She crossed her arms, as if wondering if she should believe one word out of his mouth. After the first bite, she slowly chewed until there must've been nothing left to swallow.

"Well?"

She held up a hand to silence him. Then she took another bite, a bigger one. Before she'd finished chewing, she opened her mouth and tried to speak, but all that came out was a shower of crumbs. Her eyes went wide as she covered her mouth, blushing once more.

Lucas chuckled and rocked back on his heels. "What was that?" he asked, playfully cupping his ear.

"I said…it tastes like cake."

Lucas needed to remember where he'd found that recipe so he could make it again…maybe the next time she came over. If there would be a next time after what he planned to say to her tonight.

She licked her top lip. "It's moist and dense and sweet like dessert."

"So what you're saying is, you like it."

"Yes!"

A funny warmth pooled in his blood as he watched her devour the whole piece. The woman could eat. Lucas liked that about her.

He liked a lot of things about her.

"Shall we?" he asked, pulling out a chair for her to sit.

This was not the Amish custom, for two unmarried people of the opposite sex to have dinner together, not unless they'd just announced their engagement. Hours ago, as he'd been preparing the meal, Lucas hadn't considered what Esther might read into it.

"*Danke,*" she said as she slid into her chair. "Would you hand me a napkin?"

Another warming wave.

While they ate, Esther chatted about visiting one of her friends a few days earlier—how she was 99 percent sure this friend was in a secret relationship. "At our age, though, it's not like the ministers would say anything. They want us married off so badly, they allow almost any—"

With her mouth still hanging open from the last word, she cut herself off. "Well, not *anything.* Obviously." She pressed her napkin to her lips, and Lucas noticed another blush creep up her throat. Because she'd piled her long hair onto the top of her head, it was easy for his eyes to trace the sweeping color.

He wondered what she'd said—or almost said— to make her suddenly so embarrassed.

When the silence took on an awkward feel, he coughed gently and asked, "How is your family?"

"Anna—" She, too, coughed into the crook of her elbow. "Anna's trying to grow a garden. When she lived at home, she was the worst at it. I honestly think she'd rather be milking cows at four a.m. than anything."

"She's got a black thumb, eh?"

"Completely black." She laughed. "She couldn't

even grow basil, and that's simple as anything."

Lucas took a drink of water. "Does her husband have cows?"

"*Jah.* They live with his father—mother went to heaven when he was little, so he's always stayed close to home. His pa runs the small dairy farm on the other side of the creek."

Lucas wasn't sure where she was talking about, but he nodded just the same. "I've got all this land, and I'd love to have a working Amish farm again."

"You would?" She set down her fork. "But you work at the clinic."

He pushed his plate back and wiped his mouth. "I'd like to think I could do both."

This was something else Lucas hadn't spoken aloud to anyone. He loved research and practicing medicine and couldn't imagine giving up helping people in that way. But also, he was really starting to miss the old way of life…planting with his bare hands, growing, tending, and harvesting. Visiting friends and family, gathering together as Christ's believers every other Sunday.

There was no doubt that the simpler Amish way of life had suited him very well at one point in his life. But what exactly was he willing to give up now? His car? Electric lights at home? A career he loved?

Was there a way to have everything that was most important to him?

"Huh," she said.

"You sound surprised."

"I wouldn't think you'd want to live plain again if you didn't have to."

Lucas was about to tell her all the technologies

available to aid with farming these days, but he didn't think that was her point. After all, wouldn't it be a herculean task for any sane man to give up modern conveniences after living in comfort for ten years?

"I haven't forgotten everything from my past," he replied.

"Oh," she said, then seemed thoughtful for another few seconds. "Do you feel like you're trapped between worlds?"

The question caught him off guard and made him search for a true answer as he arranged his silverware over his plate. "I never thought of it in those terms, but I suppose I do."

"Me too. No one else seems to even understand what I'm talking about." Slowly, she lifted her eyes to his. "I guess we have that in common."

Lucas didn't know how to reply, but for about the fifth time that evening, his small cabin felt very small—barely enough room for two people to breathe.

Maybe thinking the same thing, Esther pushed back from the table and sprang to her feet. "I'll do the dishes," she said, and quickly gathered the plates and cutlery.

"You don't have to—"

"The fire needs stoking," she said as she moved toward the sink. "You add some wood while I wash up. Check on Peanut, please, too, would you?"

"Peanut?" he asked, standing.

"My jenny mule. I can hear the wind howling through the trees. She's probably scared to death to be away from home. Just give her some long strokes down her back and feed her this—make sure she eats the whole thing, but no sugar cubes." She handed him a carrot.

He couldn't help chuckling. "Anything else?"

She tossed a dish towel across her shoulder. "Do you know 'You Are My Sunshine'?"

"The song?"

She nodded. "She likes it best in Dutch, calms her right down." And with that, she turned back to her work.

"Um, okay?" A bit bemused, Lucas headed out to the barn. She was right, he could tell her mule— Peanut—was skittish. First, he fed her the carrot. "Good girl," he said. "But don't think I'm about to serenade you. You smell!" The mule looked at him, blinked her long lashes, and shook her head, white mane hitting him in the face.

"Fine," he grumbled, then glanced over his shoulder to make sure no one was watching. "You are my sunshine…" he began in Dutch, his voice unsure, as he hadn't sung a note in years. "My only sunshine." He patted her rump. "You make me happy when skies are gray." The mule whinnied and nodded. "You like that, little girl?"

Surprisingly unabashed, Lucas finished the song, all the verses he could remember—the Pennsylvania Dutch returning to his mind without even thinking. Then he grabbed some logs from under the tarp and headed inside. The kitchen was spotless, with a very pleasant fragrance coming from the stove.

"What are you making?" he asked as he placed a log over the flames.

"Just warming some chopped apples," Esther

said without turning around. "A dash of sugar and cinnamon." She'd taken a long dish towel and tied it around her waist like an extra apron, causing her dress to cinch in, displaying womanly curves.

"Forgive me," he mouthed, swallowing hard. *I didn't bring her here to play house or to overstep my boundaries.* He needed to stop this before it went any further.

"Esther," he said after a quick throat clear.

Wordlessly, she removed the saucepan from the stove, then turning to him, wiped her palms across the towel. He knew what he was going to say to her. He'd been thinking about it for days, reading, pondering, and even praying for the right words.

A lot of praying, actually, he inwardly admitted. He hoped the insights he was about to share would help her see things differently, help to clear her mind of confusion and so much worry.

At the same time, the things he'd studied for her had also touched him, though they had not helped to ease his mind over Esther—the friendship he felt for her. For he knew the more clarity he would bring her, the more space it would put between the two of them.

CHAPTER TWENTY-ONE

The air and pressure in the room suddenly felt different. A change had occurred—Esther had noticed it the second Lucas spoke her name in that serious tone. He looked serious, too. Furrowed brow, lines of tension cutting into his forehead. If she hadn't felt so comfortable and at home the last hour, she might've feared he was about to kick her out of his house.

She'd enjoyed their discussion so far—well, she always enjoyed talking to him. It was so easy. He didn't judge her or get preachy, even after admitting the petty resentment she felt toward Sarah or how she was determined to top her soap sales from last month, no matter what it took. He didn't once tell her she was in the wrong.

He'd just listened.

No matter what he'd said earlier, a part of her believed that maybe it was fate or holy providence that made her storm through those medical clinic doors that day nearly a month ago. The idea brought a strange peace to her heart.

He was rubbing the back of his neck and pacing around the kitchen. "Esther," he repeated, gesturing for her to sit on the sofa. "I've been thinking about you a lot lately."

"Really?" she said, unable to not be happy at his admission.

He held up a hand. "Sorry, let me clarify. Over

the past couple of weeks, you've shared with me some fairly deep concerns about the church, your place in it, and if God has a plan for you." He paused, rubbing his neck again. "And I think you know I'm working through some tough issues of my own, and I don't just mean about my family. I'm missing something." He pressed a hand over his heart. "But I don't know what it is."

"You have an amazing life," she couldn't help blurting. "You've seen the world. You have a college degree and a high-paying job you love." She stared toward the window. "You have a fancy automobile and a hundred channels to watch on your big screen TV." She paused to gesture over the mantel. "Oh, it's gone. Why?"

"I'd stopped watching it, so I got rid of it." He shrugged at the easy explanation. "My priorities have changed."

"Oh." She waved a hand. "Anyway, I can't fathom what you think you're lacking in your life."

When she finished, she noticed that Lucas was sitting as still as a sleeping cow, not even blinking. Then he began rubbing the palms of his hands together so fast, she feared they might start a fire.

"I'm sorry. I said something terribly wrong," she said, realizing her words had hurt her friend. "I suppose I'm missing your point."

"No," he said, looking up at her. She'd never seen his face so pale. "To you, it probably does seem like I have everything I could ever want. But electricity, cars, and material possessions can't fill this." He placed a hand over his heart. "I'm searching, too, and I'm maybe more confused than you about where I fit in the world."

Again, Esther didn't understand. He'd left home on purpose to help Jacob; then he continued to live in the outside world to work with sick people. He left the church. Was he saying he now had regrets about that?

"My quest started out as getting answers to help calm your heart," he said. "Because you asked me to. But I've been feeling things lately, and it's pretty unexpected. I've been neglecting patients and other responsibilities because you're on my mind." He began pacing around the room again. "I'm praying a lot more lately."

"I hope it's helping."

"I'm still not very good at it, but like I said, I'm feeling things I can't explain away through science."

Esther couldn't help smiling. "I think that's what we call faith."

He exhaled a quiet laugh through his nose. "Maybe. But we're not here to talk about me." He stopped pacing and looked at her. "I know you have doubts—big ones, scary ones. I have to believe it's natural for even the most faithful people to feel that way sometimes."

"Isn't that wrong? Shouldn't my faith be pure and strong no matter what?" She felt herself choking up. "I feel guilty about my doubts and bad thoughts. Surely that's *Gott*'s punishment."

Lucas opened his mouth but then closed it again. He closed his eyes, as well, and Esther wondered if he was saying a prayer. A moment later, he looked at her.

"Can you do something for me?"

Without thinking, she nodded.

"For the next little while, I'd like you to forget about all that. Tell yourself that your feelings aren't wrong, that they're not wicked or sinful, that you're just working through something and soon everything will be okay. Can you do that?"

Tears began creeping up her throat, causing her chest to rattle. *"Jah."*

Lucas walked to a bookshelf and slid out a thick binder. For a moment, he stared down at it, then held it close to his chest, as if it were a cherished possession. As he began walking toward her, she immediately recognized it as the scrapbook the community had made for him when he'd had an accident while working with a young bull.

Making scrapbooks had become a tradition in their congregation for the last few generations. When someone got hurt or went through a tragedy, friends and neighbors gathered to make the person a personalized keepsake filled with uplifting scripture passages, hymns of encouragement, and even *Englishers'* poems and verses that were spiritual in nature.

Esther had one of her own, but it was hidden beneath her bed. She hadn't pulled it out since the day they'd buried Jacob.

Carefully, Lucas sat beside her on the couch, displaying the front cover. It was white with a hand-painted red rose. Thick, loopy gold script read: *Lucas Brenneman, son of Ephraim, grandson of Lucas Aaron and Emma Marie. To bring joy to your healing.*

"Do you know what this is?"

She nodded.

He turned to a page in the middle. With a tightening of her throat, Esther recognized her twelve-year-old handwriting.

"Do you remember this?" She nodded again. Along with a passage from St. Matthew, she'd included her favorite quote from Wordsworth:

We have within ourselves enough to fill the present day with joy, and overspread the future years with hope.

Seeing her simple penmanship and remembering how those words had touched her as a girl, tears sprang to her eyes.

"I had such faith back then," she said. "Where did it go?"

"Do you think it's gone?"

"Sometimes." She ran a finger over the page. "Then I see this and I can't help...remembering."

"I remember, too." His voice was low, contemplative. "Powerful, isn't it? The memories we carry with us."

She nodded as she sniffed back a tear.

Lucas turned the page. Colorful scraps of paper were glued to the white sheets, each with handwritten messages by one of their dear neighbors.

Love all, trust a few, do wrong to none. —William Shakespeare

These things I have spoken unto you. That in me ye might have peace. In the world ye shall have tribulation: but be of good cheer; I have overcome the world. —John 16:33

I believe that the sun has risen: not only because I see it, but because by it I see everything else. —C. S. Lewis

Together, they turned page after page, taking turns to read aloud each scripture, quote, and passage.

"The Lord is my Shepherd…" Esther began, the words of the psalmist flowing freely from her lips.

"Fear thou not," Lucas read, "for I am with thee: be not dismayed; for I am thy God: I will strengthen thee; yea, I will help thee; yea, I will uphold thee with the right hand of my righteousness…" The prophet Isaiah's words seemed to fill the room, while also refilling Esther's soul with something she hadn't felt in a long time.

"This might sound a little backward," Lucas said, "but I think it's completely natural to doubt. After all, that's why we have faith. It's what religion is based on. We can't *know* scientifically that the world was created in six days. We can't *know* Moses parted the Red Sea or that Christ sat on a hill and taught us to turn the other cheek. But we can have faith it's true. That's our job, to believe and live as if it's true. That's what faith is."

His words made so much sense, it was scary. And they touched her heart more deeply than any Sunday sermon she'd heard since Jacob died.

Lucas Brenneman—runaway Amishman—knew what he was talking about.

She believed what he was saying, which was just about the strangest thing ever. *Gott* knew her heart, was aware of her struggles, and He loved her anyway—maybe He loved her more because of them. Had she forgotten?

Then she couldn't help but wonder… How could Lucas stay away from the church if he, too, had so much faith?

She was about to ask him when he cut into her thoughts. "Read the next one."

Esther swallowed, then cleared her throat. "If any of you lack wisdom, let him ask of God, that giveth to all men liberally, and upbraideth not, and it shall be given him." She paused after finishing the verse from the epistle of James.

"What do you think about that one?"

She thought for a moment. "*Gott* wants us to go to Him with our questions."

He nodded for her to continue. "And...?"

"And He knows everything and won't hold back His love." She paused again. "If we ask, He'll answer."

Lucas touched his pointer finger to his mouth. "Exactly. Do you know the next verse?"

Esther bit her lip, the words not coming to her remembrance.

"But..." Lucas began, not consulting the scrapbook or the Bible, "let him ask in faith, nothing wavering."

Esther felt warmth spread through her chest. "I did that."

"How did it make you feel?"

She took a moment to really consider the question.

Had she asked unwaveringly? Had she prayed with an open mind? Or had she allowed other things to block her faith? Like sadness, rejection, and all those awkward times when she had to go alone to a dinner party, or the singings, or a dozen other activities. She'd watched friends, even younger friends, get married and start families. Now her own sister. Was that why she felt left behind? Because they had new lives and she'd missed hers?

"How did you know I needed to see this?" She touched the scrapbook. "How did you know what I needed to hear?"

"This was made for me." Lucas patted the scrapbook that lay across both their laps. "Who said any of it was what *you* needed to hear?" He turned to the next page, where someone had slipped in one of Elizabeth Browning's poems. Though the lyrical words were correctly interpreted as *Gott*'s pure love for His children, Esther knew *Englishers* read the lines as romantic love between a man and a woman.

"'How do I love thee?'" Lucas began, reciting the poem by heart. "'Let me count the ways. I love thee to the depth and breadth and height my soul can reach, when feeling out of sight, for the ends of being and ideal grace.'"

"Why do you have that one memorized?"

Lucas exhaled softly. "*Maam* taught it to me when I was a boy. It might've stuck more than most others. Here." He passed her a clean white hanky.

"*Danke*," she said, patting all the damp places of her face. "I haven't felt this much peace in… You did all this for me. I don't understand."

He scooted closer. "Your friendship has become very important to me. I forgot what it's like to be around good people, unselfish souls who try hard and who desire to live a righteous life. I'm talking about you, you know," he said, giving her a playful nudge. "You're the good person on the righteous path."

"But what happens if I want something that's not on the righteous path?"

Lucas smiled. "You're a smart woman; I don't have a single doubt you'll figure it out."

Another weight lifted off her shoulders, and she wanted to hug him out of pure gratefulness—platonically, as he'd put it once. The memory made her smile.

It was mind-boggling, the many ways her heart had been touched tonight. She still didn't have all the answers, but she was closer, and she was not going to give up. If she couldn't give Lucas a hug of gratitude, how was she supposed to thank him properly?

"Is there anything I can do for you?" she asked. "You've given me a wonderful gift."

He shrugged nonchalantly. "Just keeping my promise."

"It's more than that, and you know it."

When she didn't go on, he nodded silently. "Can I just say you're welcome and be done with it?"

"Sorry." She shook her head, wiping away a final tear. "That's in no way good enough. I'm going to give you something someday. Something you didn't know you wanted or needed, and I'll be the only one who can give it to you."

"What is it?"

"I don't know yet, but whatever it is, and when-ever you need it, you know you can come to me." Esther realized it was an empty vow full of frivolous words, but she meant them anyhow.

"Okay," he said, wiping his palms over his knees. "I can't think of anything you can give me right now—or I mean, I can, but, well, I won't…" After a sigh, he ran his hands over his face.

To Esther, it wasn't completely clear what he meant, though her heart began to race when she considered the possibilities.

"Anyway," he added as he quickly stood up, "do you want tea?"

"Please," she replied. "Need help?"

"You're my guest. I promise I do know how to boil water."

She laughed, feeling fully at home in her own body. "If you say so."

"Does your father still have a booth at the Lancaster farmer's market?" he asked.

They chatted about vegetables and their rising prices as he made the tea. Meanwhile, Esther continued flipping through the scrapbook. Lucas Brenneman had definitely been one of the community's favorites, popular with the boys and the girls. Adults loved him, too. It was clear judging by the number of pages in his book. One page was devoted to pressed flowers that had long since lost their bright colors and fragrances.

No doubt, those had been added by an eager Amish girl who'd been dreaming of making Lucas her beau. He'd been a hard worker back then—had he even realized most of the girls in Honey Brook had a crush on him?

Herself included—before Jacob had started asking to drive her home after the singings.

Esther couldn't imagine how difficult it must have been for a sixteen-year-old to leave a place where he'd been so loved and respected.

Jacob had also contributed to the scrapbook. But he'd written a knock-knock joke that he'd probably heard from an English acquaintance, because Esther could not figure out the punch line. It was heart-warming, though, seeing his neat print in his brother's book.

"Whoops," Lucas said. She stood, expecting to find a puddle of hot water on the kitchen floor. Instead, he was looking out the window. "It's almost dark."

"It is?" Esther moved to the door and opened it wide. The sky was streaked in pink, orange, and yellow, but the colors were fading fast, the sun only moments from setting. "What time is it?"

"Past six thirty."

Whoops was right. She needed to get home before her father sent out the brethren to track her down. How would she explain being discovered here?

"I have to go," she said. "I hate to, but—"

"Me too. I'll get Peanut," he added, walking past her and out the open door. She missed the smell of him. So clean and manly.

"Thank you."

A moment later, he was back. "Look, it's going to be completely dark before you get home. Can I take you?"

"In your truck?" she asked. For a moment, she contemplated the excitement of flying down the road as fast as the gusting wind. "Not a good idea," she said. "My folks will wonder where the buggy is in the morning, and Peanut can't stay here all night. You'd lose your voice singing her lullabies."

He laughed and bobbed his head, a dark curl of hair falling across his forehead. "Looks like I'll be driving you in the buggy, then." Without another word, he jogged off toward the barn.

Not bothering to argue, she put on her cloak and gloves, saying a silent though very sincere prayer for such a wonderful evening, and for *Gott* really and truly being there for her, even when she was too stubborn to feel Him. When she heard a sound from the barn, she continued her prayer with how grateful she was for the time she'd spent with Lucas.

"Bless him, Lord," she whispered under her breath. "He's searching, too. Give him all he stands in need of...when he asks in faith, nothing wavering."

"Ready?" he asked, leading Peanut gently by the reins.

"Ready!" She climbed into the buggy. "But, Lucas, if you take me all the way, how will you get home?"

"I'll call a buddy of mine," he said, tapping the pocket of his pants where there must've been a cell phone. She wanted to pull it out of his pocket and examine it, press the numbers and speak to someone on the other side of the world.

Even though her own father kept a phone in his office in the barn, Esther understood that modern technology should not be part of her world. Even if Lucas having one gave her a silly thrill.

He climbed in beside her, and she threw the wool blanket over both their laps. "Best get a move on," he said, then clicked his tongue, encouraging Peanut to walk.

The evening air was even chillier than before, and the wind was really picking up. Still, Esther couldn't keep the huge grin off her face. She felt close to him, like she could ask him absolutely anything.

"Lucas," she began after they'd been chatting for a while about how to grow the perfect tomato plant. But before she could ask the question, a black car came out of nowhere, speeding by them so fast that it caused Peanut to veer off the path. Esther screamed in fear and grabbed Lucas's arm. Half a moment later, she watched in terror as the buggy hit a bump and began sliding into the shoulder.

CHAPTER TWENTY-TWO

Lucas feared he was much too out of practice to save the buggy from completely breaking apart. But then every driving lesson his father had given him as a boy flashed through his mind, pushing his body into autopilot.

The most important thing was to remain calm. The second was to make sure—if it overturned—that it would fall over on *his* side, not Esther's.

Maybe due to the recent rain, Lucas felt the moment the right-hand wheel hit a deep, soft spot of dirt. Next he heard a loud crack. Esther shrieked and leaned into him, clutching his arm.

"Keep ahold of me," he shouted, feeling her grip tighten.

As if in slow motion, the left side of the buggy began to tip up. After another loud snap of wood, despite all his efforts, everything began sliding to the right. The sound of bending iron coupled with Esther's screams was deafening as the buggy rotated.

When all was finally silent, Lucas opened his eyes. He was facedown, staring directly at a pair of closed eyelids, while he lay flat over Esther's body.

"Hey," he said, trying to roll off, but he was wedged in there pretty darn tight. "Are you okay? Esther, can you hear me?"

When she didn't answer, he sprang into action, fearing the worst. Had she hit her head or had a dangerous internal injury? It hadn't been a hard landing, but after working in trauma for two rotations, he knew anything was possible.

Before he'd had time to even get to his feet, he heard a soft laugh. The sound slowed his panicking heart.

"What's so funny?" he asked, lifting himself onto his elbows so he could look at her.

While she continued to giggle—tears in her eyes now—he rolled onto his knees and got to his feet. After a quick assessment, he noted that her body wasn't at any awkward angles; therefore, nothing major was broken.

"What's so funny?" he repeated, wanting to join in her laughter out of pure relief.

"Everything," she said. "That was so much fun."

"You were screaming bloody murder."

"While having fun."

Lucas planted his hands on his hips. "Esther, you think nearly dying in a buggy crash is fun?" He reached out for her hand, their fingers clasping as he pulled her out the door of the tipped buggy. Not dropping her hand, he gave her another once-over, making sure she wasn't bleeding or in any kind of distress.

"Peanut!" She gasped. Lucas regretted letting go of her hand but immediately tended to the mule, feeling heavy raindrops on his back. He'd never had a particularly special way with animals, but for some reason, he felt a connection to this funny white mule with the black face markings who loved to be serenaded.

"Is she okay?" Esther called, her voice coming

from inside the buggy. She was smart enough to stay out of the rain.

Lucas stroked Peanut down the back a few times, then examined her legs. "Shaken but not hurt," he reported.

"Peanut!" She called out in a singsong voice. "Don't fret! You love the rain, remember, good girl?"

Lucas chuckled from his belly. This woman's love for mules and goats and aardvarks and probably any animal knew no bounds.

"Lucas! It's starting to pour. You better get back inside here."

He took only a brief pause, assessing his own injuries—nothing more than mild abrasions on both palms—before returning to the shelter of the buggy. Esther was inside with the blanket, her face pink and glowing.

"Now what do we do? Papa's gonna kill me."

Lucas wiped his brow. "I'll call my buddy Mike. He's got a truck and horse trailer." He made a quick call, relieved that his friend was available.

"Despite this"—Esther gestured at the wreckage around them—"I've had such a nice evening—seriously." Her voice was firm, and she began chewing on a thumbnail. "For the last few months, I've been really down, as if no one in the world comprehended how I felt. Earlier tonight, you said my friendship means a lot to you." She paused, sliding her hands into her apron pockets. "It's the other way around. Having you in my life has changed everything. Do you know that?"

Before he could even think of a reply to such touching words, headlights cut through the twilight.

"Mike's here," he said, part of him relieved for the interruption. "Stay put, and I'll help him with Peanut." Before leaving, he pulled the blanket up to wrap around her shoulders. She looked small and helpless, maybe a little vulnerable from what she'd just admitted.

Luckily, Lucas had to concentrate on settling down the anxious mule while he and Mike assessed the damage to the buggy. "Esther?" he said a good twenty minutes later, crouching so he could look into the buggy. "It stopped raining, and we need to right the buggy. Come out?"

Her dress got snagged twice, and he saw more of her legs than she probably realized, causing the blood pumping through his veins to feel red-hot. After not much of a struggle, she was standing on the road again, wrapping the blanket tighter around her body.

"Still feeling okay?" he couldn't help asking, the medic in him always on alert.

"Fit as a fiddle." She twirled in a circle. "Quit your worrying about me."

"Nice try."

"Stop it." Playfully, she swatted the air.

Even during a near-tragedy, she could still make him laugh.

"Why don't you talk to Peanut while we work on the buggy?"

After a nod and an expression of concern, Lucas could easily make out her whispers of calm, assuring words to her mule. He wished he could hang around to listen to the whole thing, but the buggy needed tending to. It took him and Mike a few tries, but finally the thing was standing upright again.

"Wheel's busted," Mike said.

"Affirmative," Lucas agreed, wiping his brow. "I heard it snap when we hit the hole back there. Besides that, doesn't look like there's much damage—"

"It's my buggy," Esther suddenly interjected. "No one else will notice a few scratches."

"Broken wheel's more than a scratch," Mike added. Lucas noticed how his buddy seemed to be keeping his eyes averted from Esther. Was he not used to his plain folk neighbors yet? As he was about to officially break the ice, Esther stepped forward.

"Hi," she said. "My name is Esther Miller. Thank you so much for coming."

"Mike Ramirez." He stuck out his hand but then flinched it back, maybe unsure of the correct protocol.

Lucas wanted to laugh.

"It's very nice to meet you." Esther smiled and shook his hand, looking as confident as ever. "The speeding car came too near us; then it all happened so fast."

"Scary." Mike crossed his arms and nodded, looking truly concerned. "And it's no problem. Anything for Doctor B."

"I'm not your doctor, man. I've told you a hundred times."

Mike turned to Esther while pointing at Lucas. "Guy's a medical marvel in my eyes but won't let me call him 'doctor.'"

"Because I'm a physician's assistant, and you

had a snakebite, man." Lucas rolled his eyes to heaven. "Even children know how to draw out the venom."

"Not this city slicker. The wife and I bought a place out here last year. We're still figuring out country life."

"Some brains just take longer," Lucas said, patting his buddy on the back.

"Watch it," Mike said, "or I'll tell the story of how you got lost for three days by following the Susquehanna River. I mean, who gets lost *following* a river?"

"It was dark," Lucas said, looking up at the sky. "And I misplaced my compass."

"Misplaced? You dropped your phone down a ravine."

"No, I didn't." Lucas paused, wondering if he had any pride left. "That was on a different hike."

Esther suddenly burst out laughing.

"Something to share?" Lucas asked. It was about time the woman interrupted.

"You two fight like brothers," she said, wiping the tips of her lashes. A second later, she peered at Lucas as if something was on the tip of her tongue. He was no mind reader, but he had a sneaking suspicion she was about to bring up his family again.

Instead, however, she began chewing on a thumbnail and asked, "I was just thinking—can you fix the wheel?"

"Of course." Lucas felt his eyebrows smash together, mock indignantly. "Why? What's going through that head of yours?"

"I can ride on Peanut the rest of the way home

while you and Mike fix it."

"Ha-ha. That's your plan?"

She nodded. "And when you're done, you'll sneak the buggy back to my house like nothing happened. But it better be there before six a.m.—that's when Papa and Benji get up."

Lucas opened his mouth to laugh at the suggestion but then stopped himself. She wasn't joking. "I do think I can manage that." He looked at Mike. "You?"

Mike gestured at his truck. "My girl's got a hemi."

"What girl?" Esther asked.

"I know!" Lucas cut in, holding up a finger. "Because cars are referred to by the feminine pronoun."

Mike's eyebrows pulled together, but then he nodded. "You are correct, sir."

"*Englishers* are confusing," Esther said after shaking her head. "In any case, I better get going."

Lucas moved to her side, reaching for the loose reins. "You're not really going through with this, are you? There's no saddle."

Esther ran a hand along Peanut's thick spine. "I've been riding her bareback since I was little. Peanut's never hurt me. She's gentle as a baby."

Lucas was not convinced. "I think we should drive you home in the truck—"

After cutting him off with a loud huff, Esther grabbed the reins, placed a palm on the middle of Peanut's back, made one practice bounce, then flipped a leg over the mule's body, landing right on top.

All Lucas could do was stare. Then he rewound

the scene to watch it about a million more times, picturing her beauty and grace while literally stealing his breath away.

"Good girl," Esther cooed, bending forward to pat her mount's neck and stroke her silky ears. "Good girl, Peanut. Who's the best girl?"

A moment later, she glanced down, no doubt witnessing both men gaping up at her, jaws hanging slack like two hound dogs.

"Good luck with the wheel," she said, wearing a wide, confident grin. "And don't forget: six o'clock."

"Uhh, right," Lucas said. "B-bye."

"Have a good night, now."

"Yeah… Hey—*wait*!" Lucas forced himself awake, leaping to block her way. "That was really something."

She lifted a shoulder. *"Jah?"*

After exhaling a chuckle out his nose, he asked, "When will I see you again?"

"Honestly, I don't know. I'm running out of excuses—even to myself. I feel like we're sneaking around."

"I know." Lucas bowed his head and nodded, comprehending the sentiment. The back of his neck felt wet from the rain, cold from the wind, overall chills. "I'd say I'm sorry, but I'm not."

"Well, who knows, maybe we'll run into each other on the street sometime." She smiled down at him, making Lucas exhale another chuckle. "Stranger things have happened."

"Be safe, please."

"Peanut's got me." She gave the animal one of her loving pats. "Don't worry even one second about me."

He kicked a rock. "Too late."

"I'm going now," she said, using her warning tone.

"I'll believe it when I see it."

With one click of the tongue, she trotted off into the night, bareback and all.

Lucas did worry, though. There weren't many streetlights and the moon was mostly covered by rain clouds. What if that black car was still out there? Would she be okay? Should he follow behind on foot?

"Dude, you've got it bad."

"Huh?" Lucas turned to Mike, having almost forgotten he was there. "What do you mean?"

"Look, I know nothing, and I mean *nothing*. But I do know what it looks like when a guy is hung up on a girl. I'm a high school counselor, remember?"

"Thought you said you know *nothing*."

Mike laughed. "Have you asked her out?"

"Not possible."

And there were a million reasons why. The most important being Jacob.

"Because she's Amish?" Mike glanced over his shoulder to where Esther had disappeared. "She's Amish, right? And you used to be."

Lucas looked at him. "How did you…?"

"That fateful day of the snakebite." Mike held up his arm, pointing at his elbow. "You talked about it, probably to keep me calm, assuming I wasn't listening. You talked about it pretty fondly, man."

"All of that was a lifetime ago."

"But you came back here to live on purpose,

where you *were* Amish." Mike crossed his arms. "What's stopping you from being Amish again? Is it that hard to return to the flock or fold or whatever?"

Lucas couldn't help chuckling, not offended in the least. "It's not impossible. There's a reconciliation process with the church—I hear it's pretty strict."

"You backing down from a challenge?"

He was about to mention his father, and how there was no way the brethren would allow him to return to full fellowship if he refused to even speak to him. But that was too personal to talk about. Although he had discussed it somewhat with Esther.

"There are certain things I'd have to give up," he said as he walked toward the buggy, knowing they had a lot of work to do.

"Didn't you say you cut your cable last week? And you've never given the impression that you care a hoot about fashion."

"This is cashmere," Lucas said, pulling at his sweater. Then he felt instant shame for not only the comment but for having bought the materialistic piece of clothing in the first place. He'd had it for years, but was that any excuse?

Then again, it wasn't as if he *was* Amish. So why the guilt?

"It's more complicated than just doing without lights or a car," he added, perhaps for his own benefit. "I mean practicing medicine."

"Oh." Mike was silent for a moment, then nodded. "That would be a huge sacrifice for you."

"Not to sound too out-there, but I feel like it's

why I was put on the earth, not just to heal people but to educate about disease prevention and general health and nutrition."

"You couldn't do that if you were Amish again?"

Lucas sighed. The topic was giving him a headache, and he began rubbing hard at his temples, trying to jog free some kind of answer his buddy would understand. But he couldn't come up with anything to appease even himself.

"Sorry, Lucas," Mike said after a long stretch of silence. "I'm making light of something that's obviously important to you. We can drop the subject."

"*Danke,*" Lucas said.

"Hey, that's Amish talk." Mike pointed at Lucas, grinning. "I'm just sayin'."

"Okay, okay, so it's still inside me and maybe coming out more often the longer I live here, but…"

"But?" Mike prompted as they carefully dragged the buggy to the front of his truck to utilize the headlights.

Lucas recalled what Esther had said about being trapped between two worlds. He'd never felt that more literally than right now: Googling how to fuse iron to repair a horse-drawn buggy.

"But I'm not ready to completely change my life…and no," he added to cut off Mike, "not even for a girl."

CHAPTER TWENTY-THREE

Except for one corner, the house was dark. Maybe her parents had left a lamp on. After giving Peanut an extra dozen loving strokes and two carrots from the side garden, Esther trod lightly across the living room floor, ready to say another prayer of thanks before having the most comforting night of dreams.

"Esther?"

"Oh!" She whipped around, cupping her mouth to muffle the cry. "I thought everyone was in bed."

"I wanted to finish scrubbing these," *Maam* said, pointing to the pile of potatoes on the table, a small gas lamp illuminated at her side. "Wedding season's around the corner—Sarah's is first. We're feeding practically everyone in town twice."

"Let me help!" Esther screeched out of nervousness but also guilt for not helping with the meal preparations. She and Sarah had decided on the food for the two wedding day meals, but after that, Esther hadn't given it another thought.

Too wrapped up in my head, worrying only about my problems. Spending my free time making soaps or meeting Lucas.

Quickly, she grabbed a potato and began scrubbing at it with a brush. "How's the concert planning going?" she asked.

"Shouldn't you know better than I would?"

"Why?"

Maam lowered the potato in her hand. "You

were with Louisa. She's head of the committee."

Esther's heart jolted to a stop, knowing her face was about to turn beet red. "Oh. Yes," she said, grateful for the dimness of the room. "Yes." Even through the single syllable, she heard her voice tremble.

Little white lie…

Before she'd left home, she thought she'd implied to *Maam* she was delivering soap to Leah, but that must've been what she'd told *Daed*. Before now, Esther had never told a real lie, and she was obviously no good at it.

Maam went back to her scrubbing. "You had a pleasant evening?"

"Yes," Esther said, scrubbing harder, keeping her gaze lowered. "Very."

"Darling, where's your prayer *kapp*?"

Esther froze, remembering far too late that her hair was still a bit damp, as was her dress. "It blew off in the wind and I didn't notice. I got Peanut galloping pretty fast."

"Do you have a spare?"

"I can wear my thinner one from spring until I make a new one."

"One of these afternoons, why don't you take your little brothers and sister into town for some material?"

"Okay," Esther said, feeling a bit more relaxed— though that managed to add to the guilt.

"It's very late, and it looks as though you've had an adventure." *Maam* touched a loose strand of her hair. "Go on to bed. You can help me in the morning."

Esther should've protested and stayed longer, but she knew full well that her mother was a master at seeing straight to the truth. Esther couldn't risk her discovering that she'd been spending all this time with Lucas, feeling things she couldn't even admit to herself. Moreover, if *Maam* knew Lucas was back in town, she would surely tell his family. And that was not Esther's secret to divulge.

"Night, *Maam*," she said, heading to the stairs.

"Oh, Es?" her mother called in a soft whisper. "I heard Kings Mercantile got a new shipment of fabric. Why not shop there?"

You mean the store in town right next to the medical clinic? Only if you insist…

"What's going on?" Sarah was rubbing her eyes as she stood on the landing.

"Did we wake you?" *Maam* asked.

Her sister yawned, passing Esther on the stairs. "Couldn't sleep. Can I have some cocoa?"

Maam began humming and wiped her hands on a dish towel. "How about I make some for all of us?" She looked up the stairs at Esther.

She felt mighty sleepy after the excitement of the buggy crash and meeting Mike and riding home on Peanut. So much had happened that evening, she'd need a really long night's rest to take it all in.

But then she looked at her sister, staring up at her from a stool pulled up to the kitchen counter, her white nightgown flowing past her bare feet. How many more cozy evenings would they have like this before Sarah was married?

"I'll heat the milk," Esther said, undoing the tight bun so her heavy hair could fall loose, then suddenly remembering how Lucas had seen her without her head covering. At the memory, she felt the sensation of blood rushing up the back of her neck until she shivered girlishly.

"Are you okay? You look flushed." Sarah leaned away from her. "I hope you don't have anything contagious that I'll catch."

"It's warm in here," Esther said as she pulled the milk jug from the gas-powered refrigerator. "I've just come in from outside. Weather's really turning."

"You just got home?" Sarah was playing with the ruffles on the end of her nightgown sleeve. "What time is it?"

As if on cue, the clock above the mantel chimed ten times. Esther's throat went dry, not sure if she needed to reply now. What if Sarah inquired where she'd been tonight and what she'd done? *Maam* could've asked the same questions but hadn't.

Why not?

"Your sister and Amos met with the bishop today." *Maam* pulled out a saucepan for the milk.

"Oh? How did it go?" Esther asked, relieved at the smooth change of subject.

"It was fine. I have to admit, I was kind of dreading these last few counsels with him. I knew we'd be talking about…" Sarah paused to shoot a glance up the stairs. "Embarrassing things."

Esther thought back, not recalling any of her premarriage counseling meetings as embarrassing. But then she remembered she and Jacob had only just begun their sessions when he'd passed away.

"Embarrassing things?" she asked. "Like what?"

When her sister didn't answer, she looked up to

find Sarah sharing a peculiar look with *Maam*.

"What?" Esther said, picking up a wooden spoon to stir the warming milk.

Maam shrugged one shoulder, and Sarah glanced up at the ceiling—both obviously averting their eyes from her.

"You know," Sarah finally began, "that part in Genesis."

Esther pushed out her bottom lip. "Noah's ark? The pharaoh's dream?"

"No." Sarah grabbed the wooden spoon and took over the stirring. "The part about how a man shall leave his father and shall, um, *cleave* unto his wife." Slowly she lifted her eyes to look at Esther. "And they shall be one flesh."

"Huh," Esther said at first, then, "oh! Oh, that part."

"Yes." Sarah exhaled and began stirring faster. "That part."

Heat flooded Esther's chest, neck, and face—she was probably blushing right up to the tip of her head. She averted her eyes, too, and it became so quiet she could've heard a hairpin drop.

From out of nowhere, she replayed the exact moment when Lucas had fallen on top of her during the buggy crash. She stared into space, remembering the weight of him, the smell and feel of his face at her bare neck. How she'd thought for one split second that she didn't want him to move away.

A moment later, *Maam* started snickering, sounding like little Evie. When Esther looked up, Sarah's lips were pressed together hard, but then she burst into giggles.

"Cleave," Esther couldn't help saying as she joined in on the laughter. "Such a descriptive word, isn't so?"

This set *Maam* to laughing even harder, her body shaking as she wiped her eyes with her long apron. "Oh, I'm glad we finally had this little talk, girls."

The three of them burst into another fit of giggles, holding on to one another so they wouldn't collapse.

"How did Amos take it?" Esther asked, needing to dab at her eyes now.

"He's always been sheltered," Sarah said. "And the bishop wasn't exactly blunt. I fear I'll have to explain everything." She lifted the wooden spoon, testing the temperature of the milk. "Remind me to bring a drawing pad to our next counseling session."

"Naughty talk!" *Maam* said, looking like she was trying to keep a straight face.

"It was surprising, though," Sarah added. "Bishop's so old and yet he knows…a *lot*."

It was no use. Once the giggling started up again, it would not cease until the last of them went to bed. Esther pulled down three mugs, keeping an arm around Sarah's waist as she poured in a scoop of chocolate powder, knowing she'd never forget this evening as long as she lived.

CHAPTER TWENTY-FOUR

Lucas couldn't stop from yawning as he walked. A soft pink glow along the horizon was the first sign of sunrise. Following Esther's orders, he'd made sure her buggy was back home before six.

It hadn't taken long for him and Mike to repair the broken wheel. In his youth when he'd had free access to the family's buggies, he'd busted more than a few wheels, axles, and frames.

As he cut through the corner of a field, he smiled when he remembered the time his older brother, Jeremiah, had snuck out their father's best open buggy for a moonlight joyride. Even though he'd left Lucas behind, Jeremiah had woken him up in the middle of the night to help him fix a dent in the door.

While they'd worked, Jeremiah had told Lucas about his midnight antics. They'd become best friends that night and, over the next few years, spent hours together, working side by side at the family mill.

It was useless not to admit how much he missed his family—so much some days, it made him sick.

Though he still couldn't allow himself to regret his reason for leaving. Until he did, they couldn't welcome him back.

"Luke?"

Stopping in his tracks, Lucas turned, shading his eyes as he stared into the bright morning sunshine.

A man holding a hoe stood near a tree ten yards away. For an eerie moment, Lucas wondered if he'd conjured a ghost.

"Luke," the man repeated, removing his hat.

Unsure if what he was seeing was real or if his memory was creating a vivid hallucination, Lucas didn't move as the vision came closer…growing larger, taller, broader shoulders than he'd remembered, thicker arms, hair with a hint of red, unlike the rest of the family.

His intense gaze, however, and that scar on his forehead, Lucas would know anywhere.

"Jerry?" he spoke around the lump in his throat.

The man stopped mere feet away. "Brother," he said, looking as bemused as Lucas felt.

Lucas was tongue-tied. He could admit to himself now that he'd returned to Honey Brook to be near where he'd grown up—the place he still thought of as home. But he'd never actually intended on seeing his family.

Twenty-eight-year-old Jeremiah had lines on his face, shooting out from the corners of his eyes. He looked healthy and strong but weathered from ten years of labor. Judging by the length of his beard, his brother had been married a while.

"Just passing through the area?" Jeremiah asked after a stretch of silence.

"I've been here nearly seven months."

"*Living* here?" His brother's bushy eyebrows shot up, almost touching his bangs.

"I'm a PA at the clinic. Physician's assistant. Live three miles north of town."

With his brows still raised, Jeremiah slowly

shook his head. "I heard something months ago, but when you never came by…"

"Besides my office, I try to stay far from… Well, no need for anyone to know."

"Why?"

Lucas laughed nervously. "I didn't come back to make trouble or cause conflict in the community. I know how things were when I left."

"When you left…" Jeremiah repeated, leaning on the hoe. "That was a long time ago."

"*Jah.*" Lucas nodded, aping his brother's strong Amish accent. "This your land?" He gestured at the rows of pepper plants and fruit trees.

"*Aye.* When Lizzy's father took ill, we moved in."

Lucas smiled. "You married Elizabeth Hooley. You were courting her last I remember."

Jeremiah smiled back. "Took me a while to talk her into it, but I finally wore her down."

"That's wonderful to hear, *wunderbar.*" Without thinking, Lucas extended a hand. "Congratulations." When his brother eyed the outstretched limb like it was a poisonous snake, he immediately dropped it, feeling a spiky knot in his stomach.

Another ten years passed until Jeremiah reached out to shake his hand. "*Danke, bruder,*" he said. "That means a lot."

"Lizzy Hooley." Lucas laughed again, rubbing his chin. "Did you know when we were in school together, she gave me a black eye?"

His brother crossed his arms. "Why'd she do that?"

"Well, she claimed it was an accident, throwing the atlas at me when I wasn't looking. But I'd been teasing her about her freckles right before, so..." He shrugged.

Jeremiah chuckled. "She's always had good aim. So what are you doing out this way? You said you live north of town."

The list of inappropriateness was a mile long when he considered explaining how he'd just returned Moses Miller's Esther's buggy because they'd crashed it into the shoulder after he'd cooked her dinner at his house.

"You were at the Millers'?"

Mid-inhale, Lucas's breath stalled in his chest.

"I saw you come from that way." After wiping his forehead with a handkerchief, Jeremiah put his hat back on. "A mite early to be visiting folks."

Lucas felt some relief that his brother hadn't mentioned seeing him towing a buggy like a draft horse.

"Not visiting," he said, trying to stay close to the truth. "Just dropping something off—not a big deal. So...you're a farmer now. I don't recall that being your life's ambition."

Jeremiah kicked a clot of dirt. "I was always good at it. *Daed* had me in his gardens since before I could walk. Lizzy grew up on a vegetable farm and knows everything about planting and harvesting. It's hard work but—"

"Better hours than a dairy farmer," the brothers said in unison.

Reciting the old joke felt as familiar as the smell of their mother's homemade pumpkin bread. Lucas pursed his lips and looked at his brother, trying to fight back what he wanted to say to his one-time best friend.

Judging by the expression in Jeremiah's eyes, was he thinking that same thing?

"Seems I interrupted your work," Lucas said, sliding his hands into his back pockets.

"Gotta take care of these two rows today before the weather turns nasty. Lizzy's been after me." A little smile crooked his mouth. "Harvesting for grain is usually her job—she likes it. But old Eliza Fisher put her on bed rest until the *bobbeil* comes end of November."

"Baby?"

The wider Jeremiah grinned, the prouder the twinkle in his eyes. "Number four."

"You have three *kinnahs*, one on the way?" Bewildered, Lucas wondered where the time had gone.

"All boys. Lizzy swears up and down this one's a girl." He paused to stroke his beard. "Imagine me with a girl."

"I can," Lucas said. He wished he could ask to see them. He wished his brother would give him permission to look in on them from a distance. They'd never know who he was or that he'd even been there.

But that wasn't meant to be. He hated the wishes had even entered his head.

"Looks like you're on your own right now," he continued. "Would you like a hand?"

"You're not at your clinic today?"

"Not until later."

His brother's eyes narrowed. "Still know how to work a plow?"

"I reckon I remember enough."

"Well then, let's set it up." To his surprise, his brother stuck out his hand for Lucas to shake on the deal.

"Lead the way, *bruder*." The lump in his throat returned, so grateful for Jeremiah's kindness. For his brother had every right to ignore his very existence if he'd seen fit.

Instead, Jeremiah put a hand on his shoulder, and together they walked across the field toward the barn. "You're dressed mighty plain," he observed, eyeing Lucas's outfit. He hadn't changed his clothes from the night before, when he'd been with Esther.

"Never completely stopped, I suppose," Lucas explained. "It's easier to blend in around here. More comfortable, too."

"*Aye.* Got a phone?" He eyed the square shape in his pocket. Lucas tapped it as acknowledgment, and Jerry smiled conspiratorially. "Me too."

"Yeah?"

"Inside the barn. And a MacBook."

"You're kidding."

"Pretty hard to do business with the English without one. Our produce travels over a hundred miles, peaches all the way to Texas. That would be impossible without the magic of the World Wide Web."

"I'm learning just how much things have changed around here."

His brother shot him a quick glance. "A lot *has* changed, Luke. Progress might feel like it takes a millennium out here in the middle of nowhere, but it does happen."

Lucas had learned that the hard way at that first Q&A he'd done at the hospital. Seemed he'd been the one who was behind the times. Over the past few weeks, he'd been "catching up"...which actually meant he'd been simplifying his life, using his free time in more contemplative ways instead of watching TV, playing on his phone, and fussing over his car. He took in a deep breath, smelling good, turned earth.

There was no doubt that his life was changing. Lucas could only wonder how far that change would take him.

As they neared the barn, he noticed a woman open the gate and step into the field. "Jerry! Come get breakfast!"

"Okay, uh, in a minute!"

"Bacon's hot now. Bring your friend." She was holding her round belly as she took a few steps toward them. "Who's that with you?"

Lucas felt his heart beat like a drum inside his chest—once again, torn between two worlds.

"I should go," he said in a low, rushed voice. "I'll go. It's fine. She doesn't have to see me."

"Elizabeth," Jerry hollered. "You're supposed to be in bed! Remember what—"

"Lucas?"

The next moment was so quiet, Lucas heard birds flapping their wings a mile away.

"Lucas!" Elizabeth was running straight at them, faster than her pregnant body should move.

Lucas glanced at his brother for guidance, but all he was doing was staring at his approaching wife, shaking his head like she'd disobeyed him like this a thousand times.

"Oh my goodness—Lucas!" Like being hit by a runaway goat—or maybe three enthusiastic kid goats—Lucas felt Elizabeth slam against him then throw her arms around him in a lung-collapsing hug. "I can't believe it's you!"

"Elizabeth," he said, unable to not hug her back. "How are you?"

She dropped her arms and stood back. "How am *I*? Well, I'm just wonderful," she said, playfully swatting his arm. "It's been so long, I must look like a dinosaur to you."

"We're the same age," he said with a smile. "And you look great. Getting ready to pop, I'd say."

She grinned and rubbed her belly. "I've never felt better in my life. This one"—she elbowed her husband—"expects me to sit around all day like a lump."

"Yes, I do." Jeremiah took her arm. "We're going back inside right now. You know what Eliza Fisher told you."

His sister-in-law struggled to pull away. "That old bat doesn't know what she's talking about. She's been senile for years." She inhaled a gasp, then bit her knuckle. "I didn't mean to say that aloud. It's the hormones." She looked at Lucas. "I can't be held accountable for what I say."

"Inside, woman," Jeremiah said, lifting her off her feet and heading toward the house.

"Luke!" Lizzy called to him. "Come inside. Please."

When he hadn't followed, his brother looked over his shoulder. "You heard my stubborn wife. Better come on in."

CHAPTER TWENTY-FIVE

For the next few days, Esther could swear she'd barely slept a wink, yet when she eyed herself in the mirror while getting dressed, she knew she'd never looked so healthy.

The day before, she'd finished four triple batches of soap, ready to take to Leah. She'd picked an afternoon when no one else was at home, that way no one would be around to make her feel guilty. Even she had to admit the cassia leaf oil was a bit strong. *And Leah will love it*, she'd thought after filling the final mold.

Sarah's wedding dress was also nearly done, and because her sister was busy organizing living arrangements with Amos's family, as well as where all the extended family would stay for the wedding, she'd barely had time to bug Esther.

While smoothing out one of the back hems, Esther thought about Lucas. Before she'd left his house the other night, she'd copied down all the scriptures they'd discussed. Since then, every night and every morning Esther had read through each of them, feeling their meaning deeper in her soul each time.

Because of his dedication to study and his good example, he'd changed her life, helped her get a grip on the worries that had been plaguing her heart for years.

Why was she blessed to have such a dear friend?

Somehow, Lucas Brenneman had become one of the most important people in her life.

He isn't Amish, though, she reminded herself before she had to visualize another Jacob memory. *And he's frightfully stubborn about reaching out to his family or even letting anyone know he's in town.*

Oh, but the thrill she'd felt right after the buggy crash! The accident had caused their bodies to jostle against each other, and then when the falling buggy had finally settled, she'd opened her eyes to find Lucas lying directly on top—

"Why are you smiling?"

Esther gasped and opened her eyes to find Evie standing in the bedroom doorway.

"Because I'm happy!" she exclaimed, not needing to fib even the slightest. "Aren't you?"

Eve tapped her index finger to her lips. "You were dancing, too."

"No, I…" Esther quickly dropped the sides of her dress that she'd been holding up as she'd swayed before the mirror.

"And singing. *Maam* said you never sing anymore."

"I was not." Esther cleared her throat and smoothed the front of her dress. "Must've been the pigs you heard." She made the most unladylike pig-type snort.

Eve giggled. "That's definitely not what I heard, but you sound just like one."

"I'll take that as a compliment." Esther turned back to the mirror. She shouldn't be pleased with how she looked, but she couldn't help noticing how bright her eyes were and the healthy glow to her cheeks.

"Where's your bonnet?" Eve inquired, pointing to the empty hook on the wall. "I haven't seen it in days."

"I lost it the other night, er—day. When I was in the buggy."

"Bishop Abram tells us to keep it tied tight, but none of the girls ever do. Not even *Maam*."

"I know." Esther nodded. "It was an accident, and it was very windy."

"Then why were you outside?"

Esther adored her little sister, but she was growing weary of all the questions. "*Maam* said I should go into town for material to make a new one. Want to come?"

Her eyes lit up. "Oh, yes! Please!"

Esther laughed and reached for her thinner *kapp*. "Go tell your brothers."

Eve whipped around. "Oh, no. Not them."

"Whyever not?"

Her sister blew out a long, dramatic sigh. "Because they're bugging me to death."

"Evie, you know you shouldn't say things like that. It's a sin to even think it."

Another weary sigh. "But they're so embarrassing in public."

Esther laughed as she tied the strings of her bonnet—tightly, ignoring the Lancaster County fashion. "They'll grow up soon enough. You'll see."

Without much more of a fuss, Esther gathered Abraham and Benjamin, and together with Eve, they set off to town. With all the afternoon chores done, they could take their time.

A few weeks ago, while visiting an English neighbor, Benjamin had seen a baseball game on television. Since then, he'd taken it upon himself to pick up any baseball-size rock or clump of dirt and attempt to pitch a strikeout. Abraham, of course, was his batter.

This slowed their pace dramatically, but Esther didn't care. She enjoyed the smells of fresh earth, the green rolling hills, and the sunshine on her face whenever it peeked out from behind the clouds.

When the redbrick building came into view, however, she felt anything but calm. It was strange, the physical reaction caused by just seeing the building. Her heart beat fast, while her stomach filled with butterflies, and the autumn sun felt awfully hot, didn't it?

"Who's that?" Eve asked. "He looks like the man from the goat—"

"Where?"

Her sister was pointing directly at the med clinic. To her shock, Lucas stood outside, one foot propping open the glass door. Tall and broad-shouldered, his body filled the doorway. For some reason, she couldn't make herself look away.

"He waved at you," Eve said.

Esther felt a tingle at the back of her neck and wondered if she was blushing. "He's just being friendly. Everybody, wave back," she said to the *kinnahs*, attempting to play casual.

"He's staring like the other *Englishers*," her sister observed. "That's all they ever do. Only now it looks like he wants to say something. Esther, why's he staring at you?"

Esther felt herself smiling—just slightly—as his gaze settled on her. Shame on Lucas Brenneman for being so bold. He should go right back inside and stop embarrassing her.

"Beautiful day, isn't it?" he said as they passed by.

Just as Esther opened her mouth to reply, Eve grabbed her arm and yanked her to a faster stride. The familiar sound of his laughter followed as they entered Kings.

"What's the hurry?" Esther said, panting for breath. "You nearly pulled my arm out of the socket."

"That *Englisher* was bugging me," Eve said in Pennsylvania Dutch, voice low.

"Evie, we must be kind to everyone—*everyone*. Just because he doesn't go to our church or live plain like us doesn't mean he's less than us. *Gott* loves everyone no matter who we are, where we come from, or what we've done." She put a hand on her shoulder. "He loves us so much that He made a plan for us to follow, and He's with us every step of the way."

For once, the words weren't just platitudes. Esther felt the truth of each one down to her bones. She couldn't have meant such a thing a week ago, not until *Gott* reminded her—with Lucas's help.

"Benji's making a mess." Eve's voice snapped Esther out of her daze. She looked to see her brother unraveling a spool of thick red ribbon.

"Benjamin," she snapped. The boy squealed, tossed the ribbon into the air, and then ran away, hiding behind an aisle of wool fabric. "Here." She handed Abraham a five dollar bill. "Take your brother across the street for a piece of candy." Before the words had completely left her mouth, the boys shot out the door.

"See what I mean?" Eve said, shaking her head. "*Maam* has no idea how naughty they are when she's not with them."

"Maybe you can be a better example for them to follow." She smiled at her sister, who was growing up way too fast. "Come help me find what I need for a *kapp*. Maybe there'll be enough left over for two."

Eve grinned, clapped her hands, then rushed off in search of the perfect fabric, leaving Esther alone with her thoughts.

She could practically feel him next door, still smiling at her—which was not helpful. How was she supposed to live a normal day when he was so near? She couldn't help recalling the poem he'd recited to her the other evening. The one by Elizabeth Browning. "How do I love thee…let me count the ways…"

The lyrics ran a circle around her heart, leaving behind a funny sort of perplexity as she and Eve settled on a sturdy black cotton fabric. It would make a fine, sensible, proper Amish *kapp*. It would keep her hair hidden as it should be, keep her modest and humble, and under the protection of *Gott*. It would also remind her of the kind of life she'd always wanted. Right there in Honey Brook.

"Let's fetch your brothers," she said. As they exited Kings Mercantile, Esther couldn't help shooting a lightning-fast glance at the clinic to see if Lucas was outside.

He wasn't. He had more important—*English*—things to do than flirt with her. The heaviness of disappointment made her shoulders slack but, since that was utter nonsense, Esther quickly knocked it away as she entered Yoder's Home Goods. The store was bustling with business. Esther spotted her brothers at the candy counter, meticulously deciding how to spend their money.

"Speak of the devil!"

Esther nearly jumped out of her skin but then settled when she realized the shout had come from her cousin.

"Es," Eve whispered. "Why did Leah call you the devil? That's not nice."

Esther laughed. "She didn't mean it like that. It's an expression."

"Does she think you need to pray?"

"No, sweetie." Instead of taking the time to explain, she added, "Why don't you pick out a treat? It's on me." Eve grinned and dashed away, Leah quickly taking her spot.

"You can't be here," her cousin said. "Word's spreading like wildfire."

Esther took a step backward, not knowing where to look. If a rumor about her and Lucas had already started, was she supposed to hide in Leah's back room?

"You've sold out again—your soap."

"Oh. Oh!" Esther wrapped her arms around her body and gave a squeeze, almost wanting to laugh-cry in relief. "I've got some at home. I'll just—"

"That's what I mean," Leah said. "I posted pictures and reviews on the website. People are freaking out over it. Do you understand you're in high demand?"

Esther did laugh this time. "I am?"

"Stop being so modest." Leah rolled her eyes. "I've read articles on commerce and product fads. For whatever reason, your homemade scented soaps are the 'it' thing right now. Fads don't last forever, though, so if you want to make a real mark, we have to strike now."

"Gracious. Sounds so frantic."

"It is!" Leah heaved a sigh, fisting the back of her bun. "That's why I'm saying you can't be here— you have to go home right now and bring me everything you have. Everything, Esther. And I need you to make more. As much as you can. Seriously."

Esther made herself blink a few times. "I'm really a success?"

Leah actually snorted a laugh out her nose. "Huge, honey, huge. Look at my face. Do I look intense enough for you?" Her eyes were wide and steady, unblinking. In fact, it seemed as though her cousin wasn't even breathing.

Esther lifted a shaky hand to her forehead. She knew her soap was selling unusually well at the moment, but she never expected to be this successful or for such secular news to feel so…rewarding.

Bishop Abram's sermon about modesty tickled the back of her memory, but Esther didn't allow it to take root.

"It's unbelievable," she said, watching Benjamin drool over the long red licorice whips. "But I can't just go; I've got the *kinnahs* with me." She pointed at Abraham filling a baggie with rock candy.

"Hey, boys," Leah said, calling over the children. "Who wants to take a ride in Alex's truck?"

Their eyes lit up immediately. "Me!" shouted Abraham, as his other siblings echoed enthusiastically.

"Oh, Alex?" Leah called out to one of the English teens who worked at the store, not moving her smiling gaze from Esther. "Can you run the Millers home, then bring back a few boxes?"

"Twenty boxes," Esther said under her breath.

Leah actually gasped. "Twenty?" She put a hand to her chest like she was feeling faint. "*Twenty* boxes."

A blond teenage boy wandered over. He seemed respectable enough; his hair was short, thankfully not hanging over his eyes like other boys his age. "Y'all live out near Honey Brook Creek?"

Before Esther could even nod, Leah said, "Exactly. You've dropped me off there before. You can finish stocking the jams later, okay? Now get going."

The boy shrugged. "I'll get my keys. Meet you out front."

"You sure he's a safe driver, cousin?" Esther asked in a hushed voice as she watched him walk away. Why did their pants always sag at the waist like that? He needed a pair of good suspenders.

"It's less than two miles," Leah said, which wasn't the least bit comforting.

"But today's a busy trading day in town. There are buggies and bicycles on the streets. The Troyer family's taken to Rollerblading. They swerve all over the roads."

Leah didn't reply but was actually pushing

Esther toward the exit.

As they passed by her soap display, Esther noticed that, indeed, it was completely empty. "Gee, they sold so quickly. Tourists again?"

"Mostly," Leah replied. "But then—it was the craziest thing—you remember Lucas Brenneman?"

All of a sudden, Esther felt like she was choking on nothing but air, while she sensed all of her blood draining from her face. "Wh-who?" She coughed, trying to breathe regularly.

"Jacob's older brother. How could you forget him? He was a dreamboat. I heard he's a doctor at the medical clinic—"

"Physician's assistant," Esther automatically corrected, then froze in place, feeling pinpricks in her cheeks.

"What's the difference?"

It seemed like an eternity crawled by before Esther could defrost her tongue. "H-how should I know what he does for a living? I mean…I *don't*." She quickly dropped her gaze to the tile floor, concentrating on the tips of her black boots.

"Um, anyway," Leah said, "a few hours ago, he waltzes in, eyeballs the place like he's looking for something specific, then goes and buys up all the rest of your soap, slides them right off the shelf into a basket. Course there were only a few left, but he completely cleaned me out." When Esther finally looked up, Leah crossed her arms over her chest. "Now, why in the world would someone like Lucas Brenneman need pretty-smelling soap?"

Esther hoped the blush on her cheeks would not cause her cousin to think she actually knew the answer to that. "I can't imagine—"

"Kinnahs!" Leah's shout made her jump. "You don't need to pay me for your sweets today; your sister and I have a deal."

The children exclaimed more animated hoots, then raced out the front door to Alex's white truck parked at the curb. Leah opened the passenger side door to display a hidden back seat in the cab. The kids excitedly climbed in.

"Act natural," Leah whispered, grabbing Esther's elbow. "There he is."

Esther didn't bother asking who, because the moment she'd stepped outside, she caught a glimpse of Lucas in her peripheral vision. He sat on the bench in front of the clinic. Another man was with him—one of the doctors, maybe.

Before her brain could complete the decision process, she was walking across the street, striding like she hadn't a care in the world. She felt Leah try to take her hand to stop her, but she kept moving forward. When she'd gotten halfway, Lucas's carefree expression warped to impressed interest, then shock.

Immediately, he rose to his feet. "Afternoon," he said, sounding unsure.

"Hello." Esther nodded, attempting to keep her expression neutral. "I heard you bought my soap from Yoder's."

She watched Lucas swallow. "Yes, I did."

Like any other gracious businesswoman, she lifted a smile. "That was very generous of you."

For a moment, neither spoke. "Frank," Lucas finally said to the man with him, "this is Esther Miller. She makes the most wonderfully scented soaps in her own kitchen."

The man was in his late fifties and had been at the clinic for as long as Esther could remember, though she'd never met him. "Pleasure to meet you," he said. "Ya say you make soap?"

She nodded. "My own recipes."

"They sell out before she can even stock them," Lucas inserted, then lifted a crooked grin. "They make my pathetic bachelor pad smell like an actual home."

"That so?" Esther couldn't help saying. "I'm glad you like them."

Before she could get too carried away, Frank said, "Maybe I'll send my wife your way. She loves sweet-smelling things."

"That would be nice."

Frank lifted a big grin. "Well, better get back to work. Pleasure to meet you, young lady."

"Pleasure was mine," Esther replied genuinely.

The next moment, they were alone, Esther sensing all the weight of a dozen eyes on her.

"What are you doing out here?" she asked.

"Waiting for test results."

"For a patient? Anything wrong? I mean, sorry, I know something is wrong. Is it bad?"

There was a pause before he answered. "Maybe. Which is why I'm so glad I ran into you." He smiled at her, eyes twinkling. "Seeing you takes my mind off worrying."

It was impossible for her to not feel his sweet words all the way down to the tips of her toes, inside her heart. "Lucas…" she said, not sure how to continue.

He exhaled a quiet laugh through his nose.

"I can't stay anyway," she finally added, feeling Leah's eyes boring into the back of her head like hot July sunshine.

"I know," Lucas said, leaning against a brick pillar. "But when I saw you, I couldn't help myself. I really needed the distraction."

"Always teasing." She exhaled a little laugh, feeling both silly and warm at the same time. "You don't scare me, Lucas—which is why I left my family over there to talk to you. I can't imagine what they're thinking."

"I suppose we'll both have some explaining to do. Before you go, there's something I want to correct." He leaned toward her. "I didn't buy your soap to make my house smell nice."

"Why did you, then?"

"I want my house to smell like you."

Esther heard her own gasp of shock right before she covered her mouth, then moved her hand down to her breastbone. Openly flirting with her like that was not appropriate, yet when she was ready to chide him over it, the tingle in her chest wouldn't allow her to utter a single word.

"I have more things to tell you," Lucas said, a corner of his mouth pulling into a smile, his light brown eyes looking round and eager.

There he was again, the teasing, curly-haired Gilbert Blythe, that handsome young man with the mischievous, addictive grin…who'd held Esther's youthful heart in his hands. Suddenly, her head felt light, like if she wasn't careful, she might just sink to the floor.

Right then and there, if she'd been of sound mind, she would've told Lucas Brenneman to keep all the imprudent attention and flattering words to himself. Also, if she'd been of sound mind, she would have remembered that accepting his attention—any man's attention—was surely disloyal to Jacob's memory.

But for some reason, she couldn't even picture Jacob's face.

"Oh yeah?" she said, hyperaware of how close to each other they were standing.

Lucas nodded, smiling like a little boy with a secret.

"Aren't you going to tell me?"

"Later." He lifted his chin to look up at the blue sky. "There's so much, I wouldn't know where to begin."

"Good things, I suspect."

Another nod of silence. "I won't keep you, but I also wanted you to know that I might be away from town for a while."

"When will you be back?" Esther blurted, her spine going stiff as a board. It was irrational, but her first thought was that he was leaving town for good like when he was sixteen. "How long will you be gone?"

"Hopefully just a few days. I didn't want you to think I'd…" He ran a hand through his brown hair, then dropped his voice to a whisper. "I didn't want you to think I'd just leave again."

She was relieved he wouldn't be gone long, more relieved than she would've expected over a friend she'd known for really only a few weeks.

Had her feelings suddenly changed?

The idea made her inwardly cringe, for even if it were so, there was nothing to be done about it. She wanted to stay Amish—and it had been Lucas who'd reminded her of that. In fact, the more time they spent together, the more her faith increased. Which meant Lucas—Jacob's brother—had no place in her life.

"Go," he whispered, pulling open one glass door. "I'll see you the very day I'm back."

After he was gone, Esther closed her eyes, needing a moment to sift through the contradictory sensations filling her body. While also wanting to remember the words he'd said—how he wouldn't just leave…he couldn't help himself…that he had good things to tell her.

"Esther!"

She snapped awake at Leah's shrill shout. After one more quick breath, she hustled back to Alex's truck. "Let's go."

Leah was staring. "What was that about?"

Esther climbed into the truck. "I was thanking him for buying the soap. Mighty nice of him—for a man—don't you think?"

Leah lifted her shoulders and let them fall. "We're not supposed to talk to him, though. He's been shunned."

Esther made sure to meet her cousin's eyes. "No, he's not. You can't be shunned until after you've been baptized. He was practically a child when he left home." She ran her hands across her lap. "Also, it was the Christian thing to do. I was being gracious. Can we go now?" She turned to Alex. "You'll need to bring my boxes back right away."

"Right. Yes," said Leah. "Don't speed—isn't that big of a hurry. And remember," she said to Alex, "always yield to the buggies—*always*! Folks are out walking and biking. Watch where you're going."

"I will," the teen said. Esther closed her door, and the truck pulled away from the curb. The *kinnahs* giggled and whooped, totally preoccupied with their sweets and the adventure. Riding in vehicles was still a treat for them, but Esther's thoughts wandered. Her sensible, obedient mind knew the difference between proper and improper, though for some reason, her heart was slow to catch on today.

CHAPTER TWENTY-SIX

"Call on line one." The voice came through the speakerphone on Lucas's desk.

"Thanks, Stephanie." He grabbed the receiver. "Greg, what have you got?" He listened a few seconds, made a note on a piece of paper, then said goodbye.

After sending a quick text, he took off his lab coat, grabbed his keys, and left the office.

"Let us know how it goes!" Stephanie called from behind the reception desk as Lucas rushed past.

"Will do."

If a thing like this had to happen, it was good that it was happening fast.

That morning, a young man named Tanner had come into the clinic complaining of sore muscles, lethargy, and chills. He was Amish, but Lucas didn't recognize his surname. The boy's father had explained that he'd already taken his son to see two of their community's medical experts.

Unless it was a Mennonite who had professional, credentialed medical training, Lucas had thought at the time, *there is no such thing as an Amish medical expert. But there darn well should be.*

"You've got a fever," Lucas had told Tanner. "Have you been taking anything for it?"

The boy had shaken his head.

"Aspirin," his father had said.

"I'll give you some ibuprofen," Lucas had said while checking Tanner's pulse. "It will help with the body aches, too."

Lucas didn't like how thin Tanner was. He'd said he was fourteen—so he should've been more filled out.

Fourteen… Lucas had thought. *The same age Jacob was.* That had sent up the first red flag.

"How's your appetite?"

The boy shrugged. "Not that hungry, I guess. Eating makes me feel…" He touched his belly.

"Upset stomach? Diarrhea?"

He'd nodded and looked at the floor.

"You didn't tell me that," his father had said.

"Can I touch the sides of your throat?" Lucas asked.

David, the boy's father, nodded, his eyes wide and anxious.

His lymph nodes were swollen and tender. When he'd pressed on them, Tanner had winced. "Are you bruising more easily than normal?"

The boy nodded.

"Any headaches?"

"About every other day."

"Tanner," his father had said. "Why didn't you say anything?" He looked at Lucas. "I thought he might have the flu. The schoolhouse needs a deep cleaning."

"It could be the flu," Lucas had told him, even as a familiar cold dread slithered up his spine. "But I'd like to do a blood test. Right now. We've got a lab in the back, if that's okay."

"Papa?" Tanner had said, sounding very young

and scared as he'd leaned into his father's side.

David had put an arm around him. "It's okay, buddy. We'll figure it out and you'll be fine."

There was no way Lucas could *not* picture Jacob. How would their own father have reacted if he'd taken Jacob to an actual hospital or even this medical clinic? Lucas didn't have time to dwell on the matter—besides, it would only make his anger flare up.

Less than five minutes later, Tanner's blood was running through the machine. Lucas had told the boy and his father to stick around town, maybe go out to lunch, because Lucas would want to discuss the results with them as soon as possible. This had not brought smiles to either party, but they'd promised to come back in an hour.

While waiting for the results, he'd gone outside to discuss the case with Frank, the administrator of the clinic. That was when he'd seen Esther coming out of Yoder's. He'd been so wound up that simply seeing her across the way had lifted his spirits. They'd exchanged smiles, a few whispers, and he'd told her he had more things to say.

Of course, she could never guess that he'd spent most of the previous day with Jeremiah and his family. How they'd welcomed him in with barely a sideways glance. Not only had he worked the farm with his brother, but while inside the house, he'd checked Lizzy's vital signs, agreeing that yes, she needed to take it easy until the *bobbeil* came.

Also while he'd been there, Jerry's oldest son had fallen from a tree and sprained his wrist. It felt wonderful to help him, to assess that the bone wasn't broken, to show Jerry how to make a sling, and to advise the boy how he must allow his arm to rest so it could heal. All without having to visit their community's "medical expert," Eliza Fisher. Who knew what she would've suggested?

Lucas had also told Esther that he might be away for a day of two—not knowing yet if Tanner would need further treatment or even a trip to the hospital. After saying goodbye to her, he'd walked with heavy steps back inside the clinic to check the results.

The platelets had been low. Abnormal levels of white and red blood cells. Anemic.

All the readings Lucas had been dreading.

After running a second blood test, Lucas asked his colleagues to double-check the results, each of them taking turns looking at the blood through a microscope.

"I'd like your son to have a bone marrow biopsy." He told this to David out in the hallway, away from Tanner's ears.

David scratched his chin, looking worried. "What does that mean? What is it?"

"We need to see if your son's bone marrow is healthy and producing the normal amounts of blood cells for his body. The blast count is abnormal—test results show that his levels are low."

The father shifted his stance. "And that's bad."

Lucas wasn't sure how to answer. "It could be a symptom of something dangerous. That's why I'd like him to have the test."

"Can you do it here? Now?"

Relief was Lucas's dominant emotion. He was so

grateful that David was open and willing to do whatever his son needed.

Unlike Papa. Lucas couldn't help making the comparison.

"Not here," he replied. "But I have a very good friend who heads the oncology department at the hospital in Hershey. We've already spoken, and he can see Tanner this afternoon."

The man grabbed Lucas's arm and spoke in a low voice. "You think my son has cancer?"

"I don't know anything yet. But in someone his age, early detection is very important. Please let me help him."

While waiting for the answer, Lucas held his breath, imagining how his own father had refused treatment for Jacob when he'd shown the very same symptoms.

Please, Lord, Lucas silently prayed, the words coming to him almost effortlessly now, *let this man be open to modern medicine. Let him see there is another way besides relying only on faith and prayer. Please help him want to do anything and everything to save his son's life.*

David's answer came a second later. "Of course. What do we do?"

Oh, danke, Gott. *Amen.* "If I drive, are you able to go into Hershey now?"

The man nodded immediately. "I'll call my boss; he's very understanding. But please, tell me how your friend will test the bone marrow. I'll need to explain it to Tanner in my own way."

"Well…" Lucas rubbed his chin, needing to think plain. "He'll collect your son's marrow through a very long needle."

"Where?"

"From inside his hip. Because of the angle of the bone, it's the best place to get a large sample. Some hospitals allow the area to be numbed before-hand—for the pain." They both looked through the small window into the exam room where Tanner sat on the table.

"Would you recommend it?" David asked.

Another rush of relief pushed through Lucas's veins. "Absolutely."

David licked his top lip and nodded. "May I use your phone?"

"Please," Lucas said, ushering him into his office. He shouldn't have been surprised when the man dialed a number by heart. The acceptable use of technology really had changed since he'd been away.

"It's fine at work," David said, hanging up. "Will we have to spend the night?"

"I don't know, but I'll be with you the whole time. I'll tell you everything that's going on."

"Danke." The father looked at peace for the first time. "Thank you so much."

Lucas put a hand on David's shoulder. "I can drive you home first, if you'd like to talk to your wife."

David shook his head. "One of the men I work with is going there now. He'll explain it."

The next few hours were a blur, but Tanner was a trouper, enduring all the poking and prodding and awkward instructions with bravery.

While Lucas waited in a private office with David, he couldn't stop the memories from flooding back...

Jacob facedown on the sterile table. The long Jamshidi needle sliding into his hip bone. It was unorthodox, but Lucas had been in the room the whole time, for the hospital in New York City had not allowed anesthesia. The brothers had looked into each other's eyes, Jacob gripping Lucas's hands. Jacob hadn't cried, but had borne the pain like the strong man he would never grow up to be.

"He'll be in recovery for a while," Lucas explained to David after speaking to Greg. "The extraction was a success, and they got a large sample. We'll get results in a week or two."

"Two weeks?" David stared out the window.

"I know that seems like a very long time to wait, but it will fly by."

"What should we do in the meantime? Tell me, what do you suspect?"

Leukemia, Lucas wanted to say. But it was completely unethical for him to give any kind of diagnosis—not even the hint of one. That would come from the specialists. Besides, it was unfair to compare Tanner with Jacob. Their conditions were not identical.

Even though Lucas had spent years studying pediatric blood diseases, he was not the right person to ask.

"We'll know more soon," he said. "In the meantime, see if you can get Tanner to eat more, sleep, mild exercise. Let's get him feeling as strong and healthy as possible."

David's lips began to tremble. Lucas would do anything to take the fear and pain of uncertainty away from his new friend.

"Does your son have a favorite food? What does he love to eat the most in this world?"

David sniffed and ran a wrist across his nose. "His mother's roast beef."

"Excellent. Protein will help. What else?"

David lifted his chin. "Carrots and peas straight from the garden. My wife planted extra this summer and we still have a crop."

"Wonderful." Finally, David met his eyes and Lucas gave him an encouraging smile.

"Blackberry cobbler, too," the father added. "My oldest daughter makes it especially for him."

"Well, that should definitely be on the menu to-night."

David blinked. "We can go home?"

"I think that can be arranged." Lucas smiled and patted David on the shoulder. "Tanner should be ready to leave soon. But remember, he does need rest, and let's not forget to treat his symptoms, too. Okay?"

David nodded. "Ibuprofen every four hours for fever and chills. Iron pills twice a day. Food, rest, ex-ercise."

"Exactly. You're a regular pharmacist."

David exhaled a little laugh while running his fingers up and down his suspenders.

"I'll also prescribe a mild painkiller with caffeine for the headaches," Lucas continued. "It can be taken alternating with the Ibuprofen."

"Lucas," David said, his gaze moving to the floor again. "I don't know how to thank you."

"It's my job."

The Amish man shook his head. "I might live a

more sheltered life than you, but I do know that running two blood tests, setting up a biopsy, and personally driving us an hour each way to the hospital is not your job." Finally, he looked up. Tears clung to the red rims of his eyes. "You helped us so much today. Why?"

Lucas tried to swallow down the lump in his throat. "Because I could," he said honestly. "Because…" The lump swelled. "Because I see how much you love your son. You'd do anything for him. Because everyone deserves a chance."

David wrapped his hand around Lucas's forearm, rocking it like they were shaking hands. *"Danke,"* he whispered. "I'll never forget all you did for us, and my family will pray for you."

His heart was so touched, so full that Lucas didn't know what to say. Perhaps no words were needed, because David removed his hat and bowed his head, lips moving in silent prayer. Lucas knew he would never forget this moment, either.

"Keep busy this week," Lucas said after David whispered "amen." "Plan activities for the whole family. We don't know what the test results will bring, so my best advice is to be optimistic. Don't dwell on the unknown or worst-case scenario. Be strong for your family."

David stood a little taller and replaced his hat. "I will."

"Greg will call me when he has news. I'll come to your house the minute I have anything to share. If that's okay."

"Of course!" David said, taking Lucas by the shoulders. "You're welcome there anytime, my friend. No matter what happens, you're family now."

That lump swelled almost painfully in Lucas's throat. Unexpectedly, strong emotions were coming at him from all angles, stemming from his chance meeting with Jeremiah and being openly welcomed into their home. Getting to know Lizzy again and his three nephews. The invitation to return another time.

And also, the growing, gnawing desire to see the rest of his family, to be welcomed again at his mother's table. If his attitude toward his father didn't change, could that ever be possible?

Especially, though, he thought about Esther and how her kindness had reminded him of all the good he'd learned as a child. Even now, that same truth rang true again. Without even knowing it, she'd given him hope. She'd also given him her friendship, her laughs and secrets.

Maybe she's given me even more, he thought. *When I saw her across the street, my first desire was to run to her, to tell her all the things I'm feeling. I even wanted to…*

The way that thought continued caused him to slam his eyes shut in guilt.

"Can I see my son?"

Lucas snapped back to the present to find David staring eagerly at him.

"Is it time?"

He pressed a hand to his heart and smiled. "I'll take you to him right now."

CHAPTER TWENTY-SEVEN

For three nights in a row, Esther stayed up late, re-reading certain passages from *Anne of Green Gables* by light of the battery-operated lamp on her nightstand. Her favorites, of course, were the scenes with Anne and Gilbert. After reading the books several times, it was easy to see the blooming romance coming between the couple, even when Anne tried to convince herself she never intended to marry. Readers knew deep in their hearts that she truly cared for Gil, and when their solid friendship easily turned to love, Esther's heart burst every time.

The next morning, after a restless night of dreams, Esther returned the well-read paperback to its place on the family bookshelf downstairs. The sweet feelings while reading the novel unexpectedly caused Esther to have real-life sweet feelings of her own.

She longed to fall in love again. But were even contemplations of moving past Jacob disloyal? She was really beginning to wonder.

"Esther?" *Maam* called. "Could you do me a favor and visit one of the neighbors?"

After three days of keeping herself extra busy—early mornings making soap followed by full days of mechanical wedding preparations and dress fittings—Esther was more than willing to get out of the house.

Maam was in her sewing room putting the final touches on a sweet little pillowcase. "Get one of the large baskets in the pantry, would you, please? Fill it with chicken broth, applesauce, and a big jar of pears. Sarah made raspberry tarts this morning. Throw in a few of those."

"Someone not feeling well?" she asked. "Sounds like a healing basket."

Maam snipped a thread with a pair of scissors. "Eliza Fisher's been out to Jeremiah Brenneman's farm, put Lizzy on bed rest. Her folks are down south for a few days where it's warmer."

Hearing the familiar surname, Esther nearly tripped over her own feet. "You want me to go to the Brennemans'?"

Maam nodded.

Because she'd been accidentally dreaming about him, Esther was not ready to see Lucas, even though she knew he would not be at his brother's farm—or anywhere near his family. "Why can't you take it? Or Eve—she's been playing with the goats all afternoon," Esther said, even while realizing her voice sounded like a whiny child's.

"You have plans in the next hour?" *Maam* looked up. "You've been going into town an awful lot lately and getting back after dark." She held a steady gaze on Esther. "Or will you be going to Louisa's again?"

Esther tried to swallow. "No, um—no. I was just…"

"Darling, Lizzy has three babies and one in a month or so. They have that farm that's too big for just them to handle. With Lizzy on bed rest, who do you think is cooking, cleaning, and taking care of the *bobbeils*?"

Hot guilt and spiky neglect spread through Esther's body. Of course she needed to help. That's what neighbors were for. Unlike the English who might pay for a maid or nanny, the Amish way was to take care of one another. If she hadn't been so wrapped up in her own drama, she probably would've thought of it herself.

Lizzy was only a few years older than she was. When they'd been teenagers, she'd watched with embarrassing envy at how close she was to the two Brenneman brothers her age. Now the family needed all the help they could get. It wasn't their fault that Esther had a secret concerning Lucas.

"Instead of just dropping off, shall I stay there to help?" Esther asked, vowing to atone for her thoughtlessness. "They might need someone to put the *kinnahs* to bed or even watch them all night. If they need that kind of help, *Maam*, could you spare me?"

When her mother smiled, her blue eyes crinkled. "That's very considerate of you. I know the Zook and Stolzfus girls have been over there, but they might need a break." She stood and stretched her back, then tucked a stray hair into Esther's *kapp*. "Do what you can, and let the Spirit guide you."

"I will." Esther couldn't help grinning at the new project. "I'll bring a change of clothes with me just in case."

"Smart cookie."

After giving her mother a big hug and kiss on the cheek, Esther flew up the stairs, refreshed by the task to give service.

After strapping her bag over a shoulder and taking a firm grip on the basket of goodies, she set off. She hadn't been to the Brenneman farm in far too long. Members of their church took turns hosting the prayer meeting every other Sunday, but Jeremiah and Lizzy hadn't hosted in quite a while. Maybe because of their small children or Lizzy's ill parents.

All this time…maybe the reason I felt like I didn't fit in was because I haven't even tried. Had she been so obsessed with her own issues that she'd let moments of kindness and service pass by? Maybe if she made the extra effort, she and Lizzy could become friends.

An unexpected flutter beat against Esther's heart as she suddenly ached to have any kind of connection with the Brennemans. One that had nothing to do with Jacob.

Esther picked up the pace when she saw the red barn and whitewashed house of the Brennemans' property. It truly was a lot of land for just one family, and she spotted only two men working in the field.

One of the Zook girls was hanging laundry in the side yard. Esther waved a greeting before knocking on the front door. "Lizzy?" she called. "It's Esther Miller. May I come in?"

Lizzy was suddenly beside her on the front porch. "Esther, hi! *Guten tag.*" Despite the shadows under her eyes, the expectant mother looked radiant.

"I heard you were on bed rest."

"I know, I know." Lizzy rolled her eyes. "Please don't say you're here to lecture me, too. I've been lectured for the past week, and I'm done with it."

Esther chuckled. "No lectures from me, but I did bring some treats."

"I see that," Lizzy said, eyeing the basket. "Come inside." She swung the door open and entered the house. Esther followed behind to see a very clean living room and smell something yummy coming from the kitchen.

"Hallo!" the sixteen-year-old Zook daughter called out. Esther had to think quickly to remember her name. The Zooks had fifteen children.

"Ruth, hallo! It smells delicious in here. What are you making?"

"Thimble cookies."

"The *kinnahs* want to help with the thumbprints later," Lizzy added. "But we're actually trying to keep them busy outside while the sun's still shining. Rain's in the forecast for tonight. The weather could turn any day now."

Esther set the basket of food on the kitchen counter. "Well, I'm here if you need me—or even if you don't!" she quickly tweaked. "I'd love to play with the *kinnahs* or clean, cook, give you a hand wherever I can." She straightened her newly sewn black *kapp*. "Or I can run errands. Anything you need." She moved toward Lizzy. "Honestly, though, aren't you supposed to be off your feet?" With a grin, she linked an arm though Lizzy's and led her to the sofa. "Sit."

"Goodness," Lizzy said with a smile. "Yes, ma'am."

"Elizabeth?" Ruth said. "After I finish the cookies, do you mind if I take Sadie home?" She looked out the window toward her younger sister at the laundry line. "Some of the youth got permission to meet tonight, and I'd really—"

"Ack!" Lizzy cried. "Of course. You girls have been a wonderful help, but please, if you have other things to do, don't feel the need to stay. Despite the gossip, I can manage myself."

"No, you canna," Esther said, planting her hands on her hips. "Not on your own; that's why I'm here now. Ruth, you and your sister can go whenever you'd like, and God bless you for being so helpful. I must tell your mother."

"Yes," Lizzy said, not putting up a fight. "Thank you so much!"

"In fact…" After making sure Lizzy wasn't about to make a run for it, Esther headed toward the kitchen. "I can finish the cookies. Why don't you head out now? I'm not so old that I don't remember youth group. Do you have your eye on anyone special?"

Ruth blushed and shook her head. "I don't know. Maybe."

"Well then, you better scoot. Don't want to make anyone wait too long."

Ruth looked at Lizzy. "Go!" she said, then made a shooing-off gesture with her hands. "Have fun! It was wonderful having you."

In less than a minute, the Zook sisters disappeared down the gravel path, leaving a trail of excited, giggling voices. Honestly, youth group had been very enjoyable. Why had Esther stopped attending just because she'd grown a little older? Just because she hadn't gotten married, was that a reason to not at least be a chaperone like Louisa?

Things are going to change in my life, Esther pondered. *I'm never going to be mopey or withdrawn again. That's not how I want the rest of my life to be. Even if I never marry, there will always be a place for me in Honey Brook if I choose to make the effort.*

But she did want to marry. She wanted her own home and family and husband who she adored…she still wanted all the things in her childhood dreams.

Except now, and despite her own heart, she was trying to block out the new feelings she had for the man of those dreams.

"I never knew you were so bossy."

Esther snapped awake, a wooden spoon unmoving in her hand. "Well, what is the English phrase? Desperate times call for desperate measures."

Lizzy adjusted her position so she was facing the kitchen, her feet up on the sofa. "I wouldn't say the situation's desperate, but I do want to thank you for offering to help."

"It's not an offer," Esther corrected as she found a cookie sheet and readied to spoon out the dough. "I'm here for whatever you need and for as long as you need. I'm just ashamed it took me so long to get here."

"*Danke.* My husband says I can be too stubborn at times. But I thought that was why he liked me in the first place." She smiled. "It's hard for me to ask for help, so I really do appreciate your just taking over. It's nice having someone else giving orders around here. I think you and I are going to get along fine."

Esther laughed. "It's good to find a kindred

spirit, as they say."

Lizzy draped a light blanket across her body.

"Are you chilly?" Esther asked. "Would you like me to stoke the fire or make some tea? These cookies can wait."

Lizzy shook her head. "This blanket is perfect, but thank you. And sorry, but those cookies cannot wait. Not only did I promise the children, but there will be two very grumpy men outside if they don't get the treats they were promised."

Esther chuckled and spooned out a measurement of dough. "Then, I'd better get started."

The ladies happily chatted about this and that, and Esther felt wonderfully comfortable both talking and joking with Lizzy and being in her home. She felt so at peace, with its warmth and coziness and simplicity. She and Jeremiah surely had a wonderful marriage.

John, Lizzy's three-year-old, rushed inside for a glass of water, a trip to the potty, and a big hug from his *maam*. Yes, this was a remarkable place to live.

Would Esther ever have such a home of her own?

Taking a short break from baking, she whipped up three peanut butter sandwiches, milk, and some of the applesauce she'd brought. Making sure Lizzy stayed right where she was on the sofa by the fire, she'd set up a little picnic on the patio for the three *kinnahs*. They'd managed to pause their play with the new baby chicks and ducks long enough to eat.

"Do you have preserves in the fridge?" Esther asked once they were back inside, as she pulled out the last batch of cookies from the oven. "Or I can use the jar I brought from home. For the top of the cookies."

Lizzy scrambled to sit up straight. "What kind did you bring?"

"Boysenberry," she said, displaying the jar. "But I added some lemon zest to this batch."

"Sounds wonderful," Lizzy said. "I could probably eat the entire jar with a spoon."

Esther smiled, loving the warmth of true appreciation. "Once you're back on your feet, I can show you how to make it."

"Sounds fun. I guess I should admit..." Lizzy's voice dropped. "It has been difficult with the children—I can't chase after them when I'm this big." She placed her hands over her belly. "Jerry works so hard, and he's great with them when he's home, but he's got a lot going on right now." Esther watched as Lizzy began pulling at her index finger. "This was too much land to take on, but when *Daed* got sick... Well, I couldn't imagine my folks selling the place. Jerry jumped right in, promised to keep the farm going. It's been tough on him, I know, because we can't afford extra help just now."

Esther gazed out the window toward the two men who'd been working side by side for at least the two hours since she'd been there. If the other man wasn't a hired hand, Esther couldn't help wondering who he was.

"Lizzy," Esther said, walking one of the warm cookies over, "I was being serious earlier when I said I'm here for as long as you want. See?" She pointed at her bag on a chair by the door. "I brought pj's, my toothbrush, and fresh clothes. It would mean a lot if you let me stay a day or two. Allow me to really help."

She waited while Lizzy took a bite of the cookie and chewed slowly. "It's my worst flaw," she finally said, "but I've got this pride thing."

"I know," Esther said.

"Hard to ask for help."

"So I see."

Lizzy exhaled a laugh. "Esther," she said after pulling in a deep breath, "it would mean so much if you could stay until my mother is back tomorrow afternoon. Would you please take care of my family and me? Wait on me hand and foot? Cater to my every need?"

Esther burst out laughing. "Since you put it that way, how can I refuse?"

Lizzy reached out and took both of Esther's hands. "You can't," she said. "Because that cookie was delicious and I want a hundred more, and because I've loved talking with you, and this will probably scare you to death, but I'm afraid you're going to be one of my closest friends for the rest of my life."

Esther couldn't help smiling and feeling just a bit choked up. "I'm getting that same feeling," she admitted, squeezing Lizzy's hands.

"Now that that's settled," Lizzy said, sitting back, "what do you have in mind for supper?"

"I spied a sweet little fryer in the icebox." Esther arched her eyebrows. "I'll stuff it with citrus, season with garlic and rosemary, baste every twenty minutes."

"And…?" Lizzy's eyes widened.

"Yams from the cellar—prepared both savory and sweet. Corn bread, fresh green beans, and sun-ripened sliced tomatoes."

Lizzy closed her eyes and moaned, rubbing her belly. "You're reading my mind."

Esther chuckled and returned to the kitchen, replacing her soiled apron with a fresh one from a drawer. It was pink and had a faint floral print. She examined it for a second, wondering where something so decorative had come from. It certainly didn't fit in with the other plain clothes.

"Are you judging me?" Lizzy's voice made Esther jump.

"Of course not," she said, tying it on. "It's just rare around here, that's all. But it's lovely."

Lizzy propped herself up on her elbows. "Lovely that I'm a terrible cook?"

"What?" Esther looked across the room at her. "I was talking about the…" She smoothed down the pretty apron. "Nothing. And I don't think you're a terrible cook."

"You've never tasted my cooking."

Esther laughed while removing the chicken from the fridge. "True, but your *kinnahs* look healthy. Pink cheeks and thick hair. That's a sign of hale health in my book."

"When I'm on my feet again, I'll have you over for dinner. Then you'll know the ugly truth."

"I'll consider myself warned," Esther said, cutting up an orange, lemon, and a small lime, filling the kitchen with wonderful, uplifting smells. Perhaps a citrus-blend-scented soap would be in her next batch.

"Bring a date," Lizzy added. "We'll play games

and make an evening of it."

At the suggestion, Esther's hand hovered over the cutting board. "I, uh, I don't date. I mean, I haven't since…" Not knowing how to explain or even finish the sentence, Esther stared down at the slices of fruit.

"You have to get over him."

Esther was startled when Lizzy was suddenly at her side, barefooted with the blanket around her shoulders. She couldn't help nodding. *I know*, she wanted to say. *I know it's a waste of time to even think about him in that way.*

"It's time," Lizzy added, putting a hand on Esther's arm. "Jacob's been gone two years. It's not healthy to be in mourning for so long."

"Jacob?" Esther couldn't help blurting, ashamed of the surprised tone in her voice.

Lizzy tilted her head to the side. "It's easy to see you haven't been the same since he went to heaven. Even now…" She cupped Esther's chin. "I see heartache in your eyes. Jacob was one of the good ones, and we shall miss him forever, but don't you want to fall in love again?"

Words flew around inside her head, making it impossible for Esther to reply. She did know, however, that this was definitely a discussion for a different time.

"I think so," she said, wanting to be honest. "But I don't know if I'm ready." Before Lizzy could probe any further, Esther drew in a deep breath and put her hands on her hips. "Now, unless you need help with a trip to the bathroom, you are not supposed to be standing."

"Bossy," Lizzy muttered but then winked.

"Tell me," Esther said as she returned to the kitchen, "why did Eliza Fisher say you need rest?"

Lizzy sighed and ran a hand down the blanket. "Apparently my blood pressure is high—that was enough for her to make the order." She shook her head. "Truthfully, I thought it was all nonsense until I got a second opinion."

"Same diagnosis?" Esther asked, rinsing out the cavity of the chicken at the sink.

"Jah," Lizzy replied. "But I also have gestational diabetes. I have to prick my finger for a blood test every morning. It analyzes my sugar levels."

Esther couldn't help gaping at her. "Old Eliza Fisher told you to do that?"

Lizzy shook her head. "Oh, no. That was Luke."

"Luke." The word hung in the air as if it was one she'd never heard.

"Luke," Lizzy repeated. "Jerry's brother."

Jerry's brother…

The name and description would not connect in Esther's mind. Quickly, she ran through all the names of the Brenneman siblings. Was there one she'd forgotten? For something in her brain would not allow reality to set in.

"Maybe you don't remember him." Lizzy's voice floated through the air. "He left home ten years ago. You were probably interested in Jacob by then anyway."

"Yeah—yes, I know him—*of* him," Esther said, feeling her eyebrows pull together in confusion. Last she knew, Lucas had no intention of seeing his family.

"One morning last week, Jerry ran into him just

outside our property line. Course we were plenty shocked." She paused to smile. "Words canna express how extraordinary it was to see him. We missed him so much. He's been out there working with Jerry all morning. In fact…" Lizzy sat up straight and craned her neck to look out the window. "Yes, I thought I heard their voices."

Esther's stomach hit the floor.

"Here they come now."

CHAPTER TWENTY-EIGHT

It had been a long time since Lucas had spent this many hours working outdoors. Years since he'd used a tractor, backhoe, or even harvested autumn corn. But being in the fresh air, toiling side by side with his brother in the rich Pennsylvania soil, was more soothing to the soul than any Western psychotherapy.

After spending time with Tanner and David at the Hershey Medical Center, Lucas was ready to give his mind a rest. Especially since it would still be another week until the test results from the bone marrow biopsy would be ready.

"Time for a break?" Jeremiah asked, pulling off his gloves. "I'll be dead on my feet if I don't have some water."

"Already worn out, brother?" Lucas grinned. "Assumed you'd have more stamina than me. I'm the one stuck in an office all day."

"Hilarious." Jeremiah waved him off. "Some of the girls from church have been helping Lizzy all week. I was promised they'd provide us with fresh baked snacks."

"She's been taking it easy?" Lucas asked as the two men walked toward the house.

"I think so. I've told her to." He sighed. "But you know how she is. She thinks she knows what's best for everyone. Stubborn woman."

Lucas couldn't help chuckling, his spirits so high

thanks to the time he'd spent with his family. That first morning when he'd seen Jeremiah had been a complete shock. But the warmth and kindness he'd received had been almost overwhelming. And when Elizabeth had invited him inside, in a matter of minutes, awkwardness from the past had evaporated like steam.

Even now, gratitude swam through his body, making his heart beat stronger than ever. He had his brother back. Lizzy and the *kinnahs*. He had a family again, and he'd never felt so blessed.

None of it would have happened were it not for Esther, he reminded himself as they neared the house. *Silly Peanut and the broken buggy wheel...*

His heart beat even stronger when he thought of Esther. In fact, his heart felt almost whole.

"Something smells incredible," Jeremiah said as he opened the front door, removing his muddy work boots before entering the house. Still halfway lost in thought, Lucas followed the example. "Have you been baking, woman?"

While stepping out of his second boot, Lucas heard Lizzy laugh. "If it smells incredible, do you really think it's *me* who's been baking?"

Lucas entered the house to find Elizabeth obediently on the sofa, and it did actually appear she'd been sitting and had not rushed there when she'd heard them enter. Jerry was right—she could be stubborn.

"How ya feeling, my little shoofly pie?" Jerry knelt down to give his wife a kiss.

"I feel good," Lizzy replied.

"I'll be the judge of that," said Lucas, taking her

brother's place before Lizzy. He checked her pulse—which was strong and steady. No visible fever or swelling of the feet. "Give it here," he said, knowing she knew he needed to take her blood pressure.

After a groan, Lizzy straightened her arm, allowing Lucas to attach the mechanical strap around her wrist.

"Rest it across your heart."

"I know, I know," Lizzy said. Her irritation made him chuckle. "How does it look?"

"Better," Lucas said after taking note of the reading. "Now, show me the tracker." He held out his open hand.

At first, Lizzy glanced away, but then she exhaled and removed it from under her blanket.

Lucas pressed buttons to read the last few results. Her blood sugar levels were finally looking more normal. Though he knew she'd definitely have the condition until after she gave birth.

"Good girl," he said with a smile. "Maybe you can have a cookie tonight."

Lizzy huffed. "I just had one—and it was worth it."

Lucas chuckled and stood up. "Is that the wonderful smell in the air?" He looked down at his sister-in-law. "Don't tell me you've been in the kitchen?"

"Not me. Esther's been here since before lunch."

After blinking in confusion, Lucas turned his gaze toward the kitchen.

Almost like a vision, Esther stood by the oven, not moving. Then suddenly, like she'd been shocked, she flinched and bent over the counter, pushing pieces of orange inside a chicken.

"Do you remember Esther Miller?" Lizzy continued. "She says she doesn't remember you."

"I did not say that." Esther's voice was quiet but firm.

"I, um, I do. Hallo." His pulse paused momentarily as he waited for Esther to look at him. The chicken, however, was getting all her attention.

It was a surreal moment—but so many moments in the last few weeks had felt surreal—seeing Esther in his brother's kitchen. It didn't make sense in his mind. Had they found out? Had Esther come looking for him and told Elizabeth everything?

But why would she do that? At this point, Lucas had nothing to lose by their secret being discovered. While Esther... If anyone found out, she'd have everything to lose.

"Hallo," she replied. "Of course I remember you."

He could only smile as a familiar warmth whooshed through his veins. Only minutes ago, he'd been wondering when he'd see her again. Be in the same room. And here they were. He didn't bother speculating over the how or why; he was too glad to care.

"She's been an enormous help," his sister-in-law said. "And we've had a fun afternoon, haven't we, Es?"

"Surely," Esther replied, finally a pretty smile brightening her face.

"Will you take me upstairs before you eat?" Lizzy asked, reaching for her husband.

"Anything you say." Jeremiah grinned. "Though I have been sweating like a pig."

"You think I care?"

Silently, he picked up his wife in his arms and disappeared up the stairs, leaving behind a longing in Lucas's heart for something he couldn't even name.

Until he looked at Esther.

Blue eyes, pink cheeks, the kindest heart he'd ever known, smiling at him from across the room.

"Can I help?" he asked, joining her in the kitchen.

"Wash your hands first," Esther requested, pointing her chin to the sink. "Scrub them clean."

"Yes, ma'am," he said, feeling a silly grin coming on. After giving his hands a scrubbing fit for surgery, he stood at her side—not too close.

"Is this one of those *things* you were going to tell me the other day?"

"Perhaps," he replied, unable to keep from grinning at her teasing tone.

"How did this happen?" she whispered. "How are you here?"

"It's a long story."

"Pull me off some rosemary," Esther said, sliding the bushy plant in front of him. "That will give you something to do while you tell me."

His shoulders shook with a silent laugh. "That morning I returned your buggy, we ran into each other—Jerry and me. He was out early working the farm and he…he just called out to me like it was perfectly normal." Simply by speaking the words, Lucas heard his voice strain as his throat tightened.

Esther became still. "What happened?"

"We talked," Lucas replied, snipping off a small branch of rosemary, bringing its strong fragrance into the air. "Then he…"

Slowly, Esther turned to him. "What?"

Lucas had to swallow first—the sweet memory still too tender in his mind. "He invited me inside with Elizabeth and the children. They weren't ashamed for me to meet my nephews. We talked for an hour, I helped him tend to the crops, and for a while, it felt like old times, like nothing's changed."

"Lucas." Her voice was hushed. "I'm so happy for you."

The air around him was warm and so soothing, he couldn't help but breathe it in, exhaling all the tension. "Thank you. I never imagined it could happen so naturally. I never allowed myself to even hope." He met her gaze. "I find myself hoping for many impossible things now."

A slam against the window behind them made Esther jump. Lucas turned to see Holmes, his eight-year-old nephew, left arm resting in a blue sling, laughing and running from the house, leaving behind a chunk of mud sliding down the glass.

"They've been playing with the chicks all day," Esther explained. "They're probably ready for some adult attention."

"I'll give him that, all right," Lucas said, grinning and pointing at Holmes through the window. "But first, why are you here today?"

"*Very* long story," Esther said, sprinkling salt and pepper over the chicken. "Well, not so long." She exhaled a soft chuckle. "I actually didn't know Lizzy was on bed rest. *Maam* asked me to drop off some tarts and canned goods. I did her one better and told Lizzy I'm staying with her until her folks return."

"I didn't realize you and Lizzy were close."

Esther shrugged. "We're not—we weren't. Not until today." She began rubbing the seasoning into the skin of the chicken. "I came by to help and…" She paused to smile. "We get along well. She's just lovely, Lucas, and the *kinnahs* are so well-behaved. They even ate my peanut butter sandwiches."

Lucas smiled and handed her more rosemary. "Is that not your strong suit?"

She laughed. "I'd rather take more time making recipes with complicated details."

"Like your soap."

"Exactly. Although I know that recipe by heart. You watch those cooking shows on television. I'm sure their recipes can get complicated." She shrugged, keeping her eyes down. "Maybe you can show me one sometime."

"I don't have cable anymore."

She glanced up at him. "No?"

"TV's gone, too."

"That's right." She lowered the rosemary in her hand. "Why is that, exactly?"

"I didn't need it in my life to begin with, and I've been altering some other things, as well. That day in town, I told you I have a lot to say to you." He turned to lean a hip against the counter so he could look directly at her. "I don't know how else to put it, but I've been feeling things—spiritual things that I haven't felt in years. My heart feels softer, more receptive to the idea of making some big changes."

He sighed. "The anger toward my father is softening, too."

"Lucas." Her voice was almost a whisper. "That's wonderful."

As they looked at each other, Lucas felt a need that was more and more difficult to deny.

"I haven't decided what to do next," he added, "but I feel…happy. I didn't know it was possible after all this time."

As if it were as effortless as breathing, Esther reached out and took his hand, giving it a squeeze. Lucas didn't care one bit that she was covered in chicken guts. "I'm so pleased for you," she said in a hush, actual tears rimming her eyes.

His chest felt tight, yet his heart was wide open. Not knowing how to reply, he simply squeezed her hand back.

"I have…" She paused to inhale deeply. "I have something I need to tell you…" She turned her blue eyes to look out the window where his nephews were playing. "But I don't think it's the right time."

"Another time, then?" he said, still gripping her hand.

"If we run into each other on the street," they said in near perfect unison.

Esther pressed her lips together, then chuckled. Lucas, too, couldn't stop himself from laughing. Upon hearing one of the little boys shriek, Esther quickly let go of his hand.

"Well, this looks great," Lucas said, peering at the chicken as they both moved to the sink. "I can't wait to try it."

Esther turned on the water with an elbow and

then handed Lucas a bar of soap. "You'll be here for dinner?"

"It's the weekend. I'd normally be working on my own garden, but Jerry's got his hands full."

"That's what Lizzy said. What are they going to do?" After drying her hands, Esther opened the oven and slid in the chicken.

"I was actually considering something—a plan. But it's…" When he didn't finish, Esther looked at him, causing him to sigh. "Well, it'll never work. I don't even want to say it."

"Have one," Esther said, straight-faced, shoving a small cookie with a dollop of jam into his mouth. The sugar and butter base immediately began dissolving on his tongue.

"Yum."

"Now." She faced him, dusting off her palms. "What can't you say?"

Lucas held up a finger and chewed as fast as he could. Esther rolled her eyes and tapped her foot impatiently.

"I was thinking maybe I could buy some of his land. We'd own it together."

Esther blinked. "*Jah*, that is…something to think about." She pressed her lips together. "How exactly would that work?"

Lucas groaned inwardly, wiping cookie crumbs from his mouth. "That's the thing. It won't. Outsiders like me don't belong in the community, and it'd put a horrible strain on Jerry. He doesn't need more stress."

While wearing a blank expression, Esther slid an entire cookie into her mouth and chewed in silence.

"There must be something you can do."

"Help him while staying completely under the radar. Like I said, I don't want to cause trouble for anyone." He made sure their eyes locked before he added, "Not anyone."

A smile curved Esther's lips. "A little late for that," she said, then dropped her blue-eyed gaze to the floor. Lucas watched in fascination as a lovely blush crawled up her throat, settling on her cheeks.

"I need to clean up," she said, as if not wanting her thoughts to go down the same path as his. Neither of them wanted trouble.

"I'll see what the kids are up to," Lucas said, needing space to clear his head.

"Would you help Holmes clean the mud off the window? Lizzy doesn't need stress, either."

"Good idea." As he started to leave, he turned back. "When I first walked in, I couldn't believe it was you. I'd just been thinking about you and—"

"Me too," Esther said. "Being here like this is a tender mercy from *Gott*. I believe that."

Lucas assumed he'd used up his allowance of tender mercies, but ever since having Esther in his life, blessings seemed to keep flowing his way.

What he couldn't understand was why *Gott* bothered to bless him if he still hadn't repented.

CHAPTER TWENTY-NINE

Esther awoke to blues skies, a golden sun, rainbows, and a sweet breeze. At least in her mind. Mother Nature had other ideas.

"It's been raining for an hour." Lizzy was in the kitchen by the time Esther came downstairs. "Jerry's in the barn, but there won't be much to do before church. Would you help me get the *kinnahs* ready? Jerry insists I stay home, but I won't allow my children to show up looking like they have no mother."

"Of course," Esther said, quickly pinning on her heart-shaped prayer *kapp*. "I should've been down here earlier. Let me make breakfast, too."

"It's all done," Lizzy said, wearing a big smile. "At least you know I'm not an invalid."

The two women laughed quietly, making Esther want to grin ear to ear, knowing she had a *gut* friend in Elizabeth Brenneman.

"I have a present for you," Esther said as she picked up her heavy cloak.

Elizabeth's eyes brightened. "From where?"

"I might've run home last night—it's real close. Here, for you." She pulled two bars of soap from her cloak pockets, eager to see the expression on Lizzy's face.

"Such pretty wrapping." She took the first one and held it up to her nose. "Smells like oranges."

"With a dash of vanilla."

"Yum." Lizzy took another sniff. "Thank you for

thinking of me."

"Smell this one." Esther grinned as she held out a bar from her most recent batch. "It's different."

"I like this wrapping, too. The rose ribbon is lovely." Just as before, she held the bar to her nose and sucked in a big breath. Halfway through her inhale, Lizzy erupted in a fit of coughing. "What *is* this?" she managed to choke out.

"Clove," Esther said dumbly, watching Lizzy drop the soap onto the floor and stand up, fleeing the area. "Too strong?"

Lizzy kept coughing, waving both hands in front of her face to clear the air. "I'd say so. Mercy, it's like a whole clove tree is in there." She walked to the large window in the living room and pulled it open. "I can hardly breathe. Why is it so potent?"

"I…" Esther began. "I'm sorry." She quickly grabbed the dented bar off the floor and put it in the inside pocket of her heavy cloak. "Sorry," she repeated.

"Why are you sorry?" Lizzy returned to the kitchen, hand over her chest. "It's not like you made the offensive thing."

Unable to reply, Esther felt sweat under her arms and the back of her neck, fighting the urge to burst into tears of humiliation.

"Anyway," Lizzy said, spreading butter over warm toast. "Last night was fun."

"*Jah,*" Esther answered through a wobbly chin, slapping a quick, yet fake, smile on her face.

"I didn't realize you knew Lucas so well."

Esther froze, embarrassment from the soap suddenly gone. "What do you mean?"

"When we were younger, I assumed you were closer to Jacob."

Esther tried to steady her heartbeats and breathing before she started uncontrollably blushing. "That's true. Lucas"—she was sure her voice cracked around the name—"was older than my friends."

"That's why it seemed strange how, I don't know, *comfortable* you two were at supper last night. I'm sorry, I suppose I should've warned you he'd be joining us. I'm sure your folks wouldn't approve."

Esther felt a pit in her stomach. "You think not?"

"Well, your mother's a sweetheart. She's got the biggest heart of anyone in Honey Brook. But your father…"

Esther couldn't help swallowing. "He's a bit more rigid," she said, agreeing with Lizzy's unspoken sentiments. "But Lucas is part of your family. If you decide it's okay for him to be here, that's not our business."

"That's another thing," Lizzy began. "I'm not sure even we can—"

Her friend was cut off when the little boys came rushing downstairs, eager for breakfast. Lizzy set to work at filling their plates. Esther tried to help, but her mind was fixed on Lizzy's unfinished sentence.

Had she been about to say that Lucas would no longer be allowed to visit his family? Was the *Ordnung* so strict as to not permit a brother to visit home again? That seemed unfair. Lucas hadn't been baptized, therefore he hadn't been officially shunned. Was the church unforgiving to the point that Lucas must sever contact with his family forever?

Or maybe Lizzy was going to say something

completely different.

Esther had no idea and was too shy to ask. Instead, she did her best to feed the boys and get them ready for church.

During the singings and the deacons' sermons, Esther struggled to stay focused. She tried to follow along in her Bible, to understand the words preached, to feel the Holy Spirit, but her mind was too tied up in what lay in store for Lucas.

She knew how grateful and ecstatic he was to be with his brother again. If that was all to be taken away, he'd be crushed. Her heart ached for him all the way through Bishop Abram's preaching.

After the services, they returned to the farm—the boys drenched from playing in the rain without umbrellas and without Lizzy there to keep them in line.

"I'll get a warm bath going," Esther said to Jeremiah as they neared the house. Upon entering, Esther noticed the three younger Zook girls were there preparing a new meal.

"Hi." Lizzy waved from the sofa—wrapped in a blanket, feet propped on a chair, Bible in hand. "Look who's here."

Esther smiled, happy to have more hands on board so she could get the boys cleaned up. "Hallo, girls. *Danke* for coming." She walked into the kitchen. "What are you making and how can I help?"

"Shepherd's pie," Lizzy said, "and you can't."

Confusion made her face get hot once more as she felt her jaw go slack. Was she being dismissed from her duties already? Had Lizzy somehow…found out?

"Since it's still sprinkling, and it's the Sabbath, and there's not much to do outside on a day like this, I've asked Lucas to run an errand for me in his truck."

"Oh," Esther said, playing nonchalant at the mention of his name, all the while longing to talk more about him. Before she could open her mouth, the distinct sound of a car engine and tires on the gravel road drew near.

"*Voilà*, as the French say." Lizzy said in a sing-song voice.

A swarm of butterflies flew into Esther's stomach, knowing she was about to see him.

"I'll get the crates from the shed," Jeremiah said. "Do not think about moving." He pointed at his wife who'd just thrown off her blanket. "We'll take care of everything."

Lizzy lifted her chin and groaned. "I was only going to tell Esther the rest."

Jeremiah blew a kiss to his wife before leaving the house. Esther tried not to look out the window when a car door shut. Lucas was right outside the house now, and she'd give anything for one look-see.

"Sorry," Lizzy said. "We need your help, too. I know it's the day of rest, but aren't you supposed to be at my beck and call?"

"Whatever you need," Esther said, knowing how difficult it was for Lizzy to ask a favor.

"Lucas is delivering our apple preserves over to the Weavers' store in Lancaster. They're not open today, but we can drop off the jars any time. Today seems as good a time as any. I'm sorry to have to ask, and tell me if this is completely inappropriate, but I was wondering if you'd go with him."

Esther's tongue felt too big for her mouth. "You want me to drive to Lancaster with Lucas?"

Lizzy began waving a hand around in the air. "It's a terrible idea. I shouldn't have asked."

"It's okay." Esther couldn't help laughing. "Tell me what you need."

"Well, I worry the Weavers will be hesitant if it's only Luke. They know you—or, their father knows your father—so it should be fine. Just tell them it's from us. Jerry will call them from his phone when we think they're home from church. You know Minister Jansen's sermons can go on for hours."

Esther's mind spun like a top, but she was not about to fritter away the opportunity to be alone with Lucas. "Of course, no problem. Does, um…" She couldn't help looking out the window. "Does Lucas have the address?"

"Jerry gave it to him. Also, Esther." Lizzy sat up straight. "Take your time, please. The roads are a mess from the rain, so make sure he drives slowly. Maybe you can find a place to stop for refreshments. You've helped us so much the past two days—I'd really like to repay you."

Esther was nearly giddy inside. Had Lizzy just given her permission to go on a date with Lucas?

"You have nothing to repay," Esther said, though unable to stop from grinning. "It's been my pleasure being in your home."

"You're sweet," Lizzy said, then lowered her voice. "The Zook girls really need to learn how to cook and clean. Heaven knows what their mother's been teaching them. Their being here is definitely a better use of resources, and, since your darling *maam* expects you to be gone for a while longer, I thought a little adventure for you might be fun."

Esther's grin widened. "As long as you think it's fine with Lucas."

"Oh, please." She waved another hand. "That man needs an adventure more than anyone."

CHAPTER THIRTY

The whole plan felt unreal to Lucas. Even now, as Esther sat beside him in the front seat of his truck, it seemed he was being blessed beyond every good deed he'd ever done.

"Stopped raining," she said, then rolled down the window. She appeared the cheerful, carefree girl as she slid on a pair of round sunglasses and slanted her face out the window. When a gust of wind nearly blew off her prayer *kapp*, she grabbed its ties and sat back.

"Learned from last time?" he asked.

"Did I tell you my mother was awake when I got home that night? I nearly forgot I wasn't wearing my bonnet."

Lucas ran a hand over his mouth. "What did she say?"

"Nothing, really. She asked where it was, and I answered honestly that I had no idea."

Too easily, he recalled in perfect detail how she'd looked when arriving at his house that day: her blond hair loose and wild over her shoulders. Before his mind got too far away, he gripped the steering wheel and concentrated on the road.

"If I neglected to tell you before I left last night, dinner was delicious."

Esther exhaled a sweet, feminine laugh. "You did tell me, five times."

"Did I?"

She nodded. "And thank you—for the sixth time."

As they drove, she asked more questions about that day in the field when he'd reconnected with Jeremiah. Lucas was more than happy to share every detail. The more he spoke of it out loud, the more it truly did feel like he was home.

Far sooner than expected, they arrived in Lancaster. His brother's directions were easy to follow, and James Weaver's farm quickly came into view.

"Back in," Esther directed. "It'll be easier to unload. Wait, let me jump out first."

Before he could put the truck in park, she leaped like a graceful kid goat, running to greet James Weaver on the front porch. He watched them chat; then Esther waved her arms, directing him to pull beside the barn.

"Hallo," James Weaver said, coming to Lucas's open window. "Mighty nice of you to come all this way for your brother."

"No problem," Lucas replied. "Let me help you unload."

"Looks like your wife's already taking care of it."

For a second, Lucas was confused, until James gestured at Esther carrying a small crate of jars.

"She's not…" He allowed his voice to fade out, deciding to soak in the "what if?" feeling, as ridiculous as it was. "I'll give her a hand!" he added when his fantasy quickly flew past ridiculous.

He unloaded the biggest crate, feeling his pulse speed up as they passed each other, purposely making his shoulder bump against hers. Mostly in silence, they worked side by side, Esther's playful eye contact making Lucas want to take her by the shoulders like he had on the street all those weeks ago. This time, however, he wanted to complete the action by pulling her close.

He wasn't sure if his arms ached at the thought of touching her like that or because of the heavy crates.

In a matter of minutes, their job was done. Lucas started the truck while Esther disappeared inside the house. A few moments later, she reappeared, carrying a basket. Lucas opened her door, relishing her sunny smile as she climbed inside.

"What's that?" he asked after shifting into reverse.

"A picnic."

"For us?"

She nodded. "Mary Weaver gave me directions to a spot she said is really nice." She smiled and sat back. "Drive east. I'll tell you when to turn."

Lucas knew better than to ask questions, so he backed up, then headed due east, the sun peeking through the clouds.

"How's work at the clinic?" she asked, rolling down the window again.

Prepared to share nothing gorier than the three flu shots he'd administered, Lucas suddenly decided to go a different way. "I'm treating a fourteen-year-old boy," he began, gripping the steering wheel. "The other day when I told you I'd be out of town, I went with him and his father to the Hershey Medical Center."

"Can I ask what's wrong with him?"

"I don't know yet; that's the problem. And he's Amish."

Esther rolled up her window so the car was quiet. "Does that make his illness more difficult to cure?"

"It definitely won't in this case. The father is prepared for treatment. He said he'll do whatever it takes. I don't mind telling you that was a huge relief to hear. We're still waiting on test results. I'm hopeful but"—he paused to run a fist over his mouth—"I've seen too many worst-case scenarios. He seems like a good kid, and his father's pretty great."

When it was silent for a moment, Lucas glanced at Esther. She was chewing on a thumbnail—which he recognized now as one of her nervous tics.

"What do you want to know?" he asked her.

After a sigh, she lowered her hand. "What test did he have at the hospital?"

Now was Lucas's turn to fall silent. Esther sure had a way of drilling right down to the point. "Bone marrow," he finally said, hearing his voice thicken.

"Oh, Lucas." Esther's whisper sounded broken, too. "I'm so sorry."

Neither had to say who they were both thinking about.

"It's…" When he didn't finish the sentence, Esther reached out and placed her hand on his where it was still clutching the steering wheel. It was soft and warm, comforting in a way he hadn't realized he needed. He loosened his grip, allowing his fingers to curl around hers.

It wasn't a good idea, he knew it wasn't, yet he couldn't let go. Since she'd held his hand so tenderly the day before, it was all he could think about, wondering if he'd ever touch her like that again.

"You're a good man, Lucas," she said, breaking the silence. "I hope you know that."

He could only shrug, feeling light-headed when she placed her other hand around his.

"What's his name?"

"Tanner."

"Tanner," Esther repeated. "I have a second cousin in Ohio with that name." She squeezed his hand. "Tanner's going to get better. I know I'm not a medical expert, but he will."

"I hope you're right," he said, then couldn't resist repositioning their hands so their fingers interlocked. He took his eyes off the road for one long moment, needing to read her expression.

Moses Miller's Esther was smiling, lovely blue eyes fixed on him, the faintest hint of a blush on her beautiful face.

The urge inside him was almost painful. Why was he allowing himself to feel attracted to a woman he couldn't have?

"Sorry," he said, dropping her hand so he could take the wheel after purposefully driving over a bump. "I think we're almost there."

Esther glanced down at the map. "How would you know?"

"I have a feeling for these things."

"Oh yeah?" He couldn't help hearing the flirty tone in both their voices. He should've been man enough to control himself, but today he didn't care. "Fork in the road."

"Yep," she said, consulting the map again. "Left for a bit, then pull off by that willow."

Lucas obeyed, following Esther's orders as if they were a couple in real life—still playing the "what if?" game.

"Over there." Esther pointed at a lush meadow with ankle-high green grass and wildflowers. Trees with yellow and orange leaves created a natural perimeter.

"It rained all morning," he said, lamely pointing out the obvious.

Esther glanced at him from over her shoulder. "Is it raining now?"

He dipped his chin and chuckled. "No, ma'am."

She displayed a blanket under her arm. After parking, Lucas carried the basket, following behind, letting Esther lead the way. After turning in a circle, she finally declared this was the place and spread out the thick wool blanket—easily thick enough to protect them from the damp ground.

"You've had a good few days," she said while unloading the food, her dark red dress and black cloak flaring out around her.

"That's an understatement."

The tinkle of her laughter coiled around his heart. "Jeremiah and Lizzy are clearly thrilled to have you back. And you should've seen the boys light up when they heard you arrive."

Another gush of warmth spread through him, recalling how his youngest nephew had run straight to him, asking to play flying angel again. "I don't mean to sound dramatic, but it's like a miracle."

She handed him a sandwich wrapped in a cloth napkin. "That doesn't sound so dramatic."

"I just wish—" He cut himself off and stared into

the middle distance, wondering if he was really about to share what was in his heart. "I guess I wish for more. I wish it could be like it was."

Esther placed her sandwich on her lap. "What does that mean?"

He rubbed his palms together, then made double fists, trying to settle his suddenly twitchy muscles. "I had a good life here; I remember that. I had beliefs and faith in things more important than science could prove. Even back when I was planning on leaving home to help Jacob, I felt a higher power guiding me. And now, I'm somehow back where I started." He let out a long exhale, focusing on one puffy white cloud. "I wonder if coming full circle is even possible—"

"It is," Esther blurted as if she'd had the words ready for a week.

It was quiet for a moment, until the birds, possibly itching to stretch their wings after the rain, began chirping and singing.

"I didn't mean to interrupt," she said, "but I couldn't let you doubt that." She put her sandwich back in the basket, then shifted her sitting position so she was an inch or two closer to him. The movement made the hair on Lucas's arms stand up.

"*Gott* loves us and knows us down to the most private corners in our hearts. You're the one who reminded me of that," she added. "We're taught repentance on a literal level. If we change our hearts and confess our sins, we can be forgiven of anything." She paused, clasping and unclasping her hands until they settled in the prayer position. "Do you believe that?"

Lucas couldn't help closing his eyes, recalling an incident just that morning after he'd offered a silent prayer before breakfast. He'd paused at the end, allowing his soul to rest in a moment of meditation. When his thoughts drifted to the possibility of coming home—really coming home all the way—the peace that had swept over him was almost all-encompassing.

"I do." The words drifted out as a whisper. When he opened his eyes, sweet Esther Miller wore the most compassionate smile on her lovely face.

As a wave of unidentifiable emotion swept over his body, his chest burned, while his limbs felt nearly too heavy to move. Still, he couldn't help himself.

Without thinking, he scooted so he was sitting directly in front of her, then reached out and cupped her cheek, running his thumb over her skin. He was so close that he both heard and felt her take in a sharp inhale.

He hadn't meant to startle her, but before he could command himself to move away, Esther placed her hand over his. The earth froze on its axis until he heard her inhales, coming in erratic patterns, as were his.

Slowly, he leaned forward, touching his forehead to hers, pressing their coiled hands to his chest. He could feel her breath, the warmth and smoothness of her skin. He lifted his gaze to hers, expecting hers to be lowered. Instead, he was met with her bright, eager, beautiful sapphire eyes.

"Lucas," she whispered, her soft breath sweeping over him like a breeze, causing a heat wave to push through his body.

"Esther," he said, echoing her same serious tone.

He felt her start to shake, suppressing a silent laugh. While staying focused on her eyes, he slowly, regretfully removed his hand from her cheek.

"I don't believe my actions were unwelcomed."

"Nay," she said, though her gaze dropped to their touching knees.

"Unexpected?"

He heard her exhale a laugh. "Maybe. But at the same time, I was wondering what took you so long."

CHAPTER THIRTY-ONE

Esther could still sense the touch of his hand on her cheek, the warmth of his rough but tender skin. Feeling his breath on her face was like breathing for the first time. It had been unexpected when he'd reached out to her, but no, not unwelcome.

"I've been having…feelings," she said, still a bit nervous to admit, yet surely he could see it all over her face.

"I should hope so." He nudged her shoulder, and Esther couldn't help laughing, using the moment to take in a few deep breaths. "I have feelings, too," he added, his voice firm, brown eyes focused on her.

Somehow, she already knew this, yet hearing it caused a happy tingling sizzle to ribbon around her spine.

"I don't know when it started," he continued, "but I think about you all the time, and not just as a good friend or as the girl my brother wanted to marry—and believe me, I'm well aware of all the trouble it could cause you. It'd make trouble for Jerry's family, too." He sat back and raked both hands through his curly hair, his expression turning frustrated.

"Lucas, we're not doing anything wrong," she said, running the words through her mind first, making sure they felt truthful.

"I'm an outsider."

"For now."

He pushed a hand through his hair again. "You know it's not that simple."

As she glanced over his shoulder, focusing on a weeping willow tree, Esther couldn't help mentally listing all the worldly possessions Lucas would have to do without if he decided to live plain again. His truck, electricity at home, many basic creature comforts and technologies, and most importantly, his professional job.

Esther's throat felt tight—she couldn't imagine him ever giving up his position of helping people medically.

And though it was unspoken, she knew neither of them wanted to dishonor Jacob's memory.

"You're beautiful."

His words made her look at him. Tenderness filled his light brown eyes. He tipped his head to the side as if examining her from a new angle. She felt a silly, romantic flutter in her tummy as his gaze seemed to slide over her.

"And you're stubborn and kind," he continued.

"Lucas," she said, knowing her throat, cheeks, and ears were probably bright red.

"You've made me feel good about myself again, about other people, and maybe about the whole world in general. I'm happier now, more at peace, and I like myself better these days."

Hearing his words spoken with such boldness should've made Esther shy and embarrassed, but somehow, she felt more connected to the earth, anchored to her beliefs in a celestial power, attached to the man sitting across from her.

"And now," Lucas continued, "I don't feel

nervous about doing this." Like it was nothing, he scooped up her hand, intertwining their fingers. When he gave a gentle squeeze, tiny pinpricks traveled up and down Esther's neck, his nearness making it harder to breathe quietly.

"Lucas," she said around the lump in her throat, "you're so...well, you're so very..."

Wonderful, she tried to say. *And giving and patient and such a good listener. And handsome. And when you look at me like you are right now, I want to...*

"You like me, too," he said, smiling when she couldn't finish the sentence. "That's all I need to know now."

"*Jah*. I like you." The understated words made her laugh.

He sighed, then lifted his other hand. Without needing instructions, Esther reached out and took it, butterflies and bluebirds and angels flying circles around her heart.

"We're supposed to be having a picnic," he said, pulling back a corner of his mouth into a crooked grin.

"Chicken, cheese, and pickle sandwiches," Esther replied, wanting to freeze this moment forever. "And freshly baked sticky buns."

"Yum." When Lucas ran his tongue over his lips, Esther felt like a fire had lit inside her core.

"We should, um, eat now," she said. "Don't you think?"

Lucas slowly shook his head, that grin growing. "Not until I do this." He lifted one set of their hands, drawing the back of her hand to his mouth, giving it a short, soft kiss.

A dazzling chill ran up her spine, circling and whirling on the way down, making her feel almost faint. "Lucas," she whispered.

"Luke," he corrected.

She smiled, blinking her eyelashes. "Luke."

"It's what the closest people in my life call me."

The only thing she could do was squeeze his hand, hoping that would prompt him to kiss it again—the delicious sensation still pushing through her body.

"Shall we start with dessert?"

"What?"

He raised an eyebrow. "The sticky buns. We should eat them first if they're still warm." A moment later, both her hands were free, and Luke was dragging the picnic basket over to her.

Esther knew she couldn't just sit there like a little girl daydreaming about her handsome prince, but somehow, she couldn't get herself to move.

"Do you want a fork, or do you want to eat them like me with my bare hands?" He leaned toward her, then released a throaty growl. "I know you love my aardvark impression."

Finally, Esther's fingers and toes tingled with life, and she giggled. "Irresistible," she said, rolling her eyes. She removed the two sandwiches from the basket, placing one on Luke's leg. "Sweets after," she said, holding out her hand until he gave her the sticky bun.

"Told you you're stubborn."

"But kind," Esther said, remembering his words.

Lucas's shoulders relaxed as he looked at her. "The kindest woman I know."

She wanted to touch him again. Hold his hand, maybe stroke his cheek, twist a piece of his curly hair around a finger. The curiosity of how it would feel was almost blinding.

"How's the wedding dress coming?"

Esther had to blink a few times, and when she focused on him, he'd taken a few bites of his sandwich.

"Um, it's almost finished, actually. My sister Anna and I are doing the final fittings for Sarah's attendants. Four more dresses." Quickly, she took a bite of her sandwich.

Mary Weaver had prepared a very tasty lunch for them, and as they ate, they chatted about the wedding, Esther sharing the near disaster when Sarah was suddenly down a dress size. "She's nervous," she said, passing Luke a red apple. "I don't think she's eating enough. I'll probably have to take in her dress once more before the wedding."

"Pretty stressful time, I'd say," Lucas added after wiping his mouth.

"Not for her. Sarah's hardly done a thing, even though her fingers are totally healed. Oh." Catching the expression on Luke's face, she pressed her lips together in remorse. "I guess I don't sound all that kind right now."

Luke laughed, wadding up a napkin in his fist. "We all have room for repentance."

Just then, a gust of wind blew one of the napkins away. "I'll get it!" Esther said, climbing to her feet to give chase. Another gust carried another wrapper into the sky. While she ran one way, Luke ran the other. When they'd both retrieved the trash, they returned to the blanket.

"Here," he said, handing her the napkin.

She laughed, barely keeping her *kapp* from falling off. "Thanks."

"Let me help you with that." As if he'd done it a hundred times, Luke reached out and put his two hands on the top of her head, pulling her head covering back into place.

They stood so close, she easily inhaled his manly smell, felt the warmth of him, the weight of his hands.

"Thank you again," he said, dropping his hands but not backing away.

"For what?"

"In a roundabout way, because of you, I got to see Jerry, Lizzy, and the *kinnahs*." His shoulders lifted when he inhaled. "I thought my entire family was lost to me. But then that stupid buggy…"

"Don't blame Peanut for your reckless driving."

He chuckled under his breath. "I blame you for distracting me." He wound a loose piece of her hair around a finger, sending tingles up Esther's spine. "I blame you for every wonderful thing that's happened since the day you stormed into the clinic, disturbing my lunch."

Esther's heart pounded at the memory. "You had a dot of cottage cheese right there." Without hesitation, she touched a finger to the corner of his mouth. Luke turned his chin, kissing her finger. Her breath hitched, imagining him putting an arm around her next.

"Esther." His voice was somber. "We have some problems."

"Yes," she whispered, unafraid. "You're not Amish."

"I know."

"You still haven't talked to your father—or your *mother*, Luke."

He nodded, lowering his gaze from hers. "I know."

"Are you ever going to? I'm asking you seriously."

"I don't know." He exhaled slowly. "I don't know if I can forgive him."

"Well, that's a mighty big problem."

"We seem to have a few of those."

She bit her lip. "I was engaged to Jacob."

"I know that, too. Whenever I think about holding your hand or touching your face, I feel so guilty. It's like he's always with me."

"He's with me, too," Esther added in agreement. "Between us. Right here." She gestured at the space between their two bodies, the great distance that must always separate them.

Suddenly, Luke lifted his chin, looking her dead in the eyes. The next second, he stepped into that empty space, filling it with his body. Esther gasped as his arms wound around her, pulling her in to his chest. Before she could breathe again, he'd completely enfolded her, holding her tightly to him as if he was afraid she'd fly away.

She didn't fight the impulse but wrapped her arms around him just as tight, pressing her cheek against his beating heart, fisting the back of his shirt. She slammed her eyes shut, wanting to absorb every second.

The hug lasted a million delicious years, draining strength from her body yet filling her with an even stronger inner strength.

"It's raining." The words came as if floating from heaven.

She opened her eyes to see Luke gazing at her, a raindrop clinging to the end of his nose. She lifted her chin toward the sky, only to get pelted with dozens of them.

"We need to get to the truck."

Esther was still happily enveloped in the dreamy memory of their embrace while Luke gathered the picnic. A moment later, his hand was around hers, guiding her to the road. The storm had hit so fast that they were soaked to the skin when they climbed inside the truck.

"What's the smile for?"

"Hmm?"

He sank his two index fingers into the corners of her turned-up mouth. "Your smile can be seen from space."

At the simple touch, she melted—just a little. "Because I'm happy."

"Well, that's obvious." One side of Luke's mouth pulled into a grin. "Me too."

A euphoric tingle ran up her back, causing her to shiver.

"Cold?"

"Freezing," she suddenly discovered, wrapping her arms around herself when she shivered again. "We're all wet."

"You know what they say about how to share body heat to keep warm?"

She felt her eyebrows squish together. "No. What?"

Luke didn't say anything for a moment, but then

he chuckled under his breath, as if enjoying a private joke. "Never mind," he finally said. "Here." He straightened his right arm, holding it out to the side. Inviting her to him.

Ignoring what might be improper, Esther slid over the bench seat, cozily positioning herself inside the crook of his arm. She felt him exhale as both of his arms wrapped around her. She didn't care that they were both sopping from the rain—it felt so right to be in his arms again, to breathe in the smell of his shirt.

Before today, I never hugged a man who wasn't a relative. One of his hands moved to the back of her head, cradling it so tenderly. *Not even Jacob. He wanted a hands-off relationship before we married.* Never once had he held her hand while they'd rode in his buggy or strolled together in her father's peach orchard. Never put an arm around her like Luke.

The thought made her suck in a gasp, but she didn't move away.

"I…" Luke said, giving her shoulder a gentle pat. "I better take you back."

Relief mixed with a stab of regret pricked her heart. "Why?" After he patted her shoulder again, Esther sat up.

When he looked at her, his eyes were dark and intriguing, his ears a little red. "Because." He turned away to stare out the windshield, massaging the back of his neck. "Because I want to kiss you."

"Oh." It was a dumb thing to say, but Esther's mind was blank. Once or twice in her whole life had she imagined what it might feel like to kiss a man, but she'd never been in the literal circumstance to actually do it.

Lip kissing wasn't supposed to happen until a couple was engaged. If Esther was serious about being obedient, she needed to restrain. So she sucked in her lips, pressing down with her jaw so they stayed sealed shut. That's when she noticed the lines running across Luke's forehead, the soberness in his expression, and how his hands gripped the steering wheel so tightly, his fingers were white.

"Yes," she whispered, frightened by the sudden desire that was making her heart pound in her ears. "We better go right now."

CHAPTER THIRTY-TWO

"You need to see your mother."

They'd been on the road for a few minutes, neither of them saying much besides how the rain wouldn't let up. Not even the heater on high was making a dent in their drenched skin and clothes.

"It's not that simple," Lucas replied, still fighting back the urge to pull the truck off the road so he could kiss her.

"You said that before." Her impatient tone cut into his thoughts. "I'm being very serious now, Luke. I know you've got an issue with your father, but that has nothing to do with reaching out to your *maam*."

"Esther," he said, shaking his head.

"What?" She rotated her body to face him directly. "Were you about to say this is none of my business? Because you know it is."

He'd loved the feel of her in his arms, the softness of her body, and how she'd come right to him, no hesitation at all. Now he wanted to kiss her wholly so she wouldn't ask any more questions.

"What's the worst that could happen?" she asked.

He sighed and scratched his head, knowing she wasn't going to drop the subject. "She shuns me."

"She'd never, ever do that. What else?"

He adjusted his position in the seat. "Okay, my father finds out and gets angry with her. Or the bishop hears word. The whole family could be in a lot of trouble."

After a few quiet moments, Esther said, "Luke, I want to hold your hand, but that's not the best idea right now. What I would ask you, though, while holding your hand is, don't you think it's worth the risk?"

"Yes," he admitted. Again, Esther had drilled straight down to the heart of the matter. "But I do not need your help with it."

"Ha!" When he glanced at her, she was grinning. He wanted to reach out and take ahold of her sweet face, if only to get her to stop talking.

"Listen," he said instead, needing to be completely honest. "You've become a bright light in my life."

"Don't change the subject by flirting."

"I'm not." He exhaled a groan, driving by that familiar fork in the road. "I'm trying to tell you that I care about you very much."

She tilted her head. *"Jah?"*

"You don't have to sound so pleased about it. We're in a real jam here."

"I know." Her voice was subdued this time. "Do you think...? Forgive me, this is a very personal question but, do you think you'd ever talk to Bishop Abram?"

For the last few days, Lucas had actually been wondering the same thing. He knew he'd made a lot of changes lately, deciding to live more simply, without distractions that once seemed so important. He felt closer to *Gott* than he had in years, and the draw to return to the church nudged him more and more every day.

But taking the actual steps. Sacrificing even more. Meeting with the leaders of the church face-to-face…

"Maybe," was all he could say.

He half expected Esther to unleash an excited squeal or clap her hands and whoop. But when he looked at her—all the way over by the passenger door—she was simply smiling, just as she had when he'd told her about canceling his cable and getting rid of the TV, feeling the Holy Spirit again.

"There's still…a lot," she said.

"Yeah." He nodded, not needing her to explain further.

"Yeah," she echoed, sounding distant. "But do you think… I'm not sure how to put it."

"You've already yelled at me once today and mocked me. And I won't even mention all the scandalous hand-holding. You shouldn't feel shy to ask anything."

"Okay." She shook her head, laughing. "To be honest, what I was going to ask is if you think we'll be able to figure it out?"

Hearing her use the "we" pronoun gave him more confidence than when he'd aced his first gross anatomy exam. He hadn't had time to even begin the process of weighing his options before she spoke again.

"Never mind," she said, crossing her arms and looking forward. "I don't want you to answer yet, because I'm still thinking, too."

"Fair enough," Lucas said.

As he drove, they chatted about meaningless things—both their heads and hearts too full of weightier subjects than could be spoken right then.

"When will I see you again?" she asked as they turned onto the road leading to Honey Brook.

"I'm assuming at supper tonight at Jerry's."

Esther's eyes brightened. "It's still so thrilling that you've reconnected with your brother. I see how happy it makes you."

The heavenly expression on her face only strengthened his fortitude. Perhaps they could go on just like this for a while longer. Meet at Jeremiah's, take private walks. If they were careful, maybe she could come to his house again, sit together and talk. After all, he was perfectly capable of controlling his actions while around her.

The thought of testing his strength made him grin.

"Yes," he said under his breath. "We'll figure it out."

Right at that moment, Lucas felt like he could take on any challenge. Anything thrown his way, he could handle. The world was his—he just had to figure out how and when to make the big decisions, those really big changes.

As he turned down a gravel road, Jeremiah's house came into view. A buggy he didn't recognize was parked in front of the barn. Visitors must be calling on them. Probably someone to check on Lizzy.

When they drew nearer, Lucas noticed two people on the front porch. Jerry was facing him, but at first, he couldn't see the other man. As he was about to toot his horn and wave, the other man turned in his direction.

Lucas's heart slammed against his ribs as he immediately recognized Abram, the bishop. Without thinking, he took his foot off the gas, slowing their approach. His eyes locked with Jerry's. The second he read the dread on his brother's face and the almost imperceptible shaking of his head, panic seized hold of his body.

Impulsively, he reached out, put a hand on Esther's head, and, as gently as he could, nudged her down onto the roomy floor of the truck. "Stay there," he said, then laid on the gas, speeding past the house, all while making sure his face was turned the other way.

His heart pumped like a New York City street jackhammer as he steered around a few corners until they were safely out of view, then parked, his hands trembling.

"I'm so sorry," he said, pulling back his hand. She wasn't struggling to get free, hadn't struggled at all, actually. "Sorry," he repeated. "You can get up."

For a moment, Esther didn't move, and he worried he might have scared her or, worse, hurt her physically. Before he could ask, though, she climbed onto the seat, her prayer *kapp* askew, damp dress wrinkled, strings of hair hanging over her pale face.

Hot, painful guilt flushed through his body as he reached out to touch her shoulder, then withdrew his hand, not wanting to make it worse. "I didn't mean to scare you," he said, his throat tight, "but there wasn't time to explain. Abram—"

"I saw him," she said, her voice level, though she was breathing fast. She stared straight ahead, making Lucas recall Jerry's expression: the fear and dread on his face when he'd seen Lucas approaching. It didn't take a genius to understand what was going on.

The leader of their church was paying a visit, no doubt wondering why Lizzy hadn't been at church, which was customary. Perhaps he'd given Jerry a lecture about the importance of Sunday preaching attendance. Bishop might've even given him an official warning—it didn't take many of those before his family would be in hot water with the church, even with Lizzy on prescribed bed rest.

And then *he* had been about to drive up in his English truck. The prodigal son sneaking around with Esther Miller at his side. Just thinking about what Jerry must've been feeling—the alarm and dismay of Bishop discovering his family had been allowing Lucas in their home, to be with his children, to sit at their dinner table—made Lucas want to punch his fist through the windshield.

He'd been careless. Thoughtless. Not only could that have been terrible for his brother's family, but how could he explain why Esther was with him? Her reputation in the community, her standing in the church, and even her family's standing would be in jeopardy.

Thoughtless! he shouted inwardly. His actions could have easily destroyed the lives of the people he loved so much, it hurt.

"Why didn't you stop?"

At the sound of Esther's voice, he turned to her. "Because he'd see me. He'd see you."

"You could've talked to him."

"Not now."

"Why?"

"Because…it's not the right time."

"It's the perfect time." She turned to gesture behind them, back at Jerry's house.

"Not yet."

"Luke." The tone of her voice immediately turned tender, and she took his hand. "I'll be right beside you. It'll be okay."

Again, he pictured Jerry's face, the terror that seemed to have filled his brother's eyes as he'd approached. Not even the warmth and softness of her skin could make that picture go away.

"Unless… Oh."

After a hard blink, Lucas watched Esther drop his hand and scoot back, her face ashen and confused.

"You changed your mind. You're not going to talk to him. You didn't mean what you said. You didn't mean any of it."

Was she right?

For a moment, there were no words. No noise or even sounds of nature. The heavy, hard, slow beating of his heart was all Lucas felt as his brain continued its downward spiral. That feeling inside his chest that only minutes ago had been flying so high with happiness was now crumpled like a piece of paper thrown in the trash.

Before he spoke again, he closed his eyes. *Please, dear Lord, if her pain is half as much as mine, take it from her. Make me feel it all—not her.* After pressing his lips together, he added, *I know I deserve it.*

"I'll take you home. Good luck with the wedding. I'm sorry."

She looked at him. "That's it?"

He almost laughed, his soul feeling black and hollow. "What more is there to talk about? I was stupid. This is over—it has to be." At the sound of her ragged breathing, he longed to rip his heart out of his chest.

This had been his fault. He should've stopped everything when his feelings evolved. He should've been bold and told her flat out that it could never work. Almost robotically, he started the truck, steering onto the road, turning a corner toward the Miller farm.

A heavy, breath-squelching silence filled the cab. There were so many things he wanted to say. He wanted to explain further how he felt, that it was killing him inside to tell her it was over. But he couldn't speak. Apparently, neither could she. Either she was too sad or too angry at his dismissive words to say anything.

In the darkest corner of his heart, Lucas hoped it was the latter. If she hated him, her heartache would be shorter lived.

Without a word, he pulled to a stop thirty yards from the house. "You should get out here," he said, hoping his voice sounded stronger than he felt. "No one will see you."

Esther reached for the door handle but then turned back. Her eyes were red, yet no tears stained her cheeks. It wasn't sadness that showed on her face but confusion.

Which was somehow worse.

"Bye," he said, trying not to choke on the single, merciless syllable.

If she kept looking at him like that, he would take it all back; he'd hold her in his arms and tell her he'd made a mistake. If he had any hope of salvaging the lives of the people he loved, as well as his own, she needed to get out of his truck.

He wasn't sure when she'd left or if she'd said another word to him. The scent of clove and vanilla soap was all that remained of Esther Miller.

Spent in every way, he dropped his head into his hands and tried to breathe. For better or worse, his life had changed yet again. All those heaven-sent blessings felt so far out of reach now, leaving him more alone than ever.

His first instinct was to pray for help and comfort. He'd learned to turn to *Gott* first again. But as he sat there, pain and disappointment so fresh in his heart, praying was the last thing he wanted to do. Why would a loving God dangle hope in his path only to jerk it away?

Ironically, that was a question he ached to discuss with Esther.

He lifted his chin and stared out the windshield. It was pouring down rain, which fit his black mood. He shifted the truck into gear and drove home, clenching his jaw the entire way, wondering if he'd ever again have a reason to drive into Honey Brook.

CHAPTER THIRTY-THREE

As if in a daze, Esther didn't go straight to the house but instead, her heavy feet led her to the grove of cherry trees behind the barn. Knowing no one would be out there on a soggy Sunday, she sank to the ground and held her hands over her face.

Thanks to the rain, she could be as loud as she wanted and no one would hear.

When she helplessly replayed his words of goodbye, she began to sniffle. When she pictured his face, tears pricked her eyes. When she thought about that night they'd sat together on his couch, thumbing through his scrapbook, sharing their feelings about life and *Gott* and what it meant to have true faith, she cried so hard, she couldn't breathe.

Why had *Gott* allowed this? If He loved her and wanted to bless her, why had He put Lucas Brenneman in her path?

After two years of suffering, she hadn't meant to have feelings for anyone, and she was sure that hadn't been Lucas's plan, either. She wrapped her arms tightly around her middle, trying to keep from crumbling.

When the sun came out from the clouds, she noticed it was arching closer to the horizon. How long had she been tucked away inside the orchard?

Struggling from tired muscles, she made her way to her feet, feeling shaky, light-headed, and worn out, taking one step at a time toward home. Her dress was damp, but her cheeks were dry. She'd run out of reasons to cry hours ago.

She needed the warmth and strength of *Maam*'s arms. When she'd been a little girl, *Maam* always made the badness go away with one of her hugs or a freshly baked pumpkin whoopee pie. Esther's stomach heaved at the thought of food and also at the thought of letting *Maam* see her in this condition.

Still struggling to move forward, Esther realized what she really wanted was to be alone. To crawl into bed, pull the covers over her head, and stay there for a week—no family, no friends, no duties. Maybe after that, she could face the world again.

"Es! There you are."

Esther actually groaned when she saw Sarah walking toward her, holding up her long skirt.

"What are you doing out here?" Sarah gave her a visual once-over. "You're drenched."

"Jah." Esther sniffed.

"I looked everywhere for you. *Maam* said you were at Lizzy Brenneman's, but Lizzy said you'd come home."

"Jah," she repeated, nodding, trying to keep her eyes fixed on the muddy ground.

"Do you think we should take in my dress one more time?" She put her hands on her hips, as if checking her waist size. "The wedding's in less than two weeks."

"If you want." Esther sniffed again, wishing it would start to rain so her sister would go away.

"Hey, are you all right?" Sarah came up beside her. "Your eyes are red. Do you have a fever?" She placed a hand over Esther's forehead. "You don't feel hot." She dropped her hand and glanced around. "Es, are you out here for a reason? It's getting cold. Come home."

"No," Esther said stubbornly, her body going tense.

"What's the matter?" Sarah linked an arm through hers. "Come inside, and you can finish sewing the inner pocket of my dress."

It didn't matter that she was cold and shivering, Esther couldn't stand being touched by anyone. "Sarah, can I please have one whole day to not think about your wedding—or any wedding?"

"Why?"

She wanted to laugh. "Because you might not have noticed, but being so deeply involved in yours—making your dress, planning the meals—has been exceptionally difficult for me."

Sarah's lips formed an *O*, as if she was about to ask why.

"Sister, I know you're not purposefully trying to make me miserable, but could you take one minute and think how this might be affecting me?"

"Affecting you?" she echoed, blinking rapidly. Esther was not about to help her along, but stood there watching her sister's eyes run back and forth.

"Jacob?" There was clear hesitation in Sarah's voice.

Something about hearing the name again made Esther want to cry. "Yes."

"Oh. I'm… I haven't thought about that—or him—in a really long time. Do you miss him?"

"Of course."

Sarah cracked her thumb knuckle, then began wringing her hands. "Do you still love him?"

Esther couldn't reply right away. There was no right answer. "No," she finally said. "But I feel like I should, because when I even imagine a happy life without him, I feel guilty. And now when I actually do want to move on, the guilt is worse."

"You have a beau," Sarah stated, then held up a hand. "I know it's not Levi. I was teasing you that day."

"I don't have a beau," Esther replied honestly, wrapping her arms around her body to stop the shivering, absolutely not picturing Luke's face.

"But you like someone. You want to move on."

Esther sank to the earth, feeling the mud soak into the back of her dress. It shocked her when Sarah joined her on the wet ground. "You don't have to stay out here."

"I know," Sarah said, her voice light. "I just…feel bad."

Esther couldn't help peering at her through her eyelashes. "It's about time."

"Sorry. I can see why it'd be hard for you." She lifted her shoulders and let them drop. "Thank you for all you've done. I know I'm not the easiest person to get along with."

Esther laughed, then gave her sister's arm a nudge. "You're welcome. At least it's almost over, right?"

Sarah took in a deep breath, then blew it out through rounded lips. "The days are flying by so fast. I can't believe it's almost time." She rubbed her lips together. "I really love him. I know it's silly because

I've known Amos my whole life, but it's different now when we're together. I know he'd do anything for me, even the most difficult, painful task."

Like facing his father, Esther thought, causing her chest to heave. *That's something Lucas can't do. Not for himself—and definitely not for me.*

"About Jacob," Sarah continued, making Esther sit up straight.

"What about him?"

Sarah ran a knuckle under her chin. "A long time ago, I remember you saying you were struggling to understand his death. You didn't know why *Gott* took him so soon."

"Jah." Esther nodded, though not sure what her sister was getting at.

"You and I were alone by the fire one night, and you asked me flat out why he'd died so young. The day before, I'd heard *Maam* tell you it was *Gott's* will, so that's what I said, too. Golly, you about took my head off, you were so upset."

"I remember that," Esther said, smiling despite herself. "And I'm sorry. I was weary of hearing that explanation."

"No, I see why you were angry, but I was just thinking." Sarah drew her knees into her chest, wrapping her arms around them. "What if that really was the dear Lord's plan for you like everyone's been saying? What if He needed Jacob with Him, and He has a wonderful and exciting new plan for you, a life that's more blessed and perfect and full of love than you could ever fathom?"

For a moment, Esther sat very still; then sudden tears blurred her vision, and she pressed both hands over her mouth.

"Did I say something wrong?" Sarah asked quietly, scooting so she could put an arm around Esther's shoulders.

Esther could only shake her head, then nodded. "That was maybe the most-right thing you've ever said to me." She covered her mouth again but was unable to keep the sobs at bay.

With her whole heart, she believed her sister's words. She believed in a *Gott* who loved her so much that He wouldn't make her mourn for a man to whom she was no longer tied.

After two years of questions and guilt—and while sitting on the wet grass after a rainstorm, still nursing a broken heart—Esther was finally able to let Jacob go.

A fresh fit of sobs shook her body, releasing her.

"It's okay," Sarah said, holding her tightly. "I'll stay with you as long as you want."

• • •

Esther didn't join in on the family Bible study that evening but stayed in her room, knowing Sarah would make any necessary excuses. Not even *Maam* came in to see her. Sarah must've warned even the *kinnahs* to stay away.

All that night, her dreams were etched with volcanoes erupting, forest fires, earthquakes, every natural disaster Esther had ever read about. Her slumber was unrestful and fitful and exhausting. When she awoke to the rooster's crow, her pillow was damp.

"Esther!" It was little Abraham's voice, followed by sounds of rushing footsteps running up the stairs. "Esther! Wake up!"

Slowly and cautiously—so she wouldn't vomit—Esther pushed herself into a seated position. "I'm awake, buddy. Come in."

"Cousin Leah called on the phone in the barn. She told Papa to tell you that she needs more… um…*smoke*!"

Esther tilted her head. "Do you mean soap?"

Abraham scratched his ear. "Yes, soap. The kind you make in the kitchen."

Esther chuckled. "Okay. Thanks for relaying the message. You did a good job."

Her little brother grinned and stood up straight. "I can call her back on the phone, if you want. Simon showed me how on his phone at his house. It's easy."

"No, no." Esther threw her legs off the bed and stood. "That's okay. You did great. Thanks again."

In a noisy, boyish flash, Abraham flew down the stairs.

Goodness, Leah was out of soap again? Esther had delivered a huge batch to her just a few days ago. After checking the time, she figured she could quickly get another batch ready to process, then deliver to Leah everything she had on the shelf of her nook.

Foolishly, she'd expected letting go of Jacob would help fill her empty heart. But as she moved to get dressed, she felt more hollow than ever.

CHAPTER THIRTY-FOUR

Lucas couldn't seem to keep his head in the game. After a restless night's sleep, he'd gotten up earlier than most dairy farmers, went for a run, then worked on fixing his front fence by the light of the rising sun. The thought of breakfast made his stomach turn, so all he had was water and a cold piece of leftover hamburger before heading out the door.

After leaving three messages, Greg finally called him back. Still no results from Tanner's bone marrow test. Lucas knew answers took time, but that morning, he couldn't control his impatience and irritability.

No doubt as to why his mood was so sour. He'd tried to appear undaunted and unflappable when he'd last been with Esther, telling her their relationship was over, but his heart was having a hard time accepting it.

Never a man to stew, he thought staying busy at work would keep him occupied, but his mind kept drifting. If he'd somehow known that first day at the clinic how much his life would change because of her, would he have done things differently?

"Nay," he said aloud as he saved the notes he'd just entered into a patient's file. Despite his own stubbornness, Esther's sweet countenance and example had brought him to *Gott* again.

After closing the file, he clicked to his email,

opening a message that had come from a colleague in Boston. Lucas sat back as he read, fingering the end of a pencil. There was a job on the research team at Mass General. The money was good, the hospital was renowned, and they wanted him ASAP. Lucas sat forward in his chair.

When the Lord closes a door, somewhere He opens a window…

The old saying repeated on a loop. Was this an opportunity to start a new life? Or was this *Gott*'s way of kicking him out of the Amish world for good?

Or just maybe, Gott *is testing my desire to return to the church.*

"I'm going across the street," he said to Stephanie as he blew by the reception desk. "Want anything from Yoder's?"

"Ooh." Stephanie sat up straight. "A soft pretzel, please."

Lucas nodded but then stopped, his hand on the door. "Marinara dipping sauce?"

"Yes, thank you!"

He nodded again, then headed outside. It was a windy afternoon, and maybe even a late autumn break for nearby schools, because the store was packed with shoppers. Lucas didn't know why he was there. He didn't want a pretzel or a piece of pie or even a slice of freshly baked bread. He'd simply needed to get out of the office and out of his head.

Stopping before he marched straight to the display of handmade soap, he steered himself into the far corner. Quilts and knitted rugs were hung from hooks on the walls or stacked in neat rows on a long table, making it easy to see their unique patterns.

His eye caught a familiar thin "log cabin" diagram. A dark blue tag was pinned to its side. Lucas's heart leaped into his throat when he recognized the handwriting.

Made with love by Lydia Brenneman.

He pressed the tag between the palms of his hands, then traced an index finger over the script, wondering how long ago his mother had written it. His childhood memories were filled with his sweet *maam* holding an unfinished quilt on her lap, needle and thread in one hand, silver thimble on each thumb.

He pulled the blanket off the hook and held it in his arms, dipping his face into its softness. His throat grew tight when he sensed the faint scent of honeysuckle. A million images flashed through his mind, each one making him long for home like never before. Just when he couldn't take another second of it, a commotion at the other side of the store stole his attention.

His heart stopped dead, then went into a straight gallop when he saw Esther. She was carrying two big boxes and was literally surrounded by women—mostly *Englisher* shoppers. When he realized she hadn't seen him, he stayed out of sight.

"All right, ladies. Let's remain calm." He recognized the short, round Amish woman who flew over to Esther's aid. "How many do you have?"

"Twenty lavender," he heard Esther reply. "Twenty-five wildflower, fifteen clove—"

"Only fifteen?" the short woman said, clearly disappointed.

"I'll take them all!" one of the *Englishers* shouted.

"I got here first," said another.

"No, I did!" This English woman actually tried to tear one of the boxes out of Esther's arms.

Alarm bells went off in Lucas's head. Was Esther about to be trampled by a mob of soap enthusiasts? Before he could make a move, the short woman pulled Esther behind the barrier of the counter.

"Ladies, ladies, we're currently building a website and will begin taking online orders in the next few days. In the meantime, please leave your name and address on our mail-order form, and the products will be shipped as soon as possible." She turned to Esther. "Which will be very soon, *jah*?"

Lucas watched as Esther bit her lip, as if wondering what the right answer should be, then nodded. "I started a new batch just this morning, and—"

"Which scent?" a woman interrupted.

"Lemon."

Oddly, the woman frowned. "Just plain lemon?"

Everyone turned to look at Esther. "Well…" She rubbed her nose. "I could add eucalyptus oil—"

"That sounds fabulous!" The *Englisher* elbowed herself to the front of the line and stood in front of Esther. "Have you ever thought of cedar or sandal-wood? Gardenia! Something strong and perfumy."

"Well," Esther began, "those aren't fragrances I normally use."

"Why?"

Even from his hidden corner, Lucas could feel the weight of all the eyes on Esther.

"Because, you see, in the *Ordnung*… I mean, the Amish aren't supposed to—"

"Don't worry. New, *stronger* scents will be coming soon," the short woman behind the counter cut in. "For now, please see our list on the order form." She turned to Esther, prompting her to set the boxes on the counter. "If you could form an orderly line, everyone will leave with Moses Miller's Esther's famous Honey Brook soap."

Like a whirlwind, Lucas watched the mob of women file into a queue that reached the door. Esther's blue eyes lit up, staring at the line of people wanting her product, maybe even counting each person, hoping she had brought enough.

How could he not feel happy for her? More than anything, he hoped she'd have a fulfilling life. A lot of people found happiness in business. Perhaps this was *Gott*'s plan for her. He felt a lump in his throat, wishing he could've been part of that plan.

But he was done wishing.

After making sure he'd be blocked from Esther's view, Lucas found an open cashier at the other end of the counter. Not forgetting the pretzel for Stephanie, he left the store with it and his mother's quilt.

The fresh air felt good in his lungs as he stood outside the door and breathed in, facing the wind.

"Lucas?"

The tentative voice was quiet and held back, but he knew it in an instant.

"Hey," he said, turning to see Esther, grateful for the heavy quilt he was carrying. Grateful he had an excuse not to hug her or touch a finger to her cheek.

"Congratulations," he said. "I saw what happened in there. I think you actually *are* famous. Or at least very popular."

"Ain't so?" she said, lifting a broad kind of smile he'd never seen before.

He smiled back, but it was painful. "You're going to be busy from now on."

"I'm busting with ideas for new fragrances—stronger ones, and blends, so many blends. I've always been careful with how much oil I use in them. Why was that?"

He tilted his head to the side. "Because you decided not to, remember? Because you decided to be obedient and not fall to the pressures of the world. You know only that will bring true happiness. That's what you told me."

Deep lines striped Esther's forehead, and her brows pulled together. "That was before I knew…" She nodded toward the store.

"How successful you could be?"

She nodded, but Lucas caught the muscle in her jaw twitch. "Is that a sin?" She crossed her arms. "Before, I thought my heart was in the right place. I tried to do everything *Gott* wanted of me. I tried to live on His path, march joyously toward the future, and look what happened."

He'd never seen her like this, disappointment laced with stubborn determination in her voice. It was more heartbreaking than the day she'd told him she didn't know if she believed in the church anymore.

Was she feeling that again?

"Don't be reckless because of what happened between us."

Her mouth fell open. "You told me how things had to be, and now I'm moving on—easier this time.

That should be what you want."

He opened his mouth to reply but then closed it.

He didn't *want* any of this. He didn't *want* to be standing in the middle of the street arguing with her. He didn't *want* to be estranged from his family, his friends, and the *Gott* he loved with all his heart. He didn't *want* to have to decide if he should take the job in Boston and never come back.

"It's not what I want," he said, swallowing the lump in his throat. He let his words settle between them before adding, "Take care of yourself."

Suddenly, her blue eyes widened, and her cheeks went blotchy red. Seeing this caused a sharp pain to simultaneously hit his temples, the bridge of his nose, and the back of his head.

"Goodbye," he continued, before regret made him say more. Then he marched across the street, opened the door of the clinic, and closed it behind him.

"Thanks, boss!" Stephanie said after he practically threw the pretzel at her. "Ooh, snazzy quilt."

After closing his office door, he checked his cell to see if Greg had called. Then he hit reply on that email from Boston.

• • •

Ever since he was a boy, Lucas hated loose ends. Before he could launch himself into something new, he always needed to finish what he'd started. He stared up at the bedroom ceiling, early morning sunlight streaking across the white paint. Another restless night had come and gone, but at least now he had a solid plan for his future.

CHAPTER THIRTY-FIVE

"Esther?"

"I'm busy."

"Es?"

Esther adjusted the blue flame under her saucepan and looked up. "Yes, *Maam*."

"It's late. This is the third night in a row you're up past midnight."

Esther sighed. "I'm trying to be quiet."

Maam lifted her chin and inhaled. Then coughed. "What's that…smell?"

"Lemongrass mixed with peppermint. Do you like it?"

Maam coughed again, then cleared her throat. "It's a little *strong*, don't you think?"

"No." To demonstrate, she took in a full, deep breath, the simmering oils burning the back of her throat. She stifled the need to cough.

Maam picked up a few of the essential oil bottles that were out on the kitchen counter. "What happened to the lavender and vanilla? The wildflower was my favorite. So lovely and light. Like springtime."

"It's not what people want," Esther said, reaching for a clean mold from the top shelf.

"Which people?"

"The people at the store. The *Englishers*."

"Ah. I see."

Esther heard the concerned tone in her mother's voice, but she knew if she stopped working, her mind would drift to things she didn't want to be thinking about, such as how she'd been ignoring her family for the past few days. How she still hadn't checked in on Lizzy or added one stitch to Sarah's dress. How her heart broke anew every morning when she woke up, remembering the things she'd said to Lucas.

Staying busy was the only thing that kept her going.

"*Maam*. It's fine."

"What's fine?"

She tried not to sigh too loudly. "You might not know this, but in the business world, you have to give the people what they want if you have any chance at hitting the big time."

"The business world?" *Maam* echoed, a chuckle in her voice. "The big time?"

Esther knew how she sounded, but she wasn't in the mood to talk about what was really on her mind. Besides, if she stopped working, stopped moving forward, she was likely to break down in tears.

Thousands of bars of soap would never clean away her feelings for Lucas.

"*Maam*, I'm sorry if I'm being too loud, but I really have to get this batch done. Orders are coming in."

"Es, Es," *Maam* said. "It's nearly three in the morning, and you're running on adrenaline." She grasped the handle of the pan and moved it to the cold side of the stove. "Come sit with me a minute."

Esther's brain began a mental protest, but she gave in, never wanting to be disrespectful to her mother. She wasn't that far gone.

Maam led her to the sofa, pushed off a few pillows, then sat, pulling Esther to sit beside her. "Darling, something's been going on."

Esther didn't speak. Didn't move.

She reached out and swept a piece of Esther's hair back. "I've been watching you. You're not acting like yourself. Hmm?"

Esther shrugged, trying to hold it together for even a second longer. But she was so worn-out and so empty that her breaths became audible heaves. *Maam* put a gentle hand on the back of Esther's head and drew her in.

"Shhh-shhh." *Maam*'s whisper filled the air as Esther couldn't stop from breaking into tears. "Oh, my darling girl." Esther's shoulders rose and fell with each sob. "My good, good girl."

For what felt like hours, *Maam* held her, continuing to whisper and coo that everything would be okay. Even through her headache and tears, Esther knew the reason for her sadness would not just disappear.

"Ready to talk?"

Esther shut her eyes, offering a silent prayer—something she hadn't done for days—that her mother would understand. "I've done something," she began, sniveling. "Or I *was* doing something, but I'm not doing it anymore."

Maam nodded, her expression unreadable in the darkness. "Was it something you're ashamed of?"

"No!" she practically shouted, then lowered her voice. "Not ashamed, but I had to sneak around to do it."

"My sweet. Are we talking about a beau?"

A beau? Was that what Lucas had been to her?

No, she thought, not needing even a minute to consider. *He wasn't my beau, or not just my beau. Lucas Brenneman is the man I love!*

Even though her throat felt hot and thick, and she was ready to break down all over again, Esther stared through the darkness, trying to see something in her mother's eyes. Finally, she lowered her chin. "Are you mad at me?"

"Why would you think such a thing?"

She clasped her hands together and placed them over her pounding heart. "I never meant to disappoint you or *Daed*."

"Es, I've noticed your mood changes since we lost Jacob. I've seen you struggle and look for ways to fit in with the community. Suddenly, though, you seemed to find peace again. Lately, you've been happy and light—a big smile on your face wherever you go." *Maam* touched Esther's cheek. "I've missed that smile."

"Me too," Esther admitted, fresh tears burning her eyes.

"A smile like that, followed by tears like these…" *Maam* wiped one away with a finger. "That can come only from a broken heart."

In the darkness, Esther allowed the tears to pour. She couldn't hide anything from *Maam* now, who knew her better than anyone. "I love him," she managed to get out; saying the words didn't even shock her. "But it's impossible."

"Are you sure?"

Esther nodded, flashes of Lucas's beautiful face filling her mind's eye. The warmth of his arms, but especially the kindness of his huge heart. When she'd been with him, she'd been the strongest, best version of herself. And she hoped in her heart he'd felt the same way.

"Heartache takes time," *Maam* whispered. "You'll heal. I know it doesn't feel like it now, but you will."

Esther nodded again, but she wasn't sure even a hundred years would put her shattered heart back together.

"Is that what this new scent business is about?"

"I suppose so." Esther wiped her nose, almost laughing at the insightfulness of her mother. "You should see how the English women love it."

"Makes you feel proud, eh?"

Again, she nodded, silently remembering the conversation she'd had with Lucas about that very thing. How had heartbreak and pride taken over so quickly and thoroughly? How had she managed to morph into the very person she'd been trying so hard not to become?

"I don't want to be a disappointment," she said, feeling the honesty and heaviness of the words. "I'm tired of disappointing everyone."

"Who do you think you're disappointing?"

Esther shut her eyelids. *Leah*, she could have said. *The Englishers.* But why in the world should she worry about them? *Lou keeps asking me to sing in her choir*, she could've added. *Our neighbors,* Gott, *you and* Daed...*Luke*...

When Esther couldn't speak, *Maam* said, "I hope that list you're making in your head doesn't include me."

"Of course it does." Esther's lungs quivered as

she forced out the words.

"Darling, I love you so much. You could never disappoint me." *Maam* put an arm around her, drawing her in once more. "Do you know who else feels the same way?"

"Who?"

Maam smiled softly, then placed a hand on each of Esther's cheeks, like she was a little girl again. *"Gott,"* she said, the word coming out like a prayer. "Our most gracious Father in Heaven knows your heart; He knows your intent. He knows how difficult your life has been the last few years, and He knows how hard you're trying. I know He knows this, because I know it, too."

Esther hadn't thought she had more tears inside, but somehow, a few more managed to trickle down her face. She knew her mother's words were correct—she'd felt them her whole life—but hearing them again, right in that moment, meant everything.

"He has a plan for you," *Maam* added.

She couldn't help remembering Lucas's words and then Sarah's. "I know."

"Is it being a world-famous soap maker?"

Esther chuckled under her breath. "No."

"Is it hiding your beautiful singing voice from all the people you love?"

She sniffed, realizing that—thanks to her sister—she'd had a beautiful closure of her time with Jacob. Singing again might add one more element to that closure.

"Nay," she said, promising herself that she would go see Louisa the very next day.

"Is it okay," *Maam* continued, "if you don't know

exactly what that plan is right this moment?"

Esther prayed again in her heart; then after feeling an inkling of warmth and peace in her chest, she took in a deep breath and nodded. *"Jah."*

Maam kissed her gently on the forehead. Even though she probably hadn't washed up since before she'd gone to bed hours earlier, she still smelled of wildflowers. The fresh, soothing scent pushed another wave of calm over Esther.

"Sometimes the answer to a prayer is so very simple," *Maam* whispered, her voice wrapping around Esther's heart. "Our job, my darling, is to act."

CHAPTER THIRTY-SIX

Lucas hid behind a large green apple tree that was heavy with fruit. It wasn't a cowardly act—he simply wasn't ready to be seen. He'd been watching her for ten minutes as she'd been digging potatoes out of the ground. It was late in the season, and he was surprised there were so many left to harvest. He could tell she was surprised, too, because she'd brought only a small basket with her—which was now overflowing with freshly picked potatoes.

A gust of morning wind made her black cloak float out behind her like she was Super Woman. To Lucas, she truly was, and always had been.

From his hiding place, he'd considered approaching her dozens of times, even going so far as taking a step or two. With everything that had happened between them, he had no idea how she would react.

So he kept watching and thinking and praying—so many prayers that he would know what to do.

When she balanced the heavy basket on her hip and began heading toward the house, Lucas had no choice but to follow.

Customary thick, heavy drapes hung over each window, blocking the view of curious outsiders—such as Lucas. The window above the kitchen sink, however, was not obstructed, and when he drew nearer, he could see she was sitting alone at the long wooden table, the potatoes spread out before her. No one else appeared to be inside. No noise of playing children or chatty visitors.

Peaceful, solitary moments like this one were probably very rare for her. But Lucas didn't care. He knew it was now or never.

Instead of knocking on the back door, he simply turned the knob and quietly opened the door. She didn't move, hadn't heard him. He took one step inside, then stood up tall.

"Maam?"

He watched as she froze in place, the hand holding a potato hovering above the table. When she still didn't move, he swallowed, wondering if this had been a terrible idea.

"Maam," he repeated, not willing to give up yet.

Slowly, she lowered her chin but then turned toward him.

He hadn't noticed from his distance behind the apple tree, but thin lines ran across his mother's forehead. Her hair wasn't as dark brown as he'd remembered. And was she just a little bit thinner? Despite the ten years that had gone by, to Lucas, she looked exactly the same.

"Maam," he said a third time as he took another step inside. Was this too bold? Was she about to call for help?

"Lucas?" Slowly, she pushed back the chair and stood. Hearing her speak his name made his heart pound with uncertainty. "Is it truly you?"

"Jah," he replied in a hoarse whisper. "It's me." Blood whooshed in his ears, making his arms and hands shake. He was about to say something else— to apologize, maybe. Apologize for running away, for having stopped writing to her when he'd arrived

in Honey Brook, for not being able to save Jacob.

Before any of those words could form, his mother covered her mouth with both hands, then practically ran toward him. When her body hit his, Lucas actually felt the wind rush from his lungs. A moment later, her arms were around him, and he was enveloped in the hug he'd missed most of all.

A lump grew in Lucas's throat as he bent down and wrapped his arms around her, holding her tight, perfectly recalling the last time he'd hugged her — the day he'd left for *Rumspringa* ten years ago.

"Son, son," *Maam* kept repeating. He heard the tears of joy in her voice while feeling a burning in his own eyes.

After finally releasing each other, *Maam* looked up at him and let out a long exhale. "I can't believe you're here."

"Is it okay?" Lucas asked. Even if her answer was no, he wasn't about to leave.

Maam brushed away a tear from her cheek. *"Jah,"* she whispered. "Although…" She glanced over her shoulder toward the front door. Lucas hadn't noticed if his father's buggy had been out front. *She* might've been happy to see him, but his father was a different story.

"I don't want you to feel awkward," Lucas said. "Would you rather I—"

"No!" *Maam* burst out, then smiled like the sweet angel she was. "You're not going anywhere, and if your father can't… Well"—she smiled again and wiped her hands down the front of her black apron—"then he can sit in that old barn of his."

"Maam." Lucas couldn't help chuckling under

his breath. His mother the firecracker hadn't changed a bit.

"He's visiting with the ministers," she said. "Then he has a meeting with Bishop Abram this afternoon. I don't expect him home for a while."

Lucas felt his eyebrows rise. "*Daed* is part of the church leadership?"

"Mostly with the logistical matters," she said, unveiling a loaf of homemade cinnamon bread. Just seeing it triggered a memory in Lucas, and his mouth began to water. "Toasted, butter and blueberry jam?" *Maam* asked.

Lucas grinned. "You remember."

Maam's eyes twinkled. "How could I forget?"

Warmth spread through his chest, across his shoulders. Even though his mother was standing six feet away, it felt like he was still wrapped in her hug. Perhaps because he was literally living in the middle of an answered prayer.

Again, his throat grew thick with tears, and he coughed into a fist before speaking again. "*Daed* always seemed too busy with the mill to get involved with church matters," he said. "What's changed?"

Maam's eyes were lowered as she cut thick slices of bread. But she lifted them for a moment to meet Lucas's gaze. "A lot's changed."

Well, it has been ten years, Lucas considered. *I'm living proof of those changes.*

"Your father's getting older," *Maam* continued. "He's had an offer on the back ten acres by the pond."

"He's selling?"

"He's considering. Jeremiah's got land, too. Maybe

too much." She paused. "Jerry's married now."

"I know." Lucas smiled. "I've seen him."

Maam put down the knife. "You have? When?"

Lucas walked to stand beside her. "Last week for the first time. It was an accident, really." He went on to explain how he and Jerry had happened to meet that early morning, and all the other details. Well, he did not mention Esther Miller. No reason to go into that depressing part of the story.

"Such a blessing," *Maam* said, her words sounding thick, as if fighting back more tears. "I might even call it a miracle."

As they sat together at the wooden table, *Maam* asked questions and Lucas did his best to answer, did his best to explain his life since he'd returned to the area. He'd been a little surprised that she really hadn't known he'd been working at the clinic in town since April—living a few miles from where they sat right now.

"Caleb's nearly as big as you these days," *Maam* was saying. Before Lucas could reply, in unison, they turned at the sound of horse hooves on the gravel driveway.

Lucas sat up straight and looked at his mother. What should he do? Hide? Run away?

"Stay exactly where you are, son," *Maam* said, her voice strong and steady, giving Lucas a jolt of strength. She took his hand and squeezed.

Footsteps were on the front porch, then voices. Lucas frowned and leaned forward, straining to hear. It had been a while, but that did not sound like his father's voice.

"It's fine, it's fine," a voice said. "We don't have

to knock." The front door opened, and Lucas felt his jaw go slack when Lizzy walked in. "Lydia, are you home? It's Lizzy."

Lucas's muscles relaxed in relief, and he was about to greet his sister-in-law when someone came inside behind her.

A burst of coldness filled his stomach, then expanded. Intellectually, Lucas knew his body was going into shock, but the medical part of his brain had gone blank. Esther's wide eyes were fixed on him as she stood frozen…in his mother's doorway.

Lizzy beamed. "There you are! Oh." She stopped when she noticed Lucas. "What are you…?"

Lucas barely acknowledged her but was fixated on her companion. Esther wore a light gray dress with a matching gray apron, her blond hair pulled into a tidy bun covered by a black bonnet. The soft skin at her throat and cheeks was marbling pink.

"Esther, dear, hallo," his mother said, dropping Lucas's hand to greet her guests. A second later, she turned to Lizzy. "May I ask what you're doing here, Elizabeth? You're supposed to be at home in bed. The whole village knows it." Before anyone could speak, *Maam* straightened her apron. "I'm so sorry. Esther, I hope you remember my son Lucas from when you were a child. He's been gone a while."

During a brief pause, Lucas glanced at Esther, wondering what in the world was going through her head at the sight of him in his mother's kitchen.

"They know each other," Lizzy said. "She was at our place a few days ago when Luke was helping Jerry with the farm."

"Ah," *Maam* said, then tilted her head to look at

Lucas. The expression was not a new one to him. His mother was silently saying that they would discuss this later. For some reason, it made Luke want to hug his *maam* good and tight.

"Hello," he said, knowing *Maam* was reading every little minute expression on his face.

"Hiya," Esther replied, not quite looking at him now, her cheeks still stained with a blush.

"And I know I'm supposed to be at home," Lizzy said. "Esther's been with me today, but she had to run some errands, and I promised her that I would nap all afternoon if I could come with her in the buggy. I'm just so bored sitting on that couch. I've knitted enough booties for quadruplets!"

"Errands?" Lucas asked, dying for the chance to speak directly to Esther.

She nodded. "I needed to make some deliveries."

"Your soap," he said, feeling something drop in his stomach. This was Esther's life, though, her decisions. Why should he feel disappointed that she was determined to disobey the *Ordnung*?

Because he cared about her—deeply. That was why. Even if it couldn't be with him, he wanted her to be happy beyond her wildest dreams.

"No," she replied. "Well, yes and no. I didn't deliver soap to the store where I sell them, but I did bring some for you, Lydia." She reached into a pocket and pulled out a single bar of soap, walking toward his mother. "I know this is your favorite."

Maam took the soap and held it to her nose. "Honeysuckle," she said, then closed her eyes and took in another breath. "You have such a *Gott*-given talent, Esther."

Esther smiled and dipped her gaze modestly. "Thank you very much. I've decided to concentrate on the scents found around Honey Brook. We have so many flowers and trees and berries and other natural, airy scents that I'll never have to look for inspiration past my own backyard."

She paused; then her eyes slid up to meet Lucas's. His heart was beating so hard inside his rib cage that he was sure everyone in the room could hear it.

"I hope they sell well; the money helps my family," Esther added, smiling at something in the middle distance. "But I told my cousin at Yoder's that I won't be making as much for her as she'd hoped. I'm pretty busy elsewhere these days. I'm tutoring my little sister in memorizing one Bible verse a day, I'm helping Louisa with the wedding music now—I'm even singing a solo with the choir."

When she paused and tipped her chin, Lucas couldn't begin to read the expression on her face, but for some reason, it seemed that announcing she was singing in the choir was a very proud moment for her—but in the humblest of ways.

"Between my other chores and keeping Miss Lizzy off her feet," Esther continued brightly, "my days are fuller than ever."

"And your sister's wedding's coming up," *Maam* said before Lucas could even open his mouth. "I heard you made her dress."

"*Jah.*" Esther nodded, then began running a thumb around the inside of her palm. "But just this morning, I decided to cut it up into three aprons."

"Why?" Lucas said, unable to stop himself...

knowing how challenging it had been for her to make her sister's dress in the first place.

"I decided to let Sarah wear my wedding dress."

"The purple one?" his mother said. Lucas heard the hitch in her voice and realized that of course *Maam* knew about Esther's purple dress, for she'd made it to marry Jacob. "I love that dress," *Maam* added.

"So do I." Esther put her lips together and smiled. "Not long ago, I looked through the scrapbook that our wonderful, thoughtful church members made for me after Jacob died, and…it gave me peace. Around the same time," she added with a slight glance over at Lucas, "a very good friend asked me why I didn't let someone else wear that dress I loved so much. I had no good answer then, but I know now that I was saving it for my little sister."

The room felt thick with warmth and unspoken words. Lucas had so much to say to her, but before he could move, his mother reached out and gave Esther a big hug. Seeing the two women he cared for most in the world share a tender moment filled Lucas's heart with a peace he'd never known.

Maam whispered something in Esther's ear before letting her go.

"Jah," Esther whispered. "I will."

"Can I get some of that bread?" Lizzy said, breaking the stillness of the room.

"Chunky peanut butter and strawberry jam?" his mother asked.

"Yum!" Lizzy's eyes brightened as she rubbed her pregnant belly. "This little one's been craving peanut butter all morning."

As the four of them gathered around the table, passing slices of smothered bread and glasses of fresh milk, Lucas maneuvered himself to sit at Esther's side. He knew it was self-inflicted torture, but he needed to be near her.

The conversation was happy and lively, as if no time had passed since he'd been away. Over and over, Lucas offered a silent prayer of thanksgiving for being a part of this precious moment.

"Do you mind if I go upstairs and lie down?" Lizzy asked after her second sandwich.

"Of course," his mother said. "You can have the big bed; the window is open and you'll have a nice breeze."

"I can take you home, Lizzy."

At Esther's suggestion, something reached in and grabbed Lucas's heart. He was not ready for the moment to end.

"*Nay, nay,*" Lizzy replied. "I just need a few minutes."

"Another sandwich for you? Cup of tea?" his mother asked Esther, clearly wanting her to feel comfortable. Lucas longed to squeeze his mother for the kind gesture.

"I'd love one, but I'll get it," Esther said, walking to the stove. After filling the kettle with water, she sparked up the gas burner, adjusting the flame. Lucas loved watching her fuss around the kitchen where he'd grown up. She must've felt at home there when she'd been engaged to his brother.

Seeing her now filled his heart with a frustrating pang of hope. Why must he keep hoping when he'd been the one to tell her it was over?

The thought barely had time to settle in his mind when the front door swung open, letting in an icy cold breeze. It had been ten years, but Lucas knew the man in an instant.

He waited a beat, hoping for a flash of inspiration. When none came, he simply said, "Hello, Father."

CHAPTER THIRTY-SEVEN

After their final goodbye, there hadn't been a notion in Esther's mind that Lucas would ever chance a visit home, not after what had happened at Jeremiah's and then ending their entire relationship because of it.

Yet, there he stood, looking as comfortable and welcomed as anyone. Once the initial shock had passed, Esther, too, began to feel at home. The entire Brenneman family had been warm and supportive of her, even after Jacob went to live in heaven.

Nothing, however, could have prepared Esther to see Luke's father burst into the room where she, Lucas, and Lydia stood.

"Hello, Father."

Ephraim Brenneman didn't move from his place in the doorway, but his eyes flashed from his son to his wife, then back again. Esther tried her best to stay small and invisible at the far end of the kitchen.

"What are you doing here?"

"Now, Ephraim," Lydia Brenneman said. "Everything's okay."

Esther observed Ephraim's jaw muscle clench. "You shouldn't be here," he said, ignoring his wife and pointing directly at Lucas. "You don't belong in this house."

Esther couldn't help but notice the tiny way Lucas flinched back. His father's words had hurt him.

"Ephraim." Lydia put a hand over her husband's pointing finger and eased his extended arm down to his side. "Please don't speak to him that way. You don't understand."

"I understand everything."

"She didn't invite me," Lucas said. "She didn't even know I live and work here."

Ephraim's eyebrows arched. "Here?"

Lucas nodded. "At the medical clinic in town."

Ephraim frowned and ran his wrist along his forehead. "That so? For how long?"

"Since April," *Maam* replied. "Our…our boy has been this close to us since the spring. He was here at Eastertime—"

"Lydia, you know the rules."

"Why do rules matter right this very second?"

"It's okay, *Maam*," Lucas said, reaching for his hat. "I don't want to bring trouble to the family."

His father exhaled a joyless chuckle from his throat. "Trouble."

Esther's heart broke at the sarcastic remark aimed at Luke. If she'd been a different type of person, she might've scolded the older man for being so unkind, that he should forgive Lucas and let him come home, to allow them all to move forward with their lives as if nothing bad had happened all those years ago.

The pain in Lucas's eyes made her stomach roll with bile.

"Ephraim Brenneman," Lydia said. "For five minutes, you are to climb off your high horse and listen to your son." When she inhaled, Esther heard her breath quake. "If this is the only chance we get with him, I will not have you scaring him off."

When she'd been engaged to Jacob, Esther had been at the Brennemans' house practically every day. But never, ever had she heard Lydia—or any other wife in their community—speak with such demanding force to her husband.

But she was so grateful she had.

"Sit down, love," Lydia continued, her tone smooth and calm. "Would you like your coffee now? Sweet cream with a dash of cinnamon?"

For a moment, Ephraim didn't move, just stood with pursed lips. Finally, he let out some kind of grumble from his chest. "Yes, thank you."

Lydia did not move toward the kitchen, however, but took her husband by the shoulders and guided him to sit down at the table. Next, she took Lucas by one arm and sat him across from his father. Lydia sat herself in the chair between them. "Tell us about your job, Luke."

After a quiet moment, she glanced at her husband. Esther couldn't see the look she gave him, but Ephraim suddenly adjusted his position in his chair and cleared his throat. "Er, yes, what is your job? Do you work with Frank McDonald?"

Lucas leaned forward. "You know Frank?"

"Jah." His father nodded. "Sprained my wrist last year. The good doc fixed me up quite nice."

Esther watched Lucas closely, knowing exactly what must've been running through his mind... If Ephraim Brenneman had been so against English medical help when his son was dying from cancer, why would he see a proper doctor for a sprained wrist?

Lucas didn't reply, however, making all the muscles in Esther's body clench for his sake. She was dying to be at his side, wanted him to know she was there, to hold his hand and tell him she loved him, wishing there was a way she could take his painful confusion away.

"You never wrote back."

The words made Esther blink as she watched Luke stare across the table at his mother.

"Not once," he continued. "Not even at the beginning when I was young and scared. Not once did you write."

Lydia turned her body to him. "I... Luke, I had no idea where you were."

"Every single letter had a return address on it."

Lydia stared blankly at him until, in a weak voice, she finally asked, "What letters?"

The question seemed to hang in the air; then all eyes in the room turned to the person at the head of the table.

"Ephraim." Lydia's voice was low. "What did you do?"

Her husband sat up straight and put his palms flat on the table. "I was protecting this fam—"

"Ephraim." Her voice was louder.

After a long silence, Ephraim's shoulders seemed to slump. "I thought I was doing the right thing. I didn't want you to get hurt."

This time, Esther saw with her own eyes the withering glance Lydia sent her husband. It actually made her afraid of the petite, not-so-submissive woman. When the glare had served its purpose, his *maam* turned to Lucas. "How many letters?"

"Until last year, at least one every month," he replied. "Dozens."

"You wrote to me every…?"

Lucas swallowed, and from the way his ears were turning pink, Esther knew he was struggling to keep his emotions in check. Even with his mother.

For perhaps the last time, Esther whispered a prayer on behalf of Lucas. Would the Lord please comfort him and protect his heart? Would this experience somehow be a good one for him? Could he please find peace and a way to get everything his heart desired? Lucas was the best person she'd ever known, and somehow, someway, he deserved all of heaven's blessings.

Lydia scooted her chair over so she could wrap her arms around Lucas, pressing a cheek against her son's chest. Esther watched as Lucas closed his eyes, lines shooting out their corners as he pinched them closed tightly. Then slowly, Ephraim pushed his chair back and stood, moving toward the hugging pair.

Esther jumped and shrieked as the teakettle suddenly let out a sharp whistle.

CHAPTER THIRTY-EIGHT

Maam flinched inside Lucas's arms at the loud sound. He'd felt so safe to be with her again that he regretted loosening his grip for even a second, fearing this whole day would turn out to be a dream.

Then he noticed Esther standing in the corner of the kitchen, her face as white as a hospital bedsheet. Somehow, since his father had shown up, he'd forgotten she was there. She was working fast to remove the kettle from the heat, silencing the whistle and shutting off the flame.

"I'm s-sorry," she whispered, behaving like she was mortally embarrassed.

"Es," he couldn't help saying.

"Esther," his mother uttered, right over his voice. Perhaps that was a good thing—no need to complicate the situation with their history.

Still, he couldn't stop from walking over to her. Truly, she looked like she was on the verge of fainting. "Are you okay?" he said in a low voice as he bent down to her.

She blinked up at him; those blue eyes still made his heart gallop like a racing horse. "I didn't mean to intrude."

He didn't know how to reply, for if he couldn't sweep her into his arms he was otherwise paralyzed. Before he could dip his face closer to her, longing to brush his lips across hers, she rushed out of the house.

He was still staring at the back of the door when he heard the sound of her horse and buggy leaving at full speed.

"Lucas."

After hearing his name again, he swallowed hard, blinking himself back to the present. Both parents stared at him, his mother wringing her hands in distress.

"Lucas," she repeated. "What's going on?"

If he was smart, he would've said nothing was going on and made an excuse as to why he'd reacted to Esther Miller like that—some kind of repressed memory from his childhood.

But hadn't there been enough lies?

"I'm in love with her," he said. Then he exhaled a shaky laugh under his breath at how easy it was to say the words, yet his voice had never felt more solid. "We were seeing each other for almost two months, and I think she's the most wonderful person on *Gott*'s green earth."

"Oh, Luke." *Maam* sighed. "What am I going to tell Mary Miller?"

"Nothing." Lucas almost laughed again, but gloomily. "We know it's impossible, so it ended."

"Impossible?" *Maam* echoed.

"Jah." Lucas massaged the heel of his hand into his forehead. "I'd marry her if I could," he added, unable to hold anything back, because at this point, why shouldn't he tell them everything?

"Listen, I don't know exactly how it would work, but I want to be part of the family again. I want to help you"—he glanced at his father—"with the mill and farm, and Jerry with his. I want the lifestyle I used to have, the one that always fit me best." Finally, when his breath was about to fail him, he pushed out the absolute truth. "I want to come home."

A blaring silence rang through the air, but Lucas could not regret his words. He had nothing to lose anymore, and being completely honest had a way of lightening the soul, freeing all the garbage polluting his life.

"I don't know what to say," *Maam* replied.

Lucas understood this. He hadn't unloaded on them to receive advice; he'd just needed to be truthful. "There's nothing to say," he agreed. "I'm glad I was able to tell you in person, but honestly, that's not what I want to talk about." He returned to the table and sat. "*Daed*, what did you do with the letters I sent to *Maam*? Burn them like they didn't exist?"

"Ephraim?" *Maam* said, looking at him.

His father gazed back steadily, unshaken. "There's a box in the barn under my tool chest. Well, *boxes* now, four of them. I didn't read the letters, but they're all there."

"I don't understand." Lucas ran a hand through his hair, scratching the back of his head. "If you thought you were protecting *Maam* and didn't want anyone to read them, why did you save them?"

Daed was blinking now, rapidly, like he was facing a strong, oncoming wind. "Because you're my son."

opened his eyes to see *Daed* staring at him, his lips pressing together firmly.

"It's no excuse," he said, "but I had reasons at the beginning. Your mother was so heartbroken

Lucas gazed at his father, *Maam* standing at his side. The two people who had had the most influence in his life. The two people he wished he could rely on now.

"I shouldn't have done it," *Daed* added, looking down, tugging at the end of his beard.

"Lucas," *Maam* said, once again wrapping her arms around him, holding him in a bear hug. Just as before, he could barely breathe. He'd missed his mother, his entire family. Almost instantly, he forgave even his father for hiding his letters.

Lucas when you didn't come home, especially after we lost Jacob. Eventually, I should've allowed her to read your letters, even to respond."

"Allowed?" *Maam* said, shaking her head. "Do you know how old-fashioned you sound?"

A tiny smile curved one side of his father's mouth. "I know you're angry, and you have every right to be." He reached a hand out to his wife. "I'm sorry."

Maam stared at the outstretched hand, placing her hands on her hips. "I'm not the one you should be apologizing to."

Lucas felt as though his heart had frozen like a glacier, understanding what his mother meant. He also knew the *Ordnung*; he'd learned the rules of the church every day while growing up in this very house. As head of the family, his father had every right to choose to allow no communication from Lucas after he hadn't returned from *Rumspringa*.

"Luke, I'm sorry."

He heard what his father said, but because of the crushingly disappointing end to his relationship with

Esther, his mind and body would not allow him to react naturally, to really trust again.

"I forgive you for that," Lucas said, knowing it was not his right to withhold forgiveness, especially now that he knew the truth and his father had apologized.

"Son." *Daed* put out a hand for Lucas to take, to make amends. But he could not take it, as heat from ten years of resentment still flared inside Lucas's chest. "Son?" *Daed* repeated.

"I need to ask you something," Lucas said.

"Yes?"

He stared down at the table, recognizing the carves and knots in the wood he'd made when he'd been a teenager. "You knew he was sick," he said, tasting sourness, feeling nervous waves in his stomach. "Jacob," he added for clarity, looking directly at his father. "He'd been seriously ill for years—everyone could tell. Why didn't you take him to the hospital? He had *cancer*. You would've known that if you'd allowed him to see a proper doctor. If it'd been caught early, he might've been able to fight it. By the time I got to him, it was too late."

"You?" *Maam* said, her brown eyes staring wildly at him.

"*Jah.*" Lucas nodded, wondering briefly if he should burden his mother with the whole story. But after a moment, he repositioned his chair so he was facing both parents, then started at the beginning…

How he'd known Jacob was different—had different weaknesses, more weaknesses than other boys his age. How he'd made a promise to himself that he would study childhood disease and figure out Jacob's ailment and thus its cure. How he'd finished high school, then college, then gone to work with a cancer research team.

Tears filled *Maam*'s eyes when he explained about the leukemia diagnosis, the bone marrow surgery, chemotherapy, and finally taking his brother to the beach, the one place Jacob had always dreamed of going.

"Was he cured when he came back from *Rumspringa*?"

It was difficult, but Lucas shook his head. "It's called remission," he replied. "Even the best experts can't predetermine how long a patient's remission will be. I'd worked at getting Jacob as healthy as possible, but I didn't know…" He couldn't finish the sentence when *Maam* began to cry.

"He was different, but not better."

Lucas turned to his father, who was staring out the window. "What do you mean?"

"I could tell he still wasn't right, but he was calmer about it, like he'd accepted a new fate." As his father continued to describe Jacob's health, the story matched what Esther had told him. His brother had become pious and serious, prayerful and obedient to a fault.

"One night," *Maam* said, continuing the narrative, "he caught a cold."

"It wasn't a cold, Lydia."

Maam closed her eyes and held up a hand. "I know, Ephraim, I know."

"He was feverish and weak," *Daed* added. "He had a cough that wouldn't go away." When *Maam* began to cry again, he put an arm around her. "He was having trouble breathing."

"He couldn't sleep," said *Maam* through her tears. "We gave him hot baths, warm bone broth, peppermint tea, wrapped him up like a mummy—I thought if he sweated enough…" Her voice trailed off as she looked at Lucas. "I suppose those all seem silly to a real doctor."

Lucas didn't bother explaining that he hadn't gone to medical school but was a physician's assistant who specialized in research. That wouldn't have helped the situation.

"Not at all," he replied. "That's pretty much how I would treat a bad cough at the clinic."

"But like your *daed* said, we knew it wasn't just a cough," *Maam* said after patting her damp cheeks with a corner of her apron. "He wasn't getting better, and he had to sit up all day and night or else he couldn't breathe."

"RSV," Lucas whispered under his breath.

Maam reached for Lucas's hand, gripping it tightly. "What is that?"

"Respiratory Syncytial Virus," Lucas explained. "It's, um, it's pretty common when—"

"It's an infection," *Daed* cut in. Lucas stared at him. "It happens a lot when someone's immune system has been compromised. Which, obviously, is leukemia's main job."

"Ephraim?"

"How do you know about that?" Lucas said, probably asking his mother's question.

Daed began pacing around the living room, fingers scratching the sides of his beard. "Do you remember when I took Jacob to the farmer's market in Lancaster?"

Maam nodded. "I do. Why?"

For a long moment, *Daed* didn't speak but continued to pace. Finally, he stopped and stood before them. "There was no farmer's market."

"What are you talking about? I packed a bag for both of you. You were gone for three days. Where were you?"

"Hershey. At the hospital."

In confusion, Lucas's mind spun, his fingertips feeling cold and numb. Was he going into shock again?

"You took Jacob to a hospital?" His mother asked the question he could not.

Daed nodded. "I didn't know what else to do. My boy was…" He wiped the back of a sleeve across his nose. "It wasn't until we arrived there that Jacob told me everything—what you'd done for him, Luke."

Lucas slammed his eyes shut, unable to meet the penetrating gaze of his father or mother. "I failed," he said. "I tried to help, but in the end, it was for nothing."

"That's not true." Suddenly, Lucas felt his father's hand on his arm. "Son, that's just not true."

It took a moment, but when he thought he could control the emotions pressing up against him, Lucas looked up. His father's eyes were wet, red-rimmed, probably matching his own.

"What happened at the hospital?" Lucas asked after a hard swallow.

Before replying, *Maam* gestured for them all to

sit down again. She took her place between the two men, reaching out to hold both of their hands.

"The ER wouldn't see him right away, until Jacob talked to a passing doctor," his *daed* continued. "I don't know exactly what he said, but he probably told him he'd been treated for cancer." *Maam* squeezed both their hands. "We were taken to an exam room almost immediately. They ran some tests that I didn't understand, yet Jacob…he grasped every word the doctor said." *Daed* paused to lift a strange kind of smile. "He was very brave, especially when they explained about the RSV."

"Respiratory…something virus?" *Maam* asked. Then they both looked at Lucas quizzically.

"Because Jacob had been so sick before," he explained, "the cells in his body that were supposed to fight off simple things like a cough or cold weren't working anymore."

"There was nothing the doctors could do," *Daed* added. "After three days, he…" At the last word, his father's voice broke. "Our son wanted to come home. He said he was ready to go to heaven but wanted to be with his family."

Maam was crying again, and Lucas was hovering on the verge, finally understanding, finally comprehending the pain his parents had been feeling for years—especially his father.

"I'm sorry," Lucas offered, ready to forgive, while also finally ready to truly repent.

"Luke," *Maam* said, "none of it was your fault—your brother was sick."

"No," Lucas said, squeezing her hand, then reaching out for his father's—not afraid anymore.

"I'm sorry that I thought you didn't care." He averted his eyes to stare down at the scuffed table. "I'm sorry I didn't think you'd do whatever you could to help him. Please forgive me. Please." He was looking at his parents, but he was also speaking to his Heavenly Father. "All this time I assumed… and so wrongly…" When he didn't know how to go on, he simply stopped speaking.

He didn't have to anymore—at least not on his own. For the next hour, he and his parents talked, *really* talked. And he felt as close to them as he ever had, maybe more so, since they were all adults now. A weight lifted off his shoulders that he hadn't realized he'd been carrying around for years.

When the grandfather clock in the corner gonged three o'clock, *Daed* consulted his wristwatch.

"Your meeting with the bishop," *Maam* said.

Daed nodded. "It's an important one."

It took a lot out of him, but Lucas managed to stand. "I didn't mean to take up your entire afternoon, but I sincerely thank you for…everything that's happened today. Being in this house with the two of you has meant a lot."

"Don't go," *Maam* said, rising to her feet.

"I think I have to," Lucas said, knowing the rules and the kind of trouble his family could be in if the church leaders knew he was visiting. Still, he couldn't help glancing at his father, ready to follow his lead.

Daed remained at the table, scratching his chin. "Earlier, you said you wanted to come home. Do you mean to be Amish again?"

"Jah." Lucas's palms began to sweat, though he'd answered truthfully. "But I know how it is. I chose to leave."

"You were sixteen," *Daed* said.

"What about your job?" *Maam* interrupted.

This time, Lucas had an answer ready, for the subject had been in his heart for more than a month, maybe even years. "I've been thinking that Eliza Fisher is really getting on in years," he said. "I wonder if she's eager to retire."

"Probably so," *Maam* said. "And honestly, when folks have serious issues, they're more interested in reaching out to someone with professional training these days."

"That was my thought," Lucas agreed.

"I don't know," *Daed* added. "There are still plenty of old order Amish and Mennonites who don't feel comfortable visiting the clinic."

"Maybe you could be a sort of…go-between, Luke," *Maam* said. "Folks might be more at ease if someone like you referred them to a proper doctor."

"Hmm." *Daed* ran a hand down his beard. "Interesting idea. Very interesting."

This was exactly what Lucas had been considering the past few days. And he was so relieved his parents seemed to be on the same page without Lucas having to bring up the concept in the first place. His heart beat firmly and steadily, and he was motivated more than ever now. After so much time, the puzzle pieces were finally falling into place. At least some of them.

Almost on cue, he felt his cell buzz. "Sorry," he said, "excuse me." Keeping the phone under the table, he quickly read the text message, relief spreading through his body like a B12 shot.

Thank you, Lord, he silently prayed. *Young Tanner can live a long, joyful life with his family, and his family to come. Thank you for blessing him with health, and for blessing me with knowledge and patience and a desire to serve others.*

"Pardon me for one second," he said, quickly walking out the back door. The call was brief, as if Tanner and David had been waiting by the phone in their barn. Once Lucas had explained the test results—zero cancer!—he allowed his new friends to celebrate after making them promise to set an appointment to see Frank McDonald at the clinic the next day.

"Good news?" *Maam* asked.

Lucas grinned and flipped his cell in his hands. "Very good news."

After whispering something to *Daed*, she added, "You'd really consider giving up your big salary and your truck to come home? Your prestige in the world?"

Lucas chuckled. "I don't have much prestige, *Maam*." He could've explained further how he'd give up almost anything if that meant he could come home. The last few weeks had taught him what he really wanted in his future, how he longed to live a life of service.

"You'd have to talk to Bishop Abram," *Daed* said, his voice low and with something of a warning tone.

Lucas nodded. He'd considered this, too.

"And the rest of the church leadership," his

father added. "Then the whole congregation votes." He scratched a sideburn thoughtfully. "Though that would be further down the road."

"It's a lot to think about, son," *Maam* said, resting a comforting hand on Lucas's shoulder.

"I know," Lucas said, feeling the weight of making such a huge, life-altering decision.

Then again, the way his heart felt as light as air every time he considered his future, it didn't feel like much of a decision at all.

He had spent three hours with his parents, and those two previous days with Jerry's family. For an outsider, there wasn't much more he should've allowed himself to hope for.

Nevertheless, he hoped. Even though it hurt.

"Do you have anywhere to be right now, son?" *Daed* asked, standing up from the table.

"No," Lucas replied.

"Gut." A squinty-eyed smile Lucas remembered from his childhood brightened his father's face. "I have an idea."

CHAPTER THIRTY-NINE

"You're joking."

"Completely serious. Every word."

"Huh." Louisa stared off into space while chewing on a knuckle. The early November breeze ruffled the puffy dress material at her shoulders, while the strings of her *kapp* danced around her face.

"I should've told you sooner," Esther said, in an attempt to fill the silence. "But honestly, before this morning, I hadn't told anyone everything."

"Not even your *maam*? Not Anna or Sarah?"

This made Esther laugh under her breath. "Definitely not my sisters."

Almost two weeks had passed since that day at Ephraim Brenneman's house. After running into Lucas in town so many times the past two months, it was odd to not see him at all now.

It worsened Esther's heartache when she considered that he was purposely staying away from her. As he should.

"It's hard to believe—not that I don't believe you," Louisa said, turning her body to face Esther as they sat in two of the folding chairs they'd just set up for the choir's performance later that day. "Lucas Brenneman."

Esther's heart pitter-pattered from just hearing the name. "I know."

"Jacob's brother."

"I *know*."

Lou flung her arms into the air dramatically. "Honey Brook's own prodigal son."

Esther ran her fingers along the hem of her apron—the one she and Sarah had finished sewing the day before. "He wasn't all *that* prodigal," she said. "Wasn't living in an opium den or anything." Before she went on, she paused to make sure her breathing was stable. "I've seen into his heart, Lou. I know he still believes—I know it with all my soul. There's no way I could love him like I do if he didn't."

"Es." Lou's expression crumpled as she reached out to take her hand. "I'm sorry this is happening. It doesn't seem fair."

"I felt that way at first," she admitted. "But I—*we* both had to know from the beginning it couldn't work. I don't know, it's like I was pretending or hoping to get away with it, all the while knowing…" She shook her head. "Doesn't *Gott* give us challenges to make us stronger?"

"Do you feel stronger?"

Esther thought deeply for a moment, then nodded. "I do. My faith is certainly more stable—I'm more committed than ever. I had the chance to make a different choice, to be disobedient, but I didn't."

She closed her eyes, offering another little prayer of gratitude. Then she opened them, glancing over Lou's shoulder as the first buggy arrived, families gathering for the preaching service and then Sarah's wedding.

"But that's what Lucas did," she continued. "He

sacrificed everything for just the chance to help Jacob. He has more love of *Gott* in his heart than anyone I know."

Tears clung to the corners of Lou's eyes, while Esther's tears had dried up days ago. She could wish with all her being that things were different, but to truly have the life she'd always dreamed of took a different kind of sacrifice—a very personal one that late one night, in the privacy of her bedroom, fingers clasped in prayer, she'd decided to make.

Slowly but surely, her broken heart would become whole again. Someday.

"The Hochstetlers are here." Louisa dipped her chin toward another buggy. "I'll pray for you."

Esther smiled, grateful to have such a dear and trusting friend. *"Danke,"* she replied, then shook out her hands.

"Are you nervous?"

Esther made double fists, then shook them out again. "Not one bit."

Louisa laughed and touched Esther's shoulder. "Thank you for agreeing to sing with the choir and for doing a solo. The spirit of the performance will raise a level because of you."

Esther closed her eyes and smiled, feeling an inner glow of peace, grateful she finally had the strength to share her favorite talent again after so many years. "It's my honor."

Lou placed the last hymnal on the last chair. "Okay, no more talking for you." She pointed at Esther. "Save your voice for the concert."

Esther giggled, then made the gesture of locking her lips and throwing away the key.

• • •

The words of the two preachers filled Esther's heart with gladness, but it wasn't until Bishop Abram's sermon about marriage between a man and a woman symbolizing the love of *Gott* for His children that her soul began to fly. She even caught Sarah's eye once or twice, remembering the conversation they'd had about husbands cleaving to their wives.

The purple dress looked perfect on her sister. And Esther took another moment of meditation to feel grateful that her heart had softened enough to make Sarah so happy.

Not until the moment she stood in the middle of the youth choir—two inches taller and probably three years older than the others—ready to burst into "Oh, Happy Day," did the tiniest butterflies tickle inside her stomach.

When it was time for her solo, it was as easy as Rollerblading down a smooth hill. Courage and an inner willingness to devote herself once more, boosted her spirits until she felt like an angel's voice was singing her words.

Oh, how I wish Luke was here, she couldn't help thinking as she began the second verse. *I wish he could see me now—how I'm stronger and more devoted, and how knowing him helped all this happen.*

In an effort to share her jubilant spirit with everyone in the congregation, her eyes began to scan the audience. *Maam* was beaming, and even Simon's little boys seemed fixated on the performance, though Esther knew that had little to

do with her talent. As she started the last verse of
the song, her eyes fell on the back row where a few
standing people—obviously arriving late—moved
into place.

For a moment, her body went into autopilot
while singing the last few words of the song. How
had just thinking about Lucas muddled her vision so
much that she believed he was standing in the back?
Could the hallucination really be wearing a black
brimmed felt hat and a *mutza* suit, the traditional
suit worn only by *Amishmen* to church and
weddings?

She looked away, blinked, then looked back. The
mirage stood tall and handsome, just like the real
man. And then it…smiled at her.

Goose bumps slid up the back of her neck,
causing her to tremble. She blinked again and again
until realizing that, yes! Lucas was at the preaching
service—at her sister's wedding.

His smile broadened, and he tilted his head to
the side. Only then did Esther notice he was flanked
by his parents. His *maam* had a hand looped
through his arm, while his father's arm was holding
him around the shoulders.

Both were in tears.

The scene was so dreamlike that Esther doubted
whether it was actually happening.

Minister Abraham began speaking, one of the
deacons said a closing prayer. The choir was then to
sing one final song as people mingled to congratu-
late the newly married couple.

Esther's focus began to mist over again but then
suddenly sharpened when Lucas broke from his

parents and began walking forward. Straight at her.

He wasn't smiling now, but his features were carved with an expression of intense determination, those brown eyes holding steadily on her. She tried to sing along with the choir, but even those around her seemed distracted.

"Hey," she heard someone whisper to another. "Isn't that Lucas Brenneman?"

"He ran away years ago…"

The whispering chatter grew louder the nearer Lucas came. Esther's heart pounded with wonder until it was all she could hear.

Out of the corner of her eye, she noticed someone approaching from the other side of the congregation. Bodies seemed to part like the Red Sea as the bishop made a beeline for Lucas.

She couldn't think, couldn't swallow, couldn't breathe! A part of her wanted to shout out to Lucas that he needed to run before Bishop saw him if he wanted to protect his family. But wait, his parents were here.

Lucas noticed Bishop Abram—the man who'd once wrongly blamed him for vandalizing his barn. Instead of fleeing, Lucas actually turned toward him. Esther watched in complete awe as the two men shook hands, both smiling ear to ear. As he continued to pass, Bishop pulled Lucas near, whispered something in his ear, then they both looked at Esther. Lucas nodded at the bishop, then patted him on the shoulder.

With his intense brown eyes fixed on her again, Lucas pointed. When he spoke, she read his lips perfectly: "I'm coming for you."

Another set of happy goose bumps danced along the back of her neck, tingles spreading across her chest. Just an arm's length away now, she lifted a hand, reaching out to Luke's already outstretched hand.

Sparks shot through her the moment their skin touched; then, with a little tug, he pulled her forward, away from the choir. She didn't fight but felt like she was actually floating on air.

"Luke," she said, trying so hard to piece everything together. How he'd shown up with his parents, walked through the crowd unmolested, but especially that quick exchange with the bishop. The smile they'd shared, the joke, the pat on the shoulder as if everything…

As if everything was okay.

"Luke," she repeated, but he didn't reply. He simply led her by the hand, out from the middle of the still-singing choir. A few steps later, when they had a bit more breathing room, he stopped walking, turned to her, and gently pulled her close into a warm, firm, welcoming hug.

Like she was the one who'd finally come home, Esther's eyes fluttered closed in relief. She wrapped her arms around him as securely as she could, holding on to the back of his coat, her face happily buried in his clean white shirt.

Behind the blissful buzzing in her ears, Esther heard gasps and giggles and tinkling whispers. "I knew it all along." This voice she recognized as Lou's.

Just as she needed to fill her lungs with air, Luke relaxed his grip, though lowering his face so it was mere inches from hers. "Hi," he whispered.

"Hiya," Esther replied, knowing her face was glowing. "Mind telling me what's going on?"

He laughed quietly. "Do you want to hear the whole story right this second?"

She laughed in return. "I guess not. How about a recap?"

"*Gute mariye*, Lucas," a man said, placing a hand on his shoulder. "Welcome back."

Without loosening his grip on her, Luke glanced at the man. "*Danke*. It feels great to be home."

"Home?" Esther said, gazing into his eyes.

Luke grinned sweetly, though with a definite mysterious glint. He took her by the hand and quickly pulled her away from the gathering and around the corner of the house. Other than a few men setting up long tables for the wedding lunch that she was supposed to be helping with, they were alone.

"Esther," he said, pulling her in again. She sank into his arms, her face nuzzling against him. "I missed you—"

"Brief recap," she said, stepping away so she could look up at him. Just seeing his cheerful smile made her heart skip.

"You saw the beginning of it at my folks' house."

She nodded. "When I left, I wasn't sure if it was going well or badly."

"It was pretty tense at first, but in the end it went well," he said. "*Daed* and I...we forgave each other. There was a lot neither of us knew and a lot of unnecessary resentment—mostly on my part." His gaze drifted to the side. "But we talked and listened and I told them about my life." He ran a finger down her cheek. "I told them about you."

A breath froze in Esther's chest. "What did they say?"

"They love you." One of his hands began rubbing her back. "And they easily saw that *I*…" His eyes grew intense as he leaned close. "I love you, Esther," he said in a whisper.

It felt like she'd swallowed her own heart, but then it began to beat true and robustly inside her chest. "I love you, too," she said, the words flowing out like a song. "I told my *maam*."

He pulled back an inch. "Your mother knows?"

"Well, she didn't know I was talking about you at the time. She just knew I was sad over a man."

"I'm sorry. I didn't handle any of that very well." He dipped his chin and pressed his lips together into a line. "Lizzy swore she knew it from the first time she saw us together at their house."

"Lizzy knows?"

"Sweetheart." He pulled her into another hug, swaying her back and forth. "Everyone knows now."

She couldn't help giggling, sighing against his body, relaxing into him as if she belonged there forever.

"That very day," Luke continued, "*Daed* took me to the church leaders. We talked for a long time. I've been back to visit with them every day. Last night, Bishop Abram said I could come home."

Hearing the crack in his voice, Esther looked to see tears in Luke's eyes, yet they shone clearly with a virtuous glow.

"What about your job?"

"I have a better one now—or I hope to soon. And with folks who really need me."

"Here?" She couldn't help smiling.

He chuckled. "We haven't worked out all the details yet, but it's looking really good. And my father supports my decision." When he blew out a long exhale, Esther felt his body relax. "I can't tell you how much that means to me."

Esther beamed up at him. She had an inkling about the relief he was feeling but didn't want to interrupt.

"It's been ten years," Lucas continued. "Ten productive yet empty years. I can't regret my education and experience, but you know how much I've missed home. All this time, I thought it wasn't possible to even hope." He pressed his lips to her temple. "Until you made me think."

"You made *me* think."

"You gave me hope again, and I'll be grateful to you for the rest of my life."

"Luke." She tipped her chin. "You changed my life. I don't know how I'll ever thank you."

A crooked smile curved a corner of his mouth. "I think I know a way."

Esther mirrored his flirty smile. "Oh?"

"Close your eyes. Trust me."

Willingly, she obeyed.

"Picture your house," he said, his mouth at her ear, swaying them again. "Picture your bedroom, the closet. See it?"

"Jah," Esther whispered.

"Now picture that dress, the one your sister is wearing right now."

For a moment, she didn't know what he meant. Then her heart began to pound. "I see it," she said as a warming tightness grew in her chest, knowing it would take only a slight alteration for that light purple dress to fit Esther again.

"Picture putting it on next November," Luke continued. "Then picture me."

Esther couldn't help opening her eyes now. When she did, Luke was down on one knee. It wasn't traditional for the Amish to kneel like the *Englishers*, but since when was anything with Lucas Brenneman traditional?

"Aren't you supposed to ask to court me first?"

He dropped his chin and laughed. "I thought that was implied."

Esther had to press both hands over her heart, fearing it might leap right out. "I love—"

"Shhh," Luke hushed, making her giggle. "I love thee, Esther Miller, with the breath, smiles, tears, of all my life, and, if God choose, I shall but love thee better after death..."

Of course, Esther recognized the *Sonnets from the Portuguese* by Elizabeth Browning. Hadn't they recited number forty-three to each other more than a month ago? That windy night they'd sat on his couch with his scrapbook.

How could she have ever imagined the impossible was finally possible?

"Will you have me? Marry me?"

For another moment, Esther allowed her eyes to flutter closed. She could picture herself in that dress, and Luke in his new black suit, bowtie, black brimmed hat. She saw their families, their farm,

Luke's future medical office in the barn behind his house—*their* house. Then she saw the rest of their future.

"I will."

"*Gut,*" he said, nearly cutting her off. "Because I've been near aching to do this."

He stood tall, tossing his hat boyishly over his shoulder, then cupped her face.

At first, his lips swept across hers lightly, enough to make her knees buckle, causing him to slide his arms around her to stabilize her wobbly stance. His second kiss—holding sweet promises of days to come—solidly covered her lips, making her rise onto her tiptoes to meet him. They may have shared a third kiss, traced with a hint of passion, maybe even a fourth—perhaps Esther had instigated their fifth, but she couldn't tell because her spirits were floating over her body.

"*Liebchen,*" he whispered, his soft breath tickling her ear. "My only love."

"You've given up so much," Esther couldn't help saying, her insides feeling soft and gooey.

With tender brown eyes and a smile so loving it took her breath away, Luke ran his thumbs over her cheeks. "*Nay,*" he said, pressing his forehead to hers. "Because of you, I've gained everything."

EPILOGUE

The sunshine felt warm and bright as Esther stared out the window. It still wasn't barefoot weather yet, but the April showers had finally made way for May flowers. The pint-size white and yellow primulas had become her favorite to plant in early spring. Though for some reason, the light-purple wildflower known as Jacob's ladder had appeared in full bloom at the base of practically every tree no more than a week after the last frost.

Esther had come to love those beautiful, delicate flowers. Not only did they have a way of brightening even the shadiest of corners, but their light, fresh fragrance had given the perfect amount of scent to the most recent batch of soap she'd made for Leah. Though that had been more than a month ago.

Lately, it hadn't been as...*comfortable* to work in her tiny soap nook space.

"Whoa. Careful there."

Esther couldn't help smiling as Luke picked up the folder she'd accidentally knocked off the desk and onto the floor. There were four folders down there now. And it wasn't as though she'd purpose-fully displaced them. It wasn't her fault her stomach stuck out like she was carrying a watermelon.

If she wasn't careful, her growing girth might hit the wall and knock down all of Luke's framed diplomas and medical certificates.

"I think even my office is getting too small," he

said as he rubbed a hand over her belly. The simple gesture made her feel so safe and loved, thrilled at the future to come.

"*Nay*, I'm getting too big for *any* room."

When he laughed and kissed her cheek, her heart fluttered anew, just like that day in November when he'd pulled her from the crowd to propose, then kissed her for the very first time. And just like that November day a year later when they'd married, and he'd kissed her as husband and wife for the very first time.

"You're so beautiful."

Almost like he was reading her mind, Lucas set his hazel eyes on her, pulled back a smile, then leaned in, kissing her until that familiar buzz came into her ears, her knees feeling like cooked spaghetti noodles.

"You've got a patient," Esther whispered, needing to hold on to his suspenders so she wouldn't fall.

"Not for another hour," Lucas said, his breath warm and sweet against her skin, his six months' growth of beard tickling her cheek.

"This is a new one. She called just a few minutes ago."

This made Lucas pull back. "Called?"

"*Jah*." Esther nodded as she patted the side of her head, making sure her white *kapp* was in its proper place. Then she glanced down at the cell phone on the desk. "I answered it and told her to come right in, though it sounds like nothing more than a spring cold."

Luke cocked one brow at her.

She smiled and rolled her eyes playfully. "I'm

getting more used to it," she said, picking up the phone. "It doesn't scare me like it used to. I mean, not that it scared me, it was just new."

"I know," he said, leaning against his desk, looking as handsome as the first day she'd seen him again after ten years. "You're doing a great job helping me here, but I know filling out paperwork and making appointments isn't what you really want to do."

I want to be wherever you are, my dear love, she could have said, though she knew that hadn't been what her husband had meant.

"Sarah and Amos are coming over to the house later."

"To work on the addition? Tell your father I'll help finish it tonight."

"I will." Esther sighed. "Sarah came over earlier this morning, as well. Right after you'd left. I think she'd actually been waiting behind the barn until you walked across the yard and shut the door of your office."

"Oh boy. She still having problems with the other in-laws?"

This made Esther giggle, him knowing her family so well. "She chose to move in with them instead of her and Amos living at home. Pa would've added on a room for them, too, but she wanted to live on the horse farm. I don't blame her—the Zooks have gorgeous animals, and Grace can train them better than anyone in the county."

"Still strange, though," Luke said while flipping through the pages of the desk calendar. "Even I am not used to the idea of a woman working with horses. It's a man's job."

"Oh, really now." Esther put her hands on her hips. "And you're the one who's supposed to be enlightened." She clicked her tongue at him.

"Okay, okay. I guess I can be stuck in the old ways as much as anyone. Thank you for keeping me modern," he added with a wink; then he dragged a finger across her cheek, making her heart jump at the tender touch.

Instead of kissing him like her body craved to do, Esther said a small, grateful inner prayer, thanking *Gott* for His hand in her life. For bringing her such a wonderful husband, partner, and friend. Someone she could be completely herself with, whom she could confide in, pray for, laugh with, and sometimes even cry with when her back hurt or her feet swelled or Sarah was being a pain.

Back during that first November, after only a few weeks of counseling with the bishop, Luke had been welcomed into the church with full fellowship. Though he'd had permission to continue working at the clinic until someone could take his place, Luke had longed to have a simple office at home, a place where all the plain folk could come for medical help, questions, and even medicine. It had taken a while, but in late October, his desire had become a reality. Then a month later, they were married.

Esther rested both hands on her belly, feeling the miracle they'd made move inside her, feeling more loved, blessed, and content than she ever dreamed possible. Soon, their precious *bobbeil* would be surrounded by cousins and friends and neighbors and so much unconditional love.

"We'll be needing two new farm horses in a few months," Luke said, interrupting her blissful thoughts. "Your pa and I have big plans for the back forty."

"Like…?" Esther asked, feeling a big smile spread across her face as her husband smiled even bigger. "What?" she asked, giving his shoulder a playful shove.

"Well, first of all," he said, "we must start with a lot of kids."

"Kids?" she echoed, confused, pointing at her stomach.

Luke grinned and shook his head. "Kid goats."

Esther felt her eyes go wide, her throat nearly too tight to speak.

"I think we'll start with four." He reached out and took her hand. "And they'll all be named Bubbles."

ACKNOWLEDGMENTS

Thank you, Stacy Abrams, my brave and wonderful editor. Back at its inception, we both agreed this project came together by fate. I still believe that. Thanks for taking on such a fun challenge with me! Thank you to Entangled Publishing for your faith in me, allowing me this uniquely awesome opportunity. As always, thanks to my writing partner, Sue, for walking me through sticky plot points, and for introducing me to chia tea latte. Thanks to my amazing group of girlfriends who listened to me babble on and on about this book for nearly a year. A heartfelt thanks to David Whitson for sharing your story with me. You are a true inspiration! Most of all, I couldn't have done this without the support of my husband, who kept me focused and positive, and who gave me remarkably creative ideas when I was stuck. You mean the world to me!

From New York Times *bestselling author Victoria James comes comes a poignant and heartfelt romance.*

The Trouble with Cowboys

Eight years ago, Tyler Donnelly left Wishing River, Montana, after a terrible fight with his father and swore he'd never return. But when his father has a stroke, guilt and duty drive him home, and nothing is as he remembers—from the run-down ranch to Lainey Sullivan, who is all grown up now. And darn if he can't seem to stay away.

Lainey's late grandma left her two things: the family diner and a deep-seated mistrust of cowboys. So when Tyler quietly rides back into town looking better than hot apple pie, she knows she's in trouble. But she owes his dad everything, and she's determined to show Ty what it means to be part of a small town...and part of a family.

Lainey's courage pushes Ty to want to make Wishing River into a home again—together. But one of them is harboring a secret that could change everything.

PLAYING AT LOVE

Show choir teacher Tess Johansson loves three things: music, her job, and sharing that passion with her students. But when a school budget crisis forces funding to be pulled from either the sports or music programs, she finds herself going head to head with Jack, the gorgeous new football coach who broke her heart fifteen years ago. Jack Marshall wants two things: to be closer to his young daughter and to make his mark as a football coach. Being pitted against Tess, the summer love he never forgot, is like being fourth and long with only seconds on the clock.

SPEAKING OF LOVE

Successful matchmaker Mackenzie Simms decides to find a woman for her friend, handsome newspaper tycoon Rick Duffy. Though they've been each other's go-to dates for the past month, Mac and Rick couldn't be more different. But on the double-date getaway to Rick's family cabin, neither expect the new feelings that develop. Can Mac 'fess up to what's really in her heart when speaking her mind puts everything at risk?

FALLING FOR HER SOLDIER

Ellie Bell is done falling for the wrong kind of guy. Why can't she find someone sweet like Charlie Johansson, her soldier pen pal? She can't stop thinking about him...until she meets Hunter.

After connecting on a real, emotional level via letters with his best friend's sister, Charlie's ready for a relationship—with Ellie. But then her brother introduces him as Hunter. And before long, the harder Charlie falls for Ellie, the more he risks losing her.

KISSING HER CRUSH

Natalie Holden wants three things: To be the best chocolate chemist in Hershey, Pennsylvania, to prove her chocolate recipe can help teenage depression, and to get over her childhood crush. Work is Luke Elliott's passion, and landing a huge promotion is just what he needs. What he doesn't need is a crackpot trying to prove that chocolate cures depression. But Natalie Holden is his "what if" girl from high school, and there's no denying the explosive chemistry that jeopardizes their jobs and their futures.

1728